He would do anything to protect her—even
turn human . . .

"I want you to explain to me how you are human, in my living room, and why," Lisa said.

"I've been sent here to look after you. To guard you
against a black dragon in human form."

Lisa tried not to be entranced by Caleb's body. She
needed to focus on what had happened, but his very blue
eyes, his male scent, and the whisper of his golden hair as
he turned his head distracted her. He was a dragon, for
heaven's sake. He was *Caleb*, her friend with the grating
sense of humor and sardonic observations. Only now he
was a blue-eyed hunk of muscle on her living room sofa.

DRAGON HEAT

Allyson James

BERKLEY SENSATION, NEW YORK

THE BERKLEY PUBLISHING GROUP
Published by the Penguin Group
Penguin Group (USA) Inc.
375 Hudson Street, New York, New York 10014, USA
Penguin Group (Canada), 90 Eglinton Avenue East, Suite 700, Toronto, Ontario M4P 2Y3, Canada
(a division of Pearson Penguin Canada Inc.)
Penguin Books Ltd., 80 Strand, London WC2R 0RL, England
Penguin Group Ireland, 25 St. Stephen's Green, Dublin 2, Ireland (a division of Penguin Books Ltd.)
Penguin Group (Australia), 250 Camberwell Road, Camberwell, Victoria 3124, Australia
(a division of Pearson Australia Group Pty. Ltd.)
Penguin Books India Pvt. Ltd., 11 Community Centre, Panchsheel Park, New Delhi—110 017, India
Penguin Group (NZ), 67 Apollo Drive, Rosedale, North Shore 0745, Auckland, New Zealand
(a division of Pearson New Zealand Ltd.)
Penguin Books (South Africa) (Pty.) Ltd., 24 Sturdee Avenue, Rosebank, Johannesburg 2196,
South Africa

Penguin Books Ltd., Registered Offices: 80 Strand, London WC2R 0RL, England

DRAGON HEAT

A Berkley Sensation Book / published by arrangement with the author

PRINTING HISTORY
Berkley Sensation mass-market edition / July 2007

Copyright © 2007 by Jennifer Ashley.
Cover art by Franco Accornero.
Cover design by George Long.
Interior text design by Laura K. Corless.

ISBN: 978-0-425-21589-0

BERKLEY SENSATION®
Berkley Sensation Books are published by The Berkley Publishing Group,
a division of Penguin Group (USA) Inc.,
375 Hudson Street, New York, New York 10014.
BERKLEY SENSATION is a registered trademark of Penguin Group (USA) Inc.
The "B" design is a trademark belonging to Penguin Group (USA) Inc.

PRINTED IN THE UNITED STATES OF AMERICA

10 9 8 7 6 5 4 3 2 1

ACKNOWLEDGMENTS

Thanks go to my editor, Kate Seaver, both for support of this project and for being an all-around terrific editor to work with. Also thanks go to Allison Brandau, assistant editor, for all her help in detail coordination, and to those in production and the art departments for their work on the book and the cover. Thanks to my agent, Bob Mecoy, for his assistance, patience, and knowledge. Special thanks go to the ladies of the Desert Rose, Tucson, and Valley of the Sun chapters of RWA for their unflagging good spirits and support. And thanks, as always, go to Forrest, for his help and his caring.

PROLOGUE

Malcolm the black dragon preferred the Internet to television. His own brain functioned much like a microprocessor, allowing him to read hundreds of pages of news in a fraction of the time it took broadcasters to tell him what was happening around the world. Even being stuck on Earth in human form hadn't impaired Malcolm's thinking ability.

In his apartment on the second floor of a converted house on Octavia Street, he used his television to watch one show and one show only. He recorded the daily episodes of a food show, *Dressing for Dinner,* then replayed the episodes one after another in the background while he prowled the Internet for information.

The woman he sought didn't usually appear on the screen, since her job was behind the scenes, but as soon as Lisa Singleton walked onto the set to hand the hostess a forgotten ingredient, Malcolm paused the playback and fixed his entire attention on her.

He watched, his lips parted, as Lisa stretched out her arm to hand the hostess a bowl of something or other. Lisa had dark red hair and almond-shaped brown eyes, slim limbs and an attractive bosom.

But that was not what held Malcolm's attention. The young woman radiated power. Not the trivial power of witches, like the trio from San Francisco who were trying to block Malcolm's access to Lisa. Lisa exuded white-hot power—it screamed from her, even through the television airwaves recorded on this box in his apartment. Malcolm intended to get that power and use it to set himself free. The witches were trying to keep him from his goal and had even coerced a golden dragon, a warrior, to watch over her.

Dragons couldn't exist as dragons in the world of humans, not anymore, because people no longer believed in them. If a dragon wanted to travel from Dragonspace to the human world, he had to have a witch from the Earth world stuff him into a human body. Dragons had enormous power and eons ago had moved freely from world to world doing as they pleased, but times had changed. A dragon had the power of lightning and the brain power ten times a human capacity, and still they'd lost the magic to move among humans at will.

The golden dragon worried Malcolm a little. Golden dragons were warriors, and while they didn't have the mathematical brains of black dragons, they were very, very good at fighting and excellent killers. The witches had chosen well, and Malcolm would have to watch his step.

But the witches, mistrusting creatures, had not allowed the warrior dragon to cross into the human world, not wanting to let him loose in San Francisco even in human form. Their mistake, Malcolm's advantage.

Malcolm scanned the television for another advantage, someone close to Lisa he could make his slave, someone who would do his bidding and bring Lisa to him. He couldn't mark Lisa, not with that raw power flowing from her and his own power diminished, but he could trick her.

He looked at the rather handsome man on the television screen who stood next to the show's hostess, the male model who helped boost the show's ratings. Brainless, ambitious, full of himself. *Perfect.*

Malcolm smiled grimly. He turned off the television and shut down his computers. Light played on the black dragon tattoo encircling his bicep, his dragon essence. He swirled his black leather jacket over his shoulders and left his apartment to make his way downtown to the studio where the show was taped.

It was only a matter of time.

1

Lisa was late.

Behind the spare bedroom door, Caleb's dragon rumbling turned to irritated growls. Out there in San Francisco lurked a black dragon, one who stalked Lisa. Every moment she was out of this apartment the black dragon could be luring Lisa to him, coercing her, trapping her, pulling her out of Caleb's reach.

Watch over her, the witches who'd enslaved him had told him. Easy for them to say. Caleb couldn't move past the door that separated Lisa's apartment from Dragonspace, though there was a small area in which he could touch Lisa and she could touch him. If he could get past the damn door Caleb could follow Lisa everywhere and make sure the black dragon, who'd been exiled here in human form long ago, never came near her.

Black dragons were not necessarily evil, but they were coldly neutral. They were the most ancient of dragonkind, and because they were old, they were very, very smart. Their intelligence could bend steel, sharpen air, penetrate all things with a single, deadly thrust, because the black dragons knew exactly which tiny part of you was most vulnerable and exactly how to get to it. No trial and error, they *knew*. And you had no hope of surviving.

Against this, the three witches had set Caleb as guardian, but wouldn't give him the magic to get through the door because they didn't trust him. Witches had done so much evil to him over the centuries, and now when he actually liked the task they'd given him, they refused to make it easier. He could only mutter and fume while the beautiful afternoon he saw through the windows of Lisa's apartment faded, and still Lisa did not return home.

The sun had set, the June day over, when the key at last rattled in the lock. The heavy walnut door swung inward, bearing Lisa and three bags of groceries.

"Lisa-ling. About time." Caleb growled to hide his relief.

"I told you taping would run late." Lisa swung the grocery bags on the breakfast bar, lifted the red curls from her forehead, and kicked off her shoes with a heartfelt sigh. "There were leftover ingredients that would expire before we tape again, so I brought them home."

"Anything for me?"

As he spoke, Caleb wove the musical strands of his thoughts through hers as much as he could, relaxing her and taking the edge off his presence. Because of Caleb's magic, Lisa had easily weathered the idea that reality folded in the spare bedroom of the apartment she'd inherited from her grandmother Li Na, allowing Caleb to look through the door from Dragonspace.

The witches had sent Caleb to befriend Li Na before her passing, to see if she knew anything about the elusive dragon orb and to learn all about Lisa. Li Na never mentioned the orb, but she talked much about Lisa. When Caleb finally met Lisa, he already knew her history and what pleased and displeased her, and it was easy to string his thoughts through hers.

Bags rattled as Lisa emptied them in the small alcove kitchen. "Five pounds of shrimp, a couple of rib-eye

steaks, five heads of romaine lettuce, a few ounces of foie
gras and three pounds of shitake mushrooms."

"I'll take the shrimp."

"No, you won't, glutton. I might invite my grandmother's friend Ming Ue over and cook up a feast."

"Don't give me the mushrooms," Caleb said, disguising
his thought-twining with banter. "Why humans eat fungus
baffles me."

Lisa laughed with her silver, sweet laughter, folded up
the bags, and padded back out of the kitchen. The Chinese
wind chimes laced with black and red string in the living
room jingled faintly with her passing. "You can have the
steaks. I'll save them for you."

Their strands of thought connected without Lisa realizing it. Caleb could not read her mind like a telepath, but a
part of his thoughts could be part of hers. Except that
Caleb never could put his mark fully on Lisa. He did not
know why, but a small section of her mind was always
closed to him, no matter how much he poked and prodded.

"Good," he said, coiling his tail around him. "Sit down
with me now and tell me every detail of what happened
to you today."

Lisa moved across the gold and white medallion carpet
of the living room, clad in a button-up blouse and a skirt
that left her legs bare. Her red hair was gathered in a tail at
the nape of her neck. Lisa's mother was half-Chinese and
her father was of Scottish descent, a combination that had
given her dark, copper-colored hair, almond-shaped brown
eyes, and pale skin.

Caleb studied the curve of her legs, an inner part of him
reflecting that her body pleased him. He liked watching her
move because she did so with effortless grace. He was always surprised that with the pain inside her, she could still
smile and be as beautiful as she was.

Lisa sat on the sofa and stretched out her legs, leaning
her head back and closing her eyes. "I don't have time for
television tonight. I'm going out."

Caleb lifted his head in sudden suspicion. "You have

just arrived home, you brought food, and you are tired. Why should you go out again?"

She fixed her coffee-brown eyes on him, the tendrils of her thoughts floating from his grasp. "I'm going to a restaurant, Mr. Nosy. With a man."

Caleb sensed her sudden increase in body heat all the way across the room. Something was wrong. "With what man?"

"None of your business."

Another bad sign. His dragon magic could make Lisa tell him anything without her wondering why he wanted to know. "You are my friend, and I am interested in every detail of your life. What is the name of this man?"

Lisa folded her arms, digging her toes into the carpet. "It's Greg Shaw, if you must know, from the show."

Caleb thought about the dark-haired male model who hogged the lights and oozed all over the hostess Hazeltine Conant on *Dressing for Dinner.* A flicker of fire left his mouth. "Why in the name of the gods would you go out with *him?"*

"Oh, he's harmless. It's been a long time since I've been out, and I deserve a little pampering." She sighed, the bantering tone leaving her voice. "I'm lonely, Caleb."

Her sadness tugged his heart, but Caleb rushed at the chink in her argument. "You can't be lonely. You have me."

She sent him a faint smile. "That's not what I mean. There are some things I need that you can't give me."

"Like what?" He thought a moment, wondering what he could offer a human woman. "In my lair, I have rubies as large as strawberries, diamonds that remember the warmth of the mountains, not like the cold stuff you have here. I'll give you whatever jewels you want."

Her eyes widened, but she shook her head. "That's sweet, but no."

"What can he possibly give you that I can't?" Caleb curled his talons, leaving faint gouges on the hardwood floor. "I provide interesting conversation and companionship, I warm the apartment on cold nights . . ."

Lisa sprang from the couch, crossed to the space outside his door and reached in to stroke his nose. He liked when she touched him, her hands warm against his scales.

"I know you do. But humans need something more than a pet, Caleb. We need someone who needs us, do you understand what I mean?"

He tilted his head so she could rub along his jaw and ignored her jab about a *pet*. "Dragons don't need anyone. We are solitary creatures."

"Uh huh. So why are you always here watching television with me?"

He rumbled under his breath. "I like you."

As she rubbed between his eyes, massaging him where she knew he liked it best, her whole body moved, loose and sensuous under her human clothes. She smelled of the smoky scent of cooking and the fresh tang of vegetables layered over her own sweet musk and fine silver scent.

"If dragons are solitary creatures," she countered, "how do you make more dragons?"

Caleb answered while he tried again to tangle the music of their thoughts. "A female dragon wants a male only when she's ready to mate. When she gives her mating call, the male dragon is compelled to answer. And then, it's a week of constant mating. In the air, on the ground, everywhere. Nothing but continuous, tail-banging mating. The male dragon nearly always dies. And if he doesn't die, the female dragon turns around when she's done and kills him."

"Golly," Lisa said, eyes wide.

"I have mated twice and survived both times. Females will always pursue a golden, because we are the strongest, the handsomest, the most virile of all dragonkind."

"Yes, I know, you've told me about twenty times. But do you understand what I mean? You need to be with dragons sometimes, and I sometimes need to be with a human."

Caleb nudged her with his nose to urge her to continue with the rubbing. The more he thought about what she said, the more he didn't like it. Envisioning a human male wanting to mate with his Lisa—touching her body with his hands, kissing her mouth, skimming her clothes from her—made the rumble inside him build to full-blown anger. There was something about the anger he didn't recognize and that puzzled him. He only knew he considered Lisa *his*, and he didn't want a man pawing at her.

"Television is better," he growled.

"It's not the same for humans, Caleb," she said, sounding sad. "We spend much of our lives looking for someone to be with, and we don't always get it right. Maybe I need someone to take me to a fancy restaurant in a fancy car once in a while. I need something for *me*."

Caleb had heard the story, in detail, of Lisa's divorce: how Lisa had come home early one afternoon after getting fired from a food editor job to find her husband Philip in bed with their young landlady and her best friend. The three of them had been licking each other's skin, and when Lisa froze in the doorway, Lisa's husband had said, "What's the matter with you? Take off your clothes and join us."

She'd refused and run out of the house, then returned later to find a note from Philip explaining he was tired of her stuffy attitude and that he'd left her.

Lisa had cried when she got to that part of the story. She'd rested her head against Caleb's broad forehead, while he'd woven his music around her aching heart, trying to ease it. He knew all about betrayal and the pain of loss.

"You do not need Greg Shaw," he said now. "I like you, and if I were human, I would mate with you. Now, sit down and stay with me. It's almost time for *Cops*."

Lisa laughed, her sad look suddenly gone. "And that should be good enough for me?"

"Yes."

She leaned in and placed a kiss on the gold scales on his nose. "You're a sweetheart, Caleb. Thank you."

Caleb tried to brush her thoughts again, but tonight more than ever, she shut him out. He definitely didn't like that. "Don't go, Lisa," he said softly.

She straightened up, patted his neck, and backed away.
"I have to. I've talked myself into it, now I'm going."

She laughed again, half at herself, and spun away into
her bedroom. Caleb watched her go, thinking even through
his worry and pain that her laughter was worth his exile in
this place.

The date with Greg went pretty much as Lisa expected.
He picked her up in a long gray Lexus with a driver in
front, Greg's model good looks making him drop-dead
gorgeous in his suit. At the restaurant the maitre d' fawned
over them, hoping Greg's minor celebrity presence would
bring good publicity. They got half the meal free, and the
waiters brought them extra tidbits like sorbet between
courses and mango tarts at the end of the meal.

Throughout the evening, Lisa listened as Greg talked
about Greg. How Greg got started in television, how Greg
wanted to get into movies. How Greg's modeling days began and ended, how Greg had caught the eye of Hazeltine
the *Dressing for Dinner* hostess, how reviewers praised
Greg's style and delivery.

Lisa nodded or said, "Oh, how interesting," at appropriate intervals, but she could not put aside the feeling that
something was wrong, something more than Greg's over-
whelming ego. Greg watched her while he pretended not
to, his eyes swiveling to fix on her position almost as
though someone else controlled them.

She thought of the long argument she'd had with Caleb
when she had asked him to *please* not be in her apartment
if she brought Greg back. He could go fly around in Dragonspace or something. He'd done it before, and the slit in
reality had closed, and her spare bedroom with its Murphy
bed and bookcase of dusty paperbacks had reappeared.

Caleb had resisted with more than usual Caleb stub-
bornness. When she'd said in exasperation, fine, she'd go
to Greg's condo instead, Caleb had suddenly reversed
course and told her that if she was going to be with Greg, it

should be here. Li Na's apartment was lucky and filled with magic, and with Greg Lisa would need all the luck she could get.

Caleb knew how to spoil a mood. Lisa had taken a long time to talk herself into going out with Greg, and now she was second-guessing herself like crazy. Greg went on and on, watching Lisa with an intensity that was was very un-Greg-like, and her thoughts drifted to Caleb again.

Caleb was annoying, he was interfering and nosy as hell, but at the same time he was always interested in her and what she had to say. She admitted it was good to have a friend, even a snarky dragon.

Lisa was careful never to tell Caleb how beautiful he was because he was already the most conceited being she'd ever met. He gleamed gold from nose to tail, shimmering like sun on water. She'd never seen him fly, but he had great golden wings that were surprisingly soft and warm, and sleek spines on his neck that narrowed into ridges across his back and down his long tail.

His head itself was free of spines except ones that looked like eyebrows. He had a broad forehead tapering to a narrow nose and a long mouth. Each of his teeth were bigger than Lisa's hand and sharp as saw blades, and he had sarcasm to match.

His eyes were the most beautiful part of him, blue like lapis lazuli. They could be wide with astonishment or rage, or narrow to sly blue slits when he bantered with her or said something snide about what they watched on television. She also sensed a sadness deep inside them, something he hid from her.

She never thought she'd count a dragon as her best friend, but she had to admit that her life had taken a turn for the better when she'd moved into Li Na's apartment in January.

"Lucky magic," Li Na had always told Lisa, when Lisa asked why she loved coming to visit her grandmother. "My apartment is filled with lucky magic." And they would laugh.

Lucky magic, or whatever it was, Lisa hadn't felt this well in years. She remembered her sadness after Grandma Li Na's funeral six months ago, when she'd entered the apartment Li Na had left in trust to her in the converted Edwardian house on California Street. The January day had been cold and rain-soaked, the view over dull gray rooftops disappearing in a wash of fog that had lowered to bathe San Francisco.

The others had gone with Lisa's parents, who'd come in from Hawaii where they now lived, to a restaurant to eat and talk about Li Na and the funeral, but Lisa had wanted to come here to remember her. She'd loved the small Chinese woman with wise eyes who had helped her through the worst times in her life, and she would miss her.

Lisa had not visited the apartment in weeks, but it remained unchanged. Li Na had died unexpectedly, although her doctor revealed she'd been ill for the last year and had chosen to keep the knowledge to herself. The apartment was so much the same that Lisa thought Li Na could bustle into the room at any moment, eyes twinkling, carrying tea and her favorite cookies on a tray, smiling at Lisa standing forlornly in the middle of the room.

Li Na had been a warm, wise woman with a strong sense of fun. She and Lisa had shared tea every afternoon at the dim sum restaurant Li Na's friend Ming Ue owned and where Lisa had waitressed, and talked about everything under the sun. No matter how bad a day Lisa had suffered, things felt so *right* when she faced Li Na over a steaming pot of tea.

Li Na told stories of how her own grandfather had been a noble in the emperor's court more than a hundred years ago. In those days, gentlemen pursued art and literature and composed verses and mastered the art of calligraphy. Women were beautiful creatures who lived sheltered and protected existences. Li Na spoke of walking in gardens while unseen musicians plucked tunes, servants brought cakes and cool drinks, and pet birds colored the bushes like flowers.

"The women in our family were always special," she'd say, leaning across the table. "They were strong and wise and beautiful. Like you."

"Me?" Lisa would ask.

"You, Lisa. You are one of the special ones. You will see."

Lisa had moved back to San Francisco after her nasty divorce and taken the waitress job offered out of charity by Ming Ue to make ends meet. She didn't feel the least bit special and assumed Li Na was only trying to make her feel better.

Li Na had decorated her flat in hues of lucky Chinese red, including sofa, chairs, and draperies. A long picture of a mountainous country painted on silk hung in the corner, and trinkets brought by Li Na's father from the court of the Tongzhi emperor decorated a cabinet.

A television stood against the wall, but in a strange place alone and outside the cluster of furniture, where it couldn't be viewed from the couch or chairs. A brand new CD changer rested by itself on a shelf in the living room. Curiously, Lisa pressed the play button, and the overture to Mozart's *Marriage of Figaro* filled the room.

She had moved slowly through the apartment to the music, touching the things she'd remembered from her infrequent visits in childhood—a beautifully shaped river rock, a small porcelain bowl, a little book containing hand-painted Chinese characters. The porcelain bowl which held an assortment of golden charms on colored ribbons had a dragon painted on the bottom of it, a golden dragon with iridescent, overlapping scales and a decided smirk on his face.

She set down the bowl and turned to the closed door of the spare bedroom, a room Lisa had sometimes played in when she was little. Lately Li Na had been curiously reluctant to let Lisa enter the room, smiling sagely when Lisa questioned her. "All things are revealed in time," Li Na would say. Then she'd laugh like she knew the answer to a riddle that Lisa did not.

It had already been a day of strangeness. Li Na was gone. Li Na's closest friend, Ming Ue, who never left Chinatown, had come to the memorial service at the Episcopal church to which Li Na's long-dead husband had belonged to sorrowfully speak about their sixty-year friendship. Li Na had been cremated, her ashes scattered over the Golden Gate Bridge from a point that had a view both of the Pacific, the direction from which Li Na's grandfather had brought the family, and San Francisco, the city Li Na loved.

When Lisa had looked at herself in the mirror that morning, she'd found a streak of pure white lacing her auburn hair at her left temple. She stared at the streak, about an inch wide, which had definitely not been there the day before. When she'd tentatively touched it, her fingers had tingled.

Grandma Li Na had had a streak of white in her perfect black hair for as long as Lisa could remember. Now Li Na was gone, and Lisa had the streak. She'd stepped back from the mirror, troubled, then finished dressing and went to the church, ignoring the curious looks others gave her when she arrived.

Ming Ue, her face as lined as Li Na's had been, nodded once when she saw Lisa, as though understanding something. Lisa hadn't been able to ask her about it, because after the service Ming Ue's grandson Lumi had whisked Ming Ue into a car and sped off with her.

As the strains of Mozart swelled and filled Grandma Li Na's apartment, the silver streak burning at her temple, Lisa quietly pushed open the spare bedroom door.

Gold flashed, and the huge, supple body of a great dragon unfolded itself, glimmering and glistening with its own light. As Lisa stood frozen, her hand on the door, two giant blue eyes swiveled to her, studying her from behind long golden lashes.

The eyes held vast knowledge and power, and behind that conceit a glimmer that might mean a wicked sense of humor and a strange sense of sorrow. The dragon—the word *dragon* slid through her shocked brain—lowered his chin to stare at her more closely.

They studied one another for a long time, as though Caleb had been as surprised at what he found on the other side of the door as she was. A few feet of the spare bedroom floor stretched beyond the opening, and beyond that a rocky ledge on which his dragon body rested. She'd felt both the chill of the San Francisco day behind her and a cool wind, a different temperature, from the darkness beyond the dragon.

She also saw, incongruously lying next to the dragon's horned claw, the remote control to Grandma Li Na's television.

"I was looking for that." She was surprised her voice didn't shake. No wonder, she realized, Grandma Li Na had positioned the television at such an odd angle. Li Na had moved it so it could be seen clearly from the spare bedroom door, so that Li Na's pet dragon could watch it.

That thought broke through her initial stunned reaction, but before her mind could dissolve into panic, a strange music wove itself through her. The music picked up Mozart's harmonies and twined in others until her entire body sang. She wondered what would happen if she put her hand into that space between the worlds to touch the dragon, fifty feet of shining gold.

The dragon rumbled, his body vibrating a deep note that harmonized with the music in her body. "Come in and take it," he said. He didn't speak through his mouth; the words floated out into empty air, his voice deep and dark like velvet.

Lisa dreamily reached in but didn't pick up the remote. Instead she touched him, placing tentative fingers on his broad forehead, right between his blue, blue eyes. She found him surprisingly soft and warm, not the cold, metallic scales of a lizard but the hot suppleness of a warm-blooded being. Heat radiated from him, warming the chilled dank air of the apartment.

She moved her hand on the warm gold as he pressed his body closer to the door. "You're *beautiful*," she said softly.

"Hello, Lisa-ling," he answered in his velvet-smooth voice. "I knew one day I'd meet you."

2

Greg was still talking. Lisa reflected that at least Caleb was interested in what she had to say.

After her initial shock that January day, she and Caleb developed a routine. Every day after work, Lisa would sink into an armchair positioned beside Caleb's door and tell him, in minute detail, everything that happened during her day. She always felt more relaxed when she finished, and Caleb's smart-ass comments about people she encountered during her day made her laugh.

Then they'd watch television. Caleb's need for television was insatiable. Lisa wasn't certain how he pressed the buttons of the remote so gently with the sharp edge of his tail, but he did it. She grew used to falling asleep in her dark bedroom to late-night talk shows and rumbling dragon chuckles.

Whenever Lisa was too late getting home, like today, Caleb grumbled and growled and was more sarcastic than ever. A fifty-foot golden dragon in a snit was an experience.

After dinner Greg's driver drove them from the restaurant, and Lisa, numb with boredom, tried to call it a night.

"I'm so tired after all the taping today. Just have your driver drop me off."

Smiling a smarmy smile, Greg slid across the seat and enclosed her in a warm, cologne-scented embrace. "Not yet. The night is still young."

Could he at least come up with something less cliché? Lisa tried to move from his grasp, but he held her firmly. She thought again of Caleb's admonishment to at least bring him to Li Na's apartment with its good magic and felt a little better. If Caleb were there, waiting behind his door, end of problem. Greg would take one look at him and flee.

Lisa smiled, pretending to be coy. "All right then. Let's go to my place."

Greg's smile deepened as though he'd given her a cue and she'd made the correct response.

Lisa gave directions to the driver, and they sped off. Greg twined himself around her like an octopus and would not let go as they went up and down hills, heading for Arguello and California Streets. Lisa sensed in his now-strange brown eyes a deep sense of satisfaction, and it chilled her to the bone.

Caleb focused his razor-sharp dragon magic on the circle he'd drawn on his side of the door. Above him in Dragonspace purple-tinted clouds gathered with a rush and a harsh, freezing wind sprang from them. Caleb with his thick hide and golden scales did not notice the cold, but the small witch who popped into the circle on her back did.

It was Saba, the youngest witch who usually arrived to take Caleb's report on Lisa's activities. She was clad for San Francisco weather in narrow jeans and a cropped tank top that bared her midriff and the interlocked pattern tattoo on her arm. Rain plastered her short black hair to her face, and she hugged her arms to her chest.

Caleb waited, but no other witches appeared. Just Saba, looking pissed and pathetic in the dirt and rocks at his feet.

"I wanted Donna," he growled, naming the trio's high priestess. "Where is she?"

"She's busy. *I'm* busy. What do you want?"

"Magic." He spread the expanse of his wings, balancing on the rocks as the wind buffeted his body. "Witch magic so I can enter Lisa's world. I can't cross without your help."

Saba brushed gravel from her jeans, her sloe-colored eyes wise for her age. "We already have one dragon running amok on the Earth world, we don't need two."

"Donna told me to watch over Lisa, but I can't protect her tonight if I'm not in there with her."

"Why tonight all of a sudden? What's so important about tonight?"

"Because Lisa has gone out with a man on her television show. The *Dressing for Dinner* one. You've seen it?"

The wind whipped Saba's close-cropped hair about her face and she shivered, her lips almost blue. "You mean she's going out with Greg Shaw? Yeah, I've seen him. He's cute but not much gifted in brains as far as I can tell. So what?"

"When I watched the show today, it screamed at me, even through the television." Caleb put his face next to Saba's. The girl smelled a little like the forest after a rain, pleasant and refreshing. "Greg Shaw has the black dragon's mark. It's all over him. And Lisa is with him, *right now*. So give me the magic and let me go in there and rip him away from her before this minion leads her straight to the black dragon."

Saba's brown eyes widened. "Are you sure?"

"Very sure."

"Crap." She pulled out her cell phone. "I have to tell Donna."

With one swat of a talon, Caleb sent the phone spinning and clattering across the rocks. "No, you have to let me go after her, now. Witches are not strong enough to handle a dragon minion, not even the three of you together. I will get Greg away from Lisa and take the mark off him."

"You can do that?"

"I can do that. It takes a dragon to catch a dragon. Give me the magic, Saba."

Saba put her hands on her slim hips. "And if I won't? You can't compel me to do anything for you or hurt me or coerce me or mark me, remember? I wield your true name."

"If you don't help me he'll drag Lisa to the black dragon. Maybe not tonight, but he'll work on her and get her there sooner or later. Help me to help her." He bent to put his face on her level. *"Please."*

Saba's eyes widened in mock surprise. "A golden dragon saying *please*? I never thought I'd hear it. All right, I'll do it, Caleb. Because you're right, if she's in danger we should help her. But the magic won't last forever, do you hear me? Only until Lisa is completely safe."

"Fine," Caleb said, exhaling in relief. "I just want her away from him. Tell me what I have to do."

By the time Greg and Lisa pulled up in front of her apartment, she'd grown thoroughly alarmed. Greg had finally released her but sat in the car with the length of his thigh touching hers, his fingers on her knee. His voice and conversation were still that of inane Greg Shaw, conscious of his own good looks, but with a strange difference, as though his mouth ran while his brain was far away. His watchful eyes and posessive hand on her leg gave her chills.

Lisa let him talk, her foremost thought that when she got to Caleb, she'd be safe. When she opened the spare bedroom door and showed Greg fifty feet of golden, growling, teeth-bearing dragon, it would scare the daylights out of him, and Greg would run screaming into the night.

Lisa could not help feeling that someone else watched her besides Greg. His driver didn't seem to notice anything—in fact, the driver seemed the most normal person in the car.

Lisa's every instinct wanted to reach Caleb, to touch his

golden scales and look into his eyes and listen to his snarky voice saying, "So Lisa, aren't you going to introduce me to your date?"

Thinking of Caleb gave her an oddly protected feeling, and she held him in her thoughts, the flashes of gold in her imagination seeming to brighten the car.

Her cold chills returned when they entered the house on California Street. The foyer was painted an inviting milk-chocolate color, its polished walnut staircase lined with an oriental runner leading to the three floors above. The lift which nestled in the curve of the staircase would not come down from the third floor, which was normal, but for some reason the fact that the thing hovered up there seemed sinister tonight.

A door banged above them and Mrs. Bradley, who lived in the apartment below Lisa's, tottered down the stairs in her orthopedic shoes, dragging her terrier Mike by his leash.

"Lift's out, again," Mrs. Bradley said, her hair encased in a plastic rain hat.

She barely looked at Greg, but Mike stopped and sniffed in his direction. When Greg glanced at him, Mike yelped as though he'd been kicked and took off out the front door. Mrs. Bradley staggered after him.

Greg smiled at Lisa, his eyes completely dark now. "Shall we?" He gestured up the stairs.

"Sure." Lisa murmured. She took the steps in a hurry, not caring that her tight red dress rode up her thighs. She fished her keys from her small red leather bag, holding the apartment key out in front of her as she neared the door. She thrust the key into the lock and breathed a sigh of relief when the door opened, and she stepped into Grandma Li Na's apartment.

Everything was as she'd left it, the wind chimes hanging still, the scent of sandalwood and cloves that seemed to always linger here peaceful and cleansing. The carpet pulled at the narrow heels of Lisa's shoes as she hurried toward the closed spare bedroom. All was quiet behind the paneled wooden door, no buzz-saw humming or Caleb's booming voice saying, "About time you got back."

Without knocking, she threw open the door, waiting for Greg's scream, and got . . . nothing. The bedroom was empty. The Murphy bed was locked in its cupboard, the bookcase stood in its place by the window, and the small bedside table had a coating of undisturbed dust.

Lisa's fear returned. Why did Caleb he have to pick *to-night* to start listening to her?

She turned around to find Greg in the kitchen. He was opening the bottle of wine she'd left on the counter, then he clinked through a cupboard and dragged out two wide-bowled glasses. He smiled, the cold of his eyes absolute. "This is a great merlot. I first had it at a party at Brad Pitt's."

Lisa doubted he'd ever been to a party at Brad Pitt's, unless it was one of those five-hundred-dollar-a-plate charity suppers where Greg ate with three hundred strangers and Brad made an appearance and a short speech.

"Come and sit down," Greg said, moving to lounge on her grandmother's sofa, his arm stretched across the back.

Lisa did not want to go to him, but for some reason, her body swayed toward the sofa. Her mind shrieked at her to stand still, but she found herself slipping off her shoes, padding across the room, and sitting down next to him. His body heat should have warmed her. Instead, she felt coldness, like something had sucked the heat from his skin.

"That's better," he said. "Lisa, what do you want?"

His voice slid into smooth seductive tones she'd never heard before. Greg's voice was usually studied; he had his suave studio voice and his off-set bitch-about-his-lights voice. Now the tones moved to dark and rich timbres, a baritone that Greg had never reached.

"Just a glass of wine," Lisa countered. "And for you not to touch me."

A wicked note entered his laugh. "I know you do not want me to touch you. You want to fight me. But you won't. My master controls me, and I will take you to him."

"Your master?" She bit back revulsion as he leaned over

her. The scent of his overly expensive cologne engulfed her, but his body continued to radiate the strange coldness.

"You will meet him soon enough. Don't worry, Lisa, you'll like him. He's not as bad as they make out, and he needs you. He desperately needs you. You would not turn away such a desperate man, would you? You have a kind heart. I see it in you."

His mouth babbled the words, but Lisa could see he did not even hear what he said. His dark eyes came closer and closer as he sent her down to the smooth cushions of the sofa, and his words filtered into a blur of grating sound.

She felt an answering surge within her, something like anger but more powerful, like hot silver wire twining through her. She had never learned any of the martial arts, but her body suddenly knew exactly how to strike Greg and where and when it would be most effective. The white streak at her temple tingled, sending awareness through her as though instincts long suppressed were suddenly breaking free.

She never got the chance to use them. As Greg opened his mouth to kiss her, a pair of heavily muscled forearms covered with wiry golden hair came into view. Two large hands seized Greg by the scruff of the neck, ripped him from Lisa and held him high.

Lisa sat up, her jaw dropping. A tall, massively muscular man with long golden hair and eyes as blue as lapis lazuli held Greg by the neck in a powerful grip. The man looked like a wrestler, his body rock solid, his face square and hard, his skin moving like liquid bronze over muscle. He was also quite naked.

Smiling a ferocious smile he tossed Greg over the back of the couch. Greg hit the floor with an impact that would have broken a normal man's bones, but he scrambled to his feet, his face ashen, amazement replacing coldness.

The golden-haired man glared down at him. "Go tell your master he has to deal with me now."

Greg stood still, mouth opening and closing, cold seeping into and out of his eyes. It was as though Greg himself tuned in and out, struggling with whatever demon posessed him. The golden-haired man took one step toward him, and Greg yelped like Mike had on the stairs and ran.

He made it across the room and out the door in two seconds flat, the door banging so hard it drifted open again. The draft stirred Lisa's hair, but she could not uncurl her fingers from her grip on the back of the couch.

The golden man strolled to the door and closed it. His sculpted back tapered to a narrow waist, his hair hung in tangles to his hips, his athletic thighs and calves were replete with muscle. A gold armlet circled just above his elbow, glittering with a light of its own. He turned around, showing her a broad chest, rippling biceps, a flat stomach, and a groin dusted with golden hair.

What caused Lisa's utter shock, even beyond that of seeing a naked and beautiful stranger in her living room, was his voice. The timbre was rich and deep, his English idiomatic but slightly accented. She knew that voice, because it rolled from her spare bedroom every day, offering sarcastic comments on all aspects of life or dropping to a tender purr when she needed comfort.

She took several deep, dry breaths of air, and said, "Caleb?"

His smile returned and his eyes twinkled with the deep, wicked twinkle that marked Caleb's blunt sense of humor.

He spread his arms. "In the flesh."

3

Lisa finally shut off the water in the bathroom sink, snatched a crimson towel from the rack and rubbed it hard over her dripping face. She knew she had to go back out there and face Caleb, her dragon guardian who'd just manifested into a barbarian warrior.

A white-faced Lisa looked out of the mirror at her, red hair mussed, red linen dress rumpled, bare arms and legs goose-bumped, white streak at her temple matted with water. Maybe he wouldn't be there when she went back out. Maybe she'd dreamed him, maybe he'd taken pity on her and turned back into a dragon, behind his door where she could handle him.

Taking a breath, she dropped the towel on the counter and left the bathroom.

No, there he was, sitting plunk in the middle of the living room sofa, one brawny arm stretched across its back, a towel she'd thrown at him loosely crumpled in his lap. He was casual with his nakedness as though he didn't even notice it, a man comfortable inside his own skin. The remote control dangled from his fingers.

"Conan O'Brien is on the television," he said, his eyes quiet. "Want to watch?"

Lisa plucked the remote from his hand and set it on the coffee table, then she sat down next to him, not too close. "I don't want to watch television. I want you to explain to me how you are human, in my living room, and why."

She spoke very calmly, but her fingers shook and she folded them into her palms.

He touched the armlet above his elbow, which bore an etched figure of a golden dragon in precise detail along with a smattering of runes. "A witch called Saba gave me this. It allows me to pass through the door and enter your world as a human. The witches sent me to look after you."

Lisa didn't answer. Greg had scared and confused her, and being scared pissed her off. Then there was the intense nearness of this man who looked at her as though seeing her was the best thing that ever happened to him. Her body responded to his sexuality even while her brain screamed that this was all wrong. But her gaze raked over him without her consent, taking in golden-tanned skin over muscle and hair a shade between brown and blond, rumpled like he'd just woken up. The irises of his eyes were large, blue swallowing the white.

She tried to keep her voice steady. "Why should witches turn you human and send you to look after me? How can I even be asking you this question?"

"Saba was not supposed to give me the magic." Caleb ran his fingers over the armlet. "Donna will be pissed at her."

"Donna?"

"The high priestess of their coven." He shrugged, muscles rippling. "If you can call three witches who don't get along a coven. Witches are powerful when they band together, but get two in a room for an hour and they can't agree on the color of the night sky."

Lisa folded her arms and sank against the end of the couch. "If I hadn't believed you were Caleb before, I'd believe it now. You are good at evasive answers."

His blue gaze took its time sliding over her bare arms,

her thighs exposed by the dress, her calves, and her bare feet. He pulled his gaze up her body again, his eyes holding a serious light.

"They sent me to guard you against a black dragon in human form. The black dragon put his mark on Greg Shaw, who was about to seduce you and drag you to his master."

Lisa thought of the *otherness* she'd sensed in Greg, the voice that hadn't been his. "To his master," she repeated.

"It is the truth, Lisa, I swear it. I think we should watch television now. Conan has James Marsters on tonight—you know, he played Spike on *Buffy the Vampire Slayer*."

Lisa tried not to be entranced by Caleb's body as he reached for the remote. She needed to focus on what had happened, but his very blue eyes, his male scent, and the whisper of his golden hair as he turned his head distracted her. He was a dragon, for heaven's sake. He was Caleb, her friend with the grating sense of humor and sardonic observations. Only now he was a blue-eyed hunk of muscle on her living room sofa.

"Screw television," she said with effort. "I want to talk about this black dragon."

"You believe me?"

"I walked into my grandmother's apartment to find a dragon in the bedroom, who is now a man in my living room. Why shouldn't I believe in a black dragon and witches? But if you tell me Spike's a real vampire, I might scream."

He shook his head. "No, I think he's only an actor."

Lisa drew a deep breath and vowed not to laugh. If she laughed, she'd go into hysterics and be unable to stop. "Why should a black dragon be interested in me? Or Greg?"

Another shrug, another ripple of muscle. "The witches wouldn't tell me. I am a warrior dragon, and to witches that means stupid muscle who should take orders and not ask questions. Fight this, fight that, never think. Witches have always done this to me. Black dragons are ancient and too intelligent to be safe."

"And one is coming from your world to mine?" she asked.

His large, blunt fingers toyed with the remote. "One is already here. Witches trapped him here in human form long ago—why, Donna would not tell me. Witches envy dragons and crave their powers, I know this well, so it could have been for any number of reasons. Now he is trying to get free, he is trying to find the dragon orb, and he needs you."

"Dragon orb?" Lisa blinked. "What is a dragon orb?"

"I don't know. Something powerful enough to destroy the world if he uses it. The witches seem to think you can lead him to it, and they have to stop you doing that, which is why they sent me."

Caleb flicked his gaze to her again, the overly blue eyes compelling her to look at them.

"I think your witches are mistaken," she said. "I've never heard of a dragon orb, and I've never heard of a black dragon. I'm Lisa Singleton living a humdrum life, except for working for *Dressing for Dinner*, which I admit can be bizarre, and of course having a dragon in my spare bedroom. But there's nothing special about me."

As she said the words, she thought of Grandma Li Na's smile and her wise voice saying, *The women in our family were always special*.

Caleb carefully set the remote on the table again, the towel sliding as he moved. The red terrycloth didn't cover him completely, and she tried not to look at his flat pelvis, the coarse golden hairs below it, and the shadow on his lap.

Leaning to her, he lightly touched the white streak in her hair. "This must mean something. Li Na had the same thing."

His touch spun warmth through her. "Genetics," she said faintly.

"Is that like magic?"

"I don't really know."

He swirled his fingers over her hair, and she felt a familiar touch on her mind, tendrils of thoughts drifting through her head like music she could not quite hear.

"What are you doing?" she asked.

His fingers stilled. "You can feel that?"

"Yes, I can always feel it. Like you're putting me into a trance, but not really."

He raised a golden brow and continued to lightly stroke her hair. "I am protecting you, marking you as mine. Greg was trying to mark you for the black dragon."

Some part of her squirmed, wanting to resist Caleb's touch, while another part of her reached for it. To distract herself, she asked, "Who are these witches? I want to meet them."

"No, you don't. If Donna finds out I'm here, she'll send me back and then I can't protect you."

His gaze was intense like Greg's had been, but with a difference. Greg had been determined, invasive. Caleb's eyes were gentle, his touch seductive and coaxing. Greg had wanted to dominate her; Caleb wanted to soothe.

His dragon song filtered through her like gossamer in a light breeze. She felt the touch of his mind, as she had when he was a dragon, weaving the strands of her turbulent emotions into even patterns with his.

She knew in some place deep inside her that Caleb could never reach her completely. She kept a part of herself remote, a part no one had ever touched, not her husband, not her family, not Caleb. She did not know why she kept this part of herself back, but she knew somehow it was important that she did.

Caleb moved closer, leaning over her as Greg had done, but she welcomed Caleb's warmth. She remembered how Caleb had so easily thrown Greg over the back of the sofa and how Caleb had turned to make certain she was all right. She felt safe with him, protected.

Some part of her mind whispered, *But who protects you from him?*

His face was an inch from hers, his breath warming her skin. She touched his jaw, finding it sandpaper rough—the magic had gotten it right all the way down to golden whiskers.

"Lisa." He said the name like it pained him. He drew one hand up her arm, his warm, callused palm scraping her skin.

This was crazy, he was a *dragon*, but her body said, *He's a man and a beautiful one*. She drew fingertips across his cheekbone and under his hair to the nape of his neck. He closed his eyes, his big body shuddering. Through the towel she felt a firm and unmistakable bulge against her hip.

She skimmed her hands over his back and the weave of muscle across his shoulders. "Your skin is as warm as your dragon skin," she breathed. "And as smooth. I thought dragons would be cold."

"Not goldens. We like to be warm."

She moved her hands down his arms, pausing to touch the gold band above his left elbow. His entire body fascinated her. She roved her thumbs across his forearms and up to his biceps.

"The magic is only temporary," he said. "She said I could be human until you are safe."

Lisa traced the golden runes of the armband, strange designs, neat and sharp. "What happens if you take this off?"

"I don't know. Maybe I change back to a dragon. Maybe if I take off the armband in your world, I die."

"Best not take it off then."

His expression was serious. "I agree." He captured her slim hand in his large one and brushed his tongue over the tip of her middle finger. "You taste good." He closed his mouth over the finger and suckled.

Fire seared through her. Her fingers tingled and so did the hollow between her thighs. "You're a dragon."

Caleb busied himself with her fingers. "Right now, I am a human. I like humans, the ones who are not witches anyway, like your grandmother."

"She never told me about you."

"She didn't want me to scare you. She didn't want you to know until the time was right."

"I miss her."

"A part of her is still here," Caleb said. "In this place. I can sense it, can you?"

"Yes." Li Na's laughter seemed to linger here, and Lisa had the strangest feeling she'd approve of Lisa rolling around on the couch with Caleb.

Caleb lightly touched her cheek, drawing his fingertips along her cheekbone. "You feel good. Your skin is so soft." He drew his tongue along the path his fingers had taken. "Does the rest of you feel as good?"

She suddenly wanted very much for him to find out. She smiled as he licked the whorl of her ear, air biting where his tongue stroked it. "Why did I go out with Greg in the first place?" she wondered. "He's nothing compared to you."

"Because the black dragon's mark was on him. You couldn't resist it."

She trailed fingers through Caleb's hair, knowing she needed more information from him but very distracted by his warmth and the rigid towel now nestled between her thighs.

"How am I supposed to know who this black dragon is? He could be Mrs. Bradley's dog, Mike. You could turn into a mastiff and have at him."

Caleb looked puzzled by her humor. "Mrs. Bradley's dog is not the black dragon. I have heard Mike's voice, and he is not. It is someone in this city, but I don't know who." He lifted her hand and kissed her wrist, breath hot on her skin. "Will you take me out in your city, Lisa? They have dragons in your place called Chinatown, and maybe the black dragon has gone there. I will locate the dragon orb before the black dragon does and then deal with him."

The idea of Caleb running around Chinatown looking for a black dragon unnerved her. "When you say *deal with him*, what exactly do you mean?"

"I will kill him.

Lisa tried to wriggle out from under him. The towel came with her, and suddenly she had her arms around a very warm, very naked human male. "Kill him?"

"It is the only way. Obviously the witches are not capa-
ble of it. They stripped him of power and threw him into
exile but did one of them think to gore him? I need to find
weapons of this world so I may destroy him. Will you help
me do that?"

"Caleb." She put her hand across his mouth to stop him
talking. She imagined him searching San Francisco, a
golden-haired warrior with sword in hand, plunging it
through the chest of the first man he suspected of being the
black dragon. "You can't just kill someone. Not here.
There are rules."

"He is a black dragon, and the witches say he will
wreak havoc if he finds the orb. He has to go, Lisa."

She shook her head. "But here you won't be killing a
dragon. You will be killing a man. You'll get yourself arrested and thrown in prison, and me, too, probably, for
helping you."

He gave her a stubborn, very Caleb look. "A black
dragon is not what you need. I came here to protect you
from him, and the easiest way to do that is to kill him. If
you do not wish to go with me, I will find him by myself."
He released her and rose as though ready to run out and
hunt for the dragon there and then. The towel forgotten, he
stood over her, every inch an aroused male.

Lisa scrambled off the couch and put her hands on his
well-muscled shoulders. "You can't go yet. It's the middle
of the night and you need clothes. If you get arrested for in-
decent exposure, there go your chances of finding the
black dragon. And when they look up your records and find
out you don't exist, who knows what could happen to
you?"

He watched her with blue eyes that held determination
and a hint of sadness. "Then Lisa-ling, let us find me
clothes."

He started to move away, and she sank her fingers into
his arms. "I will find them tomorrow, when the stores open.
For now, you stay here."

His brows quirked. "With you?"

"Yes, with me," she said nervously. She turned around and picked up the remote. "We can still catch that Conan O'Brien if you want."

He plucked the remote from her hand and tossed it aside. "I can think of much better things to do."

He slid his arms around her and pulled her against his broad chest. Emotions raged through his eyes, worry, the need to protect her, curiosity, amazement at his venture into the human world, and desire, very strong desire.

Lisa had only just met him, just gotten used to the fact that he was human, *this* human. But no, she'd known him a long time. Every day for months Caleb's voice soothed her as he encouraged her to tell him everything that had happened to her, what worried her, what made her happy. He'd sympathized with her hardships and rejoiced with her joys. He'd let her lean against his golden scales and cry when she needed to.

He'd been there for her more than any other man—any other friend—had ever been. Even the days when she curled up silently next to him in a chair by the door, turning down the heat and letting him warm the room, were comfortable. They'd watch television together, sharing popcorn, his sarcastic comments about the shows making her laugh.

Now he was here, her friend, the person who had shared joys and sorrows for half a year.

"Caleb." She cupped his cheek in her palm and kissed him.

He moved his lips tentatively in response to hers, obviously uncertain what to do. His eyes drifted closed, the blue shielded by his golden lashes, his brows drawing into a frown as he focused all his attention on the kiss. His lips were satin smooth, moving slowly as he learned how to return her pressure.

The faint notes of dragon music floated through her head, echoed by the shimmer of the wind chimes. She felt safe held against his strong body, as though nothing would hurt her ever again. It dissolved something inside her that had been tight for a long time, and tears leaked from the corners of her eyes.

Caleb brushed away the moisture with his fingertips. "What is wrong, Lisa-ling? Do you not like me like this?"

She shook her head. "I'm too confused. I've just gotten used to living with a dragon."

"You will soon grow used to living with me this way. You belong to me now."

She shifted and groaned, half in anguish. "We should stop."

He looked at her, eyes darkening. "Why?"

She put her hand on his chest, but it was like trying to move a wall. "You're beautiful, and you're my friend, and I don't want to lose that friendship, do you understand?"

"No, I don't. We are friends, our bodies want each other, my mark is on you, and you are mine. I see nothing wrong."

She rested her head on his bare, warm shoulder. "I'm torn between wanting to kiss you and wanting to know more about this black dragon."

He nuzzled her cheek. "I don't want to talk about black dragons right now."

She licked his shoulder, liking the salty taste of his skin. He smelled good, too, spicy and musky and male. No artificial cologne, like Greg, just the clean goodness of Caleb.

"All right," she murmured. "But I'm not letting you off the hook."

His brows came down as he tried to work out the idiom. "You want to bind me to a hook?"

She had the sudden vision of Caleb's muscled forearms bound with rope, lifted over his head, him smiling down at her. He might be tied, his expression said, but he was still in charge.

Her face heated and so did the space between her thighs. She felt hot and liquid as Caleb brushed his thumbs over her shoulders and leaned to kiss her again. She flicked her tongue into his mouth, and he jumped in surprise. Then he parted his lips, letting her taste him, and swirled his own tongue against hers, learning and exploring.

It seemed so natural to kiss Caleb in her living room. The wind chimes shivered, and she swore she heard faint laughter, Li Na's laughter, on the breeze.

He moved his fingers to the first button of her dress. He tugged at the button a moment, not knowing what to do with it, then simply tore it off along with the one below it. The buttons fell to the carpet without a sound.

Caleb released his breath as he dipped his hand inside the dress. "I've always wanted to touch you," he whispered. "I need to touch you."

"All right," she murmured against his mouth. She eased the rest of the buttons from the holes, saving them from destruction.

He looked with wonder at the swell of her breasts rising over her black bra. "You are so beautiful."

She swallowed, emotions chasing through her like water through a streambed. "It's nice of you to say so."

"I wish . . ." he began, then he stopped.

The front door slammed open, rocking the wind chimes and setting the silk painting on the wall trembling. Two women Lisa had never seen before rushed inside. One was tall and red-haired, wearing a floating black garment that revealed more than it covered. The other, in khaki shorts and a button-up blouse and sneakers, looked more like she should be out picking up her kids from soccer practice.

The two of them took in Caleb's six-foot, six-inch naked body with Lisa standing in his arms, her dress open. The red-haired one gaped and the older woman scowled in disapproval.

"Who the hell are you?" Lisa demanded.

The older one said, "Well, it looks like it worked."

Caleb unwound his arms from Lisa and faced the two women in snarling dragon fury. "Damn witches. Don't you ever *knock*?"

4

Caleb's human heart pounded in outrage. Donna stood in the doorway, arms folded, her pale eyes filled with anger. Grizelda's astonished gaze slid over Caleb's naked body and fixed on his groin as though she'd never seen a man before.

"She did a good job," Donna said.

Saba was notably absent. Caleb put his hand over the armband, which was glowing and hot. "What did you do to her?"

"To Saba? Nothing. It isn't her fault that you're a manipulative, cunning serpent."

"Dragon," Caleb growled. "No relation."

Donna sniffed. "Saba is no longer welcome in the coven."

"I don't think she'll care. She has a lot of power, I sense it in her, but you never let her use it."

"You have no business in the human world, dragon," Grizelda said, as she tried and failed to lift her gaze from his pelvic region. "We were on our way to take care of the Greg situation."

"You took your sweet time. If I hadn't been here, Lisa

would have been carried off as a black dragon slave by now."

Caleb sensed Lisa quivering behind him, not in fear but in rage. She had the sense to shelter behind his body, but he felt anger spinning through her as bright as a surge of dragon power.

He owed Saba his undying gratitude. When he'd looked into the apartment and seen Greg draping himself over Lisa, primal fury had seared through him. He'd launched himself through the door to her world without thought, sliding on the armlet Saba had given him, never feeling the change that took him from dragon to human.

The black dragon's magic made Greg strong, but Caleb was stronger. It had felt good to toss the man away, felt good to see the fear in his eyes and to watch him flee Caleb's might.

And then Caleb had touched Lisa, had felt the spread of her body beneath his and breathed the salty fragrance of her sex. The wonder of it shook him, and he wasn't certain why or what had happened. He knew he did not want to turn around and go back to Dragonspace before he had the chance to explore what had begun when he touched her.

"You can go away now," he told the two witches. "Everything is under control."

"You're still ours, dragon," Grizelda said. "And we order you back to Dragonspace."

"Not until I hunt and find the black dragon. If you had let me through earlier, he'd be dead by now."

Donna gave him a cold stare. "You will obey us. You've had your fun, now give me the armband and go home."

No. Not after he'd touched Lisa and kissed her and felt her against him. Caleb wanted to stay and discover what it meant to be with her, no matter how long that took.

He closed his hand over the armlet. "I like it. I think I'll keep it."

Donna's eyes narrowed. She reached for Grizelda's hand, and Grizelda, after jerking it free of her floating draperies, took hers.

Caleb clenched his fists, knowing what they were going to do and knowing he could not prevent it. Memories of pain swept through him, so much pain over the centuries, agonies untold. He knew he could run to the spare bedroom, remove the armlet, and become a dragon again and escape it. That's what they wanted, for him to obey to avoid the pain.

"Let me have this," he said, trying to brave it out. "I've done what you asked, now let me have this."

They did not answer. Hands joined, both witches opened their mouths and sang a clear, loud note. The note echoed off the apartment walls, divided into two, then four, then eight, then burst into an infinite number of fiery tendrils and wrapped around Caleb's brain. The music trickled down his spine, finding root in his body, invading the very essence of him.

The music was his true name, comprising the disparate elements of fire and gold that made up his being. Any moment now, those elements would come apart, any moment the music would tear him inside out, but not until he'd gone through drawn-out, horrific pain. He knew it and Donna knew it. He was bound to Donna, at her mercy, and she was proving it.

The music seared his nerves, lighting fires that flared hotter with each second. He sank to his knees, air burning his lungs. A moan dragged from his throat.

Faintly, behind the music that was destroying him, he heard Lisa's voice. "What are you doing? Stop!"

The two women ignored her. Hands locked, they fixed their gazes on Caleb, hatred and anger in their voices. The pain stripped him of reason and ground through his head like glass. He pulled one hand from his ear and found a trickle of blood on his palm.

A growl ripped from Lisa's throat. The latent power he'd sensed in her surged, lifting the hair on his arms and crackling through the room like sudden lightning.

Lisa stepped between Caleb and the two women and raised one hand. Her voice was commanding. "Leave him alone."

The two ignorant witches didn't listen. Caleb rocked back and forth, wanting to laugh despite the lava burning his veins. The witches had no idea what was about to hit them.

A snap of light came from Lisa's open palm. It caught the two women square in their chests, hurling them backward to bang into the wall by the open door. The name-music abruptly ceased.

Caleb fell onto the carpet, weak and sick. Above him, Lisa lowered her arm and stared in astonishment at the two women sprawled on the floor. They stared back at her, equally astonished.

Caleb laughed weakly, the laugh turning to a cough. "See? Don't mess with my girl."

Grizelda scrambled to her feet, untangling herself from her gauzy skirts. Donna rose and brushed off the back of her shorts.

"You have no idea what you're doing," she said to Lisa. "Caleb is ours and you will be ours, and when we bind the black dragon, that will be the end of the problem."

"No, what you will do is get out of my apartment." Lisa stood straighter and stronger than Caleb had seen her, the white streak in her hair glowing. "When I want to talk to you, I'll find you."

Donna scowled. "If you let yourself be bamboozled by dragons, you're done for. You have power, obviously. Let me guide you."

Donna's eyes took on that ancient look that Caleb always hated. The woman was too eager, too interested in Lisa. Donna thought Caleb was a dumb-as-shit warrior dragon, too thick-headed to notice her interest, but she did not understand dragons very well. Witches learned their wisdom from books, dragons learned it from the world and the winds and dangers that witches couldn't begin to imagine. There was something more here than Donna wanting to assist or protect Lisa from the black dragon, something sinister, and by the bewilderment in Grizelda's expression, Grizelda had no idea what it was either.

"I wouldn't let you guide me across the street," Lisa re-torted. "And I remember telling you to get out. Now you can walk out or I can throw your butts down the stairs."

She held up her hand as she had before. Caleb didn't feel the same surge of power in her this time, but the other two obviously couldn't tell the difference. Grizelda raced to the door and was out before Lisa had finished speaking.

Donna couldn't leave without a parting shot. "You're in over your head, girl. We'll be watching, and we'll pick up the pieces of you when they're scattered all over the city."

Lisa took an angry step forward, positioning her hand. Donna gave her a last sneer, then turned around and marched out. Her khaki shorts were tight on her, straining over her too-round buttocks.

The door slammed, though Donna didn't touch it. Lisa raced across the room and did up the locks, then turned back, her chest rising sharply with her breath, her brown eyes large.

Caleb started to laugh. His skin was damp with sweat, and he was so damn cold, but laughter grated out of him. "That's my girl. You are so beautiful, Lisa-ling."

Lisa went down on her knees next to him. "Are you all right? What did they do to you?"

"It's better now." He smiled, his lips shaking. "You have dragon's magic. I smell it on you, I feel it in you." He lifted weak fingers toward her. "You and me, we're going to kick some ass."

He tried to laugh again, then coughed, a spatter of blood wetting his hand.

She smoothed his hair. "What did they do to you? What was that song?"

"My true name. My ancient name, the one known only to my soul. A dragon's true name is binding, and witches bound me with it so long ago."

"Why?" She pressed a kiss to his chilled forehead. "Why should they want to enslave you?"

He didn't want to explain the truth of it, not now.

"Because dragons have power beyond anything witches can dream of. They fear dragons but they envy them. They set up spells to draw power from dragons in Dragonspace, to enhance their own magic whenever they can. Witches don't enslave all dragons, only the stupid ones like me. I trusted them once."

He buried his face in her neck, inhaling her scent, resting against her like a wounded beast.

"Did they enslave the black dragon?" she asked.

"I don't know. But he'll have no love for witches, so he won't care if using the dragon orb to get him home to Dragonspace destroys this world and all the witches who live here. Once it's gone, the witches will be gone, too. It's logical."

"Cold-blooded," she said softly.

"He's a black dragon."

She ran her hand down his long hair. "You are so strong, and they hurt you because of it. They made me so angry."

"Puny witches shouldn't have so much power over a dragon." He lifted his head, trying to peer into the depths of her eyes. He sensed something there, he always had, but he did not know what. "*You* have power, Lisa. More power than the witches. Donna is right. You must be careful."

"I don't know how I did that." Her laugh was shaky. "I just knew I had to make them stop hurting you."

He drew his fingers along the curve of her jaw, wanting very much to kiss her again. "Thank you."

She stood up, poised to help him to his feet. "Come on. You need to rest."

"I don't want to go back to Dragonspace. Not yet."

Lisa supported him as he got up. His human legs were weak, his muscles and bones aching. Lisa tucked herself under his arm. She felt right, fitted against him. "I'll put you to bed. Your skin is so cold. You need to get warm."

Her bedroom was dark and peaceful. Caleb had never seen this room, the only one not visible from the spare bedroom door. He'd watched her disappear into it every night, feeling wistful that he could not follow.

The light from the living room threw thin shadows of the four-poster bed onto the wall hung with prints of colorful flowers, mostly red. Lisa briskly stripped the covers from the bed then helped Caleb slide under the blankets.

He lay back in a nest of pillows and sheets that smelled of Lisa. He folded one arm behind his head, pain still twisting his belly, and sent her a weak smile where she stood.

"Will you sleep with me, Lisa?"

He thought she would refuse, leaving him alone all night, hurt and adjusting to the newness of being human. He held out his hand, wriggling his fingers to beckon her. In his dragon life, he hadn't known the emotions of worry, jealousy, abandonment, sorrow. Dragons had basic emotions—fear and anger, fight or flight. But he knew that if Lisa shunned him it would break some new part of him that was very fragile.

Slowly Lisa slid her already open dress from her shoulders. Caleb had glimpsed the curve of her breasts and waist, but now he could see her fully. Across her hips, she wore the same kind of black lace that covered her breasts, but the rest of her was bare. Her long legs were strong, calves curving with slim muscle, thighs tight, abdomen flat, her navel a round O above the low-slung lace. Her loosened red hair fell to her shoulders, wisps straggling across her pale skin.

He wanted her, and he realized he'd always wanted her. In dragon form, all he could do was look at her and feel vaguely unsatisfied, but now that he was human, he knew exactly what he wanted: her in his arms. He wanted to make love to her in the human way, bodies together, mouths melding.

She waited one more moment, watching him shyly, then she lifted the covers and scrambled into the bed with him, snuggling her warm, beautiful body next to his. He gave a grunt of satisfaction and relief, too tired to do anything more amorous than gather her close.

* * *

Across town, Saba Watanabe got herself off the bus and hobbled the two blocks to her walk-up apartment in SoMa on a street where tourists didn't venture. Exhaustion grated her bones, and her eyelids were sandy, her head sporting a dull ache right in the middle of her forehead. She'd never really believed in the third eye, but she did now, because it hurt like hell.

The magic it took to create the armband so Caleb could cross from Dragonspace to this world had scoured her from the inside out. She'd had no idea that magic could eat a person up like that. She'd always felt peaceful and whole doing spells, but this one had nearly killed her. But beneath the tiredness and the feeling that she'd done something extremely foolish, she tasted triumph. She'd *done* it.

She'd handed the finished talisman to Caleb and left through Lisa's apartment just before Lisa and her date Greg had pulled up outside in the gray car. From the street Saba had turned back to watch them enter the house, distinctly sensing the black dragon's mark on Greg Shaw. Caleb had been right.

Knowing she could do nothing more effectual than shake her finger at Greg angered Saba. She'd been too spent, the spell to make the armband hurting every pore in her body.

But Caleb would take care of things. She'd gotten to know him as she collected his daily reports for Donna the last six months, and though she'd never say so out loud, she knew Donna and Grizelda underestimated him. Caleb might be a warrior dragon, but he was not as stupid as they believed. His dragon magic was strong and powerful, nothing to ignore, and he cared about Lisa.

Saba knew she'd never be as powerful as Donna, who had inherited her powers and learned to greatly enhance them. Donna was adept at tapping into magics, both those on Earth and those of dragons, to make herself extremely strong. Saba, like Grizelda, had been born an ordinary person and had been drawn to the Craft as a spiritual choice.

Saba had been trying to find herself; Donna wanted to control others.

Donna was far older than she looked, Saba had come to sense. Saba had read myths of ancient witches who kept themselves going by siphoning as much magic into themselves as possible, and she wondered if Donna was one of these. She also had enough sense of self-preservation not to ask.

Saba dragged herself up the steps inside the building, her bag of magic accoutrements slung loosely over her shoulder. It was well past midnight and the moon had set, inky blackness oozing over the sky. Not a good time for a witch. She liked the moon and the connection with the Goddess, not utter darkness, which was the time for demons and other nasties that Saba half believed in. The Japanese stories she'd learned in her childhood had been full of foul-faced demons, and she'd learned to her discomfort that some of the stories were true.

Her apartment was dark. It smelled stuffy and a little musty, which was odd because she cleansed it with incense every day and left the windows open when it didn't rain. But she was far too tired to worry about it tonight.

Without turning on a light she locked the door, crossed the one-room apartment to her bed, dropped her bag on the floor, and wearily undressed. She crawled into bed in nothing but her bikini panties, dragged the covers over herself, and was asleep in minutes.

When she awoke not much later the covers were gone, the desk light was on, and she was tied, spread-eagled, to her bed.

Saba gasped and jerked at her bonds, but they held her fast. The lamp illuminated a dark-haired man leaning back comfortably in her chair, his feet propped up on the desk as he read the hardbound journal in which she recorded all her meditations, spells, rituals, and notes. Her accoutrements had been strewn everywhere. A swirl of quartz and amethysts glittered under the desk light, her chalice lay on its side amid a heap of candles on the floor, and a swath of salt sparkled softly on the carpet.

Dressed in jeans and a black leather coat, the man sat with lean ease in her desk chair, long legs in skin-hugging denim, black and supple boots on his feet. His hair was as black as hers, pulled back into a ponytail from a square brow, revealing a silver earring glittering in his lobe. She'd never seen him before.

He glanced at her briefly when he heard her gasp. His eyes were silver. Large and luminous, they glowed brighter than the desk light, taking in her nearly naked body bound to her old-fashioned iron-frame bed. After slowly looking her over, he returned to the book, unbothered.

Saba knew she should be terrified. A man with other-worldly eyes had broken into her apartment, tied her up, rifled her belongings, and was now calmly reading a journal of her most private rituals. But after her initial surprise, she felt no fear except for slight worry about what he intended to do to her. Somewhere deep inside her she was truly afraid, but on the surface she watched him without panic.

"Interesting observations you write," he said. His voice was rich and rolling, sliding sensually across the room. "Strange thoughts in one so young."

"That's private," she said quickly. "No one reads a witch's Book of Shadows without her permission."

He glanced at her again. His strange silver eyes belonged to a powerful being, one who knew he was far, far superior to Saba. He did not have to boast, he just *knew*.

"You sleep soundly," he said. "I put my mark on you and you never woke."

Saba had a sudden, vivid flash of a dream, a man with impossibly handsome features bending over her, spinning words she did not understand, his fingertips skimming her face. She'd sighed and let him stroke her, erotic feelings overlaying her fear of a stranger's touch.

"Goddess help me," she whispered. "You're the black dragon."

He returned his attention to the journal, softly flipping a page with large fingers, as though the declaration needed no answer. "You ensorcelled a golden and let him into this world to come after me," he said, voice rich and soft. "Why did you do something so very foolish?"

It was a question, not an admonition. He sounded curious.

"To protect Lisa." Saba clamped her mouth shut, but she couldn't have stopped the words. He compelled her to speak, and she obeyed.

"Why?" He cast his gaze over her again, the silver eyes disturbing and intriguing at the same time. "Let me guess. You have no idea."

"No."

He touched the page of the journal. "If you knew anything about Lisa, you would have recorded it in this book." A tone of mockery entered his voice. "You are very frank with your feelings. And so, so damn young."

"I am twenty-six, and that is supposed to be private."

He laid the book on the desk and rose sinuously to his feet. He was tall, well over six feet, his head nearly brushing the beams of the low-ceilinged room. "If no one else will read it, why write it down at all?" He touched his finger to his temple. "Why not keep it all in here, where thoughts are truly private and secret?"

"I'd forget things," she answered weakly. "I write them down so I can remember."

"I don't forget." He came to the bed, moving quietly and surely, like a cat, muscles shifting under his coat. "I remember every thought, every word, every feeling I've ever had. I remember every wrong done me, every spell cast, the face of every witch who banished me here."

He climbed onto the bed, placing his hands and knees on either side of her. "You belong to me now, Saba, body and soul, until I release you or I die." He gently squeezed her exposed nipple between his middle finger and forefinger. "Do you know what I'll ask you to do?"

"No," she breathed.

His hands were cool as they skimmed down her abdomen

and slid beneath the waistband of her bikinis. "I want you to help me ensnare Lisa. Watch her, report to me all that she does, until I find a way to bind her. And keep that damn golden dragon away from me."

Saba nodded against the pillow, because she could do nothing else. She arched her hips, wanting his fingers to move between her thighs. "Why do you need her? Please tell me."

"She has power." He pressed his fingertips to the folds of her opening and she groaned. "I want to harness it before the witches do, because they'll have no idea what to do with it."

Dark feelings swirled through Saba's body as he began to rock his fingers back and forth. "Does it have anything to do with the dragon orb?"

He glanced at her sharply. "Why do you want to know about the dragon orb?"

"If you use it, Donna says you'll destroy the Earth. I have to stop you."

He stilled a split second, then slanted her an ironic smile. "The universe will be a better place without witches, Saba. You and I will be all right, and we'll have all the power." He moved his fingertips again in circular patterns, drawing a halting moan from her. "You would like that, wouldn't you? To be a young witch with so much power?"

She swallowed. "Caleb will protect Lisa. He asked me to make him human so he could protect her."

"I know." He leaned down, leather creaking, and drew his tongue across her breasts, his touch like a trail of fire. "Golden dragons are all muscle, no brain."

"Caleb is different," Saba whispered, unable to keep her observations silent. "He is strong and very determined."

"Caleb is a slave to the witches," the black dragon said, his breath hot on her skin. "How delightful that I've been able to enslave one of them to me."

"Yes." Saba closed her eyes, a small part of her screaming frantically, the rest of her reveling in the feel of being spread and tied before this powerful man, his breath and fingers dancing on her skin.

"What is your name?" she asked.

He laughed. The laughter was low, rich, and smooth, his hair whispering against the leather of his coat. "I'll never tell you that, witch. A witch who knows a dragon's true name is dangerous indeed. You can call me Malcolm. That is a nice, Earth world name."

"Malcolm." She writhed, hips rising, unable to stop the dance. "Oh, *God.*"

"I thought you only prayed to the Goddess."

He pressed his hand hard between her legs, pumping and rubbing as she screamed and moaned, and he caught her cries against his mouth.

5

Lisa bought Caleb clothes at a store that specialized in big and tall men, choosing extra, extra large everything, and three different sizes of jeans, not knowing which would fit him. It had been a long time since she'd shopped for men's clothing, and come to think of it, Philip had never worn anything she'd bought anyway.

As she trudged home from the parking garage where she kept her car, her hands full of bags, she remembered waking up very early that morning to Caleb's strong, naked, sleeping body stretched protectively next to hers. She'd been so comfortable and warm and felt so safe that she'd drifted back into slumber, dreaming for some reason of lying naked on the living-room carpet while Caleb poured heaps of rubies and diamonds over her body.

She'd woken again to a hard knocking sound and Caleb gone. Grabbing jeans and a blouse, she'd dashed out of the bedroom to find him in the kitchen, thumping a frozen solid rib-eye steak on the counter.

"I can't eat this," he said, looking up at her.

She breathlessly buttoned her shirt, wanting to laugh

with relief. "You have to thaw it before you cook it." A thought struck her. "I guess a dragon would like it raw."

"I like it still running." He'd grinned at her, breathtaking, this nude, bronze-skinned man with his flowing golden hair and large blue eyes. "I need to search your city, Lisa. I want to find the black dragon before he finds you."

"Not until I get you some clothes." She thrust her feet into the pair of loafers she always left by the door and grabbed her purse. "Don't you dare go anywhere until I get back."

He came out of the kitchen, tossing the frozen steak from hand to hand, wincing as the ice-cold slab met each palm. "It is too dangerous for you to go alone."

"I'm taking my car and driving to a mall. I'll be in a huge crowd. And no, you can't come with me."

Caleb tossed the steak back into the kitchen. It hit the counter, skittering across the surface to shatter an ugly garlic jar someone had bought her as a housewarming gift.

"Lisa-ling, the danger is real. My mark protects you, but not enough when I am not with you."

She remembered the darkness in Greg's eyes and felt a twinge of uneasiness, but there wasn't much to be done. "You can't go anywhere without clothes, and I have to go out and get them. You can always call one of your witches to babysit me, although I'm still pretty pissed at them for hurting you."

He quickly negated that idea. "They say they want to protect you from the black dragon but I can smell their lies. Saba, maybe, we could trust, but I don't know where she is."

Lisa remembered how the witches had so easily rendered Caleb helpless and in pain and felt her anger flare. He looked none the worse for wear now, but in bed last night he'd shaken all over and been so cold.

She also remembered the bright power that had streaked through her body and the joy with which she'd let it loose on the witches. She had no clue how she'd done that, and the white-hot feeling of that power hadn't returned.

You have dragon's magic, Caleb had said. What did that mean, and why hadn't she known about it before? Li Na had known. A few of her grandmother's cryptic hints made a little more sense now, but still didn't tell Lisa everything.

Caleb let her go with a compromise—she promised to wear the gold charms from the porcelain dragon bowl. Caleb told her to wear the blossom-shaped charm she already liked, plus three others, one shaped like a dragon, one like the moon, and one fashioned into the shape of a tiny bird's wing.

"Lucky magic," Caleb said, lifting the charms on their ribbons around her neck. "The Chinese know all about magic and dragons and look to dragons for wisdom and luck. They are very smart people."

Lisa had smiled and kissed Caleb's cheek, then tried to tamp down her desire when Caleb turned his head and kissed her full on the mouth.

Now, as she trudged up the hill back to the apartment, she remembered her grandmother's stories of China and her assertion that the women of the family were very special. *Particularly you, Lisa*, she'd say.

Why? Lisa wondered now. *Because we attract dragons?*

A small spark deep within her answered the silent question, but she did not understand what it meant.

When she walked into the apartment, the heavy bags nearly breaking her fingers, Caleb was nowhere in sight. She dropped the bags and slammed the door. "Caleb?"

He was not in the bathroom or Lisa's bedroom. The television was off and silent, the wind chimes hanging without a rustle. She took hold of the doorknob to the spare bedroom, drew a breath, and shoved it open.

Nothing. Just the bedroom, the Murphy bed folded up in place. She closed the door with a feeling of disquiet. Had he gone back to Dragonspace? Had the witches sent him back for good? Pain laced her heart, but she refused to let it grow. She didn't know anything yet. He might simply have gone out and gotten lost.

Naked. In San Francisco. She envisioned him explaining to a skeptical cop that he lived with Lisa Singleton, and no, he didn't have a driver's license and no clothes either.

"Oh, Caleb," she said under her breath as she hurried to check the kitchen. The back kitchen door stood partway open, and she heard voices from the sunny balcony that overlooked the garden.

Her heart pounded. Had the witches returned? Could she summon up the flash of power to protect him again? She clenched her fist, trying and failing to feel the hot surge she had last night. She had no idea how she'd done it. She gave up and cautiously peered around the door.

Caleb sat on the balcony in one of her cushioned wicker chairs, a towel wrapped around his middle, his muscular torso and legs bare to the sun. Next to him sat Mrs. Bradley, her square purse on her lap. Mike, leash limp on the balcony floor, investigated Caleb's ankles. Caleb was talking nonstop, Mrs. Bradley smiling and giggling like a teenage girl.

Caleb lifted his head as though he'd caught Lisa's scent, and his lips curved to a smile. He jumped up, the towel thankfully staying put, and strode to Lisa, wrapping her in his arms.

He was warm and strong and hugged her like he hadn't seen her in months. He smelled like masculine musk and also her scented soaps, because she'd showed him how to use the shower before she'd left. She'd also showed him how the toilet worked.

"Lisa," he'd said as she explained the mystery of how to run her temperamental shower, "when dragons pee—"

She'd quickly held up her hands. "Caleb, do *not* tell me about dragon pee. I don't want to know."

"—they go someplace remote and private that no one else knows. It is personal."

"Oh," she finished lamely, then explained that humans went into small rooms like this with sinks and toilets, decorated to fit their tastes. Caleb was suspicious of a room where he both used the necessary and showered himself, but he finally resigned himself to it. He'd obviously washed his hair because it hung in damp, uncombed clumps across his shoulders and back.

"Lisa-ling, you have returned," he told the neighborhood. His voice had healed, the rich tones present again. Last night he'd only been able to rasp words, which had frightened her even more than the cold, clammy sweat on his skin.

Behind his back, Mrs. Bradley gave Lisa a thumbs-up. "I like him better than the other one."

Lisa blushed. Mrs. Bradley, first seeing her come home with Greg then finding Caleb here sans clothing in the morning, must think Lisa had an interesting love life.

Mrs. Bradley only smiled at her. "I came to borrow a cup of sugar." She lifted a plastic container from her lap and shook it. "Caleb and I had a nice chat all about his missions for the CIA."

"The . . . CIA?"

"Yes, it must be very exciting." Mrs. Bradley's eyes twinkled, indicating she'd enjoyed whatever the hell stories Caleb had been telling her. "But I really must be going. Come on, Mike. Time to make our cookies. I take them to my church group, I was telling Caleb. I'll bring up a dozen for you."

Lisa thanked her in a daze. Mike panted up at Caleb, his reaction world's different from his terrified response to Greg the night before.

Lisa walked Mrs. Bradley to the front door, listening to the elderly lady chatter. Before she left, Mrs. Bradley winked at her. "Such a nice young man, and so entertaining. You snap him up, Lisa, they don't grow on trees."

Giggling, she left, crooning to Mike all the way down the stairs. Lisa closed the door and turned to Caleb who was already rifling through the bags.

"What were you telling Mrs. Bradley?" she asked, watching his bronzed skin move as he bent to investigate the contents of a bag. The towel slipped, baring one curve of hip. *Oh, my.*

Caleb pulled out a pair of jeans and eyed them critically. "I had to explain why I was sitting in your apartment without any clothes. So I made up stories about having to be extracted from a mission where I left all my clothes behind."

"Oh, very clever," Lisa said. "Do you think she believed you?"

"I don't know, but she liked the stories."

"Which you got from watching reruns of *Alias*."

He shook out the jeans, holding them upside down. "Yes, but it distracted her from the truth."

"She didn't believe you at all, Mr. Smooth. She thinks we lost your clothes in some bizarre sex game, and you're making up stories to cover."

Caleb looked at her blankly, the gold of his armlet gleaming. "You think so?"

Lisa pushed aside the enticing thought of herself and Caleb tearing off each other's clothes and whatever activities would follow that, turned her back on him, and dumped the contents of the shopping bags on the sofa. She was never going to get used to Caleb in human form.

Lisa had to help him with the clothes, which didn't bother Caleb. He saw no reason not to drop the towel in front of her so she could show him how to put on what she called *briefs*.

She turned brilliant red and averted her eyes, but he liked that she covertly ran her gaze over him as though she could not stop herself. He knew he was handsome as a dragon, but he had no idea how that would translate into a human body. He'd stood in front of the mirror a long time while she'd been gone, touching his human face, examining his pitifully small teeth and un-forked tongue. He found this human body inadequate, but if Lisa liked it, it was fine with him.

Lisa was beautiful this morning in her sleeveless blouse and low-slung jeans, the charms whispering on the bare skin in the open V of her shirt. The waistband of her jeans beckoned him to slide his arm across her hips, and the little pocket in the front would be the perfect place to rest his fingers.

Humans seemed to design their clothes to be all about

sex. The clothes outlined the body or exposed just enough to be enticing—their way of sending out pheromones, he supposed. Women decorated themselves with necklaces that drew the eye to cleavage, or earrings that focused attention on pretty earlobes and the whorl of a well-shaped ear.

Lisa waved a hand in front of his face. "Caleb? You awake in there? You have to put on your shirt."

He smiled slowly and took the shirt, which was dark blue with some kind of writing on it. He didn't have as much trouble with this as he had the briefs—he'd watched men take off and put on shirts on television, mainly on what Lisa called soaps. No one stayed with their partners very long on these soaps, which seemed to be about changing lovers and having arguments.

He shoved his arms through the two small holes and his head through the larger hole. It took him a moment to unfold the fabric down his torso, and the shirt clung in an uncomfortable way. He flexed his arms, trying to settle it.

"You have it on backwards," Lisa said, finger to her lips.

He looked down at himself. "Do I?"

"If you walk down the street with your shirt on backwards, people will either laugh at you or think you're insane."

"All that from wearing a shirt backwards? It looks almost the same as frontwards."

"Anything not normal attracts attention." Lisa lifted the hem of the shirt and scooted it up his chest. "And you are definitely not normal."

Caleb helped her push the shirt off. "I think I like having you *un*dress me even better."

She blushed, her embarrassment reaching him through their threadlike bond. He sensed that she liked looking at him but was ashamed of liking it for some reason. He did not really understand that, but he would gently explore it.

Lisa shook out the shirt and turned it around so he could put it on again. He settled it over his chest and looked down at his front. The magic that let him enter the Earth world let him read English letters, but he couldn't decipher what these meant. "I heart SF?"

"I love San Francisco," she translated. She busily did not look at him as she tore paper tags off a pair of jeans.

"Do I?" He turned around and looked out the balcony window. He'd enjoyed sitting in the sunshine with Mrs. Bradley, gazing over the rooftops to a green expanse Mrs. Bradley had called the Presidio. "Do you?"

"Do I what?" Lisa asked.

"Love San Francisco?"

She glanced at him, startled. "I do actually. The best times of my life have been here, with my grandmother, and my family, before I found out what life was going to throw at me."

He sensed her sorrow, those hurts that had nearly undone her, and sent her a thin thread of soothing music. "Try ducking blue dragon fireballs."

Her brown eyes crinkled as she grinned. "Blue dragons? Are they powerful and virile, like goldens?"

Caleb snorted. "They have no power at all. They're animals, nothing more."

"Really? I thought all dragons were intelligent."

"Not even close. Reds, greens, and blues do nothing but kill, eat, kill, eat. They might have rudimentary communication between themselves, but they're nothing like the great dragons, goldens, blacks, frosts, and silvers."

"What are silver dragons like?" she asked, folding up the bags into neat piles. She liked to do that, make neat piles of everything.

"I don't know, I've never seen one." When she looked surprised, he explained, "Silver dragons are very rare, and might even be extinct. One hasn't been seen in ages. Dragons like to keep to themselves, but I usually encounter another great dragon—golden or black or frost—every fifty years or so, lesser dragons more often. But in fifteen hundred years, I've never seen a silver."

"You shouldn't let on how old you are."

He sensed her teasing but didn't understand what she

meant. "Why not? The older the dragon, the more feared and respected he is. Most goldens live to twice my age, black dragons can live five thousand years."

Her eyes widened. "It's hard for me to comprehend that. You don't look fifteen hundred to me. You look . . . good."

He liked the way her gaze lingered on his body, even when it was covered with clothes. "I have to say you look . . . good . . . too." He held out his hand to her. "Now, show me your city, Lisa."

She led him into a world of strange smells and sounds and sights, a cacophony of textures he was unprepared for, despite the hours he'd spent looking off the balcony this morning. But the reality of a city, he quickly learned, was much more than what he saw on the flat screen of the television or from the balcony.

First there were sounds, not only the various sounds of cars and trucks on pavement, but the thump-thump of music in a passing vehicle, the shouts of people and their laughter, the shrill howl of sirens, the hiss of sprinklers in tiny gardens, the high-pitched yapping or deep baying of dogs, the sounds of children's cries. Then there were smells, of someone frying meat, of cigarette smoke drifting lazily from a window, the metallic smell of car exhaust, the diesel of trucks. They passed a grocery store on a corner with crates of produce stacked outside the door sending forth the fresh green scents of lettuce and parsley, the earthy smells of potatoes and turnips, the raw smell of meat somewhere inside.

Lisa strode through it all, head up, arms swinging, very much at home here, very much one of them. She waved to a woman watering a garden, who smiled and returned the greeting, then she dropped a coin in the cup of a panhandler who sat near the grocery store. The wizened man's dirt-streaked face creased into a smile and he asked, "How are you, Lisa?"

She belonged in this human world, in this city in

particular, her blend of ancestry like the blend of cultures he'd heard discussed on the local television shows. Caleb had never encountered a being who belonged somewhere so fiercely as Lisa Singleton belonged in this place called San Francisco.

Caleb knew he didn't belong here at all. His world was one of vast wilderness, of caverns carved from cliff faces a thousand feet from the ground, skies stretching unblemished for miles upon miles, wind that scoured the land, and a night sky white with stars. He had not seen the stars at night in this place, the view from the windows of Lisa's apartment showing him bright lights that overwhelmed that of the stars. He'd at first thought the human world had no stars, but Lisa told him you could still see them if you left the heart of the city.

He would also have to work to get used to the time it took humans to move across the face of their world. In Dragonspace, he could fly faster than most human airplanes could. He could even slide between space, traversing the width and breadth of his world in seconds if he wanted to. A full quarter of an hour passed before he and Lisa reached what she called a bus stop, a journey he could have taken in the blink of an eye.

A bus, Lisa said, would take them to Chinatown much faster than walking could. Her car would be faster, but then she'd have to find and pay for a place to park it. The bus would do. Caleb had watched the buses pass on the road and thought silently that riding in one would not increase their speed by very much.

He boarded the bus first to make certain it was safe for Lisa. He scanned the seats, scrutinizing each passenger as well as the impassive driver, alert for signs of the black dragon or his magic. When he decided all was well, he beckoned Lisa in. They took a seat near the middle of the bus, Caleb on the aisle. He gave the bus driver a wave of his hand and a nod. "You may proceed."

The driver, not looking impressed, slammed the door shut and shot out into traffic.

The bus took them up hills and down, the huge metal buildings silhouetted against the sky coming closer and closer. Beyond the sharp tang of traffic, Caleb could smell the cool sea though he could not yet see it. He enjoyed the ride, slow as it was, looking out the window with his arm around Lisa, she snuggled into his side.

He studied the other passengers, wondering who they were, pushing his dragon thoughts very carefully into them. Most were busy with their own lives, the errands they had to run, the children they needed to pick up, the bills they had to pay, or basic needs like hunger or thirst. He touched each one down the rows, brushing them with a tiny thread of dragon music, making their day lucky. A youth in the back of the bus was more troubled, thinking black thoughts and contemplating ending his life. Caleb wrapped golden dragon magic around the youth's mind and one fleeting thought, *Be at peace.*

The youth lifted his head and looked out the window, his eyes clearing. He pressed the bell, then stood up, and moved to the door as the bus slowed, squaring his shoulders, the darkness inside him lightening. Caleb gave the youth a grin as the doors opened. The young man looked startled, then he returned the grin and walked away with a light step.

"What was that about?" Lisa asked, her breath sweet on his face. Before he could answer, she said, "Our stop's next. We'll go around and enter Chinatown from Bush Street so you can see the gate."

They emerged from the bus, walked around a corner, and climbed onto another bus, Caleb repeating the procedure of not letting Lisa on before he checked things out. The driver glared as Caleb assessed the bored-looking people in their seats, and finally snatched the little piece of paper in Caleb's hand. "I *said,* You have a transfer?"

Caleb sat on the aisle again, protecting Lisa with his body, and they rode a few blocks to descend before a gateway with a green-tiled slanting roof and stylized dragons on top.

"This is Grant Avenue," Lisa said. "That's the gate to

Chinatown. It can be very touristy, but fun if you know where to go."

Caleb sniffed the air. "There is magic here," he said.

"And good dim sum," Lisa offered. "Come on. I'll take you to the restaurant where my grandmother and I always used to meet."

6

Donna sat back from her bowl of scrying water, frustrated. She'd had difficulty all morning keeping Lisa in focus, and once the pair entered Chinatown with its mix of magics both petty and powerful, she lost them. The pesky dragon must have given Lisa protective magic or showed her how to use whatever power lingered in her grandmother's apartment to keep Donna away.

Donna contemplated casting a spell to bring Saba a slow, lingering death for letting Caleb through the door where he could interfere with Donna's plans. But then, Saba was now in thrall to the black dragon and that would be exquisite punishment enough. Black dragons were cold creatures, and he'd use Saba and suck her dry.

Donna chuckled. Grizelda and Saba were weak and foolish and easy to manipulate. Just how she liked young witches to be.

Caleb could be a problem. She'd brought him in to report everything Lisa did so she could keep track of how fast Lisa's power was growing and how vulnerable she was, not to mention keep the black dragon away from her. Now that the old woman was dead, Lisa was ripe for plucking, unprotected and confused. The power Li Na had passed to her was there, but Lisa had no idea what to do with it or how to hone it, or even why she had it.

Just like Li Na to remain cryptic to the end. If Donna had her way, Lisa would never learn the truth, and she'd remain ignorant and out of control. When Donna stepped in and offered to help her, Lisa would not be able to refuse.

She wasn't certain whether she'd kill Lisa slowly or quickly and spectacularly, but she would explain to Lisa exactly why she was doing it before the end. Donna would have her revenge.

The black dragon was the biggest threat to Donna's plans. The black dragon who called himself Malcolm must not gain the orb.

She sighed and rubbed her temples. San Francisco morning sunshine poured into her bedroom, dazzling her scrying water. The dancing light reminded her of dragon's scales, and her anger escalated.

Then again, perhaps Saba had done her a favor. If the black and golden dragons engaged themselves in a testosterone battle, they might cancel each other out. Then Donna could slip in to save Lisa from the dragons who thought they were so powerful and get Lisa to give her the secret of the dragon orb.

Donna pushed away the scrying bowl and stretched, the sleeves of her silk bathrobe sliding down her arms. She would have to stoke up her own power a little more to take on Lisa and find the dratted orb, which was hidden by magics she couldn't penetrate. Lisa was strong even if she had no idea how to use the power inside her.

Sheets stirred on the bed behind her and an incredibly beautiful man with a long mane of white hair sat up. He regarded Donna petulantly with his night-black eyes, covers sliding from his muscular torso. "Want more."

Incubi, Donna thought with slight disgust. They were insatiable and rather stupid creatures, but they could be very useful.

"In a moment," Donna said.

She peered into the scrying bowl again and smiled when she clearly saw Malcolm the black dragon leaving his lavish flat in Pacific Heights. A few carefully placed spells would send him right to the golden dragon.

If all went well, her dragon problem could end today.

Chinatown was two worlds, Lisa explained as they angled up Grant Avenue. One was for the tourists, full of souvenir shops and Chinese restaurants with predictable menus. Then there were the alleys and back streets that crisscrossed the main streets, free of the red hangings, big signs, and dragons painted on every window. Back here were tiny restaurants with fantastic food, stores that you weren't quite sure what they sold, and people living ordinary lives. The alleys provided grist for movies and novels about underworld crime and secret societies, but in reality, most people lived quietly, not shutting others out but not letting the rest of the world intrude.

Lisa expected Caleb to look for the old-world Chinatown where dragons were revered, but he seemed to enjoy the tourist version. As they strolled the main streets, he looked curiously into antique shops and junk shops and shops filled with souvenirs. He spent a long time at a table full of tiny plastic replicas of the gate to Chinatown, on which were stamped I LOVE SF. Plastic cable cars, replicas of the Transamerica Pyramid and plastic Golden Gate bridges tumbled about the tables outside the shop. Caleb picked up and examined each one.

"What are you doing?" Lisa asked him after a time.

"I don't have much magic in this world, but I have a little. Anyone who takes these trinkets today will find luck."

He put down the last plastic gate, smiled, slid his arm around her waist, and gestured for her to lead him onward.

The building that housed Ming Ue's Dim Sum in an alley off California Street was a nondescript square block of gray, only the red cloths on the lintel and the Chinese menu hanging outside the door showing that it was a restaurant. But people in the know showed up in droves every day for the best dim sum in the city.

The slender young Chinese woman at the cash register glanced up sharply when Lisa and Caleb ducked through the doorway, then a sunny smile lit her face. She came around the counter to enfold Lisa in a warm hug. "Lisa, I haven't seen you in ages. Where have you been?"

Carol Juan, granddaughter to Ming Ue, grew more beautiful every time Lisa saw her. Behind Carol's beauty, however, lurked a keen businesswoman who ran Ming Ue's chain of restaurants and kept them turning profits even when times were hard, without resorting to laying off the employees, who were mostly family. She was the flower of the extensive Juan clan, and Lisa was proud of her.

"The show keeps me busy," Lisa said, returning the hug. "I've been throwing myself into my work."

Carol glanced at Caleb and raised her perfectly arched brows. "Your work?"

"This is Caleb," Lisa said, flushing.

Carol sent her a knowing smile and extended a hand to Caleb in a businesslike manner. Caleb took Carol's hand and roved an assessing gaze over her that was in no way sexual. "You are a trusted friend."

"I hope so," Carol said. She returned Caleb's gaze, not seeming to find him at all alarming. "Let me take you to your usual table. Grandmother will be so pleased to see you."

She led them into a wider room that was lined on both sides with plain, white-covered tables. This simple room contrasted greatly with the lavishly decorated restaurant Greg had taken Lisa to the night before, but what came out of the kitchen on the carts more than made up for the plainness of the interior.

At this hour, the room was empty except for three elderly Chinese women chattering to each other nonstop in one corner and two Caucasian men in business suits talking quietly over a platter of steamed dumplings. Neither group looked up as Carol led Lisa and Caleb by.

Carol seated them at the table farthest from the others and disappeared with another knowing grin at Lisa.

"She admires you," Caleb said as soon as Carol was out of earshot.

"Me?" Lisa looked at him blankly. "She's the one with an MBA from Stanford. Harvard begged for her, but she wouldn't go—too far from home, she said."

Caleb fingered the glass of water that a busboy had plunked in front of him. "I do not know who these people are who wanted her but she admires you."

"You can read her mind?"

"No, I can tell by the way she watches you. She is not jealous, but she lets you inspire her."

"That could be flattering if I believed it." Lisa sipped the water, letting the flat, cool taste slide over her tongue. "I used to work here, after things went bad with my marriage. I tried to get other jobs, in fact, I roamed up and down the coast looking for them, but nothing seemed to work out. When I came back here, my parents had already moved out to Hawaii for my dad's job, and Grandma Li Na asked her friend if I could waitress here and live in the vacant apartment upstairs. I had two bachelors' degrees, one in culinary arts, the other in communications, and there I was, waiting tables and hoping for tips bigger than a few dollars. But you know . . ."

She looked around, taking in the diners, Carol in front by the register, the Chinese cut-paper pictures on the white-painted walls. "I was happy here. It was a place where the world couldn't touch me. All the hurt seemed to go away while I was pushing around the dim sum carts and explaining to customers what all the dumplings were. Grandma Li Na would come in when I finished my shift and we'd have tea together at this table. Even though things had completely fallen apart for me, it was one of the happiest times of my life. Does that make sense?"

Caleb placed broad fingers on her wrist. "This is a lucky place, a magic place. Come here when you are frightened and in danger and you will be protected."

Lisa traced the tips of his fingers, which were perfectly human. How was it that these same hands could ripple with serpentine muscle, holding the incredible strength of a beast, and yet touch her so gently, as though he'd die before he hurt her?

"You aren't speaking metaphorically, are you?" she asked.

He shook his head. "It is touched by magic, your grandmother's magic and the magic of someone else. It's similar to what I feel in your apartment, but not quite the same."

Lisa shivered, remembering the raw power that had arced through her body the night before. "But Grandma Li Na is gone."

"Her magic lingers. She gave you her apartment, to protect you." His grin was sinful. "And you have me, the best protection of all."

"I see the transformation to human hasn't robbed you of your ego." Her amusement faded. "The witches hurt you. You hurt for a long time, you even cried out in your sleep."

An expression of pain crossed his face and something like a memory of darker pain from his past. "But when I woke up, I had you." He squeezed her hand. "You slept so soundly, and I wrapped my arms around you and brought your warmth into me."

Lisa again remembered waking up surrounded by his body, his dragon-human skin warm to touch. Even the rumbles of his snores had been soothing.

She'd already slid into a kind of intimacy with him, first with their friendship, second with the fact that they'd now shared a bed. It hadn't been sexual, but there were other types of intimacy.

"Tell me more about dragons," she said as they waited. "You said the jewel-colored ones aren't intelligent?"

"They might be more intelligent than beasts, but not by much. They hunt and eat and mate. Nothing more."

Lisa casually sipped some water. "Whereas you watch Jay Leno."

"I observe human entertainment and learn about you from it."

"And that's why you don't like to miss your soaps?"

He shrugged. "It intrigues me to try to figure out what intrigues you about them."

"I'm teasing you, Caleb."

A smile creased his mouth. "I know."

Lisa squeezed his fingers, her body responding to his smile. "Teasing means I like you. When you're not being a nosy pain in the ass."

Caleb opened his mouth to retort, but the trolley, the one she remembered having a perpetually squeaky wheel, stopped next to them. Ming Ue's nephew Shaiming, an ageless Chinese man with shining black hair and fixed brown eyes who never, ever smiled or spoke if he could help it, made a brief gesture at the filled plates on the cart.

"All that is for us?" Caleb asked, gazing at the food.

"This is dim sum," Lisa explained. "That means you can choose as many little plates of food as you want, then when it comes time to pay, they count the dishes and charge for what you ate."

Mystified, Caleb scanned the array of foods wrapped in wonton noodles and the vast variety of dumplings and egg rolls. Lisa pointed out pork shu mai, Shanghai dumplings, spring rolls, chicken wontons, and marinated chicken on bamboo skewers. Shaiming silently clunked the plates Lisa indicated to the table, then pushed the cart away, the wheel squeaking, his soft shoes swishing on the carpeted floor.

Lisa divided the bits of food and explained to Caleb the various sauces from hot mustard to mild soy. Caleb watched her manipulate chopsticks, then stared at his own thick fingers. "I do not think I can eat as you do."

Lisa signaled the busboy to bring them a fork. She could teach Caleb to at least stab the food on the tines of the fork and lift it to his mouth. Chopsticks did take a bit of skill if you weren't used to them.

The fork was brought by a small Chinese woman dressed in black. She approached the table, fork in hand, face wreathed in a wrinkled smile. Lisa rose and embraced her. "Ming Ue. Let me introduce my friend, Caleb."

Caleb had risen to his feet as well, all six foot six of him, towering over the barely five-foot Ming Ue. Ming Ue looked up at him, took his hand, and lost her smile. She stared at him in awe, lips slightly parted.

"Honored one," she breathed.

"Ming Ue," Caleb replied. "I am pleased to see you."

Ming Ue gave him a low bow, then gestured to the chair. "Please sit. Shaiming, you are so stupid! Come back here and bring more food and the best tea. Lisa has brought us a most revered guest."

Lisa sat down again, a little bewildered. "Do you two know each other?"

"No," Caleb said. He helped Ming Ue to sit and seated himself next to her. "We have never met."

"I am ashamed that the honored one has to see such a humble place," Ming Ue said.

"Your humility warms my heart," Caleb answered.

"Oh, for heaven's sake," Lisa broke in. "He's already conceited enough, Ming Ue. If you call him honored one and bring him all the food he wants, he'll be impossible to live with."

Ming Ue did not laugh. "He *is* an honored one. Do you not understand? He is a golden dragon. A warrior who has chosen to come among us." She switched her gaze to his arm band. "That is powerful magic. Most dragons cannot cross through, except in very thin places, far from humankind, without the help of witch magic. But since humankind has overrun the world, those places are few."

Lisa leaned forward. "You know? How?"

Ming Ue gave her a wise look. "Your grandmother taught me all about dragons, and I come from a family of magicians with strong magic, not like the nonsense young people dabble in these days. His aura is unmistakable. Even if you cannot see it, you must feel it."

"I do feel his power," Lisa said. "But that doesn't mean he isn't conceited about it."

Caleb burst out laughing. She'd never heard him laugh; Caleb the dragon confined himself to sarcastic humor and rumbling chuckles. His laugh was dark and velvet, beautiful and smooth like deep water. "Lisa has lived with me for months and knows me very well."

Ming Ue gave Lisa a look of vast hurt. "You never told me."

"It isn't easy to explain a golden dragon living in your spare bedroom."

"In your bedroom? There is a portal there?" Ming Ue asked. "Li Na should have told me."

"I could only look through for a time," Caleb said. "And touch things that were nearby. Then a witch gave me magic to cross to your world. I have to protect Lisa, you see. A black dragon wants her power."

Ming Ue gasped. She rose to her small height and shouted in Chinese across the dining room. Shaiming, pushing the cart from the other side did not quicken his pace, but his gaze became animated as he trundled toward them. Carol hurried from the alcove in the front, expression worried.

"Grandmother, what is the matter?"

"Come," Ming Ue said, beckoning excitedly. "Come, you must hear."

Shaiming, still unsmiling, plunked a steaming pot of tea onto the table, then sighed because he hadn't brought enough cups. Ming Ue ignored him. "We are doubly blessed. Not only a golden but a black dragon walks among us."

Shaiming stopped, his wiry hands freezing on the cart's handle. He stared at Caleb, his dark eyes glittering, his gaze sharper than Lisa had ever seen it. Carol, on the other hand, took on the patient look the younger generation reserves for their grandparents and their old-fashioned fantasies.

Lisa picked up the teapot and poured a stream of black tea for Ming Ue, pretending that the elderly woman's proclamations didn't make her nervous. "I thought the black dragon was evil."

"Black dragons are not evil," Ming Ue said, eyes soft. "They are ancient and carry the knowledge of the centuries. They are the most magical beings, having the power to both heal and destroy. A black dragon is terrifying and at the same time beautiful. And one is here?"

Caleb's gaze met Lisa's. "They are terrifying. And powerful. And one wants Lisa to lead him to the dragon orb so he can use its magic. Do you know where the dragon orb is?"

Lisa thought she detected a flicker of uneasiness in Ming Ue's eyes, but the old woman's face remained so impassive that she could not decide whether she'd seen it or not.

"If the black dragon uses the orb to create a door to Dragonspace, it could unmake this world," Caleb said.

Ming Ue took that in, troubled. "Then you must not let him use it."

"I hoped that you would know where to find him so I could stop him."

Ming Ue shook her head. "I do not know. I am sorry, honored one."

Caleb put a strong hand on her wizened one. "You are already helping. Lisa has power, of what magnitude, I do not know, and she does not know either."

Ming Ue slid her wise eyes over Lisa and nodded. "Lisa *is* powerful, as was Li Na. It is in their family."

"I came to protect her and put my mark on her. She is mine now."

Ming Ue patted his arm. "She can have no better protection than a golden dragon. They are the best warriors, the most loyal, and most lucky of all the dragons."

"Ming Ue . . ." Lisa began, but Caleb broke in, blue eyes amused.

"I will protect her with my life, but I would rather remain alive. Will you help me find the black dragon and the orb?"

"We would be honored to help," Ming Ue answered. "But I do not know how I can. I am a humble and weak old woman with little knowledge of the honored ones."

Lisa wanted to laugh but held it in check, realizing that

Ming Ue spoke almost ritualistically. Ming Ue was by no stretch of imagination humble, weak, and old. She ran the dim sum shop with an iron fist and drove her nephew Shaiming to distraction, which was probably why he never smiled. The women in Ming Ue's family were all powerful, and the men scrambled to get out of the way.

"Your help will be invaluable, Ming Ue," Caleb said, as though he, too, were following a ritual. "You humble me with your offer. Your house will be blessed."

"Thank you, honored one."

Caleb touched Ming Ue's forehead with his broad fingers. Lisa felt the brush of his magic, the musical threads of his dragon thoughts, though not as strong as when he'd touched her. Ming Ue relaxed into a smile, her wrinkled face serene.

Lisa and Carol exchanged a look. Carol obviously still did not buy into the dragon discussion and was not sure what Caleb was doing but didn't want to interrupt her grandmother. Lisa gave her a reassuring nod, and Carol raised her brows, resigned.

"Now," Ming Ue said, her businesslike demeanor reasserting itself. "What can I do? I know Chinatown inside and out, and Carol knows about the rest of San Francisco. We'll help you find the black dragon's lair."

"And when you do, you will keep well out of his way," Caleb said. "You might admire him, but he will use you for his purpose. Li Na made you promise to protect Lisa, didn't she?"

Ming Ue nodded. "That is so. I watch over the granddaughter of Li Na."

Lisa looked at her in surprise, having never heard this before, but neither Ming Ue nor Caleb noticed or answered. Caleb glanced around the dining room. "This is a good place. You have made it strong."

Ming Ue ducked her head, pleased. "The little spells I have are of the humblest nature compared to your magic, honored one."

"His head is swelling," Lisa said. "I can see it."

"Leave her alone, Lisa. She is enjoying this."

Ming Ue burst out laughing and slapped Caleb's huge arm. "This is true. I like exchanging words with you, honored one. This is a blessed day. My spells do keep this house lucky, but it is nothing compared to the might of a dragon."

"You do not always need spells where you have wisdom," Caleb said. "The black dragon will put his mark on as many people as he can, to raise an army to help him. That is the way of the black dragon. Do you know of anyone who has begun to show signs of a dragon mark? Or heard of gatherings around a new leader?"

Ming Ue frowned. Shaiming still hung onto the cart, listening avidly. "I do not leave the shop much, honored one," Ming Ue confessed. "I see few people but my family and the regular customers."

"Lumi might know," Carol broke in.

Caleb and Ming Ue looked up at her as though they'd forgotten her presence. "Ah, Lumi," Ming Ue said. "He is a good boy now."

"Lumi is my cousin," Carol explained. "He used to be involved in gangs and drugs, I'm sorry to say. He has rehabilitated now, gone straight, and runs a bicycle shop off Sacramento Street. But if anything strange was going on in the Chinese underworld, Lumi would know. He has many friends; he knows everyone."

Caleb looked at Lisa. "Can we visit this Lumi?"

"I don't see why not. I haven't talked to him in a while and should say hello to him."

"Thank you," Caleb said gravely to Carol and Ming Ue.

Ming Ue smiled again. "But first, you must have your dim sum. Shaiming has brought the best and some tea." She broke off, putting her hands on the teapot. "Which is cold. Shaiming, is that the way to treat an honored guest? Bring more hot water, you foolish man."

Shaiming slammed the teapot back to the tray and pushed it sullenly away, the wheel squeaking. The show over, Carol strode back to her alcove to usher in more diners.

Ming Ue stayed with Caleb while he and Lisa ate their early lunch, patiently showing him how to use chopsticks. Caleb caught on and managed to eat everything in front of him, pausing after every bite to tell Ming Ue how wonderful the food was. Ming Ue glowed under his praise, and Caleb played along, coming up with compliments each more flowery than the last. Lisa sat back and watched them, mystified by the dance of courtesy that they both seemed to perform so well.

He had a way with people that went beyond his dragon magic, she thought as she watched him. *Charm* was what she'd call it if he were human.

And he's charming me. But he was a dragon, for crying out loud—he'd change back into a being with golden scales and sharp teeth and fly away into Dragonspace to live out his long life. His stay here was temporary.

She said I could be human until you are safe, he'd told her. Then he'd go away, forced back to Dragonspace by the witches, and she'd lose not only this gorgeous man she was just getting to know, but the friend she'd come to trust.

Lisa was full of dumplings and tea by the time Caleb paid his last extravagant compliment to Ming Ue and announced he was ready to go to the bicycle shop and consult Lumi. He unfolded himself from the chair and reached down to help Lisa to her feet.

She looked up at him as his warm hand closed over hers. His blue gaze was on her as usual and as watchful as usual. When he caught her studying him, he gave her a little smile with the corners of his mouth and led her out of the dining room.

In the alcove, Lisa said good-bye to Carol then waited for Caleb, who had gone back to talk to Shaiming. Shaiming listened to him, head bent, then to Lisa's amazement Shaiming flashed Caleb the biggest smile she'd ever seen. Caleb laughed and clapped the man on the back. Shaiming returned his attention to the cart, grinning and shaking his head.

"What did you say to him?" Lisa asked as they walked through the narrow alley back toward the street.

"That I knew he had a little magic, too. That it keeps the cart wheel squeaking on purpose, to drive Ming Ue crazy."

Lisa stopped, astonished. "The old devil."

"He enjoys it very much."

Lisa burst out laughing. Caleb watched her, his head tilted.

Still chuckling, Lisa took his arm and steered him out of the alley, making for Sacramento Street and Lumi's bicycle shop.

7

Caleb studied Lisa walking beside him, enjoying the way her body brushed against his as they went arm in arm back to the busy street. Her hips moved in rhythm to her stride, her blouse parting at the top to give him glimpses of the woman inside, the charms clinking.

He thought about how he'd opened the front of her dress last night, and how she'd frowned at him when he'd ripped the fabric. The reward had been lovely, her breasts in black lace, soft flesh beckoning his hand. She smelled good, she tasted good, and he wanted to discover so much more of her.

Waking to find her snuggled against him, her bare legs entwined with his and her bottom pressed against his inflated cock had been heady and wonderful. He'd lain still, so not to wake her, savoring the time with her as the sun slid across the bed and bathed her skin in golden light.

When he was a dragon looking into her life, he'd wanted to cross over to be with her. Now that he was here he wanted to be nowhere else. But if he'd known what confused emotions would churn through him while simply walking next to her, watching her red hair in the sunshine, he might have stayed home. Caleb, who hadn't had a complex emotion in his life, was staggering under the weight of them now. He'd not be able to stay with her forever and that thought stirred sorrow and regret.

Lisa led him from the street thronged with cars and shoppers down another alleyway where the buildings seemed to close in overhead. Lines and awnings crisscrossed above them, casting shadows.

Lisa moved confidently down the narrow alley and around the corner before stopping in front of a shop as unpretentious as Ming Ue's dim sum restaurant. Bicycles both new and old crammed the single front window, and inside hung from the ceiling and lined the walls and took up nearly every inch of floor space.

Lisa opened the door, letting a string of bells ring sweetly against the glass. Caleb paused in the doorway, touching his fingers to the lintel, closing his eyes to feel the lines of the place. They were straight and clean, not brushed with dark magic. He whispered a dragon word and opened his eyes to find Lisa staring at him.

"What are you doing?" she asked.

Her eyes were so beautiful. The brown depths of them held an almost golden fire, pulling him to her. He leaned down and kissed the corner of her mouth.

"Making sure no evil has crossed the threshold."

Lisa slanted him a look that stirred his desires. He leaned to her again, and she smiled into his kiss and slid her arms around his neck.

Her tenderness never failed to stun him. Dragon procreation was fast, dangerous, and best avoided. Humans took their time, building affection day by day.

"You taste nice," he murmured.

"Hot mustard." She deepened the kiss, and he cupped her elbows in his large hands and pulled her close.

"Uh, excuse me?" a young male voice said. "Lisa?"

Blushing, Lisa broke from Caleb and faced the tall, black-haired young man who'd come toward them. "Hey, Lumi. How are you?"

"Just great." He grinned. "You want some privacy?"

Lisa's blush deepened. "Sorry. This is Caleb. I brought him to talk to you about something."

Lumi was thin and wiry, his face a little gaunt, but his dark eyes were lively, his smile wide. He looked as though he had once been robust but had struggled with some illness and was just beating it back. Caleb put him at about twenty-five human years old, the same age as the young woman at the dim sum shop. *Cousin*, Carol had called him. He'd heard people refer to cousins on television, which meant sons and daughters of aunts and uncles.

Caleb found complex concepts of family fascinating. Dragons moved to their own solitary territory as soon as they were large enough to fend off predators and never saw their siblings, or uncles or cousins for that matter.

"Carol called and told me," Lumi said. "Come on in the back. I have coffee unless you're already drowning in grandmother's tea."

He signaled them to follow him through the shop. A narrow aisle snaked through the chaos of bicycles to the back counter, and behind that was an opening into an even dimmer back room. Bicycles in every stage of repair filled the space, as did wheels, pedals, gears, chains, and various other bicycle parts. Caleb noted, however, that everything was neat and clean, tools hanging from hooks or lined up on the workbench as though Lumi knew exactly where everything was and could put his hands quickly on whatever he needed.

In the corner, a staircase led upward into more darkness, probably to an apartment where Lumi lived, and a narrow, open back door led out to a tiny alley. Caleb quietly observed everything while Lumi and Lisa carried on their conversation.

"Really, Lumi, how are you?" Lisa asked. She looked at him anxiously, as though worried about the answer.

"I'm fine. Honest to God. I'm completely off all that stuff, and I'm glad. Almost dying at twenty-four isn't what I had in mind as a great life. I'm clean, I'm out, I'm done."

"Good," Lisa said warmly. Lumi only nodded, but Caleb could see he was pleased by her approval.

"What did you want to see me for?" Lumi's smile came back. "To buy a bike?"

"Afraid not. I know you don't like to talk about your old life, but Caleb needs to ask you about some things."

Lumi instantly became wary. "What? I don't hang out with those guys anymore, but I'm not going to rat them out, either."

Caleb wondered what *rat them out* meant, but felt the ripples of the young man's distress filling the room. He quickly encased the crazed emotion in his dragon music, easing it and letting it dissolve.

"Someone bad is here," Caleb said. "If he's true to form, he'll try to mark as many people as he can. Do you know of anyone behaving strangely—maybe worshiping a new god or something?"

Lisa watched Lumi, as though expecting him to answer in the negative and looked surprised when Lumi grimaced. "I thought something weird was going down."

Lisa fingered a small hexagonal tube on the workbench. "Like what?"

"Like secret meetings and rumors of a new boss, but no one sees him. Guys are disappearing, but not dead, you know what I mean? They're just not where they usually are."

"And you have no idea where they go?" Caleb asked.

"No," Lumi said. "I'm out of the loop, you know? But I hear things."

"Will you listen more closely for me?" Caleb asked. "It is important that I find out what he is doing—to protect Lisa from him."

Lumi's eyes widened in appropriate fear. He seemed to understand the danger even if Lisa and her friend Carol did not. "Lisa, you don't want to be involved in this shit."

"So far, I don't know what this shit is," Lisa said. "But I'm willing to believe I don't want to be involved."

"These are bad people I'm talking about," Lumi said.

"For the most part, I'm happy they're disappearing, but some of the ones disappearing are good guys. You know, they're loyal and watch your back and help when they can. But the others—they'd shoot you in cold blood for a quarter. If they're massing in some kind of new gang, we're all in trouble."

"They're forming a cult of the black dragon," Caleb said. "The black dragon can draw disciples to him who will do anything for him. Your tongs and organized crime gangs are nothing compared to a black dragon army. They can swallow the world."

Lumi sent Lisa an "Is he crazy?" look at his mention of the black dragon. "A gang worse than the gangs I already know about? That's not good."

"He wouldn't try to recruit Lumi, would he?" Lisa asked.

"Of course he would. He will try to recruit as many as he can. He will go for those already in the underworld, because they are used to working covertly, but he'll recruit more as time goes on, until he's ready to strike. Every person who joins his army gives him more power, and he wants your power most of all. So it makes sense he'd try to recruit those close to you."

"Great," Lumi muttered.

"But he won't succeed," Caleb went on. "I won't let him."

Lumi did not look reassured.

"How do you know so much about the black dragon's methods?" Lisa asked curiously.

"What is all this talk about dragons?" Lumi broke in. "You're starting to sound like my grandmother. She believes in dragons."

"She believes in them because they are real," Caleb said. Lumi gave him another *right* look. "Black dragons are best at manipulation. If I were a black dragon, what he is doing is what I would do. He is extremely cunning and will know what kind of people are easy to control, but once he is finished, he won't protect them any longer. He wants to leave this world and return to Dragonspace and won't care who dies behind him. Black dragons have no love for humans. Before I met Li Na and Lisa, I was the same, especially about witches."

Lisa raised her brows. A lock of fire red hair escaped its confining ponytail and brushed her cheek. "I'm glad we could change your mind."

He moved the satin lock of hair with the end of his finger. "You are different from what I thought humans would be."

Lisa leaned to his touch, their thoughts tangling. "What did you think we would be?"

"All the same. Cruel. Stupid. But when I met Li Na, she just laughed at me. She knew what would happen when I met you."

Lisa's lips parted, red and soft. He moved his finger to them, stroking warm smoothness.

Lumi cleared his throat, and Lisa jumped, her cheeks pink. She seemed embarrassed by her reaction to Caleb, but her desire for him was clear. He could scent her wanting, pheromones drifting from her to encase him.

"Was Li Na the first human you'd ever met?" she asked hurriedly.

"No." He shook his head. "There was a knight, long, long ago, who made his way to Dragonspace thinking he'd slay a dragon and carry it back home to impress his people. I caught him easily, but I wasn't hungry, so I trapped him in the corner of my cave. He was interesting. Every morning, noon, and evening, he would go through a series of sword exercises, honing his skill to perfection, even though his puny sword would never harm me. He was so devoted and went through the rituals so precisely that he fascinated me. Dragons like precision." He glanced approvingly at the tools lined up on Lumi's worktable.

"Did you ever eat the knight?" Lisa asked.

Caleb shook his head, straightening a wrench on the table a fraction. "I let him go. I gave him a few rubies to take with him for keeping me interested. Those probably made him more famous in his kingdom than a dead dragon would have. Not that he could have killed me."

"Your boyfriend's nuts, Lisa," Lumi muttered. "Did you know that?"

A smile pulled at Lisa's lips. "Is that how you escape a dragon? Entertain him?"

"It is one way." Caleb gave Lumi a nod, touching him with another wisp of magic. "Do *you* know where the dragon orb is?"

Lumi looked blank. "Dragon orb? Is that a club?"

Caleb smiled at him. "No. Thank you, Lumi, for your help."

"No problem," Lumi said, shaking his head as Caleb slid his arm around Lisa's waist and led her out of the shop.

Caleb expressed interest in the cable cars, so Lisa led him toward Powell where they could pick up the line. She'd take him all the way to the top and Fisherman's Wharf if he wanted, since he seemed to relish tourist attractions.

She was enjoying showing off her city to him. He viewed the sights in wonder and curiosity, drinking in the newness of it without cynicism. He liked everything, including the tourist shop selling earrings shaped like tiny Coit Towers, which he insisted on giving her. Lisa had to laugh at him and then pay, because he didn't understand that they weren't free. Caleb looked offended at the clerk who handed them to her and told Lisa again that he would bring her any jewels she wanted, she only had to ask.

Lisa took the package and kissed Caleb briefly, liking the glow of dragon magic that touched her. She wished she could have watched his transition from beast to human, watched the gold flow down to become two human legs, trunk, torso, arms, the face shifting from long and pointed to flat and human. She wished she could have seen the scales shift to skin, the spines on his neck become the golden hair that looked unruly even after he combed it. He'd pulled his hair into a tail for convenience, and it hung long to the hollow of his back. The T-shirt and jeans out-lined his gorgeous, tight body, making her realize that Caleb the dragon must have been in fantastic shape.

He leaned down as they walked and spoke into her ear. "I like how you look at me."

"How am I looking at you?" Lisa asked, trying to sound innocent.

"With desire in your eyes."

Lisa's face heated as she realized how obvious she'd been. "You're a dragon."

"Today, I am not."

She knew the truth of it. He might be Caleb the dragon inside himself, but outwardly, he was a sexy man, and Lisa was a woman who'd too long been alone.

What might have become of the embarrassing conversation, she didn't know, because at that moment, Caleb turned his head to look into an antique shop, one that carried Chinese rosewood and lacquer furniture, Coromandel screens, and antique swords. In the middle of the shop, a man rested his hands on a glass counter, studying whatever contents were under it. The Chinese woman proprietor spoke animatedly with him, obviously pointing out the assets of the wares.

The man was tall like Caleb and wore a black leather coat and black leather pants that stretched over his firm body. A tail of long black hair flowed in a sleek wave down his back, sliding over his coat when he bent his head to examine the goods under the glass.

Caleb stopped, going from moving to standing still so suddenly that Lisa went on a few steps before his iron-strong hand pulled her back. At the same moment, the man looked up and around as though he'd sensed Caleb behind him in the street.

The two men's gazes locked. The black-haired man's eyes were silver—not gray, but a misty silver—almost glowing in his face, cold like ancient ice.

Caleb released Lisa, growling, "Stay here," and strode into the store.

Lisa hurried in after him, not about to obey. As soon as she passed the threshold, she felt it, the black dragon's mark draped over the store as Caleb had draped his over the dim sum shop. The mark was dark, made of night and shadows and the dark face of the moon. It was not evil, exactly, but it contained compelling power. Lisa knew that if she were not already under Caleb's spell, she'd have quickly succumbed to the mark.

That the man in leather was the black dragon she had no doubt. He had the dragon litheness, the power, the eyes, the confidence that he dominated everything around him.

Caleb snarled as though he, too, felt the mark, but he didn't let it stop him. Moving faster than thought, Caleb snatched a black-handled sword from a rack near the door, swung the blade around and pressed the tip against the hollow of the black dragon's throat. The sharp sword made a pinprick cut in the black dragon's skin, and a trickle of blood stained the bright steel.

The black dragon's eyes flared silver. If he and Caleb had been in dragon form, they'd have been circling each other, talons extended, warning shots of fire flung from mouths of razor-sharp teeth. Their human bodies limited them, but a physical fight still could leave one or both of them dead. And the black dragon's magic floating over this shop might mean that the dead one would be Caleb.

Wait, Lisa wanted to scream, but her lips would not move.

The black dragon looked down the length of the sword, contempt filling his silver eyes. "I thought I smelled a golden's stench on the streets."

The proprietor, who'd gone white-faced and wide-eyed when Caleb burst into her shop and held her customer at sword-point, tried to slip quietly toward a curtain at the back. She'd call the police, Lisa knew, and they'd arrive in time to find the black dragon-man stuck through with a sword and blood everywhere. They were a long way from Lisa's apartment, and she'd never get Caleb back to it in time for him to escape to Dragonspace.

Without thought, Lisa brought up her hand and hurled strings of fiery light across the room. The strands wove themselves together to create a glowing web across the curtain. She shot another web of light at the front door, covering it, and willed the lock to click closed. Two would-be customers pulled the door in a puzzled way, peered through the now-smoked glass, then moved on, seeing nothing.

The proprietor stared at the front door, then at Lisa, then at the front door again. Quietly, her eyes rolled back in her head, and she crumpled to the floor.

Lisa lowered her hand, her breath coming fast, her heart pounding. She felt the fire within her, rising from where she did not know. It terrified her and at the same time it was the most exhilarating thing she'd ever experienced. It was like an orgasm, only ten times better. Her entire body pulsed with pleasure and fierce triumph.

The two dragons had not moved. If they noticed her bit of magic, they did not take their eyes off one another.

"So you work for witches, now?" the black dragon said, his voice as cold as darkness.

"I protect Lisa from all who would harm her." Every one of Caleb's muscles was taut, a warrior ready to strike. "Witches be damned."

"They want her. They want to harness her power. I am only trying to get to it first."

"To find the dragon orb?"

"To scrag the damn witches. Let me have her, and I will free you from them."

"If you use the orb, you will destroy everything behind you when you try to enter Dragonspace," Caleb said. "Including Lisa."

"Why do you care?" the black dragon asked evenly. "Think of it, the witches gone, unable to pass your true name on to anyone else—ever. You will be in Dragonspace and you will be free."

Caleb's hand was iron steady. In spite of the black dragon's power, Caleb was the warrior, the one who knew how to fight and to kill cleanly and precisely. He did not look back at Lisa, but she felt his dragon song touch her. When he answered the black dragon, his voice was calm. "The price is too high."

"They are *witches*, Caleb. Remember what they did to Severin."

Caleb's face drained of color and his eyes blazed with a fury Lisa had never seen in him before. Behind the fury, she sensed sorrow and a vast sadness pulling at his mark on her mind.

The black dragon used Caleb's distraction. With impossible speed, he knocked the sword aside and curved his hands into claws to lock around Caleb's throat. Lisa, again without thought, shot a ball of light at him with deadly accuracy. The light struck the black dragon's side, propelling him several feet backward. He fell to the floor, on his back, and Caleb, sword raised, went after him.

In the split second before the sword came down, the black dragon caught the twisting light Lisa had thrown at him in his hands. He laughed and closed his eyes, his face relaxing into pure pleasure just before Caleb drove the sword straight through his gut.

The black dragon grunted. Blood flowed from the wound in a shining swath against his black jacket. Caleb stood over him, lips drawn back in the fury of the kill. Lisa watched in frozen shock as Caleb yanked the scarlet-stained sword from the wound and stood back to watch the black dragon die.

8

Except the black dragon didn't die. He lay on the floor and stared up at Caleb, blood running freely from his wound. The dragon was in pain, that was obvious, his face drawn and gray, lines deepening in his face, the silver glow in his eyes dimming.

Slowly he leveraged himself to his feet, swaying as blood gushed from him to stain the ochre-colored carpet. He leaned against a bronze green statue of a tall bodhisattva and wrapped his arm around his wound.

"This is another thing the witches did to me," he rasped. "I'll live out my dragon lifespan here and won't die until then, no matter what happens to me." He clenched his teeth against pain, leaning his dark head against the statue. "So poke me with a stick all you want. You won't stop me."

"No, but I can slice you to ribbons," Caleb said. "And keep you from putting the pieces back together."

Lisa felt a whisper of strength, then the black dragon launched himself at Caleb, wrapping strong, blood-wet hands around the hilt of the sword. Fire welled into Lisa's palms, shaping a ball of light, which flung itself at the black dragon without her even compelling it.

The black dragon released the sword and caught the light in his hands. A blue nimbus stretched over his fingers and wrists, and he wrestled with it, struggling to hold it, to conquer it. His face contorted in pain, but when a thin ribbon of power slid into him, his face relaxed into the beatific expression he'd worn before.

"No, Lisa," Caleb said as more light feathered Lisa's fingertips. "He is feeding off it. Your power helps him."

But Lisa had no idea how to stop it. A surge shook her from head to foot, and she let off a blast of power toward both men. The light ball caught Caleb in the side and sent the sword flying end over end to shatter a display case on the far side of the room.

Caleb fell to his knees but didn't go down. The black dragon slumped against the statue, again fighting the white light, trying to control its entry into his body. He managed it, but the effort sent him to the floor with a grunt of pain, and his eyes slid mindlessly closed.

Lisa pulled her hands apart, praying that the power would stop. Sudden reaction set in and her stomach clenched. She doubled over.

"Lisa." She looked up at Caleb's worried expression, barely able to see him.

"Did I hurt you?" she whispered.

"We need to get you home, Lisa. His minions will come for him."

She started to laugh, weakly, which turned into another session of dry heaves. Caleb gently helped her to her feet and held her against him. "Did you say *minions*?" she asked.

"Come, Lisa, before he calls for help."

The black dragon lay still and limp on the floor, eyes closed, blood streaming from his wound. The metallic stench of so much blood made her retch again. Whatever power had come from her no longer made her strong and triumphant, and she nearly fell when Caleb tried to help her walk.

"Lisa," he breathed in her ear then he picked her up and carried her through the curtains and out the back door. He hurried through the rundown alley and back to the main street, where Lisa had to explain to him how to hail a taxi.

At the same time a cab shot down California street to take Caleb and Lisa home, Saba sped her elderly Toyota into Chinatown and slammed to a halt in the alley behind the antique store. She'd driven here in record time after she'd answered Malcolm's weak-voiced cell phone call informing her he was hurt and needed assistance.

Without bothering to turn off the car, Saba leapt from it and rushed into the shop through the open back door. People were pulling at the front door, trying to peer in, jiggling the latch and wondering what was going on. Saba nearly stumbled over the body of a middle-aged Chinese woman who obviously worked in the shop. For a moment, her heart stopped, fearing the worst, but a quick check showed her the woman had only fainted.

She sensed Malcolm on the other side of the counter, under the statue of a bodhisattva, even before she raced around and found him lying motionless and covered with blood. She dropped to her knees and touched his face, her heart banging uncontrollably.

His breath brushed her fingers, warm with life, then his eyes fluttered open. The silver light had dimmed, but his gaze was no less compelling. "Get me away from here," he rasped.

He grasped her wrists, smearing blood all over her bare arms. "Oh, Goddess," she whispered. "Did anyone call 911?"

"Take me to your home, *not* the hospital. I command you."

"Are you stupid? You're bleeding all over the place."

"I said, I command you, Saba. Get me out of here. I won't die."

His words and the mark on her mind compelled her to

obey. Against her better instincts, she slid her arm around him and helped him get to his feet. He was weak and sagged against her but he was definitely alive. She felt his heart beating strong against her side, his breathing even. Still, she had to help him stagger to the car, parked askew in the alley, and spill him into the seat.

She hurried to the driver's side, jumped in, and sped off, scaring a few cats and one stray tourist in her mad rush back to Sacramento Street. She drove hurriedly and badly, praying that the police were way too busy to notice her flying through intersections with a bleeding man in the car.

Malcolm slumped against the door, his hand pressed to his side, blood all over him. He grunted in pain as she careened around corners, but said nothing.

"What the hell happened?" she snapped at him.

His face was white, pupils dilating with loss of blood. "Damn golden dragon stuck a sword in me."

He closed his eyes, resting against the door frame. It occurred to Saba that if he died, she'd be free of him and his mark, but the thought did not diminish her worry and her urgent need to help him. She decided to drive now, question her sanity later.

At her apartment, she parked more or less legally, then extracted Malcolm from her car and half-carried him up the stairs. Fortunately, she saw none of her neighbors and so avoided awkward questions, but she knew *someone* must have noticed her dragging a half-dead man into her house.

She'd have to make up some convincing story to explain it, because she couldn't afford to be evicted right now. Her on-again off-again programming jobs were off again, and she could fudge the rent long enough to land another freelance project, but not if the landlord thought she was involved in something like gangs or drugs. She'd be out on her butt with nowhere to go, unless she wanted to move across the bay to Berkeley and listen to her father go on about how she should marry a nice Japanese man and keep house for him.

"You really owe me, Malcolm," she muttered but he didn't seem to hear.

Once inside the apartment, she locked the door, and Malcolm collapsed. He landed full-length on her carpet, limp, eyes closed. Saba snatched towels from the bathroom and blankets from the bed, knowing she needed to keep him warm.

At least, that's what you did for humans who'd lost a lot of blood, to keep them from going into shock. For dragons, who the hell knew? She stuffed a pillow under his head and wadded the blankets around him. She tugged his leather coat open then used scissors to cut open the pullover shirt underneath. She unbuttoned and unzipped the fly of his leather pants and eased the waistband open.

The wound gaped, a wide, deep cut, slashed vertically across the muscles of his abdomen and covered in dried and congealing blood. Pulling the shirt away started the bleeding again, and she snatched up a towel to stem the flow. "I'm not a nurse, damn it," she said. "Or a doctor."

Malcolm's eyes slid open. "You can heal me. With your magic."

"No, I can't," Saba almost shouted. "I'm barely an initiate. I can do some rudimentary crystal magic and light candles to help with little things, but I can't heal a wound like this."

"Yes, you can." He squeezed her wrist, his strength alarming even in his evident state of pain. "You made the talisman for Caleb and not just any initiate could do that. I won't die, but I won't heal instantly, either. I'll lay on my back for weeks waiting to heal, and I don't have time. I haven't the power to speed the healing, but you do."

"And I tell you, I don't." Saba sat back on her heels, watching the strong man now lying so helpless before her. "When our coven summoned Caleb, I thought my power helped bind him, but I realize now that Donna did it all. We were just there to anchor the circle. My magic sucks and so does Grizelda's. She just has too much of an ego to notice."

"You're wrong." Malcolm's voice brushed her senses,

enticing, dark, like his mark on her mind. "You have power, little witch, but Donna has made you believe you don't. She fears anyone knowing her secrets and desires, so she keeps you at a distance. But I feel the magic in you. You are close to touching your true power. Draw the circle and invoke your deities, and I'll tell you what to do."

He meant he wanted quick and dirty magic. No purifying herself with a bath, no cleansing her tools, no meditation. It wouldn't work, and she had the sick feeling that she'd have to watch him give in to pain and die. Malcolm was strong, but despite what he claimed, no man could survive a wound like that.

"You still haven't explained what happened," she said as she gathered, with shaking hands, her bags of salt, the cup and ceremonial knife, her crystals, and a handful of white pillar candles.

"Caleb, the golden dragon happened," he said. "Protecting Lisa, who he's thoroughly ensnared. I couldn't get through his protections to mark her, but I tasted her power." His voice changed, taking on a note of wonder, even joy. "She has such power, Saba, it flows from her like honey and tastes like nectar of the gods. I tried to control it, to turn it to help me, but I couldn't. I was close, but I couldn't do it."

Saba traced a circle in salt wide enough to encompass his body. She'd done salt circles in her apartment before, and her carpet glittered here and there with tiny crystals she'd missed when cleaning up. Once the circle was complete, with her inside it, she knelt facing east and lifted her hands.

She heard Malcolm chuckle.

"What?" she asked, self-conscious. She'd never performed a ritual in front of anyone before, not wanting something so personal to be witnessed, and frankly, afraid she'd screw it up.

"You don't do your rites in the nude?" he asked, a teasing light in his silver eyes. "Not sky-clad?"

Saba let irritation flare to cover her fear. "Oh, please,

that is so made up," she growled, then began her chant to
the Goddess.

Malcolm guided her through the ritual, which Saba had
never heard of or read in any Wiccan text she'd ever gotten
her hands on. He had her lay amethysts in his cupped
hands, then she placed her own hands over them, and together they charged the stones. She felt his dragon power,
the fire element, seeping into the amethysts, melding with
her own earth element. Saba was half-Japanese, and the
mountains that formed the backbone of Japan were in her
blood even though she'd never seen them outside of pictures. The snow-covered cone of Fuji-san figured in several
silk paintings that hung in her apartment now, the mountain itself calling to her from across the world. One day she
would travel to Japan and see for herself the mountain that
had been revered by her people for centuries.

Malcolm's fire magic and her earth magic continued in-
fusing the amethysts, the power building until she worried
the crystals would shatter with it. Malcolm instructed her
to clean the wound with the water from the chalice, which
she did, and then to pile the amethysts on the wound.

He flinched as the first stones touched his skin, gritting
his teeth against pain. She circled the wound with the stones
then built a small pyre of them over it. The amethysts radiated so much energy that the air around them glowed purple. Malcolm's face contorted as pain took him, but when
Saba reached to move the stones, thinking they hurt him too
much, he told her sharply to continue the ritual.

Saba laced her hands through his and placed them over
the stones, chanting the words he told her to. The stones
rocked with fire and earth magic, combining with water
magic from the chalice that cleansed the wound and with
the air magic of her breath repeating words. He began to
speak with her, his rolling, baritone syllables combining
with her lighter ones.

Magic cascaded through her, and Saba gasped with it.
She'd only come close to feeling like this once, during her
dedication rite, when she'd felt the true presence of the

male and female divine *with* her. She'd never felt so powerful, or so loved, before or since.

The power that coursed through her now was similar, but brighter, sharper like steel. It was Malcolm's power, the fire magic of the dragon that witches had been taught to both fear and covet. Dragon magic could kill them, but properly harnessed, it could propel them to heights they never dreamed of reaching.

Malcolm was giving her his magic freely, for his own benefit of course, but he was letting her take it and use it and enjoy it. Tears ran down her face with the beauty of the power. Was this what Donna felt when she performed her high priestess rituals—that she could do anything, touch anything, see anything, be anything?

A blue glow infused the circle, and the candle flames leapt high. His magic, hers, the crystals, the words, the energy of the circle, all rushed toward a spiral of ecstasy.

They broke together, his shout mixing with hers, the feeling more powerful than anything sexual. The apex of magic held for one glittering moment, strong as steel, stretching until Saba thought she'd break with it.

And then, just as suddenly, the power spiraled down, the amethysts slowly lost their glow, and the flames of the candles relaxed into small flickers.

Malcolm lay back, breathing hard, releasing her fingers. Her hands aching, Saba brushed the amethysts from his abdomen, letting the stones clink to the carpet. The blue light that had enclosed the circle slowly faded, her mundane apartment returning to focus.

Beneath the stones, his wound had closed. All that was left of the bloody mess was clean skin creased with a white scar about four inches long.

Saba stared in astonishment. Malcolm sat up, touching the scar, seemingly healthy and whole again, none the worse for wear.

"I did it," Saba said, then her heart staccatoed as she realized what she'd said. "I did it!" Her cry rang with triumph.

"Of course you did." Malcolm slanted her a dark smile,

his eyes strong and sensual. "I knew you had the power, my witch."

He snaked his hand through her hair and drew her head back, kissing her deeply. She laughed, loving the rough feel of his tongue in her mouth. He eased her to the floor, breaking the salt circle, letting the residual power flow to the floor and down through the foundations of the building to the earth.

He laid her down, his heavy body covering hers, kissing her mouth, the power between them still tangible. "I knew you could do it," he whispered, his silver eyes filling her vision. "You have power deep inside you, and I am going to give you a gift for letting me share it."

"A gift?" Her lips barely formed the words.

Malcolm stripped her cropped shirt and bra from her, and lowered his mouth to suckle her breast. As he had the night he'd first put his mark on her, he demanded nothing from her. That night he'd pleasured her again and again until she'd dived into sleep, and she'd woken in the morning to find her hands and feet unbound and Malcolm gone.

"Please, Malcolm," she begged in a whisper.

His broad hands parted the opening of her jeans and slid them and her underwear down her legs. He seemed stronger than ever, his injury forgotten. He cupped her breasts in his palms, running his thumbs across her nipples until they stood up, hard and hungry for him.

He suckled her, nipping a little, his teeth hurting her and feeling marvelous at the same time. He kissed her abdomen, dragging his strong tongue across her navel and down to the swirl of hair that was wet for him.

Saba slid her legs apart, knowing what was coming. Malcolm laid himself between her thighs and licked her, his tongue rough and hot and pleasuring her deeply. She sensed his dragon power binding her even more thoroughly and knew she should fear him, should run as fast as she could to some place in the middle of nowhere where he'd never find her. She knew she was his slave, and against her will, she was rejoicing in the slavery.

He pushed her thighs open and stroked his tongue across her, letting his thumbs move the opening of her labia. He knew exactly how to tantalize her, how to make her squirm against the carpet, the leftover salt grating into her back. She arched her hips, wanting his mouth, and he suckled and nibbled, driving her more and more crazy. She laced her hands in his long hair, silken smooth strands warm with life, and held him against her, wanting him intensely.

His breath heated her skin, her thighs stinging where the stubble on his jaw abraded her. A dragon who had to shave, she thought with an inner laugh, and the laughter made her come.

Saba screamed, trying to muffle the sounds, but she couldn't stop them. She ground her hips upward, wanting his mouth. He kept on suckling her, licking and stroking, not letting up, even as she climaxed.

"Damn you, Malcolm," she moaned.

He pressed harder, making her take all of it, climax and beyond. The feeling spiraled her past the bonds she'd put on her own mind, the admonishment to not look into things she did not understand and not follow the spark of power she sensed inside herself.

He growled softly as he lifted his head from between her legs, his black hair hanging down like a curtain. "I'll teach you. I'll teach you so much, my witch."

Her body shuddered with release, but the release only increased her need. She tried to gather him close, but he lifted himself up and away from her. The bulge in his half-opened pants showed her he had need, too—huge, elongated need pressing the cloth of his briefs—but he closed the zipper over it and buttoned the waistband, in perfect control of himself and his physical desires.

"Please stay," Saba begged. She spread her legs wider so he'd see all of her, wet from her own juices and his mouth. She'd never been so shameless in her life.

Malcolm shook his head. "You're not ready for me, Saba."

"Yes, I am."

"You are not ready for me and what I can do."

Saba shivered, wondering what he meant, not entirely afraid. Malcolm got down on his hands and knees and put his face next to hers. He had done this before, when she'd been tied to the bed, and she realized it was the dragon in him, crouching over the thing that was his—a kill, a treasure, a mate.

"They will try to use you," he said, his breath warm on her lips. "Let them."

"Lisa and Caleb?" she asked. "Or Donna and Grizelda?"

His eyes flickered with hot silver. "If Donna comes near you, I will kill her."

"Lisa and Caleb are all right, then." She felt sleepy and languid, drained from the magic and the sexual climax.

"If Donna comes near you, call my name. I'll not let her have you back."

Saba brushed her thumb across his cheek. "I don't think she wants me back."

"She will once she knows what you can do. She wants the power, she craves it for its own sake. I only want to get home, but she will destroy for the joy of destroying. Lisa knows nothing. The old woman, her grandmother, was too powerful to manipulate, but Lisa is defenseless and ignorant of what she can do. Vulnerable to the likes of your high priestess, Donna." He nearly spit the name, his revulsion tangible.

"You hate her," Saba said, surprised.

"I have been watching her. She is beyond contempt. There's a reason I chose you, Saba, and not the other."

"Grizelda is Donna's toady. She'd never turn."

"That isn't why." Malcolm kissed her, his mouth softening to almost tenderness. He got to his feet, looking down at her, all six foot, six inches of black leather and man. "Lead them to me," he said, then he turned on his heel and left her alone.

The door closed softly behind him, and only then did Saba begin to shake.

9

Caleb paced Lisa's living room as afternoon died into darkness, his dragon self restless. His instinct to fight and kill pulled at him, but his human self was weaponless, nearly powerless, wondering what the hell to do. Out there in the kaleidoscope of sound and color that was San Francisco the black dragon lurked, along with the dragon orb and witches who knew more what was going on than he did. Caleb had stuck the black dragon through with a sword and he still lived, and Lisa's magic was ripping her apart from the inside out.

Lisa lay curled on the red sofa in her living room, her auburn hair flowing across the black throw pillows. Her white face made her brown eyes enormous, the arm that was tucked behind her head looked so fragile. A glass of blood-red wine rested on the coffee table in front of her, the only thing she'd been able to ingest since they'd arrived home hours ago. He sent musical thought-threads to her, trying to soothe and heal her, but in his agitation, the music sounded like jangled chords.

"Please stop looking at me like you're scared, too," Lisa

said as he paced by her for the hundredth time. "I didn't think you were afraid of anything."

Caleb sat on the sofa next to her, drawing her feet into his lap. They were too cold and he rubbed them gently, trying to stroke warmth into them. "I understand now why Donna didn't want me to become human."

"Why?"

"As a dragon, I have enormous powers, but only on the other side of the door. My magic is limited here, and I can't protect you as well as I could if I were a dragon. But if I am a dragon, I can't be here to help you."

"So you're screwed either way," Lisa said. "I'm sorry."

"If I knew what your magic was, I would know better what to do. You have dragon magic, but it isn't exactly the same as dragon magic. It feels different. It feels ancient and yet not. It's a beautiful power, but deadly, too." He reached for her hand and traced her fingers, remembering how they'd flared with raw magic.

She drew a breath. "I can't control it. I just acted instinctively, and now I feel like shit."

"I couldn't kill the black dragon." The words made him bleak.

"You weren't to know the sword wouldn't work. He didn't seem much affected by the magic I threw at him either. We could have captured him if I hadn't gotten sick," she finished glumly.

"I protect you first. It is not a choice."

She smiled. "My knight in shining armor. No, I forgot, you eat those."

Caleb didn't laugh. He knew Lisa feared the power inside her, but she didn't have Caleb's experience with magic and knowledge of what untamed power could do. She was in a whirlpool of danger, and this place, filled with lucky magic, was the only island of calm.

"The black dragon wants your magic," Caleb said. "He tried to drag it into him. He knows what it is, and he thinks you are the key to the dragon orb. We must find out why and where this orb is. I thought I would find out in Chinatown with the friends of Li Na, but they did not know. Either Ming Ue truly knows nothing about it or she is a very good and subtle magician."

"I'd never heard of the dragon orb, either, Caleb." Lisa stroked his broad fingers. "Grandma Li Na told me many stories about old China and dragons, but she never mentioned an orb or that I'd have this power. She dropped cryptic hints but that's all, and I didn't pay any attention at the time."

"Perhaps there are clues in this apartment that she left you. I did not know her long, but she was very magical. She must have known you would come into your powers once she was gone and left you a message of some kind."

Lisa shook her head. "I went through everything after she died. I didn't find anything I didn't either already know about, or anything odd. No orb, for instance, no stashes of books on magic or dragons, no letter saying, 'Dear Lisa, Here's everything you need to know about the strange power you can sometimes use.'"

Caleb drew her fingers to his lips and kissed them. She tasted so fine, like flowers after rain, strong and fragile at the same time.

"We need the witches," he said. "I don't trust them, and I don't like them, but they know better what's going on. It might be fun to shake information out of them."

Anger entered Lisa's eyes. "Not if they try to hurt you again, singing your true name or whatever they did. I don't like or trust anyone trying to enslave you."

"Saba might help us." He glanced at the armband glittering with the runes Saba had scratched on it. "My enslavement was my own fault."

"How do you figure that?" Lisa's limbs had already started to warm, anger on his behalf flushing her skin. "How did they get your name?"

He shrugged. "I was very young, only a few hundred years old, and I heard my first mating call. I and another golden answered it, and I fought him and won, but he hurt me greatly. You remember what I told you about female dragons, how they try to kill their mates when they're finished. I had to fight to get away from her, and I was already injured. I fell into a canyon and lay there, almost dead, when a witch who'd made her way from this world into Dragonspace to steal dragon magic found me."

Lisa laced her hand through his, watching him with concerned eyes. "What happened?"

"I was in too much pain to see or even speak, and she offered to heal me. She needed the secret of my true name to do it, and I gave it to her."

He shuddered with memories as he told Lisa the rest of the tale. Overjoyed that she had a tame dragon, weak and bound to her magic, the witch used him in every hideous way she could. He'd once heard that witches followed a creed to do no harm to others, but he decided that by "others" they did not mean "dragons."

The witch who enslaved Caleb enjoyed testing the limits of what she could make him do. If he refused, she tortured him until he begged to die. She siphoned off his magic or made him use it to help her in everything from a rain spell to outright murder. His only hope had lain in the knowledge that dragons lived far longer than witches, and her small human life, no matter how hard she tried to prolong it, would soon end.

Except that the witch who had enslaved him passed the secret of his name to her followers. They built a cult around Caleb and his powers, calling him and using him whenever they wished. He could not kill them—that restriction was built into the enslavement. The sign of the golden dragon became feared, but Caleb only wished for his slavery to end.

And then, about five hundred years ago, the calls stopped. Caleb learned that magic, witches, and dragons had passed into legend in Lisa's world. Machines and the mind prevailed, and magic and dragons were forgotten, which was fine as far as Caleb was concerned. But just when he'd hoped that all the witches who'd known his name were dead and gone, Donna the high priestess and her ragtag coven had summoned him out of sleep and commanded him to watch over Lisa. Donna knew the ancient ways, and she knew what she could do to Caleb if he refused.

Lisa listened quietly, her hand in his. "We must get you free of them," she said when he finished. "Once and for all."

He leaned to press a kiss to her forehead. "Humans don't concern themselves in the affairs of dragons."

Her brown eyes were stern. "You are my friend, Caleb. I'm concerning myself. If their power over you won't let you hurt them, maybe we can find a spell or something to make them forget your name. Would that work?"

"I don't know. I can't cast spells on them, either. The first witch knew what she was doing."

Lisa sat up. "Well, then we'll consult other witches. Maybe Ming Ue knows some. I never realized she had so much knowledge about magic and dragons, and she might have connections. Or maybe Saba knows the answer. She helped you with the armband. If we get her away from the other two, perhaps she will see reason." She took on a determined look, the power in her rising. "And if she doesn't see reason, there's no restriction that says *I* can't harm the witches."

She was so beautiful, her face filled with indignation on his behalf, her lovely body quivering as she spoke. She cared about him, which was a new sensation to Caleb.

He put his fingers under her chin and kissed her. Her lips moved in response, soft as down under his. As she had in Lumi's shop doorway, she slid her arms around his neck, letting her fingers drift under his hair to massage his nape, while she softly swept her tongue into his mouth.

She tasted like the wine she'd drunk and sweet spice. He wished he had centuries of time to explore the attraction he felt for her. He wanted nothing more than to lay with her on this sofa, or on her bed, learning her body with his hands and his mouth, understanding what it was to mate with her, to *be* with her.

Lisa pulled gently away. She ran her thumb across his lower lip, wiping away moisture. "We should be talking about finding the witches."

"I want to kiss you for three days."

Pink crept into her cheeks. "That might be fun." She sat up again. "First things first. How do we find Saba?"

"I don't know. When I needed to contact the witches, I had a calling ritual, but now that Donna's severed Saba from the coven, it might not summon her any longer. I don't want Donna to know I'm calling Saba in any case. She lives here, in San Francisco, but I don't know where."

Lisa gestured to the armband. "Does that tell you anything?"

Caleb fingered it, feeling soft gold and the warm scratches of the runes. "The letters are part of the spell. Perhaps if I concentrate on it long enough, or turn back into a dragon in Dragonspace and sink my thoughts into it, I can trace the magic back to her physical location."

"Or you could look her up in the phone book."

Caleb stopped in midthought. He knew about phone books from their ads on television, but it had never occurred to him to consult it. Another indication he didn't know much about the practical side of being human.

Lisa swung herself from the sofa, looking much stronger, and rummaged in the drawer of the end table. "Do you know her last name?"

"No."

Lisa hefted a large, supple paper book, then looked at it thoughtfully and set it on the table. "We'll try the Internet. There can't be that many Sabas in San Francisco."

She sat down at a desk across the room and turned on the computer, one of the few possessions of her own she'd brought to the apartment. Caleb fingered the book, opening it at random and looking at the list of names marching down the page in tiny type. So many names. If the black dragon used the orb and began the destruction Donna feared, all those names would be of people who no longer existed.

"Here we go," Lisa said. Caleb closed the book and went to her, looking over her shoulder at a softly lit screen. "I've found three Sabas with addresses in San Francisco. I hope she lives in the city, not down the bay somewhere, but I suppose we can search all those towns, too."

"How do we know which one is her?" Caleb asked. He leaned over to look more closely at the screen, which let him glimpse the soft swell of Lisa's breasts inside her loose shirt. She smelled good, like soap and Lisa. He touched a kiss to her neck where her warm red hair swirled.

She smiled. "Stop that. Which do you think it is?"

Caleb studied the three names, able to read the letters, but human names were meaningless to him. These weren't their true names, they were the names they gave other people to identify them. True names sang. These names were merely lines on a screen.

"Saba Watanabe," Lisa read. "Watanabe is a Japanese name. Is Saba of Japanese descent?"

"She is Asian," Caleb said, interest rising. "That may be her."

"It's an address in SoMa," Lisa said, using the nickname that meant the district south of Market Street in downtown. She tapped her finger on the white device she called a mouse and a map appeared on the screen with a small star near the middle. "If Saba Watanabe is the right person, she's there." She touched the screen. "Scary, isn't it?"

"How do I get to this place?"

"I'll drive you."

He placed his hands on her shoulders. "No. I want you to stay here. This is the safest place for you." He sensed again the maelstrom of danger, with Li Na's apartment the calm in the storm.

"You want me to turn you loose in San Francisco?" Lisa asked, brown eyes wide. "I'm imagining all kinds of strange and potentially hazardous problems."

"Give me this map and explain how to get there. I will be fine, Lisa. I fly from one side of Dragonspace to the other in a heartbeat and never get lost."

"Yes, but do they have militant gay bars in Dragon-space?" Lisa murmured.

He bent down to catch her words. "What?"

"All right, I'll print out the map, but we're going to-gether. I don't want you running off exploring or chasing after the black dragon or trying to find the orb on your own. It's dangerous."

"It is more dangerous for you. If you leave this apart-ment, the black dragon will be able to track you. He's tasted your magic, and he'll be able to use it to find you. Here you are protected, both by my mark and the remnants of Li Na's magic."

"Yes," Lisa argued, "but Greg was here, minion of the black dragon, remember? He knows where I live, and I'm willing to bet the black dragon does too. Donna and Grizelda and Saba know as well, for that matter. Everyone knows where I am."

"And while you're here, they can't touch you. Have you wondered why the black dragon simply hasn't come here? He knows you are protected with strong magics. But once he's healed himself of the wound I gave him, he'll be wait-ing for you to come out."

"Exactly why you shouldn't go out alone. You can't kill him, but he can probably kill you, and I can't stand the thought of that. I at least have this." She wriggled her fin-gers. "Whatever this power is, it stopped him from hurting you."

"I am a warrior dragon, Lisa. I know how to fight."

She made an exasperated noise. "Neither of us is going to give in, are we?"

He softened his touch, caressing her bare shoulders. "Lisa, please stay here. You cannot control your power, and I need you to be safe. Please."

He moved threads of his dragon thoughts through hers, music soothing, willing her to understand how terrible the danger was. Here she was inside a fortress. Out in the city she was vulnerable, and he could not both look for answers and protect her at the same time.

She sighed, relaxing under his touch. "All right," she said heavily. "I'll stay here and call a taxi for you. But you'd better come back soon and whole, or I'll—" She shook her finger under his nose, then let her hand drop, her eyes filling with tears. "I don't know what I'd do. I can't lose you, Caleb."

His entire body warmed as he leaned down and briefly kissed her. "You won't lose me," he promised. "Not yet."

Caleb left the apartment in the taxi that Lisa said would take him to Saba's home. She came down herself and handed the driver the map along with money, before kissing Caleb hard on the lips and retreating back into the house.

Mrs. Bradley had come down with them. Caleb had asked her to keep Lisa company tonight while he went out, and Mrs. Bradley had chirped that she'd be happy to. She and Lisa could make cookies. Lisa had given him a severe look, knowing Caleb wanted Mrs. Bradley to keep Lisa inside, but she complied.

Caleb let his lips linger on hers, savoring the taste and feel of her, before he climbed into the taxi and pulled the door shut.

The ride downtown was interesting and swift, the driver keeping up a chatter about his life in San Francisco, his wife who liked to nag him, and his daughter's upcoming wedding, with asides to snarl at drivers who got in his way.

"This is it," he said, pulling up to a narrow brick building with brick arches over the windows. "The lady told me to wait."

Caleb didn't argue. He unfolded himself from the car, pulling on the long black coat Lisa had purchased for him that morning against the cool night air. At the doorway was a series of little lit-up buttons, including one that had WATANABE handwritten beside it. He pushed the button, wondering what would happen, and jumped when Saba's tinny voice came out of the air. "Yes?" she asked warily.

"Saba?"

The gurgling noise he heard meant she'd recognized his voice. "Caleb. What the hell do you want?"

"To talk to you. Where are you?"

A sharp buzzing sound made him jump. Saba sighed. "Come on inside. Mine's on the third floor."

Caleb put his hand tentatively on the door and pushed. It clicked open, then swung heavily shut once he'd stepped inside, the lock falling into place.

Unlike the pretty interior of Lisa's apartment house, this one had cracked floor tiles, a narrow hall, and a steep staircase leading upward without a lift. He climbed to the third floor and saw Saba peeking out at him from a half-opened door.

"What are you doing here?" she asked, her voice tired.

Caleb didn't feel the black dragon mark until he'd stepped inside the one-room apartment and she'd shut the door. It was subtle—the black dragon hadn't been heavy-handed with it, obviously wanting Saba to be his minion without anyone knowing about it. Caleb spun around to see Saba standing defiantly between him and the door, her slim arms folded, short black hair tousled.

"He marked you," Caleb said.

"Yes, after I turned you human. It wasn't exactly my fault."

"No, very likely not."

He curled his fingers in frustration, knowing he could not erase the black dragon's mark and put on one of his own. Saba was a wielder of his true name, and he could not mark her or harm her or do anything magical to her. In this room, the small slender witch in a cropped T-shirt held all the power.

He took in the room, the mussed bed, the candles and other witchy accoutrements strewn about the desk, the computer that looked newer and more complex than Lisa's, and the salt on the carpet. He smelled, over the mark of the black dragon, the purple-tinted magic of a healing spell.

"You cured him," he said.

"Yes." Her expression hardened. "You hurt him."

"Don't feel sorry for him."

She uncrossed her arms and let her defiance increase. "He doesn't want to harm Lisa. He just wants to go home."

"He'll harm her one way or another. Where is the dragon orb?"

She looked surprised. "I haven't the foggiest idea."

"Does Donna know where it is?"

"I don't think so, and I don't think she'd tell me even if she did."

She sounded disgruntled. Caleb picked up a black pillar candle that lay on its side on the desk and set it upright, saying nothing.

Saba rubbed her arms like she was cold. "Malcolm thinks she's after power of her own and could care less whether the dragon orb destroys the world."

"Really?" Caleb asked, fingers on the soothing wax of the candle.

Saba shrugged. "It's what Malcolm thinks. Donna's very strong. I think she could do whatever she wanted with the orb. Malcolm just wants to use it to go home." The black dragon's mark swirled around her palpably as she repeated the stubborn words.

"Where is the black dragon?" he asked her.

"I couldn't tell you even if I knew." The smoky threads around her faded. "I have no idea where he lives."

Caleb sensed her sadness and frustration. The black dragon had certainly ensnared her. "Where does Donna live, then?"

She shifted uneasily. "Why do you want to know that?"

"I want to ask her more about the orb. And find out what she knows about Lisa, and the black dragon. Because no one will tell me anything, and I want to know."

Saba looked unhappy. "She's already made it clear she wants nothing more to do with me. She won't be thrilled if I lead you to her. She might even try to send you back to Dragonspace."

Caleb touched the gold armband. "Your magic brought

me here, not hers. You will not let her break your spell and
send me back. You will tell her, *Too bad, it's my spell.*"

"Are you trying to cause dissent between witches?
Dragons and witches hate each other. I can't take your side
against another witch."

"Not even to help Lisa? Lisa is not a witch—at least, I
don't think so. She has so much power, the like of which
I've never seen before. I want to protect her, but I don't
know how to do it here."

Saba studied him with dark eyes, then her face softened
into understanding. "You're falling for her."

"Lisa is my friend."

"Doesn't hurt that she's pretty, and now you aren't a
dragon looking through a door."

Caleb hesitated as the musical thoughts of Lisa sang in
his mind. Lisa smiling at him as he chose what show to
watch on the television, Lisa pirouetting around the apartment, body lithe under her loose clothes, Lisa tucked next
to him in the bed while he lay recovering from his wounds.

He smiled, slow and warm. "No, it doesn't hurt that
she's pretty."

Saba shook her head, her aura radiating sympathy.
"Now you know what humans go through."

"My feelings, they are complicated," he agreed. "Which
is why I need to protect her. Help me protect her, Saba."

Saba was quiet a long time, thoughts chasing each other
behind her eyes. She sighed. "I know where Donna lives. I
go to coven meetings at her house, at least, until she threw
me out. Grizelda's still her toady."

"Can you show me?" Caleb asked. "I have a taxi waiting
downstairs."

Her brows went up. "You're efficient."

"Lisa is making the driver babysit me." He grinned.
"She doesn't trust me out on my own."

"Can't imagine why," Saba muttered, then she reached
for her coat and led him out the door.

As they sped away in the taxi, the driver following the

orders Saba gave him, Caleb said, "Malcolm? What kind of name is *Malcolm*?"

Saba glared at him. "It's a perfectly good name. There's nothing wrong with it."

Caleb shaped the word a few more times, then made a face and gave up. Saba continued to glare, so much that he had to chuckle. She might not like the fact that she was in thrall to the black dragon, but she was defending him as hostilely as Mike the terrier would defend Mrs. Bradley.

10

Grizelda's frustration built to a breaking point as she watched Donna, who was seated cross-legged on the floor of her basement, laying out her ritual tools.

"But I want to learn," Grizelda wailed.

Grizelda had come here tonight with questions about Caleb and Lisa and the dragon orb and had found Donna getting ready to begin a ritual. Grizelda didn't know which one, because it wasn't a full moon tonight and not a sabbat or an esbat. A witch didn't need a major celebration to do a ritual, but Grizelda believed that doing a precise ritual at a precise time was the way to power.

She was not sure about the two men in the room, either. They wore dark blue velvet robes, nothing different from what she could buy from various New Age shops in town. The robes clung to them in sensuous waves, letting Grizelda know they were naked beneath. Their faces were beautiful and identical. Twins, but she'd never seen them before. Grizelda knew many people in the Wicca community, but these men were so striking—white-blond hair, chiseled features, and large black eyes—that she would have remembered them.

Donna wore a robe, too, a white one, unadorned. Whether she was naked beneath, Grizelda could not tell, but she did not think so. Donna had taught the coven that performing rituals sky-clad was unnecessary.

"Donna, you promised to teach me," Grizelda said, watching while Donna laid a black-handled knife and a cup on the altar. The knife looked very sharp, which was odd, because the ceremonial knife, the athame, was usually blunt, for ritual cutting only.

Donna finally answered. "You are young and inexperienced, and frankly, rather stupid. You seek to know mysteries not meant for you, and you don't even know what you're ready for."

"That's why I need a teacher," Grizelda argued. "And now that you've closed the coven to Saba, you'll need my help more than ever."

Donna sent her a look of such contempt that Grizelda's heart squeezed with hurt. "I hardly need *your* help."

Grizelda fell silent while Donna positioned a pentacle on the altar. She thought Donna put it the wrong way around, but she dared not open her mouth to tell Donna she'd made an error.

"What is Lisa's magic?" Grizelda tried. "I've never seen anything like that. My butt still hurts from landing on it."

"It's very powerful," Donna said. "Very rare in a human being. Lisa is dangerous. I intend to do something about her."

Grizelda's unease flared at the matter-of-fact tone of Donna's voice. She'd thought Donna all wise and powerful when they'd met, had been so proud to be chosen to be one of Donna's coven and share in the power of the dragon's name. But Grizelda did sometimes wonder why Donna had chosen her and Saba. Donna was right, Grizelda's path through the Craft had so far been rocky, and she had to struggle to feel even the simplest energies from crystals and candles. Why had Donna chosen witches with so little experience to help her?

"Why is she so dangerous? From Caleb's reports, she seems a normal person. Except with this power."

Again the look of contempt. "Lisa has stronger magic than any you will ever encounter, and she has no idea how to control or use it. She has knowledge of the dragon orb, but it's buried deep." Donna's voice dropped to the reasonable tones that had persuaded Grizelda to follow her in the first place. "We need to show her how to use her powers, how to keep her from destroying things with it, herself most of all. And if she can help us find the dragon orb and keep it from Malcolm, so much the better."

Grizelda relaxed slightly. What Donna said made sense—Lisa could hardly be allowed to go around throwing white light at people with Caleb standing behind her egging her on. And if the black dragon got his hands on Lisa and the orb, he could destroy the world. Whatever Donna was doing must be right.

One of the men looked at Grizelda. "I'll teach you." His voice was sinuous, his smile even more so.

Grizelda clenched her teeth against sudden revulsion. "I'd rather have Donna," she said nervously.

"If you want to learn something," Donna snapped, "watch now. And be quiet."

Grizelda folded her hands in her lap and shut her mouth, bile in the back of her throat. The man looked away, thank the Goddess, and turned his intense gaze to Donna.

Donna lit the candles on her altar, having already closed her circle, and invoked the four quarters—north, south, east, west. The two men in blue stood on either side of Donna, one on the east, one on the west. The altar faced north.

Donna began chanting. Grizelda expected a prayer to the Goddess and the horned god, but what came out of Donna's mouth was pure gibberish. Perhaps it was Latin or Greek, but Grizelda didn't think so. Nor was it an Asian language—growing up in San Francisco had attuned

Grizelda to the languages of Japan, China, Korea, and Vietnam. This sounded like nonsense.

The two men opened their robes and let the velvet slither to the floor. Grizelda had been right, they wore nothing beneath. Their penises were rampant and erect, and she saw, being unable to look away, that they'd shaved every bit of hair from their pubic area.

Caleb had been naked when they'd burst into Lisa's apartment, but he'd worn his nudity easily—he was a dragon, a beast with no need for clothes. He'd shown no embarrassment and no expectation that they'd be embarrassed to see him. He made a beautiful man, the golden dragon did, a body reflective of all the goodness of the god and Goddess.

These men flaunted their bodies, made damn sure anyone looking at them was uncomfortable. The one at the east of the altar grasped his own scrotum and let his semen fall into the chalice. Grizelda gasped out loud, and the man smiled at her.

Heart thumping, Grizelda glanced into the dark corners of the room, hoping the Goddess herself would manifest, perhaps in the form of Juno or Isis, to strike him down for profaning the altar. Then Donna turned her head, took the other man's erection in her mouth and began to milk him. The air in the room dimmed, taking on a blacker hue, smoke from the cauldron and the tapers weaving gray smoke into the thickening air.

Grizelda scrambled to her feet, pushing her filmy draperies aside impatiently, shaken to the core. She understood now why Donna had put the pentacle upside down— this was dark magic, terrible magic, a perversion of all that was right in the Craft.

"Donna, no," she cried. "Remember our most important rule—that anything we do will come back to us threefold. This will harm you, the universe will make sure of it."

Donna licked the man's cock from base to tip then turned a blazing glare on Grizelda. "You stupid little cow.

Do you really think you know the secrets of the universe because you went through an inane dedication ceremony? Do you think the Goddess and god *care* that you want to celebrate them? Do you think they even want you speaking their names?"

Grizelda's heart pounded with fear and rage. Her dedication ceremony, done deep in the woods under a full moon, her body naked to the silver light, had been the happiest event of her life. She'd finally realized that she *belonged*, that there were kind and loving deities who embraced her, even if she'd been silly and awkward and uncertain all her life.

"How dare you?" she said, her voice shaking. "You are not one of us. You are perverting the Craft."

"I see," Donna said calmly. "And you know everything there is to know about the Craft, do you? Let me tell you, you know nothing. Power is for power. I have it, I want it, I will use it. Why do you think I let you in here tonight when I could have barred the door to you?"

"To teach me *this*?" Grizelda said indignantly. "No, thank you."

"For the ritual," Donna corrected her, her voice suddenly cold. "I need two of everything for it to work. Once it's performed, my power will rise threefold. That is your rule of three, Grizelda."

"I'll not help you." Grizelda began striding toward the basement stairs.

One of the white-haired men stepped smoothly in front of her, his black eyes taking on a green glow. Grizelda halted, scared and angry, then tried to go around him. He blocked her way with ease, his fingers on her arm cold and strong as steel. She realized that his white hair was feathery, and a hint of scales traced the line between face and scalp. Glancing behind her, she saw thin black wings, leathery like a bat's, folded tight against the other's back.

"They're not human," she breathed.

"They're incubi," Donna said. "And what they do not know about pleasure is not worth learning. You'll enjoy it."

"Demons. They're demons."

The incubus smiled, showing his teeth, which where shining white and slightly pointed. He made a quick move, and Grizelda went down on her back, the breath rushing from her lungs. Her head struck the floor, sending waves of pain through her. Bright lights wavered before her eyes and then the incubus was on top of her. His strong hand wrapped her hair and pulled her head back so he could plunge his tongue into her mouth.

Grizelda fought harder than she'd ever fought in her life. The incubus was strong, but finally her fist connected with his windpipe. As he staggered back, gasping, she broke away and ran, flinging herself up the stairs and out of the house in blind panic, her dress torn, her face covered with blood and tears.

Caleb came upon Grizelda in an alley not far from where he left Saba and the taxi. Grizelda hunkered on the damp ground, curled into a ball, her flimsy black garments hardly protecting her from the cool rain that had begun to stream over the city.

He went down on one knee and put his hand on her shoulder. When he touched her, Grizelda snapped her head around, opening her mouth for a terrified scream, which Caleb stopped by his hand over her mouth. She gave him a defeated look with wide eyes.

"What happened?" he asked, pitching his voice to soothe.

Grizelda quieted, but the fear did not leave her eyes. Caleb slowly removed his hand from her mouth, and she drew a long breath.

"Donna is practicing black magic." Tears leaked from the corners of her eyes.

Caleb could not quite read her mind, but he felt the terror pouring from her and disgust and dismay. Anger stirred in him. As with Saba, he couldn't put his mark on Grizelda to help her heal because she wielded his true name, but he could help her using more mundane means.

"You are safe now," Caleb said. "Saba is waiting just down the street, in a taxi. She will take you to safety."

Grizelda hesitated a moment, then she nodded. Caleb touched her face, feeling sorry for her even though she'd helped summon and bind him.

"Donna says she just wants to help Lisa," she whispered. "But how can she with dark magic and demons? It's all wrong."

"Demons?" he repeated sharply, old anger rising.

"Incubi. They're horrible."

Caleb's anger turned dangerous. Demons were unwelcome anywhere, but they oozed their way into Dragonspace and the Earth world from the pits of hell to wreak havoc as they wished. Too many people believed in them, allowing them to manifest, usually as attractive creatures to seduce their summoners before they understood the danger.

Demons were no match for the might of a dragon, although enough of them could do much damage, even to a dragon, as Caleb had personally experienced. He hated demons, evil vermin who had been the cause of the greatest sorrow of his past.

"What is she doing with these demons?" he asked Grizelda.

The young woman shuddered. "Foul and filthy things. How can she?"

"She probably wants to enhance her own power. Demons have much magic in their own nauseating way."

"I don't want anything to do with that. I only do white magic, good magic." Grizelda seized one of the amulets around her neck. "The Goddess protects me."

"You are smarter than Donna." Caleb rose to his feet. "Witches can be consumed by their own power if they aren't careful. Stick to dancing under the moon, or whatever it is you do."

Grizelda sniffled and wiped her eyes, smudging them with eyeliner. "You're not so bad, for a dragon."

"Goldens are the best of all dragons."

"But you're full of yourself."

He smiled slightly. "Lisa says that. Go now and tell Saba what you told me. I'm going to have a peek at Donna."

Grizelda bit her lip. "Be careful."

"I'll think about it." He strode away, his dark raincoat swirling. He heard Grizelda scramble to her feet and the click of her too-high heels as she hurried toward the street and the waiting taxi.

Caleb climbed an almost vertical alley to an obscure street and a normal enough looking house with a neat yard. A whiff of Donna's magic came to him before he even reached the house, and he nearly gagged on its foulness. It drifted through the air in dark strands, visible to other magical beings. Saba and Grizelda, and he added reluctantly Malcolm, were right not to trust her. Donna was working dark magic no dragon would stoop to.

He also smelled the demons. One came at him as he slipped into the shadows behind the house, a tall, white-haired incubus, white skin shimmering in the darkness. Caleb slowed. In Dragonspace Caleb could flame demons to instant ash, but here he'd have to fight.

The demon sprang. The thing was laughing, sure of its power, triumphant that at last he could best a dragon. But though Caleb did not have all his dragon powers, he still had much of his dragon strength. He caught the demon as it leapt, spun the white body around, and in a lightning-swift move, broke its neck. The incubus slid to the ground without a sound.

Caleb shot a glance at the calm house and slipped back into the shadows, leaving the body in the driveway. There were wards around the doorways of the house, but none on the basement window. Either Donna was careless, which he didn't truly believe, or she'd left the one crack so the demons could get in and out.

That's why he didn't trust witch magic, Caleb thought as he peered through the window. They needed physical things—sketched runes, crystals, candles—for protections, instead of simply casting the aura of their thoughts like dragons did. But then again, witch magic had captured him and allowed him to come here, so he had to grudgingly concede that it worked.

Donna rolled on the floor of the basement with another incubus; he was impaling her as she screamed in ecstasy. Caleb made a noise of revulsion. Demon magic was foul, and Donna was busily pulling it into herself. He saw the sickly white glow move from the demon's body to hers and her ecstasy grow as it did.

He'd seen enough. Donna did not have the orb or she'd be using it. She was trying to fortify herself with demon magic, which told Caleb clearer than words that she was evil, despite her façade of the helpful, motherlike witch who only wanted the best for everyone.

If he could have killed her now and gotten her out of the way, he would have, but the spell that enslaved him would not let him. That didn't mean, he thought with some satisfaction, that others couldn't do the deed for him.

He turned away from the window and left the house. In the driveway, the demon's dead body had decomposed to ash and a foul green ooze. Holding his breath, Caleb stepped over it and made for the alley that would take him back to the taxi.

Lisa lay awake for hours that night contemplating all Caleb had told her after he'd returned from seeing Saba, and wishing he hadn't departed again. Caleb had turned up near midnight, telling her he'd found Saba but that she knew nothing. And by the way, Saba was now in thrall to Malcolm the black dragon, she had healed him, and Donna was having sex with incubi in her basement to stoke up her own magic.

Caleb then told her he had to go back to Dragonspace for a time; why, he wouldn't say.

He'd stripped off his clothes and kissed her good-bye, but when she asked questions, he touched her mouth, stopping her words. "Do not leave the apartment until I return, and let no one in—except Mrs. Bradley. She's the only harmless person in this city. Don't talk to Donna whether she calls on the phone or comes here, and *don't let her in.* Same goes for Saba—who knows what the black dragon will make her do?"

"Caleb . . ."

"I'll be back as soon as I can." He kissed her again, his eyes darkening, and he let her go with reluctance.

He walked into the spare bedroom, his perfect body moving with grace. Lisa raised her hand to him just as he slid the armband from his elbow and tossed it to her.

"Keep that for me."

She caught it. There was a flash of gold, a hint of wing, and suddenly, fifty feet of dragon filled the space behind the doorway.

Caleb watched with his dragon eyes as Lisa reached in and touched his scales, marveling at how warm and soft they felt, his powerful muscles beneath. Now that she'd seen him as a man, she realized that there was nothing strange about him shifting back to his dragon shape—it was simply another aspect of him, Caleb of the glowing blue dragon eyes and sexy smile.

"What did Malcolm mean today when he asked if you remembered what they did to . . . Severin, did he say?" she asked. "Who was Severin?"

Caleb's eyes took on a look of vast sadness she'd glimpsed in him before.

"Severin was my son," he said, his voice quiet. "But that is a story for another time. I want to return before your night is through." He narrowed his eyes to slits, fixing them on her. "*Don't* leave the apartment."

"I won't. Hurry," she added softly.

Caleb's mouth rippled into his usual grin. "I will fly on swift wing."

He turned, his golden body filling the doorway, a black mist beyond seeming to stretch to eternity. Caleb took one step into it, then plunged suddenly downward.

"Shit!" she heard him shout.

She leaned as far into the doorway as she dared. "Caleb! What happened?"

"I fell off the ledge," he snarled.

Lisa started to laugh. There was a great heated updraft, a leathery swish of wings, and Caleb rose, a golden flash against the black. Then the mist coalesced, growing lighter and lighter, and suddenly, she looked into the empty spare bedroom, which smelled musty with disuse, and Caleb was gone.

Now Lisa lay awake in bed, starting at every tiny noise in the apartment. Donna consorting with demons, the black dragon enslaving the one witch who'd helped Caleb.

She thought about how Ming Ue had known right away that Caleb was a dragon, and how she'd gone quiet with awe when Caleb told her a black dragon was wandering around San Francisco. Ming Ue had magic, too, and so did stolid Shaiming. Lisa wondered briefly if her skeptical friend Carol also had magic but didn't know it or believe it.

Then there was this power in herself that Lisa could not control. She remembered how the power had nearly consumed her when she'd raised her hand to throw magic at Malcolm. She'd known instinctively what to do, but afterward she'd been weak and sick and had no idea how she'd summoned the power. Caleb was as astonished by her power as she was; he hadn't known anything about it, either.

Lisa's entire world had turned upside down in the last few days, as soon as Caleb had become human. His name jingled musically in her head, though she knew that *Caleb* was not his true name, but one that sounded human. The thought of his hard, naked body made her squirm with warmth. From the twinkle in his blue eyes, she knew he'd noticed her noticing him all day, and he liked it.

The wind chimes in the living room tinkled faintly as they did sometimes when the oscillating fan wafted air to them. Caleb had admonished her to keep the windows closed even though it was stifling, so she'd turned on all the fans in the house to move the air around.

To the faint jingle and the shushing sounds of the fans she at last drifted to sleep to dream of wandering a dark and trash-strewn alley somewhere in the city. She knew she was still in San Francisco because she could smell the salt water of the bay and see the lights of the Bay Bridge looming above the buildings. A man stood silhouetted not far from her, tall and well-shaped, and her heart leapt.

"Caleb?"

"If you want me to be."

Caleb's deep voice rolled out of the darkness and the man stepped into the light. He was naked, with Caleb's golden skin and mane of unruly hair and cocky grin. His eyes, though, instead of being lapis blue were black.

"You are dreaming of me, Lisa-ling. I like that."

"Am I dreaming?"

"Of course. In dreams you can do whatever you want. You know what you want to do."

Lisa's lock of white hair tingled at her scalp. "What do I want to do?"

"Touch me." He came closer. He had Caleb's scent of maleness and his knowing smile. "You want to touch my body and enjoy it. You wonder what it would be like to have sex with a man who is a dragon, a wild and magical beast. It would be good, Lisa-ling. I promise you."

Her hand rose of its own accord, fingers resting on the man's shoulder. The play of muscle beneath was real enough and she traced the cords of his biceps.

"Touch me," he whispered. "All of me."

Lisa let her fingers drift down his chest, golden hair catching on her fingertips. She moved her touch across the hard ridges of his abdomen.

"Submit to me," he said. "I'll make it hurt good."

Lisa's mind felt heavy, her thoughts in a fog. She pulled her fingers away.

"Caleb would not want to hurt me."

"Caleb is a dragon. He doesn't know how to be gentle. I'll teach you to like it hard, so you'll be prepared for him."

"He would be gentle for me," Lisa said stubbornly, trying

to shake the fog from her head. Wisps of mist wrapped her arms like ropes.

"He won't know how not to hurt you. Let me teach you to love it rough. You know deep inside you want it to hurt, it turns you on. I will be Caleb for you and hurt you until you beg for more."

Lisa forced herself to take a step back. "What are you?"

Caleb's form shimmered and became a man just as tall and handsome but with stark white hair, eyes black and empty. A whisper of leathery wing drifted across his back. "Anything you want me to be. Come with me, Lisa, and let me hurt you. You will like it."

The tendrils of mist tightened around her arms. The man smiled, showing pointed teeth, his eyes like holes into nothing.

"Go away. Get out of my dream."

"I am incubus," he hissed. "I am made for dreams. I will take you to my mistress, who will teach you obedience."

He pinned her face between his hands and crushed a kiss to her mouth. She flinched at the invasion of his tongue and his vile taste. She tried to cry out, but he pressed his thumbs to the corners of her mouth, opening her wide to kiss her harshly.

She felt a surge of power within her and heard her wind chimes jangling like crazy. She took a long, gasping breath, nearly choking on the cloying sex smell of the incubus, then her eyes flew open and she was lying, panting and sweating and alone, in her own bed.

Lights blared in her living room and the CD player belted out *The Marriage of Figaro,* the powerful strains of Mozart drowning the disappointed hiss of the incubus. Lisa threw back the covers and scrambled out of bed, but she was alone in the room in her light nightshirt, the incubus nowhere in sight. Music surrounded her and blocked out thoughts of the dream.

"Caleb," she called.

She heard nothing but the rising crescendos and runs at the end of the piece. She padded out to the living room on the cushion of noise and found it empty. The fan had fixed on the wind chimes, sending them jingling and dancing and adding their sweet music to the clamor.

The overture ended and the CD player fell silent. The fan rotated past the wind chimes, and they settled down into a soft tinkling.

Lisa found the remote control for the CD player on the floor, facedown. The fan *could* have gotten stuck and perhaps blown the remote off the table which landed on the play button.

Weeks ago, she might have accepted that explanation, but after today she didn't think so. Li Na's lucky magic surrounded this apartment, Caleb claimed. The incubus had tried to harm her or steal her through her dreams, and the magic and music had stopped it.

Beyond the bright living room, the darkness of the balcony gaped like a maw. In the silence Lisa thought she heard the faint thump of a foot, the leathery whisper of wings. Bile in her throat, she pulled the curtains tight over the windows then clicked on the CD player again. She filled every slot with discs from Mozart to Stevie Ray Vaughan and started it up.

She spent the rest of the night on the sofa, right under the wind chimes, with the lights on and music surrounding her.

"You were to bring her back," Donna told the incubus who stood before her, his wings moving slowly behind his naked body.

"The magic was too strong. She floated free in her dreams, but the magic in the house pulled her back before I could take her."

"Caleb has done his job too well," Donna mused. "I told him to keep the black dragon from getting his hands on her, but the simple-minded warrior dragon is shutting me out as well." She smiled. "Ah, well, more fun when I have Caleb help me kill the woman he has come to care for.

Even better when I tell him why. What goes around comes around."

The incubus didn't understand, that was clear, but he smiled anyway.

Donna's satisfaction surged. "Lisa will pay for what she did to my sister. I can't change what happened, or what will happen, but once Lisa knows what and who she is, she will understand why I am killing her, why I am killing the last of her kind. Her power will be nothing to mine when I am ready."

Incubi were simple creatures, interested in sex and death and nothing else. But they were useful and had so much raw power she sang with it.

She held out her hand. "Come here."

The incubus, knowing what was about to happen, widened his smile and sauntered across the room to take her hand.

In the morning, Lisa rose from the sofa, groggy and tired, and shuffled in the bathroom to take a shower. Sunshine poured through the windows, erasing the fears of the previous night, but Caleb still hadn't returned.

Lisa faced a new dilemma this morning—taping of the cooking show would recommence today, and she had to go to work. She hoped Caleb would breeze through the bedroom door before she had to leave and everything would be all right. Hazeltine wouldn't understand about lucky magic and why Lisa couldn't come in—she'd simply hire another assistant and there would go her job.

She could take a cab, Lisa reasoned, and wear the charms from the bowl with the dragon on the bottom she'd worn yesterday to go shopping. She'd be in the cab from door to door, and that would be safe, at least from everything but the cabbie's driving.

She examined the charms as she took them from the bowl, each hanging from a colored ribbon. Made of soft gold, the moon represented the Goddess and water, the dragon represented fire, the blossom represented the earth, and the tiny bird's wing represented air, Li Na had told her. Four elements, balanced and equal. When they were balanced, the fifth element, Akasha, untouchable yet powerful, would be present, Li Na had taught her. She felt a little better as she put them around her neck, the gold clinking softly.

She called a taxi and waited inside until it came to the door. Mrs. Bradley came up the stairs from walking Mike as Lisa went down, the older woman and the terrier ordinary and cheerful.

"Good morning, Lisa," Mrs. Bradley chirped. "Where is that nice young man of yours, Caleb is it?"

"He had to go home for a little bit. He'll be back."

"I hope so, he's so chatty and friendly." Mrs. Bradley winked as she went on past. "Besides, he's a hunk."

Lisa shared a smile with her then she went on downstairs to the taxi. Her grin faded as she plopped in the back seat of the taxi—checking first that the driver wasn't either the black dragon or a white-haired incubus.

What do I do if Caleb never comes back? The thought caused her a moment's alarm and a pain in her heart. She couldn't imagine returning to life before her warrior dragon had become human and wrapped his arms around her. Kissing him alone was an almost orgasmic experience. What would happen if he took her into his strong arms and made swift, sweet love to her? Her cheeks grew hot, and so did the space between her legs. It had been a long time since just thinking about a man had made her wet.

The studio, brightly lit and filling with people who'd stood in line for hours for the privilege, made her feel slightly better. Also, there was no sign of Greg, to her relief. She hadn't forgotten the darkness in his eyes, and the fact that he was the black dragon's minion. The word *minion* still made her want to laugh, but it was an apt description.

Hazeltine, however, greeted Greg's absence with a temper tantrum. "Pulled him from nothing and made him what he is," she snarled, running down the hall backstage with her hairdresser frantically chasing her. "Oh, hello, Lisa. Greg's disappeared, the ungrateful, cheating little . . . He's gone off with some woman, I'm sure of it—he went out with someone the other night and no one will tell me who."

Her eyes narrowed, and Lisa shook her head. "No idea," she said hastily.

"Well, I can't do *Dressing for Dinner* without a dinner guest. Someone call his agent. I'll have his guts for garters."

Fortunately, Lisa was called away to a food problem, leaving Hazeltine to shriek and swear and shout at some other poor assistant. It took Lisa a half hour to explain to one of the shoppers that medallion tomatoes and cherry tomatoes were two different things, and by then there wasn't time to go buy tomatoes of any kind. Lisa boldly walked onto the set, ducking microphones being adjusted by sound men, found the recipe, scratched out *medallion* and wrote in *cherry*. Hazeltine would never notice the difference.

The audience settled in, the cameramen took their positions, people scuttled across the set looking over last-minute things, and Hazeltine walked out, to applause, to have her makeup checked.

Taping the first show took most of the morning, but Greg never appeared. They took a break and began taping another show in midafternoon. Lisa remained in the studio wearing the charms and saw no sign of Greg, the black dragon, witches, or incubi.

She watched from behind the set as the next audience filed in, and Hazeltine came to breathe heavily next to her.

"Greg is a dead man," she said, then her sour expression lightened into something like pleasure. "Oh my. Look at *him*."

Lisa followed her gaze and saw Caleb striding down the middle aisle of the studio dressed in the sweatshirt and jeans Lisa had left for him. Women turned as he walked by, eyes widening in appreciation.

"Lisa," he shouted, just as the cameras started to roll.

The audience clapped appropriately and music blared as Hazeltine stepped onto the set.

Caleb bellowed over the noise. "Lisa!"

Hazeltine glared. The cameras kept rolling.

Lisa hastened from behind the set up the aisle to where Caleb the warrior dragon strode toward the stage. The audience turned heads to watch, Hazeltine forgotten. Caleb met Lisa halfway down the aisle and clapped hands to her shoulders. "You were not to leave your apartment. It isn't safe."

"I had to come to work," Lisa said over the noise.

"Why?"

The audience quieted, settling down to listen. On the stage Hazeltine tried to start talking about aspic, but no one paid her any attention.

Lisa tried to speak as quietly as she could, keeping her voice from the microphones. "I need the money, Caleb. How do you think I bought your clothes?"

"You do not need money if I am with you. I will take care of you."

They had the full attention of the studio now.

"This is real life." Lisa tried. "If you don't have money in this world, you can't live. If you don't have a job, you don't have money. I know you don't understand."

He scowled. "*You* don't understand. My hoard is carpeted with gold, all of which I will gladly give you."

"Gold . . . ?"

"Carpeted. You can have every piece of gold I possess. I will give it to you if you will stay home and be safe."

"Take the gold!" someone shouted and the audience agreed with him.

"There's more to it than money," Lisa said. "This is my *life*."

"I am in your life now. I am compelled to protect you—even if I don't like Donna, I have to obey her and take care of you." He didn't bother lowering his voice. "I *want* to protect you. I have ever since I first saw you."

The audience said, "Awwwww."

"Well, you're here now," Lisa said, flushing. "And I wore the charms. I need this job, Caleb. It's the best I ever had."

Hazeltine had given up. She appeared at Lisa's elbow and placed her clawlike hand on Caleb's large arm. "I'm missing a helper," she said, baring her teeth. "Why don't you fill in for him?"

Caleb stared at her, his dragon attention caught. Lisa tried to signal him to say no, but he would not look at her. Hazeltine knew damn well that her ratings dropped on any show in which Greg did not appear, and she wanted a good-looking man to draw the female audience.

"You want me to be on television?" Caleb asked her.

"Of course." She appealed to the audience who started a rhythmic, encouraging clapping.

Caleb appeared to think about it, and Lisa wished she knew what was spinning in that dragon mind of his. At last he gave Hazeltine a grave nod.

"Yes. Thank you. I believe I would enjoy it."

11

Malcolm clicked off the television in Saba's apartment later that evening, shaking his head. *Dressing for Dinner* had ended with clips from upcoming episodes, some of them taped that day. In the last one, the upright figure of Caleb the golden dragon had filled the screen, towering over the pink-haired woman who hosted the show.

Caleb had looked confidently into the camera, neither smiling nor boastful, like he belonged there. He'd even lifted his hand in a very human wave.

Malcolm turned to gaze at Saba curled on the bed against the headboard in her jeans and cropped shirt and bare feet, and Grizelda sitting in the chair by the desk.

"You were right to bring her to me," Malcolm said. He'd brushed the lonely Grizelda with his mark and already she looked happier. She was not the wisest of witches, but she would be useful.

Grizelda had related the entire story of Donna and the demons and how Caleb had found Grizelda and helped her get to safety.

"I am very disappointed in Donna," Grizelda said.

"Demons are disgusting. At least dragons practice clean magic."

Malcolm had wiped the fear and revulsion of being accosted by the incubus from her mind, and she'd looked at him in gratitude. Saba watched without smiling. Strange how easy it was to put a simple creature like Grizelda at ease, but Saba still resisted him with all her might.

He wished she would not resist. He liked the taste of Saba and wanted to explore more ways to pleasure her. If all went well, though, he'd not have the time, which for some reason made him feel faint regret. All the pieces were in place for him to rid himself of the golden dragon while at the same time harnessing Lisa Singleton's magic to send him home.

Donna was up to something involving Lisa and the dragon orb, but Malcolm didn't much care what as long as it did not interfere with his plans. What that witch did to Lisa or the orb or the human world after that he did not care.

He felt another frisson of worry that Saba might be harmed if Donna used her demons or the dragon orb, but he could solve that by taking Saba to safety until the danger was past.

His dragon logic satisfied, he drew his fingers across Saba's thigh and turned his gaze to Grizelda. "You have been very helpful," he said. "Now, do you understand what to do?"

Grizelda smiled and nodded. "I do."

Caleb wanted to return to the apartment right after the taping finished for the night, but Lisa introduced him to the concept of a *restaurant*.

They went to one near her house, a small dimly lit place where couples lingered over glasses of wine, and the aroma of food wafting from the kitchen made his mouth water. The taxi had dropped them off right at the front door, and Caleb insisted they take a table far in the back where he could watch every single person who came and went.

Over the meal Lisa told him all about the dream of the incubus and how the magic of the apartment had kept it from taking her.

Caleb grew alarmed and angry. "Donna sent him."

Lisa nodded around a mouthful of greens. "It would be a strange coincidence if he came on his own. But why should she tell you to protect me and then send a demon after me?"

"She told me to protect you from the black dragon," Caleb said, trailing his fork across his empty plate. "I'm betting she told me to keep you safe so that she could have you for herself."

"Because of this magic in me?"

"Yes. I wish I knew what it was. It's like dragon magic, not witch magic. Witches use earth magic—they draw circles and light candles and use the solid magic of rocks and trees and water. Dragons use fire magic, with thought. Dragon magic is much more efficient."

Lisa smiled at him. "Of course."

He didn't know why she found his observation funny but he did know he liked it when she smiled. "You should not have left the house today. Not even for this career you want."

"If Hazeltine fires me, I have to start all over again. I'm hoping to use this show job as a stepping stone to something bigger. I know it's hard for you to understand."

"While I am here, you don't need this career."

She made a face over her glass of wine. "Don't say that. You sound just like my ex-husband."

Caleb growled. "You compare me to a man who betrayed you with two women?"

His voice sounded loud in a sudden lull in conversation around them. Heads turned, and Lisa flushed.

"*Caleb.*"

"I will never do this to you. I would never hurt you." He laid his hand over her slim one, liking the way her fingers felt against his skin. "I will protect you with my life."

Her half-smile came back, the one that crinkled her eyes. "As long as I do everything you say."

"That is the best way."

She laughed. "I'm not very obedient. Philip found that out."

"I have noticed. But while there is danger you must trust me. I will take care of you."

"For how long?" Lisa toyed with her wineglass. "When the danger is gone, the magic will wear off and you'll go home." She touched his arm where the gold armband lay hidden by his sweatshirt. "Then I'll be alone again."

Caleb fell silent. He would be glad when he eliminated the danger to Lisa, but he would have great sadness to never see her again. It would hurt in a way he hadn't hurt in a very long time.

Caleb glanced up at Lisa and found her studying him, her brown eyes warm. *No*, he corrected himself. *It would hurt as nothing had hurt him ever before.*

I want to stay with her in this San Francisco place and watch television and touch her. I want to be with her.

He'd never experienced such a longing to be with another. Being human was doing strange things to him.

"You never told me why you went back to Dragonspace," Lisa said. "To enjoy yourself flying?"

"I do enjoy flying," he answered. "But I went for another purpose, to bring back more protection for you. If you'd had this last night, the incubus would never have gotten near you."

He took a handful of glittering diamonds from his pocket and dropped them to the table.

Lisa gasped. Her wineglass tilted dangerously, and she quickly set it on the table. The diamonds were laced with sapphires in a diadem that Lisa could wear in her hair. The gems caught the candlelight, throwing spangles across Lisa, Caleb, and nearby tables. Diners lifted their heads, looking over at them and making soft noises of awe.

"Good lord, Caleb."

"The stones have powerful magic," Caleb said in a low

voice. "They are very old and remember the fire that created them. They will protect you against evil, especially demons."

"Protection from demons. What a bonus." She looked up at him. "Where did you get this?"

"I rescued it hundreds of years ago when I was a young dragon. Stones grow cold when they are too far from home—they want to remember what it was like when they were part of a living seam in the mountain. I can't put back the stones I find, but I can give them a place that is as close to home as I can make it. I keep them in my cave with others of their kind and warm them with my fire." He shrugged. "I never had someone to give them to before now."

"So not only is it expensive," she whispered, "but it's an expensive *antique*?"

"The stones have soaked up my magic and will help protect you. Diamonds are very powerful."

The diamonds and sapphires glowed with their own light and had a strength about them that heartened him.

"Is that why dragons hoard gold and jewels?" she asked. "It isn't greed?"

"It is compassion," Caleb said. "That is why we keep them forever. They don't want to leave."

Lisa touched the diamonds. "Well, these stones look *very* happy."

"They're yours now."

"Oh, Caleb." Lisa stared at the stones for another long moment, then she leaned over and brushed her mouth across his. "Thank you."

Caleb sank into the kiss, letting his fingers drift to the nape of her neck to pull her closer. She drew back a little, her lips moist, her eyes heavy.

"Wait," he said. "Kiss me again."

"We're in the middle of a restaurant, and everyone is staring at us."

He pushed back his chair, his arousal rising behind his tight jeans. "Then let us not be in the middle of a restaurant."

Lisa looked up at him as though she'd begin the argument

of whether or not she should obey him, then she smiled. "All right," she said. "Let us not be here."

They walked the half block through dark streets to Lisa's apartment, Caleb's hand protectively on the small of her back, his attention on every shadow. She felt his dragon magic embrace her when they entered the house—he'd marked the entire building, filling it with the lucky magic of dragons that Li Na had always believed in.

Lisa stopped on the stairs a few steps above him—the lift not working again—and put her arms around his neck. Caleb's eyes softened, the warrior giving way to the man beneath.

"Thank you," she said. "I know you are trying to protect me, and I know it wasn't your idea, but thank you for invading my spare bedroom."

"I enjoy invading it." He nuzzled her cheek and kissed her.

He could kiss like fire, this dragon-man, awakening every need she'd buried for years. Philip had dug the grave with his philandering, and the year and a half after that had made her fill it in with cold earth. And then Caleb came along and started her blood pumping again.

It began as a tingling in her fingertips, evoking an answering tingle in her nipples, which tightened against her light shirt. His warm, broad chest covered hers, the stairs letting them stand with their faces even. It was easier to kiss him this way, not having to bend her head back to take in his vast height, but then again, she loved how his body bent over hers, so large and protective.

His lips were smooth, his tongue slow. Heat trickled down her spine, legs weakening. He felt need, too, if the hard bulge that pressed her was any indication. She slipped her hand to it, pressing her palm against the zipper of his jeans.

He made a little noise in his throat and cupped the back of her head, pulling her against his mouth. Her heartbeat sped. Her bed was wide and soft and a perfect size for the two of them. Of course, she thought as she ran her hand firmly down the zipper again, if the hall stayed quiet, the stairs might be where they ended up. The thought of being caught in the act by one of her neighbors both terrified her and excited her.

She wouldn't *really* . . .

Her thoughts trailed off as Caleb slid his fingers to the first button of her blouse. Perhaps Caleb saw nothing wrong in making love in an open stairwell—perhaps dragons didn't care whether they were seen.

He dipped his hand inside, fingers brushing the skin of her breasts. The bulge beneath her hand grew larger still, and she found herself tugging at the zipper, wanting the length of him heavy against her palm. She'd already seen the naked perfection of his body, now she wanted to feel it, to grasp him with her fingers and know that he was aroused because of her.

"Caleb . . ." she began.

"Lisa, is this wanting?" he whispered.

"This is my stairwell at eight in the evening. We could get arrested if we don't stop."

He undid another button of her blouse, proving he'd mastered buttons at least, and cool air touched her breasts. He slid his mouth to hers again. "I do not want to stop."

She did not, either. She opened her lips for his kiss, not minding his hand drifting to cup her breast inside her lace bra. Daringly, she loosened the button of his waistband, and he moved his hips a little so she could wriggle her fingers to the top of his zipper.

A vibration began in the area of her thighs, a constant, insistent vibration that warmed her at the same time it distracted her. Caleb broke the kiss and looked down at her, brows drawn. "What is that?"

"Oh, hell," she said, realizing. "It's my cell phone."

Sighing, she plucked it from her skirt pocket, hoping it wasn't Hazeltine remembering something she'd wanted to add to one of the shows and could they do it over again?

Caleb nuzzled her neck, his hands planted on her hips, as she flipped open the phone. "I hate these things," she muttered, then looked at the number. "Oh, wait, it's Lumi." Her heart beating faster, she pressed the button and answered.

"Lisa?" Lumi said. He sounded nervous. "You wanted me to tell you if I thought something was going down. Well, something's going down. You and Caleb might want to get over here."

"Why?" she asked. Caleb kissed the sensitive place below her ear, his breath warm. "Where are you?"

"At a warehouse in Potrero, down by the cargo docks. I think your black dragon is starting something."

Caleb heard. He lifted his head and pulled the phone from Lisa's hand. "We are coming," he said loudly into it. "Do nothing against him."

"You got it," Lumi said, then clicked off the phone.

Caleb rested his forehead against hers as she dropped the phone back into her pocket. "Lisa." He caressed her cheek.

"Don't even think about telling me to stay behind."

Caleb smiled suddenly and kissed her on the lips. "I was not. Your magic, it would be handy to have at my back."

In the bicycle shop, Lumi put down his phone, sweating hard. "There," he told the girl in gauzy black standing next to him. "Will your master be happy now?"

"He will," Grizelda said. She patted his shoulder. "Malcolm will reward you well, I promise."

12

The diadem was not the only thing Caleb had brought back from his dragon cave. Lying on the sofa in Lisa's apartment was a huge, broad-bladed sword with a leather-wrapped steel hilt.

"Good lord," Lisa said.

"It is good to go well-armed if my powers are diminished." Caleb hefted the sword a time or two, then strapped it to his side with a leather belt and sheath he'd brought as well.

More than one person cast a curious glance at the big man with the big sword as she and Caleb walked the few dark blocks to her parking garage, but their glances never went beyond the curious. It was not always safe in night-time streets to be too inquisitive.

Lisa drove to the address Lumi had supplied. It was down in an old warehouse district south of Central Basin within sight of the cargo docks. Huge container ships reared against the night sky, outlined with lights, the enormous cranes used to load and unload them lit with flood-lights as they clanked and groaned in their tasks. The bustling activity didn't reach the dark silence of the warehouses that lay empty and abandoned to the west of the docks. The moon, round and full, drifted in and out of dense clouds, bathing the area first in silver-white light, then in inky darkness.

Caleb sat uncomfortably next to Lisa, his big frame barely contained in her small two-door car. He'd had to stash the sword in the back seat, and he'd ridden with one hand on its hilt while she'd navigated the hills and traffic and side streets of south San Francisco.

"We are being led to a trap, you know," Caleb said into the silence.

Lisa jumped, then righted the steering wheel before she drove off the road. "Why do you think that?"

"Lumi has been marked by the black dragon. I felt it in his voice. A person is different once a dragon has touched him."

"Then why are we going to a deserted warehouse to meet him?"

"I want to know what he has in mind. And to rescue Lumi if I can. I like Lumi and do not want to see him hurt."

Lisa gulped as she turned down the road Lumi had indicated. "Wait a minute. Malcolm is a dragon. He'll know you'll know that he put his mark on Lumi. He'll know you can sense it."

Caleb chuckled. "Yes, he knows I know. And he knows I know he knows. This will be fun."

"Caleb."

"I want to kill him, Lisa. This way I will not have to track him down. Black dragons are masters at hiding themselves when they want to be hidden. They are subtle and cunning. Goldens are much more honest."

Lisa gritted her teeth as she let the car roll to a halt next to one of the warehouses, parking in a circle of shadow. The light looked more inviting, but she wanted to see what was around her without being blinded before she got out to explore.

"I hope you're sure," she said.

"I am sure," Caleb answered, his voice quiet and tight.

"He'll be ready for us."

"Of course he will be." Caleb opened the car door. "As I am ready for him. Look, there is Lumi."

Lumi approached the car, his tall, lanky form unmistakable. Caleb hauled his large body out and stood up as Lumi leaned down and looked in Lisa's open window. "I'm glad you're here," he said. "I wasn't sure what to do . . ."

He choked his words off as a wide steel blade rested against his neck. "You reek of lies, my friend." Caleb's voice was soft. "I can smell them."

Lumi deflated. "I'm sorry, Lisa. She came and told me everything would be all right if I brought you here. I believed her."

Caleb growled. "Where are they?"

"Wait a minute," Lisa broke in. "Her who?"

"Grizelda. He sent her to fetch me and bring me to him." Caleb nodded. "The lure of soft skin and lips."

"Sorry," Lumi mumbled.

Caleb lowered the sword from Lumi's throat, to Lumi's obvious relief. He laid a brawny hand on Lumi's shoulder. "It is not your fault the black dragon used you. I'm the one who sent Grizelda off with Saba. Though she is probably better off marked with a black dragon than under the power of Donna."

"I never saw any Donna." Lumi looked around nervously. "They're behind the warehouse, on the dock."

Caleb tilted his head, seeming to listen to the sounds and silence of the night. On the docks, streets away, containers boomed to the decks of the cargo ships, and far out into the bay a boat blew a foghorn. Around the warehouse there was nothing, not even the hum of moths against the floodlight on the building.

"Leave the car, Lisa," Caleb said in a low voice, drawing the sword from the scabbard. "And stay close to me."

Lisa eased herself out of the car and clicked the door closed, not slamming it tight. She moved to Caleb's left side, leaving his sword arm free.

Lumi eyed her uncertainly. "Shouldn't she stay here? It might be safer."

"And have him send someone behind my back to snatch her? No. Be very quiet and follow. No place is safe except with me."

"Why is he so sure?" Lumi whispered to Lisa as Caleb began walking softly to the end of the warehouse.

Caleb heard. "I am a warrior dragon."

"So, you spend your life fighting?" Lumi asked.

"No, I spend my life *avoiding* fighting. But when I have to fight, I'm very good at it. Now, no more words. Take me to the black dragon."

He shouldered his sword, and Lumi, looking glum, started off. Caleb and Lisa followed him quietly around the corner of the warehouse to the side bathed in shadow.

Six men dressed in black waited for them, training pistols of varying sizes and calibers on Caleb and Lisa when they came around the corner. They didn't take Caleb's sword, but why should they? Lisa thought. They stayed out of reach and could shoot faster than Caleb could swing.

Beyond them, in the full glare of a floodlight, stood Malcolm, and behind him was a circle of flickering blue light. The girl Grizelda stood inside the light, holding a candle, as did two of Malcolm's men who looked dismayed that they held candles instead of weapons. On her knees in the middle of the circle, her hands outstretched, was a smaller young woman Lisa hadn't seen before, but she assumed she was the third witch, Saba.

Malcolm, as tall as Caleb, was dressed in black leather, a black T-shirt stretched across his muscular chest. He wore his sleek midnight hair pulled back in a tail, revealing his face of sharp cheekbones and silver eyes.

"Thank you, Lumi," he said in his quiet, slightly accented voice. "Please take your place."

Lumi, looking unhappy, trotted across to the circle. The light parted to let him in, then sealed up behind him. Grizelda lifted a candle from the ground, lit it, and handed it to him with a smile.

Malcolm looked none the worse for wear considering he'd been stabbed through the middle by Caleb only yesterday. Lisa admitted that Saba had done a remarkable job healing him. He seemed good as new.

Lisa searched for the magic she'd so easily summoned in the antique shop, willing the white nimbus to her fingers, but she felt nothing. Could she throw the lightning before the men could shoot? She had no idea, and she also had no idea where the power had gone. It certainly wasn't coming to her now.

"You will not hurt him," Caleb growled to the black dragon. "He's an innocent."

"Lumi?" Malcolm answered. "Of course not, he has been useful. I also thank you for sending Grizelda to me. She was the easiest of all to mark, afraid and wanting refuge from Donna. Lumi couldn't resist her."

Lisa balled her fists and said nothing. Caleb stood in front of her like a rock, his body unmoving, but she felt anger coursing through him, held back only by his warrior's experience at facing enemies. He would not let go yet, but when he did . . .

Malcolm continued. "Everyone has been very helpful. Donna's insistence on recruiting Caleb only assisted me, because it led me to Saba."

His face softened a moment almost into affection, then the cool neutrality returned. "What I want is simple. Saba will channel the energy of her circle into thinning the way between the universes. Then you, Lisa, will open the door for me."

"I will?" Lisa asked.

"You will. Not because I threaten you and those you love, but because you will return me to Dragonspace where I will stay and leave you and yours in peace." His mouth twisted. "Believe me, I want nothing more than to leave this plane of existence and go *home*."

The anguish in the last word was palpable. Lisa had no reason to trust him or believe him, but the loneliness in the man's eyes was real. How long he'd been in this world, she had no idea, but she sensed his desperation, his need to try anything to get away. She'd felt much the same during her sojourns away from her family, struggling in career and marriage, but all she'd had to do was drive up the freeway or get on an airplane. Malcolm was stuck.

Or, perhaps Malcolm was working magic on her so she'd feel sorry for him. "Why do you need to open a door when there is one in my apartment?" she asked. "Why haven't you stormed in there and jumped through?"

He gave her a thin smile. "The witches made that fold for Caleb, for your protection. No other dragon can use it, and there is so much magic in your home it makes me sick to go near the house, in any case. I have tried. Caleb was not even supposed to come through the door. He had to have additional magic for that, courtesy of Saba."

Lisa glanced at the circle. The young, slim witch in jeans and black jacket sat back on her heels, her eyes on her altar. In front of her was a chalice and a black-handled knife, candles, and a heap of crystals. Through the mark that bound her to Caleb, Lisa could sense Saba's power, melding with the blue magic of the circle. Lisa felt only a flicker of such power from the Goth Grizelda—the black dragon had pinpointed Saba as the most powerful, and Lisa agreed with him.

"My Saba can get me home," Malcolm said. "But only with your help."

"What about the dragon orb?" Lisa demanded. "I thought that was your holy quest, to get your hands on this orb and use it to destroy our world."

His silver eyes flickered with impatience. "No, I wanted to use it to take me out of here. I cared nothing for what it did otherwise. But with your magic and Saba's, I don't need the dragon orb. Powerful magic can create a door without harm, and with you and Saba together, I will have that magic. I no longer care about the orb, nor do I particularly want to bother destroying this world."

"But you might destroy Lisa," Caleb rumbled. "If creating

the door needs such magic, you will drain them dry, Lisa and Saba both."

Malcolm's gaze slid back to Lisa. "Saba is powerful, and Lisa is so protected, that I think this will not happen. I did not realize how much raw power Lisa had until I saw her in Chinatown yesterday."

He reached a broad, brown-skinned hand toward her. Instantly, Caleb's equally strong hand clamped to his arm. The two dragons eyed each other, predators sizing each other up.

"Kill him," the black dragon said clearly to his men.

"No." Lisa put herself between them. "Leave him be, and I'll help you."

Caleb's eyes swam with flecks of light. "Lisa."

"If I am strong enough, we can be rid of him," Lisa said, trying to keep her voice calm. "If all he wants is a door to another world, then we'll make one for him and shove him through. End of problem." She glared at Malcolm. "Don't let the screen door hit you on your way out."

Malcolm smiled at the idiom. "You are a wise woman, Lisa Singleton. As was Li Na. I enjoyed my many talks with her."

Lisa's heart beat faster. "Funny, she never mentioned you."

"She would not have. Protecting you was her greatest concern."

"Why did you wait, then?" Lisa asked. "Why wait so long before you tried to use me if you knew about me all along?"

"Because when I found Li Na, you had not come into your powers. You did not inherit them until your grandmother died, and she was anything but vulnerable. I knew I'd never best her." He smiled. "But she enjoyed bantering with me. I miss her."

Lisa bristled. "Please stop talking about my grandmother like you were friends. Can we get on with this?"

"Lisa, it might kill you," Caleb argued.

"I don't think it will, somehow. I don't know how I know that, but I think it will be all right." She took Caleb's warm, broad hand in hers. "If you anchor me."

Caleb's anger poured from him in waves, his dragon power nearly knocking her over. "He is lying. Black dragons twist the truth for their own use, and he is twisting it."

Malcolm broke in. "So you like seeing a dragon in thrall to witches? I thought you of all dragons would spit on the witches to release another dragon enslaved." He stepped close to Caleb. "You let me get away from this hell, and I'll have enough power to help you release yourself from the witches. You can't move against them, but when I am back to my full dragon self, I will be able to. Dead witches can't use your true name."

Caleb's gaze flicked to Saba and Grizelda in the circle. "They are innocents. Donna used them and now you are. You would kill them, their use over?"

"I said I'd take care of your problem. The method, I'll keep to myself."

Caleb grunted. "This is why black dragons are not to be trusted."

Malcolm gave him a grim smile. "This is why golden dragons are thickheaded. If you can't eat it or screw it, you don't bother to understand it." To Caleb's look of anger, he said, "I swear to you, Caleb, I'll help you. It's the least I can do."

Caleb remained stubborn. "It is too risky to Lisa, and if you do not care about that, I do."

"But you can die here," Malcolm pointed out. "If my men shoot you, your thin human flesh will be full of bullets, and you will bleed and die. I imagine it hurts, if the agony of having a sword through the stomach is similar."

"You are perfectly all right now," Lisa said.

"Saba healed me." Again, Lisa saw the flash of almost affection. "She is amazing."

It was his affection that swayed her. Lisa agreed with Caleb that the black dragon was manipulative, cunning, and a liar. But she somehow believed that when he said

Saba would not be harmed, he meant it. The look in his eyes, the softening of the cold, was real. Affection was not something a man like him would readily show, and he possibly did not even know Lisa could see it.

"Let me try," she said to Caleb. "Stay beside me, and I'll be all right."

Caleb did not soften, but he held her hand. "I don't want this, but I, too, would like to see the back of him. If there is the slightest hint that you are being hurt, I will stop him."

"Fine with me," Lisa said. "I'll stop him, too."

Malcolm's eyes flickered with brief uncertainty, then his confidence returned. "Thank you," he said.

"Malcolm." Saba's voice floated to them. She and the circle were surrounded by a thick nimbus of blue, and her voice filled the air solidly, as though she spoke through an amplifier. "I need you."

Malcolm gave her a nod, his eyes softening, then he held out his hand to Lisa. "Shall we?"

Lisa took his hand, feeling his fingers warm and strong around hers. Caleb had her other hand, his anger still rippling from him. She sensed the incredible power of the two dragons on either side of her. Even subdued in this universe, they were formidable. What would it be like, she wondered, if the two of them had their full dragon powers? She imagined flying between them, two powerful males soaring through the heat of Dragonspace, the world unfolding beneath them. She drew a long, shuddering breath. It would be . . .

"Glorious," Caleb whispered in her ear. "I long to fly with you, Lisa-ling."

"But I can't fly," Lisa started to say, but they'd reached the circle.

Saba rose. She looked small and vulnerable despite the power radiating around her. Her hands were bathed in blue, and electric sparks swam from her fingers to join the magic of the circle. She was shaking, her face white, her almond-shaped eyes burning with dark intensity.

"Malcolm, I don't think I can do this."

"You can," the black dragon answered. "You are far stronger than you know."

Saba did not look reassured. She glanced at Lisa and Caleb, and an expression of envy crossed her face.

"I'll help you," Lisa promised. "Once he's gone, you will no longer be bound by him."

If anything, Saba looked sadder still. "I'm almost ready."

She turned back to the altar. Lisa watched her tense her shoulders, ready to draw the energy of the circle and those who stood at its quarters into herself before releasing it.

She lifted the chalice and then the knife, using the tip of the blade to trace small patterns that Lisa couldn't decipher into the air. Lowering the knife, she laid it back on the altar and began to chant a rhyme asking the Goddess to enter into the circle and help with her magic.

Then she closed her eyes, clenching her fists. Lisa saw tendrils of magic seep from Grizelda, the candles, the altar, and the statue, and slither into Saba's body. Saba's muscles tensed, her form jerking as magic began to fill her. She made a noise like a small moan, and Lisa saw Malcolm take a step toward her as though ready to interfere.

Then Saba opened her eyes. They were hot and black, swimming with white sparks. The blue energy from the circle suddenly flowed directly into her, and she lifted her hands high and drew a sharp line in midair. Power flowed swiftly out of her blazing fingers, lighting a bright crease through the night sky.

The other four in the circle suddenly fell to their knees, candles guttering. Saba cried out in pain.

"Lisa," Malcolm said, urgency in his voice.

Lisa clung to Caleb's hand. "Hold onto me," she whispered. She focused on the slit in the sky, drawing all the energy inside her she could muster, bringing a little from Caleb. She lifted her hand and pointed it at the bright slit.

Nothing happened. Lisa felt emptiness inside her, not even the barest surge of the magic. Caleb glanced at her, blue eyes filled with concern. Lisa ground her teeth and tried again.

Still nothing. She'd thought that if she wanted and needed the power enough, it would come. She certainly wanted to rid the world of this black dragon—she was willing to risk making herself sick again to do it.

And yet the magic refused her call.

Malcolm snarled at her. "Do it. She cannot stand much more."

"I can't. I don't know why."

Around her, men trained their weapons on her. They must be heavily under Malcolm's influence, she thought fleetingly, if seeing Saba and the crack in reality didn't faze them.

Lisa tried again. She remembered how she'd felt when Donna and Grizelda had attacked Caleb by singing his true name, the surge of fury that they would try to hurt him. She remembered her urgent anger when Malcolm had lunged at Caleb in the antique shop in Chinatown, and her instinctive impulse to stop him. She tried to reach deep within her to find that fury, but though her anger had not abated the magic fizzled as she attempted to touch it.

"Do it," Malcolm demanded again. He strode to Lisa and grabbed her by the hair. "It's killing her."

"I don't know how," Lisa gasped.

Caleb seized Malcolm by the throat and ripped him from Lisa. "You have to make them stop."

Malcolm twisted away. "I am getting the fuck out of this dimension, whatever it takes."

"I don't know how to help you," Lisa said frantically. "I don't know why I could use the magic before and I can't now."

Malcolm regarded her with narrowed eyes. She sensed the cold dragon logic behind his gaze, the clicking of thoughts that several thousand years had honed to sharpness. "I know why," he said coolly.

He backed up, standing almost in the nimbus of the circle, and pointed at Caleb. "Shoot him," he ordered.

The men, obedient to his will, moved pistols to Caleb.

"No!" Lisa screamed. She tried to push Caleb out of the

line of those pistol barrels. He wouldn't budge, but at least Malcolm's men held their fire.

And then one of the men did fire. She heard the report of the pistol a split second before the bullet entered her body. There was a brief spurt of pain, then strange numbness, as though nothing had really happened. She heard Caleb's roar of rage, like a beast in a trap, and wondered if he'd been shot, too. She heard Malcolm's voice promising terrible things, and Saba's scream of anguish which died to sobs.

The circle's blue light crackled, then vanished, leaving them in a silent, empty parking lot within a wavering circle of yellow floodlight. Lisa sagged in Caleb's arms, the world blurring before it went gray.

13

"Lisa." Caleb gently lowered her in his arms, fingers touching the wound where the single bullet had pierced Lisa's chest. She was still alive, her breathing fast and shallow, her eyes half-closed, gaze fixed and unseeing.

He heard Malcolm shouting at the gunman followed by a crackle of bone. The man who'd shot Lisa crumpled to a groaning heap. Behind Caleb, Saba lay flat on the ground, unmoving.

"Someone call 911," Lumi said, panic in his voice.

Caleb sensed the others gather around, Grizelda open-mouthed, Malcolm's men still numbly holding their guns. Malcolm dropped to one knee, leather coat swinging, and reached for Lisa. Lumi, guilt heavy in his eyes, knelt on Lisa's other side, trying to help Caleb hold her.

"There isn't time for an ambulance," Malcolm bit out. He looked up at Caleb, sliver eyes losing their coldness, pain haunting their depths. "This isn't what I meant to happen. We can't lose her."

Caleb could barely think. Lisa's hands were growing so cold. She was drifting away from him, farther than she'd ever been even when he was on the opposite side of the door. "Black dragons are healers."

"Not here, I'm not," Malcolm answered, voice harsh. "I have limited powers here."

"Your witch healed you. Make her heal Lisa."

Malcolm's gaze darted to Saba's limp body, the wind from the bay stirring her dark hair. "Saba is spent. It would kill her to try. You have to take Lisa to Dragonspace."

It made sense. In a magical world like Dragonspace, even human bullets could be rendered harmless by the right magic.

"Find a black dragon called Balin. Tell him I sent you."

Caleb gave him a short nod. Black dragons, for all their distant coolness, knew the secrets of healing, and he'd heard of this one and knew where to start looking for him.

"Lumi," Caleb ordered. "Drive Lisa's car. Get us to her apartment."

Lumi wiped tears from his face and nodded. Gently Caleb touched Lisa's jacket pockets until he found the jingling keys that would run the car and open the apartment's door.

Lisa never moved as Caleb drew out the keys and handed them to Lumi. Caleb's fingers were stained with blood, Lisa's life-blood.

Lumi sprinted around the warehouse, and after a moment Caleb heard the roar of the engine. Lumi squealed the car around the end of the building, through the open gate in the huge chain-link fence, the smell of exhaust overriding the acrid smell of spent magic.

Lumi screeched to a halt next to Caleb and Lisa, and Malcolm helped Caleb lift Lisa into the car, resting her on Caleb's lap in the front seat. Lisa didn't respond as they laid her against Caleb's shoulder. Malcolm touched her face, his silver eyes still, as though he tried to call up his powers of healing but could not. Caleb regarded him narrowly. When he returned from Dragonspace, whether Lisa lived or died, he'd make Malcolm pay for what he'd done.

Malcolm slammed the car door, Lumi jammed his foot

hard on the gas pedal and the car shot away. They turned
out of the warehouse lot and raced down the dark corridor
between buildings, back to lighted and well-trafficked
roads. Caleb bounced back and forth on the seat as Lumi
swerved and swung the car, and he cradled Lisa tightly,
trying to keep her from being rocked too hard. Her face
was cold and gray, color draining from it by the moment.

"You have to go faster," he told Lumi.

"I'm flooring it. If I smash us in the car, it won't matter."

Caleb didn't argue, but his insides churned with impatience. Dragons could move by slip-sliding through space,
but plodding was all these creatures could do here. They
had to build machines which were far from safe to fly.
They risked death every day, these humans, for the sake of
speed that was still far too slow for Caleb.

Lumi swung around a corner then onto a crowded freeway heading north, the glittering lights of downtown
spreading before them like jewels on black velvet. Lumi
swerved back and forth through traffic, then dove off onto
streets again, the hills and other cars slowing him down as
they zigzagged through the city.

Caleb realized that Malcolm had ordered him shot not
so much because he wanted Caleb dead, but because Malcolm had figured out that Lisa used her magic only when
Caleb was in danger. In Chinatown she'd acted as a dragon
would, protecting what was hers, turning magic upon those
who would harm what she loved.

Malcolm had assumed she'd use the magic to stop his
men shooting Caleb, and then he'd have absorbed that
magic into the spell, opening the door to Dragonspace. But
Lisa hadn't known how to call the magic even when
needed, and so she'd done what humans did—tried to push
the loved one out of harm's way. For her instinct, she
would die.

He held her close, knowing he took a risk taking her
back to Dragonspace. She might not be able to survive the
transition—she was not a witch, and even then only the

strong witches were able to cross. She had strange magic, but might it work against her in Dragonspace? And could he find this black dragon in time to heal her?

He had to try. It was either that or watch her be taken to a hospital and hooked up to all kinds of machines that he'd seen on television shows, while her life slowly drained away. Magic couldn't help her there.

It took far too long before Caleb began recognizing tall houses and shops near California and Arguello Streets— the grocery store he and Lisa walked by on their way to the bus or to fetch her car, the restaurant they'd eaten in earlier tonight, its lighted windows showed serene couples lifting bites of food to their mouths.

Lumi slammed both feet to the brake, and the car skidded to a halt, half turned toward the curb in front of Lisa's apartment. Other cars screeched around them, horns honking, rude words sailing from open windows.

Caleb kicked open the door and got himself and Lisa out, lifting Lisa as gently as he could. Lumi, his long-legged stride quick, reached the door of the house first and yanked it open.

Fortunately, they met no one inside. Caleb sprinted up the stairs, not bothering to see if the lift was in order, to the door of Lisa's apartment. Lumi fumbled with the keys, taking an exasperatingly long time to find the right one. Finally, he unlocked the door, and Caleb carried Lisa in, his heart pounding, unashamed tears wetting his cheeks. Lisa's breathing was ragged, her half-closed eyes remained glazed, and she was so cold.

Caleb shoved open the spare bedroom door. He looked down at Lisa, her face white against his arm. "I hope this works," he whispered.

"You hope?" Lumi echoed.

Caleb held out his arm. "Take the armband off me. It's under my shirt."

Puzzled, Lumi slid Caleb's sleeve up and yanked the gold band down Caleb's arm. At the same time Caleb leapt through the door, feeling the wings sprout and elongate from his back, his hands curving into talons and his legs expanding with muscle. His human clothes tore away and he sprang from the pebble-strewn ledge, his wings propelling him upward. He cradled Lisa safely against his warm, scaled chest.

Behind him Lumi said, awe in his voice, "Holy shit. You really *are* a dragon."

Caleb flew. His wings created downdrafts like minitornadoes, scattering scrub and dust far below him. Wild cattle streamed before him, panicked at the predator that had appeared from nowhere. Caleb left them alone and slipped through space, emerging high above a dense forest that climbed foothills to mountains. Waterfalls cascaded down cliffs, cool air wafted upward to chill his underbelly. He shot fire to keep the air warm, to create thermals on which to float ever northward toward the mountains of home.

He had to search out the black dragon to heal Lisa, and the best place for Lisa to rest while he hunted for him was Caleb's own cave. His magic permeated it, his hoard was warm with it, and its magic would keep Lisa alive until he could find the healer.

Caleb's wings split the air as he drove himself higher, fifty-feet of dragon and a hundred feet of wingspan propelling him forward and up. His shoulders ached, but he could not stop to rest. His very sensitive talons felt Lisa's life essence beneath her skin, faint and growing fainter by the minute. Here in Dragonspace, Caleb was mighty and powerful and magical, and still he was helpless to save her.

He dove between a crevice in the mountains and at last, lighted in a shallow cave in a cliff face—*home*. His magic raised orbs of light that fell across a floor covered in gold. A narrow opening led into an inner cavern, a huge room stretching hundreds of feet outward and upward, stalactites hanging from the ceiling far above like stone chandeliers.

The light followed Caleb in and burst into a glitter of

gemstones, precious and semiprecious, that covered the floor and piled high along the walls, interlaced with gold and silver coins, necklaces, rings, cups, plates, and ornaments. The jewels and gold flowed into one another in interlocking patterns, melded after so many centuries, remembering life under the mountains. A dragon's hoard radiated magic, the more powerful the dragon, the more powerful the magic.

Caleb laid Lisa in the very center of this hoard, raking his talons through the jewels to pile them on either side of her. She looked so small and vulnerable as she lay on the makeshift bed, her human skin fragile and soft. He drew his talon gently down her front, splitting the clothes that bound her, revealing her pale naked body, her chest stained with blood. Her human flesh hadn't been able to stop the bullet, the tiny bit of metal that could take a frail human life.

Caleb touched the end of his nose to Lisa, wishing he could kiss her. Dragonspace was vast, dragons were solitary creatures, and finding the black dragon healer would be difficult even though he knew where to start, but he would try until he died. Leaving Lisa to the care of the jewels and his gold, Caleb left the inner cavern, sprang from the cliff face, and flew rapidly away.

As soon as Lumi sped off in the car, Malcolm lifted Saba in his arms and carried her across the parking lot to her own car. He would not speak to the others who waited for him to tell them what to do. Saba was unconscious and though she looked unhurt, her skin was cold to the touch.

He arranged her on the passenger seat, then got in the other side, having taken the keys from her coat. He'd learned to drive during his time in exile, and he easily started the car and drove away.

He did not take Saba to her tiny apartment in SoMa. Instead, they went to his own luxurious flat in an apartment house on Octavia Street. Malcolm could come and go here unnoticed if he wanted to because he'd extended his dragon mark throughout the house and all along the park opposite it. The magic of the mark protected the residents of the neighborhood and also gave Malcolm privacy when he needed it.

He carried Saba inside the house and up to his corner apartment on the second floor. The house had been built in 1870 by a railroad baron who'd spared no expense in architectural details, moldings, staircases, and flooring. The result was a place with rich walnut paneling, soaring ceilings, thick doors, and large rooms. The house had been restored, so the luxury that the railroad baron enjoyed was now savored by tenants who had the money to live in splendor. Malcolm, for his part, had chosen it for its convenience, maid service, and the fact that everyone pretty much left him alone.

Once inside his flat, Malcolm carried Saba into his bedroom and laid her on the four-poster bed. He stood looking down at her as she lay unmoving, her face white and drawn. He knew the humans' beliefs about his kind—their legends said dragons felt no guilt or remorse, nor deep love or affection. Black dragons especially were sharp-minded, intelligent beings who looked at the world through calculating eyes and had dismissed emotion long, long ago.

"I wish that were true," Malcolm whispered. He touched Saba's dark hair, damp with sweat, smoothing it from her forehead. He leaned down and kissed her temple, feeling her pulse flutter beneath his lips.

He had to get her warm. He stripped the boots and her thin lace socks from her feet, then peeled away her jacket, blouse, and bra. He unzipped and slid her jeans from her legs, then hooked two fingers under the waistband of her bikini underwear and pulled it off. She lay naked on his pristinely made bed, body still and limp. He skimmed back the covers on the other side of the bed, laid her on the sheets, and pulled the quilts over her.

After settling her, he prowled his house as he always did, checking that not only physical locks were in place, but also the marks around his windows and doors to warn him of intrusion were undisturbed.

His heart burned. He'd nearly killed Lisa trying to use her for his own benefit, and in retrospect, that was probably why her magic hadn't worked. Malcolm knew the secret of her existence—so did Donna—but Caleb and Lisa herself were ignorant.

By trying to harness beauty and power, Malcolm had almost destroyed it. Being trapped here had made him insane with wanting to get away. That insanity had led him to ignore his cool logic and act on anger and desperation, which led to stupidity. He'd hurt Saba, who had done her best to help him. He'd put his mark on her, but he felt beneath it her true pity for him and a willingness to help him no matter what the danger. He'd been so eager to throw her humble offer away.

Saba stirred and murmured in her sleep. Malcolm slid off his coat and let it fall to the floor, then he stripped off his own clothes. He clicked off the light, the brightness of the moon illuminating the stark lines of the black dragon tattoo around his arm. He walked naked to the bed and got in, gathering Saba's cold body against his. He pressed a kiss to her hair, then remained there, holding her, for the rest of his sleepless night.

Lisa's first thought as consciousness swam back at her was, *It itches*. Her hand moved between her breasts and she scraped fingernails across her skin, sighing as the tingling abated the slightest bit. She cracked open her eyes and instantly shut them again, blinded by brilliantly colored light.

She was lying on something hard and sharp, and the air of the room was cool and somehow *vast*. The last thing she remembered was dining with Caleb on California Street, trying to explain to him what shallots were, her eyes widening when he gave her the beautiful jewels.

No, that wasn't quite right. She remembered urgency,

fear, haste, a worried voice on a phone saying, "Something's going down."

Kissing Caleb on the stairs, his mouth slanted over hers, his broad back under her hands. Driving quickly through dark streets, Caleb's thigh brushing hers, a bright sword slung across the back seat.

After that, everything blurred. Who had been on the phone, where had they driven, and where the hell was she now?

Lisa pried open her eyes. The brilliant light returned, and she realized that it came from all around her. Lamps, or at least clear spheres that hung from nothing, radiated yellow light. The red, blue, purple, gold, and white brilliance came from a sea of glittering jewels and gold flowing across the floor, layers upon layers of it, a carpet of riches beyond imagining. The gems and gold pulsed with power, but softly, like a mother's gentle heartbeat.

"Good God," Lisa whispered. She sat up, her naked body shifting in the pile of jewels. "Dragon treasure. But which dragon's?"

The whisper of the gold vibrated on the same frequency as the musical strands of thought Caleb put into her mind. Was this place Caleb's? She knew nothing for certain, not where she was or why or how she'd arrived, or what had happened after she'd stopped the car in front of the dark warehouse. She remembered that much, at least: sitting in the still car while Caleb stood and hefted the heavy sword with grace and ease. When she tried to remember more, pain welled up inside her, shutting the memories into darkness.

A sudden rush of air made her ears pop, a vibration of something huge entering the cave beyond this one. She heard the sound of claws on rock and then gold light filled the room, radiating from the dragon who emerged into the cavern. Music filled the air, the same music he'd woven around her the day she'd met him. The gold on the floor sang back to him.

"Caleb," Lisa said in relief.

Caleb stood still, like a dragon statue, his neck curved,

head turned to fix his gaze on her, much as he'd done the first day she'd opened the door and found him in her spare bedroom. His huge blue eyes regarded her without blinking.

"It is you, isn't it?" she asked. But of course it was. She felt Caleb's thoughts weaving around her as always, except they were bewildered. "Why did you bring me here?" She slid her hands down her naked sides. "I feel so strange."

"You were shot."

Caleb's mouth didn't move, but his voice echoed through the cavern while music merged with the words.

"Shot? I don't . . ." Lisa put her hand to her chest, right where it burned, and looked down. Her skin was covered with dried blood, so thick over her heart that it was black. "Caleb . . ."

Memories flashed through her—of the circle of blue light, of Malcolm the black dragon, his eyes silver fire, demanding Lisa bring her magic to bear. And then the barrels of pistols trained on Caleb, and Lisa knowing she could do nothing to save him even while she tried to push him out of the way.

The vision faded, broken by the song of the jewels and gold and Caleb. The song surged, and something surged inside her, too, a vast power that filled her and grew stronger by the second. *Oh sure,* Lisa thought, *now, the magic comes back to me.*

Caleb remained still, his golden scales reflecting the light of the jewels at his feet. The power inside Lisa filled her like liquid silver, flowing from the top of her head down her trunk and out to her limbs.

Her body vibrated and quivered until radiant light poured out of her hands, catching in the already glittering jewels. Caleb snapped his eyes shut at the sudden glare, but Lisa kept hers open, the powerful glow somehow giving her strength.

She felt strong, stronger than she ever had in her life, stronger even than when Li Na had held her hand and told her she was special. *Oh, Li Na, is this what you meant?*

Lisa's body elongated, stretching thin from floor to

ceiling, swirling with silver and white light. Suddenly she understood everything, Caleb, Malcolm, the desperate need of the witches to touch this magic.

"Lisa," Caleb whispered.

"Caleb," she said in astonishment. She felt wings sprout from her back and stretched them, feeling bone against membranous flesh. She raised her arms and shot around the cavern, easily reaching the ceiling and swooping to just brush the jewels on the floor.

She darted past Caleb, her body changing and reforming to fit through the slender space between him and the roof of the outer cave. She enjoyed the look on his face— total shock, dragon eyes wide—as she slid past him and out into the wild air of the night.

Caleb stumbled as Lisa whooshed past. He stood unmoving while he watched her transformation from human woman to a being of translucent light, brilliant silver at her core.

Caleb had been unable to track down the black dragon, and he'd returned to see Lisa standing in the middle of his hoard, touching her bare chest with a puzzled expression on her face. She'd been healed, perfectly healthy and sound. He'd touched her with his dragon thoughts and found her whole and unhurt. The bullet had been gone, the wound closed.

And then, she *changed*.

He came out of his stunned surprise and dove from the cave after her. This was Dragonspace, full of dangers Lisa couldn't imagine, even if she now was a magical, radiant silver dragon.

She was already far ahead of him, the musical threads of thought between them stretching thin. *Lisa*, he sent after her in desperation.

Lisa did not slow. The silver of her laughter came back to him, rising far into the dark mists of the sky. Stars shone thick above them, untainted by the pollution or artificial light of the human world. The galaxy spiraled endlessly to the horizon, dusting the mountains with faint white light.

If she flew too close to the stars, he'd lose her. Dragons who flew into the heavens became enamored with it, so dragon legends went, the closeness to the gods too heady to resist. Those dragons melded into the night sky, becoming stardust as they flew, and people made up stories about constellations that looked like dragons.

Caleb didn't want Lisa to become stardust. He didn't think her grandmother Li Na had wanted that for her either. He wasn't certain how he knew, but he suspected that Li Na wanted Lisa to ground herself in her world, find her powers, and live happily ever after.

Lisa, he called again, pumping his wings hard. Lisa shot through the sky, a streak of brilliant silver that drew him on. *A silver dragon*, his stunned mind repeated. The rarest and most magical creature in the universe.

Caleb flew valiantly, swooping on thermals to gain more height, while his mind raced with questions. Silver dragons were so magical that they could go anywhere, be anything, without the restrictions put on other dragons. They didn't need magical armbands or special doors between the worlds or magic circles raised by earth witches—when they decided they wanted to traverse to another universe, they simply did it.

Chill wind bit him, the air thinning as Lisa flew higher and higher. He chased her, steam streaming from him like a comet's tail. No wonder Donna was so interested in Lisa's power. No wonder Malcolm wanted to harness it. Saba and Grizelda and Lisa herself had been dupes, not to mention Caleb.

Damn witches, Caleb growled to himself, willing his wings to move faster. He was the only one in all of this who did not want to use Lisa for his own gain. He cared about her, she was his friend, she was Lisa, and he'd protect her to his last breath. Silver dragon or beautiful woman, it made no difference to him.

"Lisa, damn it, wait for me."

He hadn't flown this much in a very long time and sitting in the doorway watching television hadn't helped him. He pumped his wings furiously then stretched them to glide, desperately chasing the bright silver streak too far ahead.

He'd never have caught her if she hadn't stopped and hovered in midair, coalescing into a solid dragon form to wait for him. She was bright pure silver, scales rippling across supple flesh, muscles strong and lithe. Her eyes were brown, Lisa's eyes, but spinning with silver flecks, wide and dragonlike and full of mirth.

"Caleb." His name rang from her like the sweetest of music. She danced on the thermals, swooping like a hawk as he caught up to her, then her dragon body dissolved into translucent lights and swirled tightly around him.

"Caleb." She laughed his name again and plunged upward, becoming a dragon again as she climbed into the sky.

The sound she sent back wrapped around his senses like threads of fire. He recognized it at once, having been caught before—the siren song of a female who wanted to mate.

"Hell," Caleb muttered, even as he spread his wings and chased her.

He scanned the horizon as he flew, expecting half a dozen dragons to pop up from behind the mountains and zoom in on them any moment. All males within range would respond to a female's call, unable to resist, and the call of a silver dragon would likely bring dozens. Caleb would have to fight off every one of them, and fight he would or die trying. No other dragon was going to come anywhere near Lisa. She belonged to *him*.

Her call came again, and he imagined Lisa's laughing voice saying, "Catch me, Caleb!"

He sent back a snarling male cry, loud, possessive, and angry. He beat his wings frantically, propelling himself up and up and up. Cold nearly froze his blood even through his thick hide, but he knew she could go higher still—hell, she could go into orbit.

But the chase fired him, making the cold immaterial. The chase was what dragon life was all about, the rapid beating of the heart, the burning of blood, the flames shot into the air for pure joy. The memories of being human and wandering the strange city of San Francisco and eating dim sum and rare steak were already fading. He was all dragon now, rejoicing in flying through freezing air and chasing the streak of light that was his mate.

She let him catch her. That was the only explanation for why Caleb was at last able to soar above her. She laughed at him as he drifted gently to her and covered her body with his, his belly against her back. He wrapped his wings tightly around her, trapping her to his body, her silver form solidifying under his touch.

She turned her head and nipped his shoulder, and then they were free-falling back down the long way they'd climbed, plummeting from the edges of the atmosphere toward the earth. The rush of wind only intensified Caleb's feeling of being one with his mate. They soared downward, his wings tight against Lisa's body, his teeth in her neck, and her laughing.

The ground came up faster than he wanted. At the last minute, Caleb released her, and they climbed again for height. Lisa moved faster than he did, able to transform her body into a stream of light, stretching quickly toward the stratosphere. Caleb's flight was more ponderous, his wings beating so much air that it sent a gale into the forests below.

When they reached the point where the blue of the sky gave way to black, he caught her and dragged her silver body against his again, wrapping his wings around her.

They plunged down. This mating was dangerous, and glorious, and made him happier than he'd ever been in his life. His other mates had been nothing like this. Lisa was playful and affectionate, murmuring happily in her mind. But then, he'd never met a silver dragon before—he'd never met *Lisa* before.

Their descent ended at the top of a dense forest, both of them breaking apart and rolling away to fly upward once more. Caleb met her at the top of their climb, roaring triumph that he'd made it up faster than she had. She only laughed at him, then dove over his body, nipping at him as she went.

He grabbed her, catching her in his wings, and down they plunged. They dropped and climbed like this three more times, the mindless pleasure of the last coupling nearly making Caleb forget to let go at the bottom. But Lisa slithered free of his grip before it was too late, lights chasing through her body, laughing at him as he frantically rolled away from the ground and flew after her.

The sun was rising when they landed near a lake and refreshed themselves with a long drink of water. Lisa's body, in solid dragon form, was smaller than his, maybe thirty feet in length, and less than his in girth. Her wings were iridescent, jewel colors catching the sun's light as she spread them.

Caleb drank about a hundred gallons in one gulp, his mouth dry from the plunges in and out of the atmosphere. He wondered why no other male dragons had arrived—the call of a silver should have drawn dragons for thousands of miles.

Lisa gave him a smile, as though reading his thoughts. "I called only you," she said. "I wanted *you* to catch me."

He chuckled. "So, are you going to kill me when you're done using me as your sex slave?"

Lisa drank, water rippling from her smooth silver skin. "No. I have a better idea."

She rose from the lake and launched herself into the air, turning once more into streaming lights and sending her siren call back to him.

"All this flying might kill me anyway," Caleb muttered, and he hurtled into the air and flew after her again.

The being *Lisa* twined with that of the silver dragon, who rejoiced at finding life as a dragon again. The large golden warrior who chased her was gorgeous, with beautiful blue eyes and musical thoughts and the strength to keep up with her.

A name swam to her, *Caleb*, along with a vast feeling of fondness. She'd met him before and cared for him. How strange.

Somewhere inside her Lisa worried, *I'm a dragon and I just mated with Caleb as a dragon. Oh my God.*

The silver dragon, on the other hand, stretched her wings and rejoiced in the wind. *I am free again and strong.* She looked behind her at Caleb streaking toward her like a golden comet. *And I'm in love.*

The silver dragon had mated before in her life, but never with a dragon who displayed such exuberance and affection. Dragons mated because of the irresistible call to procreate and for pure sexual pleasure, but this one wanted *her* and she wanted him. She sent her thoughts back to twine around his, silver and golden music weaving together.

She wasn't entirely the silver dragon any longer, she knew that. The women she'd shared her long life with were still inside her, including this new one, Lisa, who was kind and warm-hearted and wanted life. She'd been lonely and hurt, but soon she'd understand that she'd endured it for a purpose—her troubles had driven her back to San Francisco where she needed to be to inherit her destiny when Li Na's human body finished with life.

As much as the silver dragon loved flying and playing with this golden, she knew she had to return. She could not leave the human world unprotected for too long.

The silver dragon turned unerringly, feeling the pull of the slit in the human world Lisa had come through. That world and the people who lived there no longer felt alien as it had at first. Now it was home.

She slid and flew across Dragonspace, Caleb directly behind her. They moved over glaciers then through dry, rocky plains, making straight for the way to the human world. She heard Caleb flying hard, a burst of effort letting him catch up to her just before she streamed through the open door of her spare bedroom into her apartment and the

Earth world. Caleb snagged the gold armlet Lumi had left outside the door and shifted into the human Caleb just as he fell into the apartment.

They landed on the soft Oriental carpet in the living room, Caleb shoving the armlet in place above his elbow. Lisa leaned back on her human hands, naked and breathing hard, the streak in her hair burning like silver fire.

"I'm a dragon," Lisa gasped.

Caleb pushed her down to the carpet, his eyes blue and hot with desire.

"I'm a dragon," she repeated, still feeling the shimmering silver dragon laughing inside her. The dragon was delighted that Caleb could follow her into the human world and stay with her. She had learned in her long life what it was to be in love.

These thoughts swirled deep inside her, the dragon receding as Lisa's awareness took control again.

Caleb kissed her, his mouth rough with wanting. "You're a *silver* dragon," he said. "The most magical creature in the universe."

"Yes," Lisa panted. "How the *hell* did that happen?"

14

The sun was high when Saba managed to slide out of bed without waking Malcolm. He lay facedown, his head turned on the pillow, one arm curved next to him, black dragon tattoo on his bicep. The sheets were low on his back, baring his bronze-colored torso and a swell of pale backside. His dark lashes curled against his cheeks, his face relaxed in sleep.

He looked so harmless like that, Saba thought as she quickly dressed. Just a handsome man asleep in a bed, his gorgeous body half bared. Not the kind of man who'd charge into her life, take it over, and then almost kill her in the space of a few days.

Everything used to be so simple. Casting her circles at esbats and sabbats, gazing at the moon and feeling the presence of the Goddess, lighting candles inscribed with runes for safety, health, prosperity, and peace. Listening to her father extol the virtues of his Japanese friends' sons, hinting that one of them must need a nice wife. Scanning computer magazines hoping someone in San Francisco needed a young woman specializing in complex database programming for a large salary and good benefits package.

Life used to be very straightforward. Then Donna had lured her into a coven to raise the power of a golden dragon to protect a young woman from a black dragon. Saba had felt honored to participate in such a rite and indignation at the black dragon and his ability to destroy the world.

And then Malcolm had walked in and tied her to the bed. The trouble was, Saba did not feel *evil* from him. He was dangerous yes, but not cruel. He truly believed that Saba had the magic to help him and that using Lisa was his only ticket home. He hadn't meant for Lisa to be shot. She'd felt his anguish even when Saba had lain half-conscious inside the broken circle.

Even so, it was time to get out of here. Saba needed to restore herself, and she couldn't do it here, not in this ornate, expensive apartment—damn, where did he get the money for a place like this? The ceilings were high and intricately molded, designer chandeliers hung in the main rooms, costly leather armchairs faced the fireplace in the cozy living room. He had weapons, too, hanging on the living room walls, antique Chinese swords, and one she recognized as Japanese, truly ancient and probably extremely valuable.

His bed in the white-painted bedroom was wide and soft and covered with expensive sheets and the best kind of pillows. Malcolm might not like his exile, but he sure had figured out how to live well. Existing here hundreds of years and having a brain like a computer must have given him a hell of a return on his investments.

Saba sighed, hungry. Using too much magic always left her depleted of energy, and she needed carbs in the worst way. She'd stop on the way home at her favorite bakery on Van Ness and grab a bear claw or something.

Quietly, she slipped down the hall to the large front door at the end, unlocked it, and turned the handle.

Malcolm's large hand appeared above hers and pressed the door closed. His naked body was warm and tall against her back, his strong arms pinning her to the wood. "Do not leave yet," he said in his deep, rich voice.

Saba studied the door, polished walnut carved with grapes, probably the original restored at hideous expense. *Antiques Roadshow* would love this place.

"Why not? I can't do any more spells for you, Malcolm. You've wasted me."

"It is safer if you stay here." His breath moved her hair, tickling heat inside her ear.

She felt his magic take hold of her, making her want to stay with him. It didn't hurt that his erection gently bumped her back and his strong, tall body covered hers from behind. He never asked for sex; he only pleasured her, as though he refused to take any pleasure for himself.

She also knew that he had callously told his men to shoot Caleb so that Lisa would use her magic to protect the golden dragon. Malcolm was desperate for Lisa's magic, and he'd manipulate anyone to get it.

"I only want to go home," he said, as if reading her thoughts.

"But you killed Lisa to do it," she said, tears in her eyes. "And me almost."

He slid his arms around her waist and rested his cheek on her head. "Lisa is alive. Caleb saved her in time. I felt the change when they reentered this world not many hours ago."

Her throat ached. "So it's fine that you're a manipulative bastard, because no one actually got hurt?"

"No." He pressed a kiss to her hair. "That is why I want you to stay with me. You will heal and be whole if you stay here. I never want to see you unwhole again."

Saba turned around. He let her, loosening his hold and sliding his hands to rest lightly on her hips. The dragon tattoo on his arm was sharp and clean, black lines on brown skin.

"Are you apologizing to me?" she asked him in amazement.

"I think I might be."

"Terrific."

His closeness unnerved her, six and a half feet of naked man, the scent of male musk, the long black hair that slid over his shoulders to brush her fingers.

She swallowed. "I'm sorry I'm not strong enough to send you home myself. You keep saying I have so much magic, but I don't."

"You do." His hands moved along the curve of her waist, thumbs resting beneath her breasts. "You are a powerful witch, Saba, and you will become a force to be reckoned with. I see it in you."

She hadn't decided yet whether he told her these things to manipulate her, or if he was mistaking her for someone else. "I can't be a witch at all without my tools." A dismaying thought struck her. "You didn't leave my altar tools behind in that warehouse parking lot, did you? My best chalice, my nicest athame . . ." He gave her an uncomfortable look and she let herself blaze anger. "You did leave them, didn't you?"

"Grizelda will care for them," he answered.

She twisted loose with an exasperated groan. "Do you know how much trouble it will be to cleanse and reconsecrate everything? My crystals shattered during the ritual so I'll have to replace every one of them. Do you know how expensive crystals are?"

"I can see you feel better," Malcolm said, eyes sparkling.

"Dragons just don't understand witch magic."

"Dragon magic doesn't need the trappings of Earth."

"Dragon magic doesn't have the survival strength of earth magic," she countered. "You have a big burst, yes, but not a long-term effect."

Malcolm smiled a little. "Earth magic is slow."

"Fire magic is showy."

"Witches are stubborn."

"Dragons are arrogant."

She waited, brows arched, for him to answer, but he merely broadened his smile. "You are a ferocious little witch. When I leave this place behind, I will miss you."

"Well, I won't miss you," Saba returned. She felt a tug in her heart as she said it, and she swallowed before going on. "You've made my life complete chaos, drained me of any energy and peace I had, not to mention leaving my best chalice in a *parking lot*. Besides that, I'm hungry."

He kissed her, cutting her thoughts off in midformation.

His kisses amazed her. That a man so strong could kiss so tenderly, brushing her lips with his gentle mouth, was astonishing. She slid her arms around his neck, furrowing his sleek hair, giving in.

He kissed the corner of her mouth, light as a feather's touch. "Then I will take you to breakfast."

"I thought it was safer if I stayed here." Her voice cracked.

"It is safer if you are with me at all times. Donna will be looking for you. She has filled herself with demon magic, and she will drag whatever knowledge she thinks I've given you out of you, probably not in a pleasant way."

"Do you still want the dragon orb?" Saba asked, a little worried. "The door didn't work, so it's still your best bet for getting home, isn't it?"

He looked down at her, eyes softening, and brushed a lock of hair from her forehead. "No, I don't want it. I'll not destroy the Earth with you in it."

"Well, how nice of you."

"I have always looked for other methods. The dragon orb was to be my last resort. I still believe you and Lisa can open the way for me."

Saba laid her hands on his strong shoulders. "I think you're optimistic about me. But buy me a bear claw, and you can say anything you want."

He nipped the side of her neck. "Do not leave yourself open like that, or I might tell you, over my latte, how much I love the taste of your quim."

She went hot. "Do you?"

His teeth scraped her neck, his tongue a streak of fire. "I think I've showed you that. If you don't believe me, I'll show you again. Right now."

Saba shivered, remembering his tongue laving her between her legs and how hot her juices flowed into his mouth. "I really am hungry. But . . ."

Without a word, Malcolm unzipped her jeans and tugged them down her hips. He pulled her underwear down as he sank to his knees and blew his warm breath over the curls of black hair between her thighs. Then he leaned forward and slid his tongue inside her.

Saba gasped and threaded her hands through his long hair. "Malcolm," she breathed. "I guess the bear claw can wait."

Caleb smiled, feeling the welcoming spread of Lisa beneath him on the carpet. He was breathing fast from the exertion of flying and chasing her, but his human body was hard with wanting and not in the least sated. He wouldn't be sated with her for a long, long time.

Caleb had no idea how to mate with a human woman, but his body seemed to understand what to do. As she lifted her hips to him he parted her thighs and pressed the tip of his huge, aching hardness to her opening.

Her eyes, brown swimming with silver flecks, widened. The revelation that she was a silver dragon stunned her as much as it stunned him, but his shock was dissolving in a wash of need.

"Please," she whispered.

Caleb slid inside her so wet and slick that he entered all the way with no resistance. He closed his eyes as her tightness squeezed him hard, unbelievably erotic. He wasn't certain what to do now, other than love this feeling of being *in* her, but she gripped his hips and moved him back and forth, forcing him to a rhythm that he quickly joined.

So *this* was human mating. He ground his hips harder, each stroke more wild and burning than the last, loving it, loving her. Sweet gods, this feeling surpassed anything he'd ever felt, even in fifteen hundred years of dragon life.

Her hands moved down his back, nails scratching, her feet wrapping around him to pull him even more firmly against her. The wet heat inside her scalded him, her opening so slick he slid in and out with little effort.

He felt her little pulses around him, her climax beginning. Her desire scented the air, adding to the incredible feeling of being in her. He kissed her hot mouth, and she fastened her lips around his tongue and suckled. Hard, harder, her mouth a counterpoint to her sex pulling him in and in and in.

Then beneath him she turned to lights again, her body dissolving into translucent colors, but he still felt her around him, squeezing his cock tight, so beautifully tight. He felt her dragonness and her humanness and her *other*ness all at the same time.

"Fuck," he cried.

She became Lisa again, entirely woman, beautiful and smelling of vanilla and spice. Dark excitement swept over him and he groaned. He'd wanted to stay inside her for hours, letting her squeeze him, but his human body had reached its limit.

With another groan, he came. She squirmed beneath him, her own climax taking her.

"Lisa," Caleb said, voice hoarse. He pumped into her, needing to stay in her until the very last minute. Lisa held him hard, her face damp with perspiration, tears in the corners of her eyes.

Everything stilled, the only sounds the faint stirring of the wind chimes and the noises of the waking city outside the window. Caleb lifted a shaking hand and raked her hair back from her forehead. "Lisa," he breathed. *Mine.*

Lisa lay against her grandmother's Oriental carpet, the nap tickling her back, and cradled Caleb's hard body on her. He lay quietly, still inside her, pressing lazy, warm kisses to her neck. His skin was hot, damp with sweat, fingers heavy on her.

Her thoughts whirled one on top of the other, fear and wonder, lust and love, and fear again. She'd been shot, carried to Dragonspace, turned into a dragon and made love to by Caleb, once as a dragon and once as a human. Her heart beat hard, the feeling of the awakened being inside her both terrifying and comforting and familiar.

"Did you know?" she asked Caleb, brushing her hand through his tangled hair. "About the silver dragon?"

"No." He licked her skin, his tongue slow.

It was frighteningly easy to dissolve her body into a string of lights, flowing away from him and resolidifying on her feet. He rolled over to watch her, and she looked down at his bronzed form stretched out on the white and gold carpet, a living statue of male perfection.

Her dragon, her warrior, at her feet. He folded one arm behind his head and studied her, unmindful of her scrutiny. He lay his other hand on his taut belly and watched her with blue eyes heavy with lovemaking.

"Why am I a silver dragon?" she asked.

"I don't know." He sent her a lazy smile. "But you're a beautiful one. And my mate."

Not comforted, she touched his bare toes lightly with her own. "Grandma Li Na never told you?"

"Never." He moved his foot up her leg, drawing a sensual line. "Dumb-ass golden dragons don't need to know these things."

Her heart beat swiftly with unanswered questions. She knelt on the carpet and began to massage his legs, even in her agitation loving the hard muscles dusted with wiry golden hair. "Tell me about silver dragons."

He traced his toes over her folded thigh, dipping them to the crease where thigh met calf. "I only know the dragon legends."

"Tell me the legends, then." She needed to know, she had to know and understand. A blend of fear and exhilaration was making her nauseous. Only Caleb seemed real right now, a dragon-man stretched naked on her floor, letting her touch him.

"Silver dragons are the most magical beings in the universe."

"You said."

His golden lashes flickered as he moved his gaze. "Silver dragons can go anywhere, can slide through space to any world they wish. They can look like whatever they want—a dragon, a being of light, a human, a wild beast. I've heard they can even traverse through time, flying through centuries as easily as other dragons fly through the air."

"Time? Is that all true?"

He shrugged against the carpet. "I have no idea. I wonder if Malcolm and Donna know. They know you have great power, but do they know about the silver dragon?"

She stilled her massage. "I need to have a talk with Malcolm."

"I'm going to kill him."

He said it so matter-of-factly that Lisa believed him. "No, I mean really talk to him," she said. "Find out his place in all this and what he knows about silver dragons. If you're right about black dragons being ancient and incredibly smart, he might . . ." She absently caressed Caleb's skin. "I feel the silver dragon inside me and all this power. I need to know what it can do and if I can control it. What happens if I can't control it and it takes me over? I so need to call my mother."

Caleb watched her, his eyes still. "Why?"

"To find out if she's a silver dragon, too. Li Na was, I understand that now. Is every woman in my family a dragon, or does it skip generations?"

By the way he looked at her, Lisa knew Caleb had no answers for her. The silver dragon surpassed even his understanding.

"I want to know what Malcolm knows," she said. "I think I can help him, send him back to Dragonspace, break the spell that binds him here, whatever he wants." She held up her hand. "Don't ask me how I know I can do it, I just do. The silver dragon inside me is wiser than I am."

"She's beautiful, too." Caleb slanted her a smile, lighting all kinds of fires, but his watchful look remained.

"Are you afraid of me?" she asked.

His smile faded. He hooked his leg behind her hips and pulled her forward, his strength too great to resist. She landed full-length on top of him, feeling his muscular body against every inch of her own.

"Yes. But if you kill me by mating with me, then so be it."

"You think I'd kill you? After mating, like you said lady dragons did?"

He growled, the vibration in his chest humming through her body. "I'm willing to find out."

She smiled. Despite her agitation and the wild revelations of the day, Caleb could still make her laugh. "Can a girl resist such sweet-talking?"

"I'm willing to find out," he repeated.

Lisa lowered herself to kiss him, but he threaded hard fingers through her hair and held her back an inch from his face. "I want to do it slow. I have never mated as a human."

"We just did," she pointed out.

"That was the dragon in us, still in the frenzy of your mating call. I want to start from the beginning." He pressed warm fingers to the hollow of her spine.

"I still feel the frenzy."

"So do I. But I want to touch you. Dragons don't touch."

"I remember liking your wings wrapped around me."

His fingers in her hair loosened, becoming caressing and gentle. "When you opened the spare room door for the first time, you touched me. No one had ever touched me before. I sat still for a long time, amazed at how good it felt."

"Humans like to touch," Lisa said, tracing his cheekbone in demonstration.

"I like to touch you." His voice was low, breath warm on her lips. His blue gaze flicked over her face, intently studying her. When he pressed a soft kiss to her mouth, he tasted sweet, like he'd been eating honey. "You feel different now. Like your skin is alive with power."

"It's what I always feel from you." Lisa drew a hand down his well-muscled arm, fingers catching on the cool armband. "I did from the first night you walked into my living room, all naked and sexy."

"Sexy." His smile was warm and slow. "I like this word."

"I like it, too."

He kissed her again, and she splayed her hand on his biceps, feeling the incredible strength of him. His mouth was hot, his returned kisses raw, as though he couldn't get enough of her.

He moved his hands over her buttocks, cupping her hips, parting them a little. His sex fit between her, still hard and wanting, not sated.

Lisa eased her hand between them and grasped him, liking the feel of his cock against her palm. The tip was smooth and velvety warm, and he made a faint noise as she ran her thumb slowly across it.

"I like this touching," he said.

"Dragons don't do this?"

"They don't." His eyes half closed in pleasure. "Too dangerous."

He shifted his hips so she could rub her hand up and down him. She liked the feel of his shaft, hard and strong, longer than the stretch of her fingers. She dipped her hand to the firm tightness of his balls, coarse hair tickling her skin. Caleb gritted his teeth as she traced his tip, feeling the different textures of flange and column, lingering on the sensitive skin below the tip.

He'd been so powerful as a dragon, holding her fast and not letting go as they fell together through empty space. It had been exhilarating and terrifying, though she no longer felt the insane urge to fly as high as she could before he caught her. The silver dragon still fluttered inside her, but Lisa was in the forefront now. *Only because the silver dragon wants it that way.*

What would happen when the silver dragon wanted to take over again, she didn't know. It terrified her, and at the same time she felt the dragon's soothing music. *It will be all right. Ming Ue will explain.*

Ming Ue? She halted, startled.

"Don't stop," Caleb breathed. His fingers bit into her skin, eyes heavy, cheekbones flushed.

Ming Ue knew about the silver dragon? She might. She had been Li Na's best friend, despite their differences in class—Li Na had been born into a nineteenth-century noble family while Ming Ue's family had come over as railroad workers. But they'd been very close, and Lisa had played with Carol and Lumi when they'd all been tiny. It made sense that the two women, both of them magical, had been confidants.

"Lisa." Caleb rested strong fingers on her wrist. "Don't go away from me. I've just found you."

She looked down at him a moment. He returned the look, eyes dark, his chest rising and falling with his breath.

Abruptly she leaned down and kissed the tip of his cock, then swirled in lights to her feet. Caleb jumped up, growling. She closed her hand around his shaft and pulled him with her to the wall between the bathroom and her bedroom. He landed against her, hands on the wall, still growling, his dragon ire roused. "Stay with me."

She kissed him, then she swirled into lights again, surrounding him with herself. It seemed so easy and natural to become the string of lights—she could do it without thinking. She could still feel him, his warm skin, his solid muscles, the vibration of his frustration, his firm erection. She could feel all of him at once against every molecule of her, and it was heady and furiously exciting.

When she became Lisa again she'd positioned herself in his arms, her legs around his hips, his arousal already inside her.

Caleb's eyes widened. "Sweet gods."

He made love to her in frantic silence, pressing her hard against the wall, his body dripping sweat. She'd never felt anything like it, the hot friction that seared her inside and out and made her know she was Lisa the woman. The silver dragon receded to the background, watching in wonderment and fascination.

The crazed sensations of this lovemaking were caused by more than Caleb's exuberance and her need. He cared what she felt, and he wanted to pleasure her as much as to take pleasure in her. Her ex-husband had wanted sex— Caleb wanted to be a part of her.

Lisa cried out as climax hit her. Silently Caleb held her, biceps working, sweat beading on his forehead. "Lisa," he said, his voice breaking as he came.

He shot seed inside her, hot and thick, then he held her hard against his warm body. She lay against his shoulder, breathing heavily. "Thank you, Caleb," she whispered.

The silver dragon added a satisfied, musical noise, as though she were pleased with herself.

15

Without looking up, Donna said, "What do you want, black dragon?"

Leather creaked as Malcolm sank to his heels in Donna's basement, watching her gaze into a bowl of still water. He could smell a demon behind them in the shadows, but the creature seemed smart enough to hide himself from Malcolm. The entire basement, indeed the house and the garden around it, reeked of demons and the basest forms of sexual magic.

"Lisa has returned," Malcolm told Donna. "I felt the surge as she returned from Dragonspace, and her power is different now. What do you intend to do with her?"

Donna lifted her head. Her eyes were light gray, almost colorless. "You've been screwing one of my witches."

"Saba is mine now," Malcolm said. "I protect her." He remembered the taste of Saba and allowed himself a fleeting thought of pleasure. He hadn't actually "screwed" her as Donna so vulgarly put it. He'd pleasured her, but not made love to her fully.

"She is foolish and so are you."

Malcolm ignored the jibe. "Is Lisa connected with the dragon orb?"

"Everything is connected to the dragon orb." Donna pushed the bowl of water to him, slowly so the water would not ripple. "Look."

Malcolm peered into the bowl. Dragons didn't usually scry, but they could when needed. Through the clear water he looked down at Caleb and Lisa, naked and pleasuring each other on a white and gold carpet.

Weeks ago Malcolm would have studied them dispassionately, two human creatures doing what human creatures did ad nauseum. But watching Caleb and Lisa touch each other put him in mind of what he wanted to do with Saba, and his body warmed.

He was about to indicate disapproval at Donna's voyeurism when the bowl filled with shimmering light. It was Lisa, her body elongating into light studded with colors, like a string of Christmas lights in mist. She swirled around Caleb, then manifested as Lisa in his arms.

Malcolm's mouth went dry. He had known, but having the knowledge confirmed was a shock. Only one creature could do what Lisa had just done, and they were so rare they'd passed even into dragon legend.

"So it's true."

"That she is a silver dragon?" Donna sounded more angry than awed. "Of course she is. Her grandmother, Li Na, was a very powerful manifestation of it. So powerful neither of us could get near her. But Lisa, she is weak and clueless about what she can do. I brought Caleb in to protect her from you, so you would not damage her before she could become the dragon and lead me to the orb."

Malcolm processed all this, his mathematical brain clicking. "You believe she is hiding the orb."

"The silver dragon is. That is why she is in this world at all, to protect the orb."

"Then why would she lead you to it? Caleb will have told Lisa you've been ingesting demon magic. She won't trust you."

"Because Lisa the woman is sentimental. Everything she does happens because she loves too much." She sneered. "What is the quote, *Not wisely but too well*? She will reveal the orb to me, and then I will kill her. Would you like to help me?"

Caution stirred inside him. "You cannot kill a silver dragon. They are too powerful."

"I will kill this one. She is not yet at her full strength, but I have been preparing for this for years."

"Why did you wait?" Malcolm asked. "Why not kill her before she realized she was a dragon, or when she was a child?"

Donna drew an impatient breath, nostrils flaring. "Because the magic of Li Na surrounded her and protected her, it always has. I waited until she manifested because . . ." She paused. "I want to kill *this* silver dragon, not just Lisa Singleton. She committed a heinous crime against my family, and I will make her pay."

"What crime?" Malcolm remained outwardly stoic, betraying none of his inward alarm.

"No less than murder. I cannot change events, but I can punish her for what she's done."

Malcolm raised his brows. "I've never heard that Lisa Singleton murdered anyone."

"Of course you haven't. It happened centuries ago in Dragonspace. I cannot stop it and I cannot change it, but I can have my revenge."

Malcolm fell silent. A witch out for revenge was a dangerous thing indeed. Dragons never went for vengeance— they resorted to violence only for survival. Vengeance meant violating a dragon's territory and possibly being hunted down by other dragons not wanting vengeance turned on them. Witches on the other hand were limited by human vindictiveness and an inability to get over the past.

He also recognized his danger if he refused to help Donna. She would not tolerate his interference or Saba's. Saba had power, latent and buried perhaps, but she had it, and likely Donna knew it.

Without hesitation, Malcolm lunged at Donna and grabbed her by the throat.

His fingers barely connected with her skin when a bubble of darkness shot from her and slammed Malcolm across the room. He landed on his back, spine jolting, gritting his teeth against the pain.

He scrambled to his feet, ready to fight, but he found himself in an empty basement. The black bubble receded into nothing before his eyes, and Donna and the incubus were gone. The scrying bowl lay on its side, a puddle of water widening around it.

Malcolm got himself upstairs and out of the house without seeing Donna anywhere. The witch had vanished even though the demon stink had not.

He strode down the steep alley toward the street, his heart racing, and pulled out his cell phone.

Lisa and Caleb went to bed, even though the sun was well past the noon mark. Caleb drowsed next to Lisa in the warm light, watching the sun on her skin. Strands of her red hair flowed across his shoulder, auburn on bronze. He moved lazy fingers over her bosom, and beneath his touch, she stretched a little.

"I'm hungry." She said it like the fact surprised her.

"You were mortally wounded, then became a dragon and had wild and wicked sex with me. Why should you not be hungry?"

She traced a pattern on his chest, weaving her fingers around his flat nipples. He was still connected to her by the musical threads of their thoughts, but as usual she kept some part of her away from him, even more strongly now. At the same time that he was drawing closer to her, she was pushing him away. It surprised him how much that hurt.

"If you are hungry," he ventured, "we could go back to Dragonspace, and I'll teach you to hunt."

"Actually I feel more like ice cream."

He smiled at her, hiding his uncertain feelings. "A human delicacy I have not yet tried."

"It's fabulous. Maybe that's why I wanted to come back to this world. French vanilla with chocolate sauce."

"Maybe."

She raised on her elbow, watching him, her eyes dark. "I loved Dragonspace. For the first time in my life, I felt like I'd found some place where I really belonged. All the messes I've gone through in my life didn't seem to matter. It was right to be there."

He skimmed his fingers across the side of her breast, enjoying her softness. "It is natural to feel right in Dragonspace. You are a dragon."

"But there was a pull, stronger than anything I've ever felt, a need to return to this world, this city."

"You have been happy here," he suggested.

"It's more than that. I know that I can move back and forth between here and Dragonspace to visit either place. Don't ask me how I know, I just do. But this place called me back. The silver dragon understood why, but I don't."

Caleb unfolded his body and moved to straddle her, resting on his heels, his knees on either side of her thighs. He lightly stroked the tight muscles of her abdomen and the curve of her waist. "You have such strength. I could barely keep up with you in Dragonspace. I feared I'd lose you to the stars."

"I'd never leave you behind," she said, sounding surprised. "I'll always wait for you."

Caleb skimmed his hands up her sides. "When the mating frenzy is on you, every dragon in Dragonspace will be after you. You'll have to fly fast if you don't want to be caught in a *ménage-à*-eight."

She grinned. "That's physically impossible, even for dragons."

"Mmm, just wait until you're caught in another mating frenzy."

"I feel pretty frenzied right now," she said.

Caleb lay his fingers across her mouth. "Be careful. Once

you emit a mating call, you'll have males banging down your door. Better use me to get the frenzy out of your system."

She smiled around his hand. "Of course."

"Truly, if you need to satisfy yourself with hours upon hours of lustful mating, I will be happy to service you with whatever you need. All through this day and the coming night, and the next."

"My, you're gallant."

"I know."

She looked thoughtful. "The way I feel right now, I think I'll take you up on the offer."

He touched his chest. "You honor me."

"No, I feel like—I want to devour you. Mating with you has already made feel crazy."

He ran his hands down to her hips, smoothing her hipbones with slow fingers. "Really? How crazy?"

She arched toward him. "This crazy."

He leaned down and licked her navel. "*How* crazy?"

"Touch me," she said. "Please, Caleb, touch me."

He continued his strokes over her hips and across her thighs, tracing circles that drew closer and closer to the moist space between her legs. "Like this?"

"Exactly like that."

"Lie back," he instructed.

Lisa lay down flat on the bed, her chest rising and falling as she watched him. Caleb moved his hands to hers, which lay relaxed at her sides. He traced each of her fingers, taking his time, then ran his fingertips across her palms, watching her fingers curl inward. He moved his touch up the inside of her arms and then down her sides, feathering again over the mounds of her breasts.

Her skin was so incredibly soft, and at the same time, Lisa was so strong. Her arms and legs were taut with muscle, honed by walking the hills of San Francisco.

He drew his fingers together over the warm, taut peaks of her nipples. Then down her abdomen, massaging. Back to her thighs, then down her shins to her feet, rubbing his palms in little circles. He sat back on his heels and lifted her right foot, massaging the sole with his thumbs.

"Mmm," she purred.

Sexy, she'd called him. She was sexy, especially when she smiled. Seeing her smile was like plunging into a hot bath that comforted, and at the same time slid heat over places no one else was allowed to touch. She seemed not at all exhausted from their arduous flying and dragon love-making. When they'd landed in her apartment, she'd not even been sweating.

He continued the foot massage with soothing hands, then he leaned down and nibbled her toes. Lisa giggled.

"I like when I make you laugh," he said.

"You are so gentle. At the warehouse last night you were ferocious."

Caleb lowered her right foot and cradled her left one in his hands. "As a dragon, you match me in strength." He drew her toes into his mouth and licked them. "As a human, I am much stronger than you are, and I do not wish to hurt you. I will never hurt you."

"Maybe that's why I wanted to come back here," she said. "Because you would be like this."

He flicked his tongue over her toes again. "Maybe it was your grandmother's magic."

"Maybe." She laced her fingers behind her head, watching him lick and caress the top of her foot. "I wish Grandma Li Na would have told me more."

"Perhaps it is something you had to discover for yourself." He stroked his thumbs over her instep, then pressed his mouth to her arch, where his fingers had been. "Like a rite of passage."

"Maybe you are here to show me the way."

"I hope so. Turn over."

Lisa rolled facedown onto the bed, cradling her head on bent arms. Caleb pushed her warm hair aside, then she moved in satisfaction as he drew firm hands down her back, kneading and caressing. He traced her buttocks, fitting his hands into the hollows of her hips, gently parting her cheeks and massaging with his thumbs. She made a noise of pleasure as he found the moisture between her legs.

He lowered himself, sliding his erection between her buttocks. He lay there, not inside her, but nestled in the crease of her backside. He loved feeling her squeezing him, loved smelling her so close to him, loved dipping his head to taste her skin.

He moved teasing lips along her neck, followed by his tongue. She squirmed, and when he nipped her, she squealed, then laughed.

Caleb nibbled her earlobe, growling under his breath. After thoroughly wetting her ear, he lifted himself away and kissed the base of her neck, moving slowly downward, drawing his tongue along the length of her spine.

She wriggled as he kissed the hollows in the small of her back, lingering on the sensitive skin. Then he dipped between her buttocks, and she lifted her hips, shifting in eagerness.

Caleb moved his tongue to the space between her thighs where her juices flowed. He nudged her legs apart, and she let him, readily arching to him so that he could fully lick her.

"Lisa-ling you are so wet."

Her voice was muffled by the pillows. "You've made me wet."

Caleb thrust his tongue inside her, wrenching a moan from her. "You taste like nectar." He ruffled her red curls with his breath, then licked some more, fully tasting the lips of her opening.

She gasped. "Caleb, you have to stop."

"Why?"

"Because I'm going to—" She broke off, writhing against the bed, driving herself farther onto Caleb's mouth. He chuckled in his throat as she moaned his name. She felt swollen and tight and tasted so good he never wanted to stop having her.

She scrambled away from him, facing him on her hands and knees, panting. Caleb knelt before her, hard and naked and smiling. "Come to me, Lisa."

He laid down on his back, his erection standing straight up, his wanting not hidden. Her eyes dark with need for him, she slid one leg over his torso and lowered herself straight onto him.

Caleb moaned at the same time she did, feeling the incredible heat where they joined, coupled with the exquisite pressure of her along the length of him. A few golden threads of his thoughts still tangled with hers, even though much of his power over her was gone. But what remained was a sweet joining, making their mating even more intense.

She rocked her hips, and he lightly clasped her buttocks while she rode him. Lisa touched his face then leaned down and kissed his lips, her breasts brushing his chest. She tasted of spice and warmth. "You are so beautiful," he murmured.

"So are you," she said.

"Of course. I am a golden dragon."

"Smart-ass," she gasped. She twined her arms around him, still riding him, and as she did, silver lights shot through her skin, glowing between them before she solidified again.

Caleb slammed her against him and drove into her, his breathing hoarse. He kissed her hair and her face, holding Lisa hard as she shuddered with climax, another sweet, sweet release.

I love you, Lisa.

The thought stunned and jolted him, and his body reacted by coming hard and fast. She climaxed with him, their hands locked in a fierce grip.

She rode him a little longer, then gave him a languid smile as she lay down across his torso. He smoothed her red hair as he lay back to catch his breath. Lisa did not even look tired.

They lay together for a long time, listening to birdsong in the garden below, the traffic going by on California Street. "Whew," Lisa said at last. "That was fun."

She raised up on her elbow, her eyes mischievous, giving him a warm smile. "Now, how about that ice cream?"

16

Lisa pulled a cylindrical carton from the freezer, sending frigid air over Caleb's skin. He watched the loose blouse she'd pulled on over her nakedness sway enticingly as she rummaged for spoons.

I can't love her. Now that his brain had calmed somewhat from all the sex his thoughts came crystal clear. *I'll have to return to Dragonspace soon and remain a dragon.*

Even if she could join him there, she would be a dragon, too, and dragons didn't take life-mates. They might mate, yes, but then she'd fly away, and maybe he'd want that as well once he reverted to his dragon life. And what would a magical silver dragon want with a golden anyway? Silver dragons were powerful beings, well beyond the reach of a golden who liked to eat popcorn and watch late-night talk shows.

I will lose her.

The thought brought pain to his heart and more complicated human emotions. Uncertainty, regret, longing.

The phone in the living room began a shrill peal. Lisa

shoved the carton into Caleb's hands and strolled to the phone, her buttocks moving sweetly under the blouse.

"Hello?"

Caleb heard Lumi's voice all the way across the room. "Lisa? Damn it, are you all right? Grandmother wants to murder me for getting you hurt. She won't leave me alone, and she's about to pull in every favor every thug in China-town owes her to go kill Malcolm."

Caleb walked out of the kitchen, alarm building as he thought of the small Chinese woman waving her fist under the black dragon's nose.

"Oh, Lumi, I'm so sorry," Lisa said, sounding truly sorry. "I should have called right away, but . . ." She shot a guilty glance at Caleb. "Really, I'm all right. Caleb saved me in time, and a lot of things happened. I'm fine, Lumi. It's all right." Caleb sensed the magic in her voice as she tried to calm him.

Lumi's tone remained shrill. "Grandma wants to see you, like right now. You have to tell her you're okay so she'll let me live."

"I will. But tell Ming Ue to leave Malcolm alone. He's powerful, and he could hurt her. Besides, we need him." Her knuckles whitened on the receiver.

"Sure," Lumi said hesitantly.

"Actually, tell him to get Saba and meet me and Caleb at Ming Ue's restaurant tonight, about six. We have a lot to discuss."

The phone crackled. "Lisa, I don't know if he'll obey a summons, especially delivered by me. He does what he wants."

"He'll be there. You tell him that Lisa knows every-thing. Or at least, almost everything. Ming Ue needs to fill in the last pieces."

"I don't know if Grandmother will obey a summons, either."

"You tell them. They'll understand. And Lumi . . ." She softened her voice to comforting tones. "Thank you for helping Caleb save my life."

Caleb could not hear Lumi's next words, because he'd stopped his worried shouting. He saw Lisa nod. "It wasn't your fault," she said reassuringly. "He has a lot of power, and everything turned out all right. I think it was supposed to happen. Stop crying and deliver my messages. You be there, too, all right?"

Caleb again could not hear the response, but he imagined Lumi gulping and saying, "All right," in return.

"Thanks, Lumi. See you then." Lisa clicked off the phone and laid it on the table. She turned back to the kitchen, looking pleased.

Caleb pried off the top of the ice cream tub, dipped a finger inside, and licked off the cold ice cream. Sweet, creamy goodness filled his mouth, chilly and satisfying. He dipped his finger in again.

"I don't like you meeting with Malcolm," he said around his finger. "Then again, I wouldn't mind seeing you kick his ass."

"I'm not going to kick his ass." Lisa picked up the spoons and offered him one, but he shook his head, enjoying eating with his fingers.

Lisa dipped into the ice cream. "I have something he needs, and he can pay by helping us."

"Black dragons are tricky, Lisa. They live nearly forever and spend the time thinking up devious things they can do to other dragons and witches and humans."

"The silver dragon can be pretty tricky, too. Hmm, we need chocolate sauce, I think."

Lisa rummaged in a cupboard and pulled out a large, dark-colored bottle. She popped the top off the bottle and poured a stream of shining black liquid straight onto the ice cream in the tub. Caleb caught a dribble on his finger and raised it to his lips to lick it. A rich, dark taste coated his tongue that was amazingly satisfying.

Lisa dug a spoon into the chocolate and ice cream mess and scooped a dollop into her mouth. "Oh, that is so good."

"Lumi is well?" Caleb asked her. He enjoyed watching her lick the chocolate from the spoon with her pink tongue, droplets of ice cream and chocolate lingering on her lips. He tried to reach the thread of her thoughts again, but the music was weakening, like wind chimes growing fainter. She was pulling away more each minute, and likely she didn't even know it.

"Poor Lumi," she said. "Ming Ue has been all over him, blaming him for what happened."

Caleb scooped ice cream and chocolate on his forefinger and sucked it clean, hiding his thoughts. "Malcolm almost killed you," Caleb reminded her. "While he was trying to kill me."

"I never said I'd let him off easy."

She sounded so confident, like she had no doubt everything would work out exactly as she wanted. The Lisa he'd met when she'd first opened the bedroom door to find him lurking was a Lisa who'd been kicked around by life, who wanted to do nothing more than go to work and watch television with her new dragon friend. She wanted to retreat from life and lick her wounds.

This Lisa was eager to face the world. More than just the world—she was ready to face down a black dragon and an evil witch and tell them what she thought of them. She was the same Lisa, but she was different, too. Perhaps she was pulling away from his mark because she no longer needed him and his protection.

"Talk to him if you want," Caleb said, filling up his fingers with more ice cream. "But if he doesn't behave, *I'll* kick his ass. And Donna's, too."

"You can't hurt Donna. She wields your true name, remember?"

"Maybe. But I can use what you call, I think, *duck tape*? To put over her mouth so she can't talk." He licked off the ice cream and chocolate. "Why do you need tape for ducks?"

She grinned, and his heart spun with a mixture of love and worry.

"It's *duct* tape, goofball. And I don't think taping Donna's mouth will stop her casting the name spell." She looked thoughtful, or would if chocolate hadn't streaked the corner of her mouth. "But you've given me an idea."

"Something involving ducks?"

The chocolate streak was inviting. He could lean down and lick it clean.

"You said the spell over you wouldn't break until all witches who knew your true name were dead. I won't kill Grizelda or Saba, but I could wipe their memory of your name. If they don't know it, they can't use it or teach it to others."

"You can do this?"

"I don't know. I'll try with Saba this evening."

"What about Donna?" He wiped the chocolate from the corner of her mouth, then raised his finger to his tongue. Hmm, chocolate on Lisa was even better than on ice cream.

"Donna is a different story," Lisa said.

"You *are* going to kick her ass."

"Maybe."

He grinned around his finger, trying to bury his feelings where she would not see them. "You are so sexy."

She blushed. "I'm mad at her for hurting you. What does that have to do with being sexy?"

"You gearing up for battle while you're half-naked in the kitchen with chocolate on you. That's sexy."

"*Caleb.*" She reached for a roll of paper towels on the counter. Caleb stopped her with a hand on her wrist, leaned down, and licked her mouth clean.

She softened under his touch, her lips forming a kiss as he drew away.

She's still mine. Here and now in this room, she is still mine.

Caleb set down the tub of ice cream, picked up the bottle of chocolate, and drizzled a stream across Lisa's breasts bared by the open shirt. She gasped, eyes widening. Caleb bent over and lapped the chocolate from her skin, scooping up the line of sweetness with his tongue. He stood up and squirted a little chocolate on her right nipple, then enjoyed himself suckling it clean.

Lisa's fingers threaded his hair, pulling him to her. Her nipple filled his mouth like velvet, so soft. The salt taste of her skin and the sharp sweetness of the chocolate blended well.

He came up, licking his lips. She watched him with heavy-lidded eyes, her face flushed. Grinning, he reached for the bottle and sent another dribble of chocolate between her breasts, letting it trickle to her abdomen.

Lisa took the bottle from his hand as he bent to lick her. He dragged his tongue between her breasts, right above the place where the deadly bullet had gone in. There was only a tiny pink scar now, as though the injury had occurred long ago.

He eased his tongue downward, taking the chocolate from her skin, then he knelt and laved the chocolate from her belly and navel, his tongue moving in slow strokes.

He loved the taste of her. He'd never get enough of her. He licked her abdomen back and forth, dipping toward her pussy but never quite making it. The smell of her sex tantalized him, making the chocolate sweeter.

When he had her squirming, trying to lift her pelvis so he'd lick between her legs, he stood up again and kissed her mouth. She suckled his tongue, moving against him in newfound excitement. Pushing him away, she upended the chocolate bottle and squirted a wild design on *his* chest.

Caleb landed against the opposite counter in the small kitchen. Lisa grabbed him and went to work with her tongue, licking and suckling the chocolate from his skin. His hardness had grown full length, and she bumped against it as she ran her delicate tongue all over him.

"Liiiisa," he breathed. He loved saying her name, liked the way his tongue curled over the *L* and the sound the *S* made as it slid from his mouth. He also loved the way her determined mouth pinched his skin, eager to suck the sweet chocolate from him.

She came up, her face covered in chocolate. He laughed and licked a long streak from her cheek. Lisa grabbed the ice cream tub and her spoon. She scooped out a huge gob, then glanced at his erect cock, a sly smile on her lips.

Caleb stiffened. "No, Lisa . . . ay!"

The glob of ice cream landed on him, the cream half-melted, but still damn cold. Lisa followed it with a long stream of chocolate. "I just love sundaes," she said.

"I thought it was Tuesday."

She laughed at him, and he knew he'd misunderstood her. She yanked open the refrigerator and took out a jar of red floating spheres. "An ice cream sundae." She unscrewed the jar and removed a fiery red piece of fruit on a stem. "All you need is a cherry on top."

She set the jar on the counter and plopped the cherry right on the tip of his hardness. He watched, still wide-eyed from the half-frozen ice cream, as she dropped to her knees and rolled the cherry from him with her tongue. She chewed it slowly, then leaned her head back and plucked the stem from her mouth. "There," she said, after she swallowed. "I took your cherry."

He didn't understand that reference either, and she laughed out loud. Before he could ask what she meant, Lisa opened her mouth and slid it over his erection, ice cream, chocolate sauce, and all.

"Sweet gods," Caleb moaned. He clutched the lip of the counter as she licked off the ice cream, her tongue moving around and around.

He dropped his head back, his long hair tickling his back, an erotic counterpoint to what Lisa was doing to him. She placed her fingers on the creases where his legs joined, massaging with her thumbs as she rubbed his erection with her tongue.

He gripped the counter. His knees had gone weak, ready to buckle, but he wanted to stay standing so she would keep . . . doing . . . that. He spread his legs a little, letting her get her fingers behind his balls. She stroked his scrotum, which was tight and hard, barely holding back his seed. He wanted to come, but he wanted the feeling to go on and on. *Not yet. Don't let me release yet.*

She suckled him harder, her tongue moving on the sensitive skin beneath his tip. He felt her fingers between his buttocks and groaned again. He'd let Lisa explore his body all she wanted to, and then he'd make sure he explored every inch of hers.

She licked off all the ice cream and sauce, but she didn't stop suckling. Harder and harder she pulled, until he was rocking his hips back and forth and groaning out loud, unable to stop.

"Gods, Lisa." He seized her shoulders and pulled her up, ceasing the sensations, but not his excitement. "I want to fuck you. I want to be in you when I come."

Her eyes were bright, sparkling with arousal and need. He lifted her buttocks to the counter and shoved her knees apart, positioning his tip right over her moist, sweet opening.

Her eyes went wide as he pushed himself into her. Her walls closing on him felt so *good*. She wrapped her arms around his neck, and her legs around his hips, leaning back as far as she could to take him all the way inside.

His gold armlet gleamed in the kitchen's fluorescent light, the runes glimmering softly. Lisa writhed and squealed, her red hair a mess, her body sticky with chocolate. She licked his shoulder where splotches of chocolate lingered.

He pumped into her, clenching his teeth against the wild sensations spiraling from their joining. This was primal, almost like dragon mating, but at the same time human and loving. He felt her fingers in his back, her teeth scraping his shoulder, the sweet, sweet hotness of her walls, the soft of her buttocks under his hands, her feet scrabbling for hold on his thighs. He wanted to roar with joy, he wanted to whisper her name in the softest voice he could muster.

His excitement built to a frenzy. He slammed himself into her, dragging her head back so he could devour her mouth. The position was not easy, and he didn't care. His strong arms held her hard, muscles working automatically to hold her and to drive her onto him. His balls were tight with unreleased seed, and he felt the pulsing deep within him that pushed him toward climax.

Then he had no idea what happened. She was screaming, and he shouted, his seed streaming into her. Her skin glowed with light, a bright white that blinded him, then a vibrant silver, more beautiful than the most polished silver he'd ever seen.

"Love you," he said, his voice broken. He pressed into her, this coming the headiest he'd ever experienced. *Stay with me, Lisa. Please stay with me.*

They held each other for a long time, the frenzy slowly dying, but not completely going away. The newness of being with her was too strong for satiation, although Caleb knew he'd never get tired of being with her. He knew this was insane, that he was only making the inevitable harder, but he could not push her away now if he tried.

He moved and winced a little in pain. Lisa looked up at him guiltily. "I think I scratched your back pretty hard. I couldn't help it."

He touched a kiss to her forehead. "I am pleased you couldn't help it. Thank you, Lisa, for showing me how beautiful lovemaking can be."

She slanted him a hot smile. "Stop sweet-talking me. I'll think you just want more sex."

"I do want more sex. But I still think it's beautiful. And you're beautiful."

"Ooo, you *are* a sweet talker."

"But very truthful. How long until we go to Ming Ue's?"

She stretched her arms, twining her fingers behind his head. "I said six. That gives us about two hours to get there."

A nice long time. "Good." He drew the word out, cutting her a heated look. He slowly released her, sliding her to the floor, and she rose on her tiptoes and kissed him.

"Don't you want to rest first?" she asked.

"No. Do you?"

She smiled, her eyes sparkling. "Not particularly."

"Good," he said again. He reached for the bottle of chocolate, pleased that it was still heavy and full. "Let us go into the bedroom."

She eyed the bottle in trepidation. "That could get messy. I'd better grab some towels."

"Whatever you like." He put his lips to her ear. "But go into the bedroom and lay down on the bed."

Her eyes widened, but she looked excited, not fearful. She swung away from him and made for the bathroom, her sweet backside swaying. Lord, she was beautiful.

She ducked into the bathroom and emerged with her hands full of fluffy towels, which she spread across the bedcovers in the bedroom, trying to lay them as neatly as possible.

"Get on the bed," he repeated, caressing the chocolate bottle. "Facedown."

Shooting him another worried glance, Lisa climbed onto the bed and settled herself on her stomach, moving her hair out of the way, as if she knew what was coming.

Her body was sweet and lush, and his arousal rose when he just looked at her. Human women, he knew from watching television, would do anything to make themselves rail thin, including slicing into their bodies to remove bits of it. Why, he could not fathom. A woman was beautiful, whatever shape she happened to be. She had curves in the right places and hair to stroke, and eyes to admire, and a smile to warm your heart. He wished he could make them understand how perfect they were.

He could tell Lisa, at least. And he could show her.

Smiling, he upended the bottle and squeezed hard. Chocolate streamed out all over Lisa's back, making her jump. He swiveled the bottle back and forth, drawing designs and swirls and complicated whorls then, his grin widening, he let a large puddle form right on her backside. Chocolate pooled up and slid between her legs.

"*Caleb,*" she gasped. She glanced over her shoulder, her face bright red.

Caleb gave her a dragon's smile. She might be a silver dragon and later she might despise a lowly golden, but for now, she was his mate, and he had the power.

He plunked the bottle down on the nightstand, knelt behind her, and spread her legs. Chuckling softly at her squeals of protest, he lowered his head and began his delectable chocolate feast.

17

Much later, Lisa led Caleb out of her apartment and down the street to catch a bus to Chinatown. Lumi still had Lisa's car, and while yesterday Lisa would have thought it safer to call a taxi, today she saw no reason not to walk along the streets in the sunlight, although she wasn't sure why she was suddenly so brave. Also, she wanted to see people around her—normal people getting off work or going to visit family or friends or heading to work. Humanity in all its glory.

She sat by the window, and Caleb again sat protectively next to her. She slid her hand into his, twining their fingers and letting their clasped hands rest on his thigh. It was fun, holding hands.

It had been fun in the shower, too, Lisa and Caleb washing the residual chocolate from each other's bodies. After Caleb had snacked on her, delving his tongue into places no man had delved his tongue before, she had smeared chocolate all over him and enjoyed herself. She'd delved with her tongue as well, and then she'd tried something she'd never done before, taking him in her mouth while letting him lick between her legs. Both of them had come pretty fast.

The towels saved the bed, but barely. Every towel in her house was now covered with chocolate. They'd had to share the last clean one to dry themselves after the shower.

She blushed thinking about what they'd done in the shower. Soap had made Caleb slick, and her hands had brought him to readiness and then to climax again. He'd returned the favor. She blushed harder as she remembered how, when they'd run downstairs, Mrs. Bradley had popped out of her apartment under Lisa's to say hello, beaming a knowing smile. Lisa had put her hand over her face, realizing how much noise she and Caleb must have made upstairs. Mrs. Bradley had giggled.

Next to her on the bus, Caleb covertly massaged her palm with his fingers and not so covertly nuzzled her cheek. The riders around them smiled. As they descended at their stop, a few of the boys in the back gave Caleb high fives and told him how lucky he was. Caleb had to take a moment to figure out how to do a high five, and then his slap nearly knocked the kids over.

"It is unreal how you make friends everywhere you go," Lisa remarked as they walked, hand-in-hand, around the corner onto Grant Avenue. "Those are the kind of kids who shoot people they don't like."

"I'm a golden dragon," Caleb said, as though that were a good enough answer.

A cable car clanged by on California Street, full to the brim with tourists desperately clinging to handrails while they swiveled their heads to see everything they could. Caleb watched interestedly, and not a few women on the car turned to study *him* until Lisa pulled him around the corner deeper into Chinatown.

Lumi was on the lookout for them, pacing fretfully in the tiny courtyard in front of Ming Ue's restaurant. When he saw Lisa and Caleb approaching, he jumped like a greyhound, his tall, lanky form swaying back and forth.

Lisa hugged him. "Lumi, it's all right."

Lumi squeezed her hard, his young body shaking. "I'm sorry. I'm so sorry," he repeated like a litany.

Carol came out after him, her sophisticated clothes a contrast to Lumi's sloppy jeans and shirt, but her eyes were no less worried. "Lisa, what happened? Lumi kept saying you'd been *shot*, and Grandmother is reaming everyone out, and this tall man with silver eyes has turned up—he's gorgeous, but a little scary—and Grandmother keeps swearing at him in Cantonese."

Lisa gently put Lumi aside then she hugged the startled Carol. "Everything will be all right. I'll explain."

Carol didn't relax. "Well, come inside. She's waiting for you." She glanced behind Lisa. "Hi, Caleb. I'm sorry you're not seeing our family at our best."

Noise prevailed inside the restaurant. There weren't any customers, just Ming Ue standing with her hand on a cane, glaring up at Malcolm who towered over her. Malcolm had pulled his long hair into a tail that flowed like black silk to his hips and wore jeans and a sweatshirt and a leather coat. His swarthy face was square and hard, and at present his black brows were drawn into a fearsome scowl. Ming Ue didn't look the least bit afraid of him.

Near Malcolm stood Saba, the black dragon's height emphasizing her smallness. Her short dark hair was disheveled, and she looked exhausted, but she lingered near Malcolm as though pulled by the link that bound her to him. Lisa could see the link like silver-black threads glittering under the restaurant's artificial light, a web stretching from him to enclose her. She also sensed that Saba was not entirely unhappy with the bond, and Lisa felt a twinge of pity for her.

She wondered if similar threads bound her to Caleb and realized with a jolt that his mark on her had lessened. Had the silver dragon done that or had Caleb? Caleb had said that dragons did not take mates like humans did—would the silver dragon want to be free like other dragons in her world, ready to kill the male when she was finished with him?

I don't want to be the silver dragon. I want to be Lisa and in love with a man who can stay with me. No, that wasn't entirely true. She wanted to be in love with Caleb and wanted him to be able to stay. Which he could not.

The other witch, Grizelda of the floating black lace, was there as well. Lisa glanced at her in surprise, then understood when Lumi slid his arm around her waist. Malcolm might have used Grizelda to bring Lumi to him, but Grizelda and Lumi were close in age and it was not strange that they, both slightly out of sync with the rest of the world, had found sympathy in each other.

"Ming Ue," Lisa said loudly, and the din suddenly ceased.

Ming Ue turned to Lisa. She might be a small elderly woman, but she had power, and not simply because she was a mage. She'd survived things in her youth that most Americans knew only in nightmares and had lived to create her tiny empire in Chinatown and rule it with an iron hand. Lisa couldn't follow Cantonese quickly enough, or Ming Ue's dialect at all for that matter, to understand what she had been saying to Malcolm. But by the cold, silver anger in Malcolm's eyes, he'd understood her all too well.

"Ming Ue," Lisa said. "I'm really fine and well. And I *know*."

The dangerous anger faded from Ming Ue's eyes as she looked Lisa up and down. Then her wrinkled face flushed, and her expression turned guilty. "Li Na made me promise not to tell you until the time was right."

"But the time is now right." Lisa looked past Malcolm at Saba. "Are *you* all right? That power was pretty intense."

Saba nodded. "I'm fine. But I don't really understand what's going on, and no one will tell me anything." She glared up at Malcolm, making it clear who she meant when she said *no one*.

"She's Japanese," Ming Ue said, disapproval in her voice.

"Ming Ue, we are all Americans here," Lisa said. "Or dragons," she amended. "I need to know everything you do about the silver dragon and the dragon orb. I need to understand what I am and what I'm facing. I'm terrified. You

and Li Na were thick as thieves, and I know you know what
I mean."

Ming Ue fell silent, looking more guilty than ever. Lumi
and Carol stared at their grandmother in astonishment, and
behind them Shaiming twisted his lips into a faint smile.
None of them had ever seen Ming Ue back down before.

"And as for you," Lisa pointed her finger at Malcolm.

"Please," he said in a cultured voice. "I have had all
I can take of small women shouting at me."

Lisa touched her fingers to his chest, the fleece of the
black sweatshirt soft. She released a small amount of
white-hot silver dragon power that laced its way into his
bone and muscles. His eyes widened slightly and a corner
of his mouth pulled.

"You ordered your men to shoot Caleb because you
thought I would release my magic to protect him," she said.
"You were ready to kill him to get what you wanted. I don't
know if I can forgive you for that, but I might let you make
recompense." She extended the power a little, and he
flinched.

"Would you like me to fall at your feet and worship
you?" Malcolm asked, voice harsh. "Would that make it
better?"

"No." She spread her fingers on his chest. "You have a
heart, Malcolm. I feel it inside you. But it is the way of a
black dragon to be ruthless and calculating. You use people, because you don't know how to do things differently.
And you wouldn't use people if you weren't so desperate."

His eyes darkened when she said the word *desperate*.
"After eight hundred years, the signs were finally right that
maybe I'd escape this captivity. You can't blame me for
trying."

"I can blame you for your methods." Lisa withdrew her
hand, and he exhaled in relief. "But you'll escape, Malcolm, I'll make sure of it. Although you know . . ." She
slanted him a smile. "You could have just asked me."

* * *

Caleb watched Lisa chivvy them all to sit around Ming Ue's biggest table, Lumi with Grizelda, Malcolm with Saba, Ming Ue next to Caleb, her mouth flat and unhappy. Shaiming brought tea, still pushing the cart with the squeaky wheel, still thunking cups and pots to the table ungracefully. When he set a cup down in front of Caleb, Shaiming's brown eyes twinkled and a tiny smile hovered around his mouth.

Lisa slid into the chair next to Caleb, smelling of soap and a little bit of chocolate, which overlaid the faint, lingering scent of lovemaking. *She's amazing,* he thought, wrapping his thumb and forefinger around the warm, handle-less cup of tea. She'd walked into a room full of argument, discord, fear, and anger, and had easily persuaded everyone, including a black dragon and two witches, to sit down and drink tea together.

"Everyone has a story to tell," Lisa was saying. "Starting with you." She gave Malcolm a glare. "I am curious to know why you've been exiled here. Who did it, and what did you do to them to make them exact such a vicious revenge?"

Malcolm turned his cup around on the table. Beside him, Saba tensed, and Caleb sensed that she didn't know his story either. Malcolm had enslaved her but not entrusted her, and the frustration of that poured from her in waves.

"Witches playing with fire." Malcolm lifted his teacup and took a sip of the hot, black tea. "I burned them."

Caleb said grimly, "Let me guess. You were minding your own business and they came along and tried to tap into your magic."

Malcolm nodded and took another sip of tea. At the other end of the table, Carol spoke up. "I'm lost."

Carol was the only person here not of a magical turn of mind. Having read her before, Caleb knew that Carol liked numbers and figures and business plans, things that lined up neatly on pieces of paper and on computer screens. She liked the figures in the "income" columns to be higher than those in "expenses," and she preferred black numbers to red. She might belong to the magical family of Ming Ue, but she did not know or care much about magic or witches or stories from the past.

He explained. "Some witches perform rituals that tap into Dragonspace, seeking dragon magic to enhance their own. Many of these witches aren't powerful enough to actually enter Dragonspace, and they imagine it as some astral plane where dragons sit around waiting for their magic to be needed. They even believe the dragons give up their magic freely to help the witches, but they're wrong. Most dragons prefer to be left alone and can be pretty cranky when bothered."

"You don't say," Lisa said under her breath.

"The witches take whatever magic they can find with their probing and don't give anything in return. Sometimes they'll ruthlessly drain the magic, and the unfortunate dragon caught in their ritual dies."

Lisa's eyes widened, and Saba's expression mirrored hers. Malcolm set down his teacup. "Eight hundred years ago, they tried to tap into me," he said. "Ten of them from a large coven, pooling their power to pierce Dragonspace and steal the magic of a black dragon."

Grizelda gasped from her end of the table. "Tapping black dragon magic is extremely dangerous. I tried blue dragon magic once and that hurt me pretty bad. I never did it again."

"Black dragons are dangerous because they fight back," Malcolm said. "Blues fight, too, instinctively, but black dragons are intelligent and know how to fight very well. I killed the witches. All ten of them."

Saba jumped. "Goddess, you didn't."

Malcolm slanted a glance at her, and Caleb sensed his explanation was more directed at Saba than at Lisa or Ming Ue. "They were bent on killing me—they'd caught me in a powerful web, pooling their magic to take mine, so I turned it back on them to save myself. It killed them. The rest of their coven was outraged. The ten had been their most powerful witches and seers, and they'd been trying to make their power even greater by stealing mine. The coven banded together to trap me. They didn't have enough power to kill me, but they had enough power to drag me here and seal the gate. I started out stark naked in a stone circle in Scotland and survived by being ruthless, and yes, by using people."

Grizelda bit her lip. "But that can't be right. The witches' rede is to harm none."

"None but dragons," Caleb said, lifting his teacup.

"You are quoting the Wiccan creed of this century," Malcolm told Grizelda. "In the past, many witches it is true were benevolent healers and seers, but others were bent on raising power no matter who it hurt. They weren't the ones caught by the witch-finders—these witches were much too cunning to be caught. Most of the witches burned or hanged were harmless women who only wanted to help. Humans tend to persecute those who cannot fight back."

"I think I can send you home, Malcolm," Lisa said quietly, breaking through his words. "And I will."

Malcolm's expression said he did not trust her, but Lisa did not answer him and turned her attention to Ming Ue.

"All right, Ming Ue. Spill it."

"Spill it?" Ming Ue cocked her head, looking confused. "I do not understand what that means."

Carol snorted. "Yes, you do, Grandmother. Tell us what is going on. How did Lisa survive being shot in the chest, and what is this dragon orb you were screaming at Malcolm about?"

Lisa fixed Ming Ue with her brown eyes. "Tell me," she said gently.

Ming Ue sighed. She stared into her teacup, as though she could read the story in it, then said, "Your grandmother, Li Na, was a very wise woman. She knew you would come into your legacy after she was gone, but she said you'd be all right, that you'd be protected by a powerful golden dragon." She flicked a glance at Caleb. "She also said that only great danger and a sacrifice would reveal your true nature, as has happened for all women in her family. When you allowed yourself to be shot, as Lumi told me, you were trying to save Caleb, willing to trade your life for his. And so, your nature as the silver dragon manifested."

"This happened to my grandmother, too?" Lisa asked.

Ming Ue nodded, looking pleased that she held the rapt attention of the entire table. "When Li Na was only sixteen, she saved a child who had fallen from a ferry into the bay. She did not know the child, but she instinctively knew she could save him, and she acted without thought for her own life. She grabbed the child and helped lift him to safety, but she was dragged under and the water was so cold. When they pulled her out, all believed her dead, drowned, the brave girl from Chinatown, but later she revived and that day came into her legacy."

"She became a silver dragon." Lisa clenched her hand on the table, white fingers stretching. "How long has this been happening to women in my family?"

"Oh, two thousand years, give or take."

Ming Ue smiled as everyone collectively gaped at her. She liked having an audience, Caleb sensed, liked to tell stories. "It all began with a witch, of course." Ming Ue sipped her tea, relaxing, and the rest of them fell silent and waited for her. "Two thousand years ago, a witch made her way to Dragonspace, with the intent of stealing the magic of the legendary silver dragon."

"You see?" Caleb said. "You're minding your own business, and a witch decides to mess up your life."

"This witch was cleverer than most," Ming Ue went on. "Instead of trying to tap into magic without leaving her own plane of existence, she traveled to Dragonspace herself. Because she'd studied silver dragon legends half her life, she was able to track and eventually find one. While the silver dragon slept near a clear lake, the witch stole one of its scales. The witch fashioned this scale into an orb, a perfect silver sphere, and into it she poured her own magic. Then she tried to steal the magic of the silver dragon and put it into the orb as well, but that woke the dragon. Angry, the dragon spit magic at the witch, but the witch was ready, and she caught the magic with the orb. The more magic the dragon tried to use, the more the witch stole it. Finally the silver dragon struck out physically, and the witch fled.

"But the witch was not as clever as she thought. She'd poured so much of her own magic into the orb in order to both fashion it and trap the dragon magic, that she had little left to cross back to the human world. She managed to get through with the orb, but the crossing drained her of life.

"Knowing the orb was dangerous, the silver dragon followed the witch to this world, determined to get it back. The dragon emerged deep in a green valley in China, near the Li River, where she found the orb and the witch dead. When the dragon attempted to take the orb back to Dragonspace where she would destroy it, she learned a terrible fact. The orb had absorbed so much magic, both witch and dragon, that fearsome earthquakes and devastation began when she tried to take it through the door the witch had created back to Dragonspace.

"Understanding she could not take it from the human world, the silver dragon tried to destroy the orb. But the same thing happened—earthquakes and mountains spewing flame. She realized at last that the orb must stay on Earth, untouched, because the power it contained was so great and so unstable that it might unmake the world.

"Being a curious creature, the silver dragon decided to explore, to discover what sort of people lived in this place that the orb might destroy. She hid the orb in a safe place and began to look around. She found a town full of people and changed her shape to look like one of them, so as not to frighten them. This happened two thousand of our years ago, during the time of the Han. The silver dragon made her way to the cities, trying to blend in with human beings, but she was such a beautiful woman that the emperor himself heard of her and wanted to view this marvel. He had her brought to his court to stand in front of him. What he saw was a lovely, dark-eyed woman with a streak of pure white in her sable hair. The emperor was enchanted with her and wanted to bring her to court. The silver dragon agreed, curious about this man who presumed to rule over all the people. Dragons, Li Na has told me repeatedly, do not have rulers, and the silver dragon found the emperor fascinating.

"The silver dragon met all kinds of interesting people, learned to make music, and learned how to draw pictures with ink. She soon became the most celebrated woman at court, although she never forgot about the dragon orb and used her magic to keep it hidden, checking on it as often as she could.

"She had stayed at the court for one human year when she met a man who wrote poetry for the emperor. The emperor instructed this man to teach the silver dragon how to make poetry, and for the first time in her life, the silver dragon fell in love. She used her powers of persuasion, and very likely some magic, to convince the emperor to let her marry the poet, who had likewise fallen in love with her. The emperor, an old man, gave her to the poet with his blessing. From what Li Na told me, I am certain the silver dragon would have just carried off the poet if she'd wanted to, but she liked to be courteous.

"By this time, of course, the silver dragon had realized that humans aged and died, meaning her husband would, too, leaving her alone and grieving. So she decided to make a sacrifice. She wanted to stay on Earth to make certain none of these weak humans were hurt by the orb, and she wanted to live as a human with her beloved husband.

"She decided to break her long dragon lifespan into many lifetimes. When her human body died, she would flow into the youngest female of her human family. In such a fashion, she grew old with her beloved poet and passed her dragon essence to her great-granddaughter, who was only a babe. That child was not the silver dragon, but contained her essence, her spirit. The child grew to be a beautiful woman, and when she was still young she saved a man from certain death by sacrificing her own life, thus awakening the essence of the silver dragon. When *she* died, the silver dragon passed to the youngest girl-child in her family, and so on.

"When Li Na's grandfather, who was married to a silver dragon, brought his family to America, the silver dragon unburied the orb from the Li valley and carried it safely here, to San Francisco, to Chinatown. When she died, the dragon essence passed to Li Na, and at Li Na's passing, the silver dragon came to Lisa."

Ming Ue picked up her tea and sipped it. Her listeners blinked, as though waking from a trance, then all eyes moved from Ming Ue to Lisa.

Lisa touched the white streak in her hair. "This appeared the day Li Na died."

Ming Ue smiled, her face wrinkling. "All the silver dragons were beautiful, Li Na said, and all had such a streak in their hair. It was regarded as family luck—the women who had the white streak were lucky and blessed. She told me all this, with instructions to tell you when you were ready. I am fortunate to have been the friend of the silver dragon and to have the safe keeping of the orb."

As though on cue, Shaiming wheeled the cart over, the wheel giving its usual *squeak, squeak, squeak*. Actually smiling, he set a small cloisonné bowl that looked much like Grandma Li Na's bowl with the dragon in front of Lisa and lifted the lid. Inside was a silver sphere, perfectly round and shining softly with silver light.

18

Caleb leaned to look at it, drawn to the softly glistening orb. On Lisa's other side, Malcolm leaned forward as well, reaching a long finger toward it.

"No," Lisa said.

Malcolm stopped, glanced at her, and folded his finger into his palm.

Ming Ue said, "If anyone uses that orb or tries to take it back to Dragonspace, the earthquakes will begin. We have all seen what earthquakes can do to San Francisco, but this would be ten times worse, Li Na said. It would be the end for us."

Lisa's lashes moved as she flicked her gaze over the small globe that her ancestor had given up her dragon life for. Caleb expected it to pulse with power, but he did not sense much from it, pretty as it was. He felt Ming Ue watching him and looked up. She gave him a faint smile, a wise look on her face.

Saba leaned forward on her slim arms, regarding Lisa curiously. "Do you remember all that? Coming to China and falling in love with the poet and traveling to America with Li Na's grandfather?"

Lisa tilted her head, still studying the orb. "I do, and I don't. I remember it, but it's like I'm remembering a movie, something happening to someone else." Her look turned thoughtful. "The first dragon was certainly beautiful. I see her in silk robes with her long black hair hanging to her knees, the white streak lacing back from her forehead. She smiled a lot."

"Like you." Caleb slid his fingers to cover hers, and she glanced at him, her look almost shy.

"She was curious, Li Na said," Ming Ue added. "Very interested in human beings. She liked them. They were like children to her."

"She must have liked them a lot," Saba observed. "To stay here all this time and make all those sacrifices. She could have taken the orb back to Dragonspace and said to hell with Earth."

"She did not know whether moving the orb would hurt Dragonspace as well, remember," Lisa said.

"But she might have risked it."

"She didn't want to." Lisa's eyes softened, as though she saw something in the distance that Caleb could not. "She truly liked the human world. She used her magic to help when she could, she enjoyed life, and she fell in love."

Malcolm cleared his throat, his impatient look showing that he didn't much care about the silver dragon's interest in humans. "What are you going to do with the orb now, Lisa?"

"Have Ming Ue keep it," Lisa answered at once. "It is protected here, isn't it? My grandmother saw to that, and Chinatown is a magical place."

"It's *somewhat* protected," Malcolm said.

Saba on his other side murmured to him. "Tell her what you told me about Donna."

Caleb saw his flicker of annoyance as though Saba had asked him to reveal something he wanted to keep silent about. He might have marked Saba, but the witch was strong enough to think on her own.

Quietly Malcolm told them all about his visit to Donna's basement and her goal to kill Lisa. "She said the silver dragon that is now Lisa committed a crime against her family. Murder, she said."

Lisa looked bewildered. "I've never hurt anyone in my life. Not even accidentally."

"I could not understand what she meant," Malcolm said. "She invited me to join her."

Caleb's protective hackles rose. "And have you?" Saba watched Malcolm, eyes worried.

Malcolm's dark brows went up. "Help a witch hunt a dragon? The woman is a fool. I tried to kill her and solve the problem, but her magic was too strong. And it's dark and unclean."

Caleb remained silent, his warrior instincts flaring. He'd not trusted Donna from the first, and her attempt to send the incubus after Lisa alarmed and infuriated him. *Protect Lisa. At all costs.* Including his own life, although he'd rather see Donna sliced up on the floor.

"We need to go to Donna," he said quietly, "and explain to her that she must leave Lisa alone."

Malcolm caught his gaze, his silver eyes reflecting understanding of what Caleb meant by *explain*. "First we have to find her. When she threw me off, she disappeared and I could not sense her trail. I set up some of my men to watch her house, but they have reported that she has not returned. I don't think she will."

"We will lure her out of hiding then," Lisa said. "I've done nothing to harm her family, she is mistaken about that. If it was something the silver dragon did, I have no memory of it."

"She said it was *this* silver dragon, the one that is you," Malcolm added.

"Lisa will not face her alone," Ming Ue vowed in her small, strong voice. "We will fight to protect Lisa from this witch woman."

"You won't, Grandmother," Carol said in alarm. "You're not fighting anybody."

Ming Ue scowled. "If you did not have your nose so buried in your balance sheets, you would know that it is necessary to fight for some things. No matter whether you are old and small, or young and strong."

"Grandmother," Carol tried.

"I will help Lisa," Ming Ue said stubbornly. "We all will help."

"You are a brave warrior, Ming Ue," Caleb said. "I thank you." Ming Ue looked somewhat mollified.

Lisa gazed at the orb for a time. The restaurant's fluorescent lights and the steam of tea reflected on its bright surface. "Ming Ue, will you keep this for me a while longer? I promise you can give up the burden soon."

"I kept it for Li Na," Ming Ue said proudly. "I hid it from all eyes, even yours, black dragon."

Malcolm made a little bow in her direction. "I commend you," he said. "I was never the wiser."

"But he is now," Caleb observed. He itched for his sword.

Lisa looked at the black dragon. "Malcolm is coming home with us, and I'm keeping an eye on him until this is over."

Malcolm opened his mouth to argue. Lisa held his gaze for a long time, though what passed between them Caleb could not see.

Malcolm uncurled his lip. "Who am I to defy the power of a great silver dragon?" He put his hands on the table and rose to his feet. "I'll wait outside. I need some air."

He turned away without saying anything polite to Ming Ue, or anyone else for that matter, and strode out of the room. Saba moved in her chair, and Caleb sensed her fighting the urge to run after him.

When Lisa turned away to continue speaking to Ming Ue, Saba quietly rose and slipped from the room. Lisa saw her, but said nothing.

"Tell me more," Lisa said. "Caleb says the silver dragon is very magical and able to do all kinds of things."

Ming Ue nodded, her eyes watchful. "Li Na was powerful indeed. I think there is little you cannot do."

Lisa glanced at Caleb out of the corner of her eyes.
"Caleb mentioned that the silver dragon can move through
time as well as space. It would solve many problems if I
could go back in time and find Donna before all this
started. Come to think of it, why didn't the original silver
dragon move back in time to stop the original witch from
making the orb?"

Ming Ue shook her head. "No one can change that which
has already taken place. Not even the gods." She sipped her
tea, taking her time, setting down the cup, and dabbing her
lips with a napkin. "Li Na told me this as well. The silver
dragon can return through time but not for long stretches
and only to watch. She does not truly exist there, you see.
She can observe, but not touch the people she is with, and
unless they are of highly magical persuasion and looking
in the right place at the right time, they cannot even see her."

"Hmm," Lisa said, absently turning her empty cup on
the tablecloth. "It might help me find out exactly what
Donna is up to though."

Ming Ue shook her head. "The need to travel in such a
way must be great. Not simply to observe what happened
the day before. That magic works the same way as the
magic that brings the silver dragon forth in each woman.
The need must be compelling, Li Na said. It is not a frivo-
lous thing."

Lisa kept her eyes on her teacup as though only half-
listening to Ming Ue. Lumi and Grizelda and Carol had
gone utterly silent on their end of the table, watching the
others uncertainly.

Shaiming gently put the lid over the orb in the bowl and
lifted it back to the cart. "We keep it safe, Lisa."

Lisa looked up at him, starting out of her reverie. She
had something in mind, Caleb didn't know what, but he
was certain he would like it even less when he found out.
He sensed her closing even further to him.

When Lisa and Caleb finally took their leave from Ming

Ue and emerged from the restaurant, they found Saba and Malcolm leaning against Lisa's car, which Lumi had driven here. Saba held, point downward, the large sword Caleb had brought back from Dragonspace. She and Malcolm stood close but not touching, not talking.

Saba pushed herself away from the car and handed Caleb the sword without a word. Caleb stepped back, hefting it. Then feeling wicked laughter welling inside him, he swung the sword around in a perfect arc and settled the point at Malcolm's throat.

Saba gasped. Malcolm eyed him malevolently but made no move, while Lisa watched and waited.

Caleb chuckled. "Just so we know where we stand. Ready to go?"

Lisa was surprised she still remembered how to drive. But her feet knew where the gas and brake pedals were, and her hands steered the car between the lines and those drivers whose grasp of "between the lines" was more erratic.

Flying had been so much easier, she reflected, and such a joy. She'd had no idea how to fly, and she had the vague idea that small dragons needed to be taught. But her dragon body had seemed to understand. She'd shimmied through the air, weaving between molecules to shift through space. She remembered how her body had honed itself to a string of misty lights that arrowed to wherever she wanted to go. It had been a lovely, lovely feeling.

"Lisa," Caleb said in alarm. Saba was staring over the back seat, eyes round.

She looked down and realized that her body was translucent and shimmering, filling alternately with color and bright white light, and her feet had slipped from the pedals.

A car darted in front of her. Lisa solidified into herself and slammed on the brakes, sending them careening sideways. Fortunately, there wasn't much traffic on this street and the other driver sped on his way, snarling foul words.

She gulped. "Sorry."

"Perhaps Saba should drive," Malcolm said in his mild but hard voice.

"No, it's all right." Lisa dragged in a breath. "I'll be fine."

Hands shaking, she steered the car into the street again and drove home slowly, concentrating on keeping herself solid and human. She saw Malcolm in her rearview mirror watching her with his silver eyes and felt Caleb's equally watchful blue eyes fixed on her.

She parked the car in her lot, and the four of them walked the few blocks home. Lisa's legs shook, but she found it easier to remember who she was with her feet on the ground. Caleb carried his sword over his shoulder, earning a few startled glances from passersby, and Malcolm and Saba followed, waves of their uneasiness flowing over her.

Caleb slid his hand in hers, his strong grip an anchor, reminding her that she was Lisa and that she was in love with him. She'd never dreamed Mr. Right would be a fifty-foot dragon with glittering scales and a bad attitude, but he was.

For how long, she couldn't tell. When Caleb went back to Dragonspace, Lisa would remain here to look after the orb. She understood now the compelling pull back to this world when she'd been in Dragonspace—the silver dragon had known she needed to return to be with the orb.

Protecting the orb would count more with the silver dragon than being with Caleb, and Lisa felt now the burden of that responsibility. As much as she didn't want such a burden, she knew she could never be the cause of the world's destruction or allow someone like Donna to cause it.

The personal price would be high—Lisa would lose nothing less than herself, not to mention her newfound love for Caleb. *Sacrifice*, Ming Ue had said. *Caring that went beyond personal happiness.* Ming Ue and Li Na had always seemed so wise and serene, and Lisa could only hope to find such serenity. Right now she felt like a hole had been ripped open under her feet and she was falling and flailing.

When they reached the house, Malcolm walked slowly through the front door, as though having to force his feet to do it. He tilted his head, studying the large open hall, the sofa with its chocolate-colored upholstery and the wide staircase with the lift between its curves. "The whole place reeks of golden dragon."

Caleb casually brought the sword around in his competent hands, but Lisa stepped between them. "Play nice," she admonished.

They mounted the stairs, not bothering to see if the lift worked. Malcolm slowed as they reached Lisa's apartment, clearly uncomfortable. He'd said it had made him physically sick to try to approach the house with Li Na's protective magic, and Caleb's had been added over that. Dragons, Lisa realized with her new insight, didn't approach another dragon's territory lightly because a fight to the death was likely to ensue. Malcolm's nostrils flared, but he squared his shoulders and let Lisa usher him into her lair.

"Everything's so pretty," Saba said in delight as she looked around the living room. She studied the painted Chinese scrolls, the river rock, the bowl with the dragon on the bottom that held the charms. "These must be worth a fortune."

Lisa joined her to study the painting of sharp mountains with deep folded valleys. "My grandmother kept them so well, and they're such a part of her that I don't have the heart to sell them or give them to a museum."

She felt a sudden yearning toward the mountains in the painting, and realized it had likely been painted by one of her ancestors, a silver dragon woman longing for the razor-pointed mountains of Dragonspace.

"There was very little that was Asian at my house," Saba said, oblivious of Lisa's revelation. "My parents are ultramodern—in décor, that is. In everything else, they're extremely old-fashioned. My father expected me to grow up a quiet, obedient Japanese girl ready to marry the husband he picked out for me. They haven't quite come to terms with my choices of computer programming, tattoos, and witchcraft."

Lisa smiled with her. Saba was smart and talented,

she'd sensed that when she'd first seen her in the circle at the warehouses. She also sensed a young woman who had grown up in a protective world and was now trying to fit into an unprotected one. Malcolm had easily twisted his mark on her, which added to Saba's confusion about what she truly felt about anything.

Caleb leaned on the doorframe to the kitchen and watched Malcolm pace restlessly around the apartment. Dragons didn't like to be in close proximity to each other, she understood, especially in an enclosed space. Caleb watched Malcolm with the expression of a cat watching a new cat enter his domain. They could either ignore each other and coexist peacefully, or teeth and claws could erupt at any moment.

Malcolm studied the door of Caleb's bedroom. "Is that the portal?"

Caleb nodded, arms folded across his broad chest. Malcolm's leather coat whispered as he put his fingers on the doorknob and pushed open the door to reveal the small, plainly decorated bedroom.

"It won't open for you," Saba said. "It was created for Caleb."

"Lisa used it," Caleb pointed out.

"Lisa is a silver dragon," Malcolm answered. "Silver dragons can open portals anywhere they like." His eyes swam with dark sparks. "Why do you think I tried to steal her magic? With silver dragon magic in addition to Saba's magic, I could open a gate and go home."

"I'll send you if I can," Lisa promised. "But I'm asking you to stay here for a time. We need you if Donna makes good on her threat and tries to kill me."

"You don't need me at all. You could make short work of her."

"Maybe. Maybe not. I don't know how powerful she is or when and where she'll strike. A black dragon at my side would be extremely helpful."

"A black dragon with little power except the ability to

mark," Malcolm corrected her. "Donna easily thwarted my attempt to hurt her. I'd say I'm useless to you."

Lisa tilted her head and looked him up and down. "Black dragons are smart and cunning and powerful, no matter how stripped of powers. I like the odds of winning better if you stay."

"You're good at flattery, silver dragon," Malcolm said, a hint of growl in his voice. "You might have Caleb wrapped around your finger, although it's not hard to bamboozle a golden."

Caleb shifted against the kitchen doorframe. "Black dragons live so long because it takes them hundreds of years to think of insults."

Lisa held Malcolm's gaze, as she had in Ming Ue's shop. She saw in him a man tired and desperately lonely, ready to do anything to end the pain of his exile. He'd moved beyond feeling, although she sensed he'd begun an affection for Saba that he did not quite understand. Saba should be his enemy—a witch like those who'd trapped him here—and yet he'd become protective of her.

At last, Lisa gave him a nod. "All right. I'll send you back, right now."

Before Malcolm or Caleb could answer, she turned to the open door of the bedroom. Lisa had no idea how to open a portal to Dragonspace, but she let the silver dragon take over, and the silver dragon just *did* it.

Silver fire sprang from her fingers and cut a long slit in the air. The wind chimes jangled and danced and a clear note of music spun around them. A hot, dry wind blew through the doorway, followed by the scent of heat and pine and juniper.

Malcolm's face changed, a wild hope springing to his eyes. He inhaled the breeze pouring through the opening, and the wind chimes behind them shivered and tinkled.

"Do not tease me," he said. "It's cruel."

Lisa motioned to the doorway. "Go on. Hurry up. You might want to leave your clothes behind."

He stared at her, waiting for her to reveal that it was all a trick. Lisa merely watched him.

Saba made a faint noise in her throat, and Malcolm looked back at her. Lisa saw a flicker of regret in his eyes, but the beckoning of Dragonspace was too strong for him.

He shed his coat and handed it to Lisa, then he stripped off his clothes without embarrassment and stepped, nude, to the door, the dragon tattoo stark on his arm.

"I hope you're right, silver dragon," he said. "But even if I end up in one of the nether hells, it's worth taking the chance."

Lisa gave him a slow nod. "This is not a trick, Malcolm. Go home."

"Please," Caleb muttered.

Malcolm ignored him. He stepped to the bright slit, the glow bathing his body in warm light, the wind stirring his long hair. The moment he realized it was real, a look of impossible joy crossed his face.

"Yes!" he shouted, balling his fists, and then he dove forward into the light.

19

The cold wind blew Saba's black hair every which way, and she shivered. The wind chimes danced and rang, and then, with a final icy blast, the wind died and the crack sealed. Malcolm was gone.

Tears sprang to Saba's eyes. She blinked rapidly to hold them back, worried that the others would see them. She could still feel the swirls of Malcolm's mark in her mind, but the connection was now very, very faint.

What was she crying for? Malcolm had invaded her life and tied her to her bed and forced her to do things for him, for heaven's sake. And here she was, free of him and crying about it.

She felt Lisa's presence next to her, though Saba never heard her cross the apartment. Lisa put her hand on Saba's shoulder, comforting. "He'll be back," she said.

Lisa's dark eyes swam with silver sparks, and she exuded power, the silver magic evident in her. Saba could feel it rubbing against her own witch magic, the friction causing a tingling like static electricity. Lisa was saturated with power, and it was evident from the episode in the car that she really didn't know how to control it.

"You're confident." Saba wiped the moisture from her eyes with her thumb.

"Once he realizes he has a choice, that he's truly free, he'll feel differently."

Saba shrugged. "I don't know. I think he's had enough of this world and humans and earth magic. And witches."

"A few weeks ago, I'd have agreed with you. But now he has a reason to keep this world safe from Donna and her schemes." She smiled. "He met you."

Saba's heart beat faster. She took the leather coat Lisa handed her, still full of Malcolm's warmth and his scent. "Are all silver dragons like Little Mary Sunshine?"

Lisa's smile became a grin. "I don't know. I don't know any other silver dragons."

Caleb's look toward Lisa was like a caress—the warrior dragon was far gone on her. "I think Lisa is right. He won't want Donna to kill Lisa and get hold of the dragon orb, because who knows what she'll do with it? She might destroy this world, she might use the magic to go after any world she wants."

Saba admitted he made sense even though his reasoning was less flattering to her. Malcolm wouldn't simply let Donna have her way, but she doubted that Malcolm would work *with* Lisa and Caleb. He would do things his own way, for his own reasons.

"While we're waiting . . ." Lisa began.

Saba snapped her attention back to her. Lisa was still smiling, but lights roved in her eyes, and Saba didn't quite like how Lisa was looking at her.

"While we're waiting, what?"

"There's a little matter of Caleb's true name."

Saba held up her hand, which shook a little. "I won't use it, I promise. I saw what it did to him when Donna first got us together. I'd never use it deliberately."

"Maybe not, but what if Donna compels you to help

her?" Lisa touched her hand to Saba's forehead. "I'm going to try to remove your knowledge of it. Don't fight me."

Saba had no intention of fighting. She'd seen the awful power in Lisa, and she was not going to stir that up if she could help it.

Lisa spread her fingers across Saba's forehead and temple, her touch light. Saba didn't close her eyes, but continued staring at the silver lights burning in Lisa's brown eyes.

Some people are born lucky, she reflected, *while others have to struggle and scramble for every scrap they get.* Saba had grown tired of struggling and scrambling, knowing she could not be what her parents wanted, knowing they were disappointed in what she'd become. Then Donna had come along six months ago, telling her she could be a powerful witch and show everyone what she was made of. Her offer had dazzled Saba, and she'd willingly gone to learn what the woman could teach her. All she had to do was whatever Donna said, *You're so weak, and you need me to make you strong . . .*

A bright pain filled Saba's head, and she cried out. Lisa flinched and yanked her fingers from Saba's skin. Pain flared once through Saba's body, then receded, little by little, until it was no more than a faint headache.

"Ow," Saba said, scowling. "What the hell was that?"

Lisa bit her lip. "She's imbedded the knowledge of Caleb's name too deep inside you. You're still bound to her. I'm willing to bet Grizelda is, too."

Saba hugged Malcolm's coat to her, trying to take comfort in it. "I am not bound to her. Malcolm took that away, didn't he?"

Lisa looked troubled, which didn't make Saba feel any better. "I'm sorry, Saba. I think the only way you'll get away from her completely is if Donna dies. Or you do."

"Terrific." She eyed Caleb and Lisa, wondering if the pair of them would be desperate enough to kill her in order to free Caleb from a witch who knew his name. Caleb was a warrior dragon, and she'd seen the way he'd hefted that sword. As for Lisa—who knew what she could do? Saba didn't have near enough power or experience with magic to stand up to either one of them.

"Don't worry," Lisa began.

Her words cut off in midsentence. Saba felt the sudden dark bite of Malcolm's presence, and then he was there, six feet six inches of naked muscle stepping through the bright light of the portal.

Malcolm strode past Lisa and a scowling Caleb and gently took his leather coat from Saba. He touched her forehead. "This one's mine," he said. "You two will leave her alone."

"How did you know he'd come back?" Caleb asked.

Lisa lay in bed with him, his body curled around hers, his arm heavy on her abdomen. She shifted to snuggle closer to him. "I just knew."

"Can you read his mind?"

He sounded troubled. Lisa turned her head on the pillow and kissed the tip of his nose. "Not really. I can sense his thoughts . . . no, I can sense what his thoughts are *like*, if not the actual words or visions. He was so afraid he'd be stuck here forever, and he'd do anything to get away. Now that he knows he can leave, that he's not bound here any more, he can think about what he really wants."

"I know what I really want." Caleb nuzzled her.

"What's that?" she asked, pretending innocence.

"Me being on you. And in you."

She kissed the corner of his mouth, lingering when he licked the pad of her lip. "That can be arranged."

"But not yet."

"Why not?" Lisa's heart gave a strange beat.

"As humans like to say, can we talk?"

"Talk about what?" But she knew what he wanted to say.

"About you being a silver dragon, and me being a warrior who knows only how to kill and mate and sleep."

"And protect and give a home to gems longing for the mountains and make friends with a lonely woman like me.

Donna sent you to watch me; you didn't have to be nice about it."

He pressed a kiss to her hair. "I liked you."

"I liked you, too."

If she admitted it, her affection for him had gone far deeper from the start. She'd never believed their relationship could go past friendship, because after all he was a dragon, but she'd looked forward to coming home and talking to him and laughing with him and kissing him on the nose before she went to bed. A person could love another person without it being sexual.

Of course once he'd become a gorgeous, tight-bodied godlike man, physical love had been added to the mix.

"What about now?" he asked, voice quiet.

"I still like you." She raised up on her elbow, rubbing her palm over his chest. "And I want to be with you. That hasn't changed."

"Maybe *you* do, Lisa. But what about the dragon inside you? What does she want?"

"I don't know. But I don't want to go on without you, Caleb. I can't. I like you in my life."

"We might not have a choice. No one can break free of a dragon mark, but you have. You've broken away from me."

Lisa reached for the strands of thought that had bound her to Caleb from the first day she'd seen him, the music that lingered in the back of her mind at all times. She could no longer feel it.

In panic, she reached for it. "No. Come back to me."

"I can't mark you anymore, Lisa. I tried."

"But I want you to."

He shook his head and rolled on top of her, his warm weight and bare chest against hers. "Maybe you should find out what the silver dragon wants. If it isn't me, then I'll go."

Her eyes filled. "I don't want you to go. You're my best friend."

"I've never had a best friend before. But you have a purpose here, something to do, guarding the orb. Maybe you can do it better when I'm not here to distract you."

"No." She clung to him. "I'm not giving you up that easily."

He captured her wrists in his hands, pinning them above her head. "I haven't gone yet," he said. "And I'm going to enjoy every minute of you while I'm still here."

He began to make love to her with slow heat, and she closed her eyes, wanting the pleasure though her sorrow cut through it. Caleb slid his hand between them, swirling his fingers over her mound until she was fiery hot, the added friction spiraling her into climax. She gasped and groaned, trying and failing to be quiet. Caleb didn't bother. He shouted as he drove into her, harder and faster, his thrusts almost brutal.

Lisa sent out gleaming threads of her own thoughts, seeking his golden music. Strands of silver wrapped his body, connecting with the gold that shimmered together, binding them at least for a time.

"Yes," he said, smiling. "Thank you."

Donna lay down on the metal floor, changing her body to be long and sensuous and beautiful. The incubus liked that better, even though he would serve Donna no matter what she looked like. But it was nice to reward one's slaves on occasion.

The incubus glowed with sexual energy, its white hair nearly incandescent.

"What did you find out?" she asked, stripping off her shirt then her skirt.

"The black dragon is free," the incubus said. He dropped to one knee, his muscular body rippling in a satisfying way. "He returned to Dragonspace."

"Damn. Well, one less obstacle in the way."

The incubus shook his head. It reached for Donna's camisole and tugged it off, then caught Donna's lush, winsome breasts in his hands. "He came back."

"Did he?" Donna asked in surprise. "Why?"

"I don't know. I could not hear everything they said."

"He is a black dragon. He will have plenty of motives of his own, but the trouble is, you can never tell what they are. Is he going to help them, or help himself? Black dragons are selfish creatures, ultimately."

"Let me kill him," the incubus begged.

"Not until I'm finished." She grabbed the incubus's hand and dragged it between her legs. "There. Yes." She closed her eyes, letting the creature's expertise relax her and fill her with ecstasy. Why these modern Wicca abstained from using incubi was beyond her. Not only did the demons infuse her with power, but they were damn good at sex and never grew tired. What human male could offer that? "When I am finished, I'll let you play with him. He will not be able to fight back."

The incubus smiled. "I would like that."

"Good." Donna pulled his head down to her and kissed him. A flicker of his power entered her mouth, and she swallowed it.

But she wanted more. She turned her head and called into the shadows. "Come. I summon you."

After a moment, she heard the tread of bare feet, and another man, similar to the first incubus, entered the light. He had white hair, but a streak of black ran back from a widow's peak down to blend with his white locks. Faint scales around his hairline showed he was demon, but he was as beautiful as the most beautiful human male she'd ever seen. The first incubus eyed him curiously even as he continued to stroke Donna.

"I brought him to replace your brother. I hope you'll get along."

The new incubus knelt next to the first one. They looked each other over, from faces to sculpted chests to cocks that stood out full and erect. The first incubus touched the black streak in the second's white hair. The second bent his head and kissed the first full on the lips.

Heat stirred between Donna's legs. As she watched, the incubi began to explore each other fully, licking each other's mouths and faces, using hands to learn each other's bodies. Delight spiraled through her, and she pressed her own fingers against her opening. There was nothing quite so satisfying as watching two attractive males exciting each other.

"Good," she whispered. They began to explore each other's genitals, stroking and moaning, hands expert. "Good," she repeated. "Now me."

They knew what she wanted. Before long, she was rocking in ecstasy, screaming as they moved in perfect rhythm within her. The incubi keened and moaned. She dragged their power deep within her, every stroke making her stronger.

The stupid little witches who had abandoned her had no idea of the power of demons and how satisfying it was. Maybe she'd be nice and let one of the incubi take young Saba and teach her a thing or two. Grizelda had fought off the gift that Donna had offered and run away. Foolish girl.

After the incubi spilled their seed, Donna wriggled away from them and laid down to rest her body and absorb the power she'd taken. They waited, breathing hard, erections still full, and then, to her great joy, they fell to the floor and started taking each other.

Malcolm came out of the spare bedroom in Lisa's apartment in a T-shirt and underwear and headed for the kitchen, still thirsty from his journey to and from Dragonspace. It was also a relief to escape the irritating groans coming from Lisa's bedroom.

Saba lay on the sofa under a pile of blankets, her black hair tousled on the linen pillowcase. He'd offered to let her sleep with him in the Murphy bed since Lisa had no intention of letting either of them go home, but Saba had flushed and said she'd make do with the sofa.

Now that he'd regained more of his dragon powers, Malcolm could see fairly well in the dark and kept the light off so he wouldn't disturb her. The air in the refrigerator felt cool to his lightly clad body, the sport bottle of water still more soothing inside his hand. He drank the water, wetting his throat, and softly closed the refrigerator door.

The beauty of being a dragon again, of soaring through space with the wind under his wings had been incredible. His territory was still there, untouched—a dragon's power over his lands did not diminish until he was long dead. Malcolm had refreshed his power, and then spent time simply reveling in being a dragon. The strength and magic flowed through him once more, and he'd wept.

Black dragon tears had much magic. He'd lifted a few from the ground where they'd dropped and brought them back to this space, sliding them into his coat pocket when he'd taken the coat from Saba.

Lisa had known he'd come back. He'd seen it in her triumphant smile when he'd emerged, human once more. But he knew what was at stake—Donna filling herself with magic strong enough to kill a silver dragon and getting her hands on the powerful dragon orb was not a scenario he wanted. She might get big ideas about making her way to Dragonspace and torturing and killing a black dragon for the fun of it. She was dangerous and needed to be stopped.

He did not want to admit the tug he felt to the small woman on the sofa. The thought of her facing Donna, even with Lisa to back her up, chilled his blood. If he took care of the Donna problem, he could leave Saba behind without worry.

Saba stirred as if sensing him and lifted her head. "Malcolm?" she whispered.

He moved softly to the sofa, sitting down at her feet. He took another drink of water, letting the liquid soothe his throat. "I didn't mean to wake you."

"I wasn't asleep."

He cocked a glance at Lisa's bedroom door. "They are keeping you awake, too?"

Saba smiled wistfully. "At least someone's having fun."

Malcolm set the bottle on the coffee table and laid his hand on her thigh. "Would you like to be pleasured?"

The look in her eyes said *yes*, but she flicked her gaze away. "Is that why you came back?"

"I came back to stop Donna."

"No other reason?"

He knew she wanted him to say he'd returned for her. He moved his thumb across her thigh, feeling the slim muscle beneath the blankets. "When I return to Dragonspace, I want to know you are safe. You won't be until Donna is dead."

She smiled again, but the smile did not reach her eyes. "So no sacrificing your dragon life for the sake of humanity?"

"No."

"What's it like?" Saba pulled the covers to her chin and rested her head on her folded arm. "Being a dragon, I mean, in Dragonspace? Did you find everything changed when you went back?"

He continued to massage, feeling her relax under his touch. "I found everything much the same. Eight centuries is not that long in dragon terms. To answer your question, it was glorious. To fly again, to taste the skies, to feel the beauty of the plains. I love it so much."

He could not keep the longing catch from his voice. He needed to breathe the air of Dragonspace the same way people needed their hearts to keep beating.

"I'm sorry you were trapped here," she said. "It was cruel."

He liked the way her hair wisped against her forehead and how her eyes, almond-shaped, were so dark they almost pulled him into them. "It is not your fault. Those witches were dead hundreds of years ago."

"But they were humans, like me. And witches, like me."

Malcolm moved his touch to her abdomen. "I saw many things and learned much while I was here. I find it strange that humans blame themselves for things people in ages past did. They wallow in guilt or expend energy assigning blame. Dragons forget and move on."

She gave him an "Oh, really?" look. "If that were true, you would not have come back."

"This is a different situation."

Her lips quirked. "Of course."

Malcolm leaned over her. "I truly wish to pleasure you." He liked touching her body, watching her rise to his hand, feeling her skin warm with his touch. He skimmed a kiss to her cheek.

Saba put her hand on his chest, pushing slightly. "Why don't I pleasure you for a change?"

His heartbeat quickened as he imagined her slim hand on his staff, moving in long, slow strokes while he held her and kissed her. Or better still, he could sit here on the sofa with his thighs spread while she knelt before him and ran her tongue up and down his full arousal. It was a heady and tempting vision.

"No," he answered.

"Why not?"

She sounded hurt. She thought he controlled himself because he was not attracted to her, as though he did not find her pixy face and lovely body beautiful. He tried to explain. "When I leave here, I want no ties to anything. If I take pleasure from you, it might be more difficult for me to go, and I do not want a reason to stay."

He thought it a logical solution. If he fell in love with her, he'd always be torn. If he made love to her and gave her a child, he would be further torn. Best to make it a clean break. Surely she would understand this.

Anger and pain flickered in her eyes, and she pushed him away in earnest. She grabbed the edge of the blanket and rolled away from him, covering herself completely and pressing her nose to the back of the couch. "Go to bed. I don't want you touching me."

Malcolm stared at her in surprise, expecting her at any moment to roll over and reach for him, unable to resist. She did no such thing. As she remained a lump of blanket and rumpled black hair, anger bubbled inside him. Hot words formed in his mouth, words of annoyance that a human male might say to his mate, and for one insane moment, he nearly started to argue with her.

He stopped, surprised at the feeling which was not the least bit logical. He was not human, he was *dragon*, and she had no business refusing anything he asked of her or any gift he wished to give her.

He shifted in irritation. The sooner he finished and went back to Dragonspace the better. He'd release Saba before he left, and then she'd forget all about him, and he'd forget her. It would be better that way.

That did not explain why he sat on the sofa in the dark for another thirty minutes, waiting for Saba to roll over, smile her shy smile, and say she wanted to enjoy the time she had left with him.

Saba remained motionless. The clock was striking midnight when Malcolm at last rose, picked up the half-empty bottle of water, and drifted back to the spare room to sleep. At least the two in Lisa's bedroom had finally shut up.

Lisa made breakfast. No one else had the inclination to cook, and Lisa wasn't about to let Caleb lose with her pots and pans and the open flame on her stove. She put the shrimp she'd brought home from the show to good use, making seafood omelets with a butter and lemon sauce.

Saba drifted to the kitchen to help, but mostly she leaned on the counter and watched Lisa chop herbs and sauté the shrimp. "Do you do everything perfectly?" she asked, a grumpy note in her voice.

Lisa looked at her in surprise. "No. What are you talking about?"

"You're a silver dragon, you have powerful magic, you can cook . . ."

"I'm a silver dragon because of my hundred-times great-grandmother, I didn't choose it. The cooking came from a grueling year in culinary school and more grueling years in kitchens with terrorizing chefs, not to mention Hazeltine Conant. My life was never quite right until I moved back here and started working at Ming Ue's and meeting my grandmother for tea. When I finally gave up trying to have the perfect career and the perfect marriage and the perfect life, everything fell together."

Saba picked up a spoon and absently tasted the sauce, her lips curling at the heat. "Do you have any advice for a freelance programmer who's currently available?"

Lisa thought a moment. "I guess, don't fight what feels right. Don't let anyone try to make you be other than who you are." She grimaced. "I sound like a fortune cookie."

Saba laughed lightly. "Your people are good to you. Did you have trouble when you were a kid? Being part Asian?"

"I have red hair," Lisa said, stirring the shrimp. "Most people don't know I'm part Asian. Li Na married an American, so my mother was half-Chinese, and my father is as far from Chinese as anyone can get." She thought of her tall, red-haired, big-boned father trying to eat tiny Chinese delicacies with chopsticks. "I never knew Li Na's husband—he died before I was born. My parents live in Hawaii now so we're not as close as we were."

Saba looked wistful. "My grandmother was the perfect woman, trained in the art of pleasing everyone around her and keeping things running like an oiled machine. My own father rebelled at having to be traditional, but suddenly he thinks his heritage is being lost, and I'm the one to revive it." She wrinkled her small nose. "It's not working."

Lisa spooned a pile of sautéed shrimp onto a puddle of cooking egg. "Like I said, you have to be true to who you are."

Saba sighed. "I suppose I have bigger things to worry about right now." She glanced past Lisa to the living room, where things were quiet. Too quiet. "You don't think Caleb and Malcolm have killed each other out there, do you?"

"They better not have," Lisa said darkly. She flipped the finished omelet onto a big plate and carried it out to the table, which she and Saba had pulled in front of the open French doors to catch the warm June breeze.

Caleb and Malcolm were watching television. Caleb

held the remote, and both man-dragons stared with looks of rapt concentration at a basketball game being rerun on a sports channel.

"Ah," Lisa said. "Male bonding."

20

The two looked up at her, both shifting as though embarrassed to be found actually doing something together.

"We are trying to decipher the rules," Caleb said.

"There seems to be little order to it," Malcolm added, glancing back at the screen.

"You've never watched basketball before?" Saba asked him.

Malcolm rose effortlessly to his feet. "On the contrary, I have been observing human sports for eight hundred years in many different countries—Britain, Italy, France, Spain, Mexico, America. I still don't understand any of them."

"Come and have omelets instead," Lisa said. "Eggs and shrimp. Nothing dragons wouldn't eat."

Caleb clicked off the television and he and Malcolm approached the table, splitting off to the opposite ends, eyeing each other warily. Lisa ducked back into the kitchen for another omelet, and soon she had four plates sitting on bright red placemats.

Malcolm held a chair out for Saba to slide into. She did so with a quick look at him but no smile. Lisa sensed the tension between them as she started the sauce around but decided to say nothing about it.

"We need a plan of action," she announced as they began to eat. "Donna wants to get her hands on me, and I'd rather find her instead of waiting around for her to jump at me from the shadows. Caleb and I talked about this last night and decided that the best way to circumvent the problem is to offer Donna the orb."

Saba started. "How will that circumvent the problem?"

Caleb scooped up a large bite of eggs. "We offer her the orb, she rushes out of hiding to get it, Lisa kills her, end of dilemma."

"That's your plan?" Malcolm asked, fork halting halfway to his mouth. "Lisa meets her on the street and says, 'Here's the orb'?" His voice dripped sarcasm. "Donna will be suspicious, don't you think?"

"If *any* of us offer her the orb, she'll suspect a trap," Saba pointed out.

"Not if I do it," Caleb broke in. Into the silence that fell, he said, "If she uses my true name I have to obey her, and she knows it. So if she finds out I know where the dragon orb is, she can order me to either steal it or tell her where it is."

Lisa looked at her plate. Caleb had come up with the idea while she'd lain against his body in the dark. She'd argued for a long time before deciding he was right. Donna would compel Caleb to come to her hiding place or meet her somewhere and Lisa could follow.

"It's a bad idea," Saba said in a hard voice.

"No, it isn't," Malcolm said. "I imagine Lisa could track Caleb to Donna and I can follow her."

"But Caleb would have to put himself in her power," Saba said. "Then Donna would have not only the orb but a warrior dragon on her side."

"Not for long," Caleb put in. "It is the best way to finish this quickly. I'd rather force her hand than wait until she's ready to strike. She's building her strength, and we should stop her before she becomes more powerful than she already is."

"I know," Saba said glumly. "But I worked with her. I know how strong she is and how cunning. I thought at first she was a wonderful, wise woman who would help me when no one else would. I realize now she wanted me to think that. She had me completely fooled."

"Her perfidy isn't your fault," Malcolm said. He gave Saba a steady look, which she returned as though they'd discussed this before. "Caleb's idea is good, but it leaves the small problem of planting the idea that Caleb knows where the orb is in Donna's head."

"Which is where Saba comes in," Lisa said.

"Me?" Saba pressed her hands to her chest. "I'm not strong enough to coerce demon-magic-infested Donna."

Malcolm's face went hard. "I don't want Saba in this. Me, Lisa, and Caleb, fine. Saba stays out of it."

Saba ruffled her short, black hair. "I'd be offended at your lack of confidence if I didn't agree. I really can't go up against Donna."

Lisa swirled the tines of her fork through her thin sauce, making patterns on the plate. "I only need you to do a locating spell. That's all. And we can do it right here."

"She'll have shielded against a locator spell," Saba argued. "If she doesn't want to be found, she'll have put plenty of wards in place."

"I know. But when I feel the backlash of her shield, I can send suggestions to her using the thread of her magic. If I do it subtly enough, she'll think she's being very clever."

Lisa took a calm bite of eggs and shrimp, then noticed Saba staring at her in an odd way. "What?"

"You can do that? Infiltrate a counter-spell?"

"Yes." Lisa stopped, thinking about it. "Don't ask me how I know how to do it, but the silver dragon does."

Malcolm scraped more eggs into his mouth and swallowed. "In that case, why can't you follow her counter-spell back to its source? Find her that way?"

"Because the locator shield will be very strong, with all kinds of blankets to confuse direction, and I might reveal myself if I try to follow it. She won't be looking for suggestion spells, which is tiny magic compared to the power of a shield."

"You hope," Malcolm said.

Lisa nodded. "I hope."

"I'll do it," Saba said in a quiet voice. "Don't look at me like that, Malcolm. I want to help, and I can't fight, but I can do a locator spell."

He continued to stare at her, silver eyes cold. Saba returned the look defiantly, her brows lowered under her wispy bangs. They were mismatched: Malcolm large and powerful, Saba young, slender, and inexperienced. It was like watching a mouse face down a tiger. But Saba held to it, and Malcolm was the one who looked away first.

Lisa broke in. "We'll do it *after* we finish breakfast. I slaved over a hot stove for this, so enjoy it."

She went back to eating, but Malcolm glared sullenly, Saba looked troubled but determined, and Caleb reached over and squeezed her hand. It didn't make her feel any better.

For the spell, Saba asked for a map of San Francisco, salt, thread, and a needle. Lisa cleared the plates, and Saba scrubbed off the table while Lisa found the accoutrements for her. She tried to work calmly, but she worried. Despite Caleb's reassurances, she knew that Donna could hurt him and the thought of him dying made her physically sick.

Saba spread out the map, which detailed streets from the Golden Gate Bridge in the north to Daly City in the south. She instructed the other three to sit around the table in approximate locations of the main compass points, while she took the north side.

Lisa sat on the east side, watching Saba encircle the table with salt, murmuring rhymed lines that called for the presence of the Goddess. Saba then spread salt in a fine film across the map and used the tip of a quartz crystal, which she'd taken from her pocket, to sketch runes around the perimeter. Last, she drew a length of thread through her thumb and forefingers, chanting more rhymes, and threaded it through the needle.

She lifted the thread and let the needle dangle over the map. She drew a breath and looked at each of the other three, a shaky smile on her face. "Wish me luck."

"You can do this," Lisa said softly. She sensed Malcolm sending a tendril of black dragon magic to her, the thought encompassing Saba like smoke.

Saba's shoulders straightened the slightest bit. She closed her eyes, holding the dangling needle over the map, the point hovering just above the salt. Drawing a breath, she began to speak.

> Lady of light, mistress of the moon
> I pray you to grant my boon
> That I might find the hidden one
> And so charge her to harm none.
> I ask this freely, Goddess of Earth.
> So mote it be.

A faint blue nimbus surrounded Saba and glowed from her fingers down the thread to sparkle on the sharp needle. Malcolm watched her intently, hands gripping the edge of the table as though ready to spring and knock the thread out of her hands if anything went wrong.

Lisa glanced at Caleb, who returned her look with a smile that she assumed was supposed to be encouraging. She touched his hand and he closed his fingers on hers.

Saba remained still, her energy pouring into the needle, thread, salt, map, and the circle around them. She was strong, Lisa felt, a power contained behind a façade of uncertainty. Saba needed training, but when she had it, she'd be powerful indeed.

The blue light sparkled suddenly, and the needle moved. Lisa released Caleb's hand and leaned over the map, holding her breath, waiting for the feel of Donna's magic. The needle traced a slow line through the salt, the string bending as the gleaming needle glided slowly east, toward the bay.

When the backlash came, it came with a vengeance. A wicked red light arced from the map to the needle, skimmed up the thread faster than thought, and exploded. It engulfed Saba in a brilliant red glare, twisting itself around her body and snuffing out the blue nimbus. Saba screamed. The map burst into flames that burned high and blue, like those of an alcohol burner. Salt scattered as the paper crumpled to ash, scorching the table beneath it.

Malcolm leapt from his chair and caught Saba's body as she sagged from her chair. He cradled her against him and used his dark dragon magic to dampen the red flares that flashed around her body like bolts of electricity. She moaned in pain, and he held her close, his eyes blazing fury.

Lisa studied the burn mark on her grandmother's table, her breathing hard, her fingers tingling. As soon as the first red spark had appeared, she'd sent the tiny magic suggestion back through to wherever the spell-caster lay. She'd done it in the blink of an eye, before the red light had even reached its way up the thread to touch Saba. It was done.

She stood up to find her knees weak. Caleb caught her with strong hands, helping her to stand.

"Is Saba all right?" she asked.

"I don't know," Malcolm growled. He lifted Saba in his arms. Her eyes were closed, her face drawn, though the red snakes of electricity had disappeared.

"I think it worked," Lisa said. "I sent the suggestion. Donna should move soon."

Malcolm shot her a look a pure fury. "I don't give a damn." Holding Saba close, he strode into the spare bedroom, slamming the door so hard it shook the apartment.

Caleb's blue eyes were flecked with dark specks, golden lashes lowering as he looked down at her. "Well," he said. "Now we wait."

* * *

Hours passed. Lisa and Caleb sat side by side on the balcony, the wooden slats of the railing warmed by the fading sunshine, Lisa's pots of geraniums bright smudges of red against the white-painted posts. Saba and Malcolm hadn't come out of the bedroom since Malcolm had carried Saba in after the spell. Lisa had wandered the apartment, restless, eating only when Caleb convinced her to make herself a sandwich. She hadn't realized Donna's counter-spell would be so strong, but of course Donna would not only shield herself but set up the spell to attack the magician who tried to find her.

"Lisa," Caleb said now. "I want to tell you about Severin, my son."

Lisa looked up at him. The afternoon sunlight cast shadows on his square, tanned face and skimmed highlights along his golden hair. His eyes were sad.

"You don't have to," she said quickly.

He took her small hand in his larger one, stroking her fingers with his blunt thumb. "I want to. In case anything goes wrong."

"I won't let anything go wrong."

He gave her a dragon look from under his long lashes. "She is powerful. I know you can defeat her, but who knows what she'll get up to before you can?"

"I won't let her."

He didn't answer, looking away across the gardens and rooftops to the trees of the Presidio, the historic army post that was now a preserved recreation area. "Witches have known my true name for a long time," he said slowly. "But about five hundred years ago, I went through a stretch of time when none called me. I was naïve enough to believe that they'd forgotten about me, that all the witches who had known my name had died off. During this stretch of years, I mated with a female golden and was lucky enough to get away before she disemboweled me. I patted myself on the back for mating and living for the second time in my life and thought no more about it."

"And then you found out you had a son?" Lisa asked, curious.

"I found an egg." Caleb leaned back on the patio chair, stretching out his muscular, blue-jeaned legs. "The female laid a clutch, which she guarded well, but she'd pushed this particular egg away. They do that if they think there's something wrong with it. I happened to observe her, and for some reason I decided to save the egg. I thought maybe the hatchling inside was dead, but I stole it anyway and took it to my lair. I kept it in my hoard and set up magic protection around it, and it sat there for about a year. I almost forgot about it, but one day, when I returned from hunting, the thing was hatching."

"And a baby golden dragon crawled out?" Lisa clasped her hands in delight. "Oh, I bet he was cute."

Caleb gave her a withering glance. "He was a little pain in the ass. When dragons first hatch, they're tiny and fairly helpless. What they do is climb inside the female's mouth and she carries them around, behind her teeth, until they're big enough to fend for themselves. So imagine me, staring at this tiny thing the size of one of your lizards, when it pops open its eyes, looks excited, and scuttles up the side of my face. He buried his little body behind my teeth and wouldn't come out for anything."

Lisa put her hand over her mouth. "I wish I'd seen that."

"I tried to explain to the little monster that I wasn't his mother, but he didn't care. I tried to spit him out, but I couldn't dislodge him, and I couldn't swallow my own son, so I let him stay. Didn't have much choice, did I? After a couple of years, he was big enough and finally crawled out."

Lisa blinked. "Did you say a couple of *years*?"

"Dragons grow slowly. By that time, he was as big as my hand, and able to fly around the cave. Unfortunately, about that time, he started to talk. And I mean, talk. He never shut up."

Lisa grinned. "I bet you made a great dad."

"I didn't kill him anyway." Caleb growled. "I taught him

to hunt and find jewels and how to navigate Dragonspace. I named him Severin. He didn't like the name, but I told him to deal with it."

He spoke in his grumpy tones, but Lisa knew him well enough now to know that he'd cared deeply for this son.

"He lived with me for a hundred years," Caleb went on, his voice softening. "Dragons like solitude, and I could never decide why I let him stay, but being without him seemed impossible somehow."

"He must have wanted to stay with you, too."

Caleb shrugged, muscles rippling under his shirt. "I think he liked having someone to talk to." His look turned ironic. "And that little dragon could *talk*. He asked questions about everything under the sun, and if he couldn't think of something to ask about, he'd describe in minute detail all the pretty rocks he'd found in the stream bed that day. Maybe that's why the female threw out his egg in the first place—she heard him in there, his little voice already gearing up."

Lisa hid a smile. "He sounds funny."

Caleb's expression relaxed. "He could make me laugh. He was so eager to learn everything about life and everything about being dragon." He closed his eyes, pain shading his face. "And then, a witches' coven summoned me."

"You don't have to tell me, Caleb. Not if it hurts you."

He opened his eyes and gazed for a moment at the deep blue sky over the green trees of the preserve. "I want you to know. These witches took me with them to a tribe of humans who worked a primitive kind of magic that was very powerful. The people were simple, because magic gave them all they needed, and they'd never developed much beyond basic necessities. Well, these witches decided they wanted to tap into that primitive magic. The witches tried going to the people and learning from them and asking for the magic, but the people either couldn't or wouldn't give up their magic to the witches. So the witches decided to take it."

"Like the witch who made the dragon orb," Lisa mused.

"She couldn't stand the thought of not being able to have whatever magic she wanted."

Caleb didn't answer. His eyes were bleak as he continued. "The head witch wanted me to appear to these people and pretend to be a god. They knew nothing about dragons and I terrified them, but then when I didn't hurt them, they started to worship me. They built shrines, prayed for me to do things for them—I hated it, by the way. I was a charlatan, and I knew it, but it was mostly harmless. I thought this was all the head witch wanted me to do, I thought she would use their new religion to trick them into giving her their magic, but no.

"One day she told she wanted me to lure them back to Dragonspace, promising them eternal life and heaven. There she and her coven would drain them of their magic and kill them. She offered to let me eat them when she was done."

Lisa's lips parted in horror. "That's terrible."

"I refused," Caleb said. "Pretending to be a god is one thing. Murdering an entire race so a witch can siphon their power is something else, and I wouldn't do it. She and her coven tortured me, using my true name, but I resisted. It hurt me like nothing has ever hurt me since, but I did it. Eventually they had to stop because their spells on me were wearing them out. I still wouldn't obey, and they had to release me. I thought that would be the end of it, but they were furious, and to take their revenge they summoned a horde of demons, hundreds of them, who ripped Severin apart." His eyes grew dim with distant sorrow. "I couldn't fight them all. I was too exhausted from fighting the witches. The demons killed him and ate his flesh."

Silent tears slid down his cheeks, and his strong hands closed hard on the arms of the chair.

Lisa moved from her seat and knelt in front of him. "Oh, Caleb. I'm so sorry."

"It was a long time ago."

"That doesn't matter. It was evil." Her eyes filled. "And I wasn't there to stop it. I wish I had been there to stop it."

She laid her head in his lap and felt his tears drop to her cheek, his hand on her hair. "Thank you, Lisa-ling. But it is done."

She could sense how terrible his grief had been. It had cut him deeply, and the wound had not healed even after all this time. No wonder he could barely contain his fury and disgust when he talked of Donna with her demons, no wonder he'd brought Lisa diamonds from his hoard in an effort to protect her. She'd left the diadem in his lair, dropping it when she'd become the silver dragon. She sensed that the silver dragon was far more powerful than demons now in any case.

Finding the egg and raising the baby dragon had taught Caleb about love and about sacrifice for a child. To take that from him had been cruelty in its purist form. The silver dragon had learned to love two millennia ago, and she'd also learned to rage against injustice.

Lisa lifted her head, her body sparkling with silver dragon fire.

"Lisa," Caleb said in alarm.

Lisa got slowly to her feet. The sight of tears on Caleb's strong face brought a knife-sharp pain to her heart. She had not been there to use her silver dragon powers to stop the demons from taking his son. At that time, the silver dragon had been in this world, in China with her family, watching over the humans as best she could. But back then Caleb had needed her help most of all.

Lisa leaned down, kissed him hard on the lips, and strode to the door. She heard Caleb jump from the chair. "Lisa, what are you doing?"

Inside, Malcolm and Saba, pale but otherwise unharmed, were at the table, bent over a new, unburned map of San Francisco. They looked up in surprise as Lisa crossed to the spare bedroom door. She lifted her hand and the door opened, revealing not the plain room but the chill of Dragonspace beyond.

"Lisa, no," Caleb shouted behind her.

Lisa sent him a smile. She turned and leapt into the dark

and into a place he could not follow—the spaces between time.

"Shit," Caleb said, pounding a fist on the doorframe. He felt Malcolm hulking behind him and the smaller, lighter presence of Saba. The silver dragon was gone, the smile on Lisa's face before she'd departed telling him she knew damn well he couldn't follow her.

"What just happened?" Malcolm demanded.

"She's going back through time." Caleb leaned his cheek on the door frame, still wrung with emotion. It had been difficult to tell her the story of Severin, but he'd wanted her to know it. "She's going back to try to put things right for me."

"She can do that?" Saba asked in wonder.

"She can't," Malcolm stated flatly. Black dragon anger seeped from him. "Silver dragons can move through time but not change things. Changing something would violate all kinds of temporal physics laws that humans haven't discovered yet. It isn't possible."

"That's what Ming Ue told her," Caleb said. "But I don't think she cares."

"Well, it was a foolish idea," Malcolm snapped. "Because now there is no silver dragon and its protective magic on this plane and in this time, and the dragon orb is, as humans say, a sitting duck."

Lisa knew in her heart that Ming Ue was right, that she could not alter events that had already happened or bring the dead to life. But her silver anger streamed behind her as she slid easily through centuries, needing to be appeased. She needed to do *something*.

Caleb's dragon grief pulled her toward the clearing at the base of a mountain, his sorrow cutting the air like a sword. She found him lying in the grass, stretched out like a dead thing, his dragon head resting limply on the ground.

His eyes were half-closed, the bright blue of them dull. Nearby lay the carcass of what once had been a young dragon, maybe twenty-five feet in length. It had been ripped to shreds. Kind rain was falling now, washing the blood and grime down the hill into a raging stream at the bottom.

Lisa knew Caleb would not see her. She was nothing but a stream of light through time, undetectable to him. She touched his forehead, stroking his warm, shimmering scales, and pressed a kiss between his eyes. "Find comfort," she breathed. "Rest."

Caleb's eyes flickered, as though he heard something but did not understand it. His eyes slid closed, and he breathed a long dragon sigh.

Lisa darted away, her anger giving her speed. She could smell the demons who did this, overlaid with the odor of the decadent witches. She followed the scent through another portal, arriving in her own world again but five hundred years before her own time.

She was not certain where she was. A flat plain of gorse led to stark mountains, which climbed to meet a leaden sky. Cold wind bit her, and icy rain sheeted from the clouds.

Lisa skimmed across the land, tracking the scent to a fold of hills in which a village nestled. The cottages were made of gray stone with thatch for roofs—a remote area of England or Scotland perhaps.

She found the witches inside a tavern, which was little more than a room with benches and a hole in the roof for the fire. The family who owned the tavern huddled against a far wall, casting fearful glances at them. No other guests or villagers were in sight.

The witches were able to see her. Three of them, young women wearing costly velvets and jewels from this century, stared at her in abject terror. The fourth, their leader, who had ordered the killing of Caleb's son, was more contemptuous.

Lisa let herself manifest in half-human, half-light form

in front of the startled witches, bathing them in silver radiance. "I am not happy with you," she said severely.

The head witch's lip curled. "You cannot change what has happened."

"No, but I can make you very sorry for it."

The head witch spat. Lisa got a good look at her eyes, and realized several things. One, that the witch who faced her looked much like Donna but with subtle differences. Second, that the tavern keeper planned to rush out and fetch his friends to drive out the witches, and the four women would not last the night.

The head witch faced Lisa, hands on hips, a smirk on her face. "A silver dragon. My favorite. And if, I'm not mistaken, the same silver dragon my ancestor, a great witch, hunted long ago. She died fleeing back to this world from Dragonspace. Your doing."

"Her own doing," the silver dragon said. "She wasted her magics in an impossible task and it drained her."

The witch's eyes narrowed. "I will be happy to kill you to avenge her."

Lisa pushed slightly with her power and the woman flinched. "I don't even exist in this time," Lisa said. "I've met a witch who looks like you. Her name is Donna."

The witch looked startled. "How do you know my sister?"

"She is your sister? I met her five hundred years into the future. How could she live so long?"

The witch smiled. "Our family is very strong. The strongest you will ever encounter. Maybe even too strong for you, silver dragon."

"She feeds on other magics," Lisa mused. "Like demons and dragons. Draining other creatures dry so you can survive, like vampires, sucking magic instead of blood."

"Dragons and demons are weak. They think they are strong, but they are not."

"Silver dragons are not weak," Lisa said softly. "And this one is very angry at you for what you did to Caleb."

Donna's sister looked at her in slight alarm. "He would not obey. It is dangerous to let them not obey."

"So you murdered an innocent, a child."

"A dragon," the witch scoffed.

"Caleb's child. His son. He loved his son and you took that from him."

"Dragons don't love. They don't know how."

"Oh, yes they do." Lisa turned to the family watching and solidified enough for them to see her. "Go," she said. "Hurry."

They didn't wait to ask questions. The tavern keeper grabbed his two children by the hands and sprinted for the door, his wife following, clutching his coat.

Lisa let the silver dragon take over. For the first time since she'd discovered the truth of who she was, she felt no bewilderment or fear. Strength filled her along with sharp joy as she raised her hands, silver power radiating from her.

The three witches in the corner screamed. They started for the door, fighting one another to get through it into the rain. The head witch faced Lisa, tendrils of darkness swirling around her. "You will not win," she hissed. She flung a cloud of blackness at Lisa which blotted out all light.

Lisa let go her silver magic. She had no idea what it would do, and as it left her fingers it took on a mind of its own. Silver threads, music shimmering from them, wrapped themselves around the witch. The witch countered with dark tendrils, and the silver threads flared to meet them. Shrill notes filled the tavern, sweet and loud like the finest church bells.

The dark magic was strong. Lisa felt it wrap her, trying to squeeze the life from her. She struck back with silver magic fighting blindly, and somewhere inside her the silver dragon laughed.

Suddenly the music ceased and Lisa could see again. The silver light brightened the room like the brightest summer day, chasing shadows from the place.

The witch lay at Lisa's feet, stunned, not dead. "No," she said hoarsely. "No, don't let them."

The earth rumbled beneath her like a San Francisco tremor, and the witch's colorless eyes went wide. "No," she screamed.

Lisa leapt backward as dragon claws erupted through the earth floor, black, golden, red, blue, brilliant white. Dragon heads followed, not solid but translucent, perhaps the ghosts of dragons whose magic she'd stolen.

Dragon talons closed around the witch, dragging her down. One of the black dragons looked at Lisa with silver eyes much like Malcolm's. He bowed his head as though doing homage then joined his fellows in dragging the screaming witch through the floor. The earth closed up behind her and the witch was gone.

Lisa drew a breath, feeling shaky and sick. She folded her arms over her chest, breathing hard, shocked, but inside her, the silver dragon did a little dance of pleasure.

"Stop that," she said hoarsely.

As she tried to comprehend what had just happened, she saw a line of lanterns approaching the tavern through the gathering darkness, the villagers coming to drive out the rest of the witches. Lisa drew a long breath, then layered some lucky silver magic over the tavern before she departed.

The silver dragon skimmed back through the portal into Dragonspace, flying unerringly to the place where Caleb still lay. He was deep in slumber, his scales glistening softly in a pool of moonlight.

Lisa's heart ached for him. He would hurt for so long, and some part of him would never stop hurting. She remembered his voice cracking when he'd whispered, "Love you," as they made love in the kitchen. That love was so alien to him, given from a heart reluctant to embrace human emotions.

Lisa knew she could not bring Severin back or remove Caleb's grief, but she could at least relieve him of the task of having to deal with Severin's corpse. Using a small flicker of magic, she pointed at the remains of the dragon Severin and burned his flesh and bone quickly to ash.

Two gold dragon scales glittered in the grass beside the charred place. Lisa picked them up, marveling at the supple gold, so beautiful in the moonlight. She placed one between Caleb's front talons and tucked the other into her pocket.

"Are you pleased with yourself?"

Lisa whirled and found herself facing a young woman with long black hair dressed in a tightly wrapped robe of blue silk with gold embroidery. A white streak burned in her hair at her brow.

Lisa approached her, careful to walk softly. "You're me," she said in wonder. "Or at least, the ancestor of me."

21

"Yes," the silver dragon of the past said, her mouth creased in mirth. "But you should not have come here. Entering Dragonspace for a short while in your own era is one thing, but leaving your entire time unprotected may do more harm than your vengeance was worth."

Tears filled Lisa's eyes. "I wanted to help Caleb. I felt so ineffectual sitting there while he told me his story, knowing I couldn't stop his pain."

Silk rustled as the silver dragon put a kind hand on Lisa's shoulder. "You love him very much."

"Yes."

"The ability to love is greater than any magic. That is the secret the silver dragon discovered and passed to us, and why we are still strong when lesser dragons would have withered and died. We understand love and its power."

Lisa wiped her eyes. "I wish it didn't hurt so much."

"That is its price." The woman-dragon touched the silver streak in Lisa's hair. "We love and we ache, but once we have learned to love, that can never be taken from us."

Lisa tried to smile. "Were all the women in my family

wiser in the past? It's taken me forever to figure out I'm in love with a pesky golden dragon."

The silver dragon laughed, a sound like the wind chimes in Lisa's apartment. "We come to wisdom in our own time. I fell in love early in my life and so learned of it quickly. And when you have your children, you'll learn how to love even more deeply. It will happen." She wrinkled her nose, her face young and even cute. Lisa knew that Chinese women of the past had been expected to be quiet and subservient, and she imagined the silver dragon busily turning those expectations upside down.

The silver dragon stepped closer to Lisa, looking at her eye to eye. The two women were the same height, and Lisa saw her own and Li Na's features reflected in the young girl. "I will tell you another secret silver dragons know which might help you later. Magic isn't about power—who has the most, who is strongest. It's about balance. When the elements are in balance, that is the greatest power of all."

"Balance," Lisa repeated. The word felt good in her mouth, tasting of truth.

"You'd better be getting back," the silver dragon said. "They will need you." She cocked her head, as though hearing distant voices. "I must as well. Sying is chasing the chickens again. He is my youngest and fascinated with birds."

"He feels the pull to fly," Lisa suggested.

"Maybe. Or the pull to drive his sisters and father mad." She grinned then backed away a few steps. "Good-bye."

Her form flickered into silver, then into lights, and she streamed away and was gone. "Good-bye," Lisa said.

In his sleep, the dragon Caleb shifted and murmured. Lisa went to him and softly kissed his forehead. "Rest, love."

Then she narrowed into her silver-and-lights form and streamed back through space and time to the doorway that drew her.

When she spilled through, her apartment was dark except for white moonlight that poured into the living room.

She felt a moment of disorientation, not certain how long she'd been gone—hours or days?

Malcolm rose from the sofa, his leather clothes creaking in the dark. "He's gone," he said without preliminary. "Donna summoned him—he just vanished."

"Caleb?" Lisa knew they intended for this to happen, but panic lodged in her throat.

"Yes, Caleb," Malcolm growled. "While you were off doing whatever the hell you thought was so important. And Saba's gone, too. Donna took her as well."

Lisa felt Malcolm's fury pour from him in brittle waves as she drove her car to Chinatown and Ming Ue's restaurant. In her lap she held the little dragon bowl filled with charms. Malcolm had snarled with impatience when she'd stopped to gather the charms and place them into the bowl, but Lisa silenced him by telling him they needed all the help they could get.

"Tell me what happened," she said as she navigated the tight, busy streets. "Without shouting and swearing at me. Just tell me."

Malcolm braced his hand on the dashboard as Lisa careened around a corner. "Donna summoned him, as we thought she would. One minute, he was telling Saba about some asinine television show, the next he was dragged into thin air. I wasn't terribly sorry to see him go, but then Saba started screaming like she was in pain. I tried to hold onto her, but in the end she slid away. I don't know if she's even still alive."

His rage covered his fear, but only barely. He blamed Lisa, and she blamed herself, too. She should have anticipated this.

She drew a shaking breath. "I suspect Saba and Caleb are together, and that Donna took them to force *our* hand. I'm perfectly happy to face her."

"I have no qualms about killing witches," Malcolm

agreed. "Whether you outmagic her or I break her neck, this will be her last night."

Lisa nodded, glad he was on her side—if he was on her side. Malcolm wasn't exactly tame and obedient.

They reached the alley behind Ming Ue's dim sum restaurant, and Malcolm leapt from the car almost before it stopped moving. Lisa turned off the engine and followed him inside.

They found what Lisa expected to find, tables overturned and dishes broken and Ming Ue sitting despondently among the clutter in the light of a single bulb. Carol was shouting through the telephone to an electrician to please come out and fix the lights. Shaiming sat by himself at another shadowed table, quietly drinking tea.

"He took the orb, Lisa," Ming Ue said as soon as they entered. "There were demons following him, and they tore up the restaurant, laughing. I was afraid they'd hurt Carol, and my magic wasn't strong enough to stop them."

Lisa laid a hand on Ming Ue's shoulder. "I'm so sorry. Caleb had to come. He didn't have a choice."

Ming Ue looked troubled and angry. "I know. He explained. But I will have to close, and Carol will scream about how much money we are losing, and fixing the electricity will cost a fortune. I don't think we were up to code in the first place."

"I will pay for the damage," Malcolm said. "You will not be closed long."

Ming Ue's eyes widened. "A black dragon would do such a thing?"

"I would be pleased to. Make as many refurbishments to your restaurant as you like. I'll enjoy myself taking it out of golden dragon hide."

Lisa was already rushing outside again, passing Carol who watched her over the phone with wide eyes. "Hurry," Lisa called to Malcolm.

"She has the orb by now," Malcolm pointed out as he slammed into the car. Lisa stomped on the gas pedal and the car hurtled through the alley. "Caleb took it to her. It's only a matter of time before the earthquakes start."

"No, he didn't," Lisa said, pulling onto California Street, narrowly missing a high-speed taxi. "The orb he took her isn't real. It's a decoy Li Na gave to Ming Ue to draw attention from the real orb."

Malcolm swiveled in the seat to stare at her. "How the hell do you know that?"

"When Ming Ue first showed it to me, I didn't sense the power from it that I expected. It has some power, but it's false. Ming Ue knows, I think. But when Donna discovers it's not the real orb, who knows what she'll do?"

"She'll kill Saba, you mean."

"Yes," Lisa said reluctantly. "I didn't know she'd snatch Saba, too."

"Because you had to go enjoy yourself time-traveling in Dragonspace."

"It wasn't for enjoyment." Lisa swung the car around another corner and raced it down a hill. They bounced across the intersection at the bottom and tore down the next street. "It was important, and I learned things."

"What things?"

"Nothing I can explain right now. Hold on." The light at the next intersection had turned yellow. Lisa floored it, screaming through, the car bottoming on the edge of the next hill down.

Malcolm gripped the dashboard and the handle above the window, muscles flexing under his jacket. "If Saba dies, you will pay for it. I don't care if you are an all-powerful silver dragon."

"Do you love Saba?" Lisa asked Malcolm.

Malcolm started to answer, then she felt the weight of his silver gaze. "No." The word was emphatic, more so than necessary.

Lisa squealed around another corner, toward the area the needle had started to indicate on the map before the backlash of the counter-spell. She could faintly sense the threads she and Caleb had entwined when last they'd made love, but she wished she had a more specific direction than a feeling of "this way."

"Not much farther," Lisa said. "I hope."

Malcolm turned his head to look out the front window, his mouth set in a hard line. He said no more as Lisa pulled the car to a halt in a narrow space underneath the Bay Bridge. No streetlight flooded this black space, and the moon did not penetrate the darkness. It was magic darkness, and it crawled over her skin like oil. "Here," she said softly.

"Yes," Malcolm answered. "I feel her. Saba. She's still alive, lucky for you."

"The question is where?" Lisa clutched the bowl with the charms tightly as she and Malcolm approached the car again. They'd walked up and down under the bridge but seen no one and nothing to indicate anyone had ever been here. Barges and ships outlined with lights floated through the bay, and cars roared onto the double-decker bridge above them, reinforced since the disastrous '89 earthquake. Considering the homeless population in San Francisco, Lisa was amazed to see no one down here. If people desperate for a spot to lay a blanket avoided this place, something bad must be going on.

Malcolm lifted his gaze to the dark water where Treasure Island, once a naval base and still partly closed off, perched. "There, perhaps. Or Alcatraz or Angel Island."

"Too many tourists," Lisa said. "She could never hope to be unseen all the time, and I think a witch with demons would stand out. But she's close, and she has Caleb. I sense it. I *scent* it."

"Golden dragons do stink," Malcolm bantered lightly, but she could tell he said the words out of habit.

"Remind me again why I'm helping you?" Lisa shivered, hugging her arms to her chest. "Come on, they have to be somewhere."

Almost at the same time, the two of them swiveled their

gazes to a long, low bulk that floated into the glare of the city's lights and just as quickly out of it. Lisa had only seen it for a moment, but that was long enough.

"That barge," she said, pointing.

"Yes," Malcolm agreed tightly. "How do we get there?"

"We fly. Hold this." She thrust the bowl with the charms into his hand. "Whatever you do, don't drop it."

It seemed so easy to change herself, so easy to call the magic. Lisa felt the glow within her strengthen, first becoming shimmering light, then solidifying into glimmering silver, taking her dragon shape. Her muscles hardened, and huge iridescent wings unfolded from her back.

As the light from her body flashed through the darkness beneath the bridge, the moon suddenly shone through the roiling clouds, caressing her silver scales with white light.

She gripped Malcolm securely in one of her talons and pushed herself up and out across the water. Her wings caught, the moon flashing on them in a blaze of silver sparks.

"They won't see us coming or anything," Malcolm said.

"Donna expects us," Lisa answered, not needing her mouth to form words. "And the people of San Francisco will think I'm fireworks."

Malcolm did not answer, but she felt his belligerence still radiating from him. At the same time he'd taken a leap of faith, trusting her. Lisa could so easily open her talons, letting him fall down into the dark waters of the bay where he'd quickly drown and he knew it.

Lisa landed on the deck of the barge. It was a large one, with at least two hundred feet of deck space. A four-story building crowded on the back of it, windows bathed in a faint white glow. Otherwise, the barge ran with the minimum of lights necessary to keep other craft from running into it.

The barge stank of diesel, a huge engine grumbling under their feet. Barges like this crossed San Francisco Bay all the time and slid out into the Pacific to move up and down the western coast. This could be an ordinary barge with just the crew inside the deck house, heading back to the docks for their next load of cargo. Except Lisa knew it wasn't.

She elected to change back into Lisa to walk toward the deck house. She took the bowl of charms that Malcolm had carefully carried and strode with him across the dirty and oily surface of the empty barge.

"You didn't have to bring clothes," Malcolm observed.

"What?"

"When you shift to and from your dragon form, you don't remove your clothes or put them back on."

Lisa looked down at herself, eyeing her denim skirt and white blouse as though surprised she wasn't naked. Malcolm and Caleb had been naked each time they emerged from their dragon forms. "I don't know why. I just didn't think about it."

"Hmm," he said, as though making a note to himself.

They said nothing more until they reached the entrance to the stern cabin and walked inside.

The barge was definitely not ordinary. Inside, all the floors and inner walls had been removed, so the building was one huge, empty room with windows climbing to the top. The bridge with its controls for running and steering the barge still existed on a platform high on the wall, reached by a series of stairs and catwalks. Exposed pipes ran down all the walls to disappear into the floor, and the strong stench of oil and diesel hung over all.

Saba sat in a corner on the metal floor, her knees drawn to her chest, a red nimbus surrounding her. Caleb leaned against the wall nearby, chains wrapping his large body. A tall man with long white hair handled the controls high above. He wore nothing to cover his very white skin. Two men identical to him flanked Donna on the floor below. Lisa stopped, her hackles rising as she recognized one of them as the incubus who had invaded her dreams.

Beside her Malcolm hissed, "Demons."

Donna had forsaken her soccer mom clothes. She dressed in robes, dark velvet and probably costly, but they weren't ancient—Lisa had seen something much like them for sale on an Internet site.

As soon as the door clanged closed behind Malcolm and Lisa, a small missile shot toward them. They dove apart, and the orb that had been in Ming Ue's restaurant crashed against the metal bulkhead and shattered.

"Bring me a toy, will you?" Donna said, her voice clear and ringing. "I want the real one, Lisa, or I'll kill the little witch. Caleb I'm going to kill anyway, so I won't offer his life as a bargain."

"Sorry, Lisa." Caleb shifted, chains clinking. "I'd squash her if I could."

The golden threads that meant Caleb caressed her, and she twined them with silver music. *Don't worry*, she tried to signal to him.

Donna ignored them. "I know how sentimental the silver dragon is about humans. You'll give me the orb so I won't murder this girl, even though you've barely met her. You can let the black dragon fly her off to a meadow somewhere to pick daisies together."

"I'm not giving you the orb," Lisa replied evenly. "Get used to the idea."

"You murdered my sister," Donna said. "I couldn't stop it, and I couldn't stop you going back to do it, but I can make you pay. You got your vengeance, now I am taking mine for my sister. Give me the orb and I might be merciful and do it quickly."

"I've already said no. I didn't kill your sister, her own foolishness did. The dragons she drained got their own back."

"Which would never have happened if you hadn't weakened her."

Lisa's dragon ire rose. "She murdered Caleb's son in a cruel and brutal way, and I could not let that go."

Caleb rumbled in rage. "Her *sister* did that?"

"Yes. I tried to help you. I'm sorry I couldn't do more."

The music of Caleb's thoughts whispered with sorrow. "I would never blame you. I blame witches who can't leave dragons in peace."

Donna glanced at the nimbus surrounding Saba. "Enough

chitchat. I really will kill her." The light flared a sudden, bright blue, and Saba screamed.

"Stop!" Malcolm grabbed the bowl from Lisa. "She can have the fucking orb. I say to hell with this world. Saba and I are leaving."

He started to stride forward, but Lisa said calmly, "Malcolm, wait."

Malcolm swung around in fury. "She'll kill her, and it will be your fault."

"I have no intention of letting her kill Saba, or Caleb, or even you. Do you trust me?"

"No," he said sharply, but he remained where he was.

Donna said, "You are so stupid," and turned her magic on Saba. Saba screamed.

Lisa skimmed over the floor, her body nothing but light, and blocked Donna's path to Saba. Immediately the blaze of magic died, absorbed and neutralized in Lisa's body.

Donna gave her a deprecating look. "Ah, the silver dragon. Ever the defender of humankind."

Lisa, human once more, cocked her head. "You have much power. So does the silver dragon. I am not afraid of finding out whose is greater."

"I shouldn't if I were you. Unless you know how to steer a barge." Donna smiled

"What's that got to do with anything?" Malcolm growled.

"We've turned and started heading back toward the city. This barge, if not properly steered, will ram itself straight into Fisherman's Wharf and all the tourists indulging themselves on their one week off a year. I'm aiming for a nice big shopping center with all kinds of restaurants and little places humans like to go. So many deaths. You give me the orb and come with me, and your friends can save them all. Won't that be nice?"

Lisa met her gaze. "Let Saba go and release Caleb from his enslavement, and *I* might be nice."

"You've heard my terms," Donna snapped. "Give me the orb, and let them bravely save everyone. Don't, and a lot of people will die. That would break the silver dragon's sweet little heart, wouldn't it?"

Lisa gave her a sunny smile. "What makes you think I came here to bargain with you?"

For the first time, a flicker of uncertainty crossed Donna's features. "You can't use the dragon orb against me. You know what will happen as well as I do."

"Just kill her, Lisa," Caleb said, his dragon rage palpable. He might be human and strapped in chains, but that didn't mean he wasn't dangerous. "She's boring me."

Lisa gently pried the bowl from Malcolm's still fingers and walked toward Donna in slow steps. "If you willingly give Caleb and Saba their freedom, I might go easy on you."

Donna smirked. "You think yourself so smart, that you tricked me into revealing myself. You thought you'd come down here, scold me, and send me off somewhere to punish me, didn't you? Did you never bother to think that I was trapping you? I wanted the orb and the silver dragon, and now I have them both."

She snapped her fingers. The door behind Lisa and Malcolm opened and about a score of white-haired demons poured through. More came in through the upper windows, leathery wings hissing as they floated to the floor. The problem with these demons was that they all carried automatic weapons.

Donna went on. "I, of course, took the precaution of bringing in backup. I don't need magic to hurt your friends, you know." She smiled, large and white-toothed. "Demons just love to kill people."

Malcolm growled, a feral rumble that rivaled the engine for strength. Demons covered the floor, looking like ultrahandsome men but in truth mindless beings who lived on death. They were rather like the sharks who were no doubt circling the barge even now, waiting for the frenzy of the kill.

Lisa knew she could keep bullets from doing herself harm as the silver dragon, but Caleb and Malcolm were as mortal as Saba. If the demons shot them, they'd die.

"Leave them out of it," she began, though she knew what Donna's answer would be. "Let this be between you and me."

"I'm not that idiotic. If I throw away any advantage, you win. Give me the orb, Lisa."

Lisa hugged the bowl to her chest. She really had no idea what would happen if Donna held the orb, but she believed Ming Ue's claim that it would begin the destruction of the world. As the silver dragon, Lisa could easily escape through a portal into Dragonspace and leave the destruction behind, but Lisa was thinking about more than her own hide. That was what Donna didn't understand.

"No," she said.

Donna gave her a look a pure fury. She pointed at Caleb. "Shoot him."

"No," Lisa screamed. Malcolm grabbed the arm of the nearest demon and wrestled with him for his weapon. Lisa launched herself and her magic at the demons, but too late. Her magic burst over the demons, downing them like dominoes, but enough of them fired.

Time seemed to slow. Dimly, she saw Malcolm wrench a gun from the demon he fought and bash his head in with it. Sickly green demon blood stained the floor. In the corner, Saba chanted words with all her might.

Lisa counted the bullets that entered Caleb's body, at least twenty hitting the mark. Caleb slammed back into the wall, his deep blue eyes glazing over.

Anguish poured from her. She had no idea what words she screamed, but her throat was raw with them. The nimbus around Saba suddenly dimmed. The young witch dove through it, her face twisting in agony, and scrabbled over the short distance to Caleb. She reached up to Caleb's arm, closed her hands over the gold armlet and yanked it down.

Lisa cried out again. Taking off the armlet might tear Caleb apart as the magic forces tried to shift him to his true dragon form. Lisa snaked her silver magic to him, wanting to hold him in, even if the bullets had already killed him.

"No!" she heard Saba shout. "Let it happen."

Lisa redirected the magic to slam down more demons. Caleb's body rippled and gleamed, forces trying to turn him inside out. Several of the demons rose again, insane grins on their faces, and let more bullets fly at him. Saba dove for the corner.

Donna, while her demons fought for her, came at Lisa. Lisa clutched the true orb, the bowl, knowing she could use the magic within it to save Caleb if she dared. She would destroy the Earth, but Caleb would be free.

Donna chanted a darkness spell that engulfed Lisa. She could no longer see Malcolm, or the demons, or Caleb. She held tight to the orb, realizing Donna was trying to make her use it, to make her know that trying to protect people made no difference.

"Give it to me," Donna said. "One of us will destroy this world, you or me. I bet you won't want it on your conscience that it was you."

Lisa tried to form a reply, but she'd run out of words. Seeing Caleb die was worse than her own death. She loved him. That love for him had manifested the silver dragon inside her, and that love would now tear her apart with grief.

"Take it," she whispered.

There was a sudden explosion, the sound of chains bursting and links slamming against metal walls. Lisa saw a flash of gold, a beating of huge wings, a wild sound of golden chimes. Then a voice growled. "Demons. Yuck."

"Caleb?"

The dark spell fell away just as Donna's hands wrapped around the bowl and yanked it from Lisa.

Lisa ignored her. She stared, open-mouthed at the huge golden dragon, fifty-feet long and gleaming with his own light that rose above them. His scaly front was pockmarked with bullet holes, but while the tiny bullets could easily tear up human flesh, dragon flesh repelled them like the heaviest armor.

Two demons became puddles of green fluid and ash as Caleb trampled them. Demons trained the guns on him, but the bullets danced off his hide. Caleb snaked his head around and gushed incandescent fire all over them. More demon ash piled on the floor along with melting metal that had once been weapons.

Malcolm brought up his captured gun and trained it on Donna. "Saba," he said. "Get out of here."

Saba remained in the corner, the gold arm band dangling from her hand. "I'm not going out there. There might be more demons."

"I hope so," Caleb said. "I haven't had this much fun in years."

He pumped his wings and flew upward, directing his fire at the demon on the bridge. "Not him," Lisa yelled. "He's steering this thing—oh."

Fire destroyed the demon to nothing, and half the controls melted with it. The barge lurched as the engine cut.

Caleb flew down and landed with a thump on the deck, his face at Donna's shoulder. He could not hurt her since she still wielded his name, but he didn't mind curling his lips to show his razor-sharp teeth.

"You're mine, dragon," Donna said. "And now I have the orb. I could amuse myself forcing you to kill your friends, but it no longer matters."

"Lisa would not give you the orb if she didn't know what she was doing," Caleb said. "Right, Lisa?"

Lisa hesitated. Malcolm looked at Lisa in anger, Saba in alarm.

"Right, Lisa?" Caleb asked, sounding worried.

"It's all about balance," Lisa breathed, praying the silver dragon of the past knew what she was talking about. "How much balance have you got, Donna?"

22

Donna gave her a frosty look. "I am a witch who has trained and extended her life for hundreds of years. How much balance do you think I have?"

Lisa stepped forward, narrowing her focus to Donna and the pale eyes that once had looked so ordinary. Now Lisa read the evil in them, a woman who lived for nothing but her own power and vengeance, uncaring who she hurt.

"It unbalanced you." Lisa heard her voice swell, the echoes of all the other silver dragons down the centuries joining her. "By absorbing the magic of evil, you've nearly unmade yourself."

"It doesn't matter, you little idiot. If I have the orb, then I have *all* the magic. Air, fire, earth, and water. And with it the fifth element, Akasha, ultimate and all-encompassing. Perhaps the silver dragon is right that the energy will start an earthquake that ends this annoying city and maybe the entire world. All I have to say is, oh well."

Donna upended the bowl, sending the charms clattering to the metal floor.

"Only if you have balance," Lisa and all her other selves

said, their voices stretching and vibrating. "The Earth will be shattered because of imbalance. What do you think it will do to you?"

"And you have perfect balance, I suppose," Donna sneered. "You who cut your life into a thousand and more pieces. You gave up all that precious magic and a long life so you could get married." She spat the word.

"I loved," Lisa answered. "I was born, I aged, I died. I gave birth to children and watched them grow, some I watched die and I grieved." Her other selves shivered in sorrow, Lisa's movements like the reflections of a person caught between two mirrors. "We loved men, some who were great, others who were ordinary, but all who were kind and loving and had generous hearts. I helped the people I could and wept for those I could not. I would say that it was worth the sacrifice."

"You chose weakness. You felt the silence of death and the helplessness of being a child. I chose life and strength."

"No," the voices of all the women the silver dragon had been said. "You did not."

"Oh, please." Donna closed her hands around the bowl with the dragon on its bottom and brought it to her chest. "You are pathetic. And now you will pay."

The outline of the bowl blurred and in its place a sphere began to pulse, filled with silver light brighter than the moon. Donna smiled as the silver-white light began to engulf her. For a moment, nothing more happened. Then suddenly, the barge rocked heavily, as though a large wave had swamped it.

Caleb swore. Lisa said, "Malcolm, see what is happening."

Lisa heard Malcolm run across the metal floor, a lighter tread joining him—Saba. The door slammed open, bringing in a wash of cool sea air.

"It's an earthquake," Malcolm confirmed. "It's starting."

"And I will finish it." Donna lifted the orb above her head, smiling up at it.

And then she screamed. Her face distorted, white and

silver light pulling it every which way. Her body elongated, stretching like Lisa's did when the power of the silver dragon filled her. This was silver dragon power and more, the power of the earth and wind and fire and the savage power of the seas, and the element Akasha, untouchable, that wove its way through them. All five elements dove into Donna, searching for an outlet, power contained and held dormant for so long that the backlash was enormous.

Donna's body could not hold it. Lisa sensed her struggling, calling on her witch powers to bend herself to accommodate the forces.

All the silver dragons inside Lisa reached out to her. "Balance," they said, voices chiming. "Harmony is greater than power, because it creates and heals instead of destroying. Creating is slow but so, so strong."

"Help me," Donna cried.

Lisa held out her hand. "Seek the stillness inside you. Draw the power of the orb there."

Donna's face distorted again as she closed her eyes and willed herself to find silence in her soul.

"Why are you helping her?" Caleb demanded from what seemed a long way away.

"Find it," Lisa urged. "Find it."

Donna's face began to flow back to human lines, and the crazy fires of the orb began to dim. Lisa held her breath, willing the woman to understand. Donna opened her eyes, still filled with white light, and then she smiled in triumph.

"I did it," she said. "The power is *mine*."

"Get down!" Lisa screamed. Malcolm and Saba dropped to the floor, and so did Caleb, flattening his huge body with amazing speed.

Donna swelled with light and power, her laughter suddenly giving way to screams. Again her body distorted, swelling and cracking with wild light, and then, quite suddenly, she exploded.

A blare of incandescent light filled the room, followed by bursts and flares of fireballs whizzing far above them to the high ceiling. The fireballs sizzled against metal walls and seared through the thick, dirty glass, shattering the windows and sending a hail of shards on the four below.

Caleb gathered Lisa, Malcolm, and Saba to him with a sweep of his forearm, shielding them with his stronger body. Lisa pressed back against his supple gold scales, Malcolm cradling Saba's body on her other side. The magic dove and swooped above them, triumphant in its release. Lisa fancied she heard faint silver laughter woven through the sizzling stardust.

And then, just as suddenly, the bright light went out. The dragon bowl dropped with a muffled clank to the deck, and all was dark, but for the dim, bluish glow of the ordinary control lights of the barge.

Caleb's muscles unclenched one by one as he eased his claws across the deck with a brutal squeal. "Is it over?"

Malcolm scrambled up, lifting Saba to her feet, then he enclosed her in his arms and pressed his cheek to her hair. Lisa, too, rose, her limbs rippling as the other silver dragon women occupied the space with her. Caleb wondered what it was like for her, if the memories of all her other lives invaded her thoughts and whether any of the silver dragons remembered Caleb.

"It isn't over," Lisa said, hundreds of voices joining hers. The deck heaved and pitched, waves grating the hull of the barge. "The earthquake is still going, and this barge is still rushing toward shore."

"Ah," Caleb answered. "Not good."

Lisa walked to the fallen bowl, the silver radiance from her lending light to the air. She knelt on the deck and retrieved the bowl, then picked up each of the charms—the dragon, the moon, the blossom, the bird's wing—and piled them back into it.

Caleb extended his neck to put his head next to hers, watching what she did. "Were the charms part of it?"

"A big part." Lisa looked up at Caleb and pressed a kiss

to his nose. "They keep the orb magic stable. Donna was too foolish to understand that."

"Can you stop the earthquake?" he asked. "It's going to be bad, isn't it?"

"Yes." She gave him a somber look. "But we can try to prevent it."

Caleb rubbed his face against her body, inhaling the perfume of her. She smiled her sweet Lisa smile and rubbed between his eyes, right where he liked it.

"You're sexy, you know," he said. "I think that even when I'm a dragon."

Lisa blushed. "The end of the world is happening. Remember?"

"That doesn't mean you don't have great legs."

She growled and planted another kiss on his nose. "Stop it. Get Saba and Malcolm and have them come over here. I need you all."

Caleb moved away, chuckling under his breath. He managed to pry Saba and Malcolm apart and make them follow him to where Lisa was scratching out a small circle with the edge of the moon charm. "Which way is north?" she asked.

Malcolm studied an instrument panel and pointed to the wall with the door. "That way."

Lisa made a mark on the circle. "Saba, will you stand there? I'll need you to represent north and earth. Caleb, stand just opposite." She hurried to the other side and made another mark. "You'll be fire." She made a third mark. "West. That will be you, Malcolm, water. I'll stand east, and represent air."

"Do you want me as a dragon?" Caleb asked. He coiled his tail around himself and stood with his feet pressed exactly to the mark she'd made.

"Yes. You have more power—at least, I hope you do. I didn't know you could exist as a dragon outside Dragonspace."

"I didn't either," Caleb said. He raised his head high and shot a small stream of fire from his mouth for the pleasure of it. "So few believe in dragons here anymore. But maybe because you do, and everyone in this room does, and Ming Ue and Shaiming do, then I can exist at least for you." He lowered his head and held it level with Saba. "Did you know I could?"

Saba gazed at him with unperturbed dark eyes. "To be honest? No."

"Ah," Caleb said.

"If you'd remained a human, you'd be dead," Saba pointed out. "I took the chance."

Caleb breathed out, but warm air only, no fire. "Thank you."

"I wish," Malcolm said tightly, "that you would have brought him back as a *mute* dragon."

Caleb rumbled. "Black dragon. Another phrase for smart-ass."

"You know, Malcolm," Lisa said as Caleb drew back to his space, "if Caleb can exist here in his dragon form, so can you. The binding spell that kept you here powerless is broken."

Malcolm started as though he hadn't thought of that. He glanced at Saba, arms folded across her slim chest, and at Caleb. Then, as he had in Lisa's apartment, he started to peel off his clothes.

Lisa politely averted her eyes, but Saba did not. Poor girl. Once unclothed, Malcolm closed his eyes, reached his arms above his head, and *changed*. His black tattoo distorted, then human muscle and bone flowed into a dragon body, sable and gleaming, black like the deepest night. His body was long, powerfully muscular, and his wings rose above him, full and tight.

He opened his huge eyes, silver like glistening lamps, and looked down at them from his great height. Saba stared up at him, her face white.

Malcolm regarded her for a long time, his eyes cool with black dragon hauteur. He was an ancient dragon, Caleb could tell, probably three thousand years old. He fanned the air with his huge black wings, then folded them back into his body and lowered himself to the mark on the circle. "I'm ready," he said. "Let us save the world."

It wasn't that simple. Lisa held the bowl between her hands and told them to each touch it, Saba first, then on around the circle, clockwise. Caleb's and Malcolm's talons nearly dwarfed the bowl, but they managed to touch it delicately.

She sensed Caleb's power and Malcolm's, both equally as strong, but very different. Caleb's power was raw and energetic, much like the fire he represented in this circle. Malcolm's magic was old and honed and very, very strong. The phrase *still waters run deep* definitely applied to him.

"Earth, air, fire, and water," she murmured. "Sun, moon, mountain and heavens, sea and sky. Four points of the compass. Balanced. Equal."

She felt her other selves within her reach out with their silver dragon magic, pouring it into the orb to restore the balance. She saw people in her head she did not know, men smiling, dark eyes warm, children laughing up at her, older women putting hands out to touch her. Lisa felt the heat of passion as the silver dragon awakened to human desire for the first time and then the many times after that. She felt the brutal pain of pushing a human child into the world, the wonder when she heard its first cry. She felt the stab of grief when holding the wrinkled hand of a husband or friend as they slipped into death, felt the fear and then peace as her own senses began to darken.

So much existed within her. She was the same silver dragon through the ages, but Lisa's silver dragon self was unique, her own. The silver dragon might have sacrificed her long life, but joy had returned to her a thousand-fold.

Saba's powerful earth magic flowed in next to Lisa. The young woman's eyes were closed, her short hair mussed by the fight. She had a sweet face that hid vast, untapped power that would soon come to the fore.

And then Malcolm's magic, coolly logical, made of

mathematical intelligence, power bent to precise coordinates. After that Caleb's magic which made her smile. It was so like him, hot and fierce, deadly when focused, yet playful and warming.

"Earth, air, fire, and water," Lisa repeated. "Four points of the compass. Balanced, equal."

The elemental magic flowed into the bowl, which jumped and bounced in Lisa's hand, the charms dancing and clinking. She'd always been drawn to this little bowl with the dragon on the bottom, even when she was a little girl and fascinated by Grandma Li Na's Chinese things. She sensed Li Na in the myriad women inside her and waved a silent hello. Grandma Li Na smiled back at her.

The three in the circle worked with Lisa, the dragons and the witch, none of them grabbing the power for themselves, or tilting the balance in any fashion. They knew what they had to give to make the magic work, to restore the balance to this world, and they were willing to contribute it.

Slowly, very slowly, the waves shaking the barge subsided, the roll lessening, imperceptibly at first. Lisa continued to concentrate on the bowl and the four magics filling it, smoothing out the strength to build the orb's equilibrium.

Finally, the barge floated gently, lifting and settling as it would on a calm, sunny day. The windows far overhead had tinged golden with the morning sun. A beam of that sun flowed in and bathed the bowl in light. The radiance warmed Lisa's fingers, and she said softly, "It is done."

The other three let out a collective sigh, removed their touch from the bowl and opened their eyes. Saba blinked at the daylight. "Is it morning?"

Lisa laughed. She felt her other selves receding, the silver dragon's task done. A pang of regret touched Lisa's heart, and then she let them go. It would not be forever until she saw them again.

"I hope it's morning," Lisa said. "Or else the sun is confused."

Caleb rose on wings that flashed gold fire. He flapped them once, carrying himself up to the windows of the bridge. The ash and green goo of the demons had gone, as though the magic in the room had washed everything clean.

"It's daylight," Caleb said. "A pretty sunrise. Except we have a problem."

"Oh, no," Saba said. "What now?"

"We're moving along pretty fast. Anyone know how to steer a barge?"

Malcolm joined him, huge back claws gripping pipes to hold him upright. "It would be easy, if a golden dragon hadn't fried the controls."

"I could have let the demons keep shooting at you, I guess," Caleb returned. "Would have meant one less problem for me."

"The golden dragon answer to everything," Malcolm rumbled. "If it annoys you, kill it."

Caleb ignored him. "I wonder what this lever does."

"Don't touch it until I work out what all the controls are for. The ones that still work, that is."

Below them, Saba glanced at Lisa, her look ironic. "Think we should help them?"

"I don't know." Lisa folded her arms, staring up at the black and golden bodies. "It sounds like they're having fun."

Above them, something clanked. The bow of the barge swung suddenly around, the deck listing horribly. Lisa and Saba stumbled into each other then across the floor until they banged into the wall. Malcolm snarled curses.

Caleb blew out a tiny stream of fire. "We turned, didn't we? We're not heading straight for the wharf anymore."

"No, we're heading for the bridge. Why don't you let me steer a while?"

"You don't know how to do this any better than I do."

Malcolm growled again and the barge made a sudden surge the other way.

Once it straightened, Lisa and Saba jumped to their feet, clothes covered in oil and dirt.

"That's it," Lisa called. "Both of you come down here. We're taking over."

Two dragon heads swiveled to look down at them, one pair of blue and one pair of silver eyes staring.

"Now," Saba said.

Malcolm released his hold on the metal pipes, claws screeching, and drifted down on outstretched wings. When his feet touched the floor, he folded the wings, bowed his head, and flowed into his human form. Naked, he casually lifted his clothes from where he'd left them and headed for the door. "I'm going outside to see what's what."

Caleb stayed behind. Together Lisa and Saba, with the help of Lisa's dragon magic, got the barge stopped and pointed out toward the Golden Gate and the open sea beyond. "We'll leave it drifting," she announced as she and Saba descended the catwalk. "The police or national guard will investigate and tow it back to the docks."

The others had no objection. They flew back, silently and swiftly as three dragons, Malcolm carrying Saba safely in his talon. They landed under the bridge in growing daylight, where Lisa's car, looking soiled and prosaic, waited.

Above them, morning traffic crept across the bridge, commuters on their way to work. Ships moved through the bay, the water now calm and quiet. Joggers ran through the streets near the entrance to the Bay Bridge, and somewhere a radio blared music. If San Francisco had experienced an earthquake last night, the city bore no sign of it. All looked ordinary and normal under the misty light of the rising sun.

"It looks like nothing ever happened," Saba said.

Lisa nodded, wondering if restoring the balance to the orb had restored the balance to the world.

Next to the car, Malcolm dressed without embarrassment, lifting his long black hair to spill down the back of his coat. Caleb, still in dragon form, eyed the gold armband Saba held out to him then looked at Lisa. His blue eyes sparkled wickedly.

"Kiss me once, Lisa," Caleb said. He tapped his talon to his scales. "Right here, between the eyes."

"Then can I go home and get some sleep?" Lisa asked. "I'm beat."

"One kiss. Then we go."

Lisa stepped up to him. She placed her hands on his warm scales, felt his long, soft lashes brush her as she closed her eyes and pressed a kiss to his face.

The scales vanished, a draft of air hit her, and suddenly she was holding six feet and more of naked male, arm band restored, his lips seared to hers. He kissed her with all the possessiveness of a dragon for a beautiful jewel, and of a man for a woman he loves.

She melded to him, feeling herself respond to him, every pore of her tingling for his touch. She drew her foot up his bare leg, wishing they were alone and that he could simply take her hard against the hood of her car.

They weren't alone, of course. Malcolm cleared his throat, and Saba laughed. "Get a room, you two," she said.

"Preferably one not right next to mine," Malcolm growled.

Caleb drew back, holding Lisa against him, smiling his Caleb smile. "Both good ideas," he murmured, then he looked down at himself. "You didn't happen to bring some extra clothes, did you? Mine are in shreds on the barge."

23

Caleb buried himself deep inside Lisa in the warm sun-light on Lisa's bed. He'd thought her beautiful before he knew she was the silver dragon, and he'd think her beautiful forever. She twisted beneath him, lifting her hips against his, her eyes half-closed, her face flushed and touched with sunshine. The same sunshine gleamed on the armband above his elbow.

Malcolm and Saba hadn't returned to the apartment with them. After a visit to Ming Ue to reassure her that all was well, Malcolm asked Lisa to drop Saba and him off at his lodgings on Octavia Street.

Ming Ue had told them she'd felt a small tremor but no earthquake. Restoring the orb seemed to have erased any damaging effects. Lumi and Grizelda had been at the restaurant, come to help make repairs. Ming Ue seemed forgiving of Caleb, understanding that he'd been under the power of the evil witch.

Now that Donna was dead, Lisa had no trouble erasing the memory of Caleb's true name from Saba or Grizelda. She'd stood both witches together and gently removed the knowledge. The two young women hadn't even flinched or noticed when she was finished.

Caleb was truly free, Lisa had said, softness in her eyes. No one could command him again.

"Except you," he'd said. "What do you want me to do, Lisa?"

That had led them back to the apartment, into Lisa's bedroom, and onto the bed.

He pressed harder inside her, skimming his fingers over her damp skin. Lisa writhed beneath him, whimpering softly.

"That's it," he whispered. "You are so strong, you can take so much."

"No, I can't," she began, "I'm exhausted."

"You're doing it, sweet Lisa. You're taking all of me."

She murmured in excitement and he laced his dragon mark over her, twining his thoughts with hers as much as he could. "You're mine," he said. "My own mate."

"Yes." She lifted her hips, her red hair tangled on the pillow. *"Please."*

Caleb knew her words came from her fevered arousal, her physical need for him. When this was over, when they'd calmed, the silver dragon would make her choice of what she would do for the rest of her life, and that choice might not include him.

For now, he would soak up every second with her that he could. He pressed his hips into hers, the bed swaying dangerously. "That's it. Come for me, love."

"I'm too tired from saving the world."

"No, you are not. Enjoy it, love it." He gasped, a dark wave of feeling swamping him. "No, too soon. Gods, no."

Her fingers bit his skin as he came, too excited by the feel of her around him to stop. He slid his hand between them, pressing his thumb over her mound, rubbing and massaging until her eyes widened and her shout joined his. They climaxed together, holding each other hard, the bed frame rattling.

Caleb gave one last, swift thrust, and suddenly, the bed

broke, the legs giving way, and the slats parting to send the mattress to the floor. Lisa burst out laughing and Caleb joined her, feeling the joy of being inside her while she laughed, and catching her sweet laughter in his mouth.

"Oh dear," Lisa said, wiping tears from her eyes. "How embarrassing. I sure hope Mrs. Bradley has her television turned up."

Saba was hungry. She consumed a plateful of eggs and bacon, half a loaf of toast and then had a salad on top of it, all of which Malcolm brought home from a nearby restaurant. She was exhausted, the magic Lisa had required of her completely draining her. Malcolm and Caleb and Lisa seemed none the worse for wear, but they were dragons. Saba was a human with only so much energy.

She'd wanted to talk to Malcolm about everything they'd seen and done, but Malcolm was uncommunicative. He shut himself in his study, a finely decorated room with leather furniture, and stayed on the phone most of the day. The few times he came out, Saba suggested she go home, but Malcolm had ordered her to stay, and still enslaved to his mark, she had obeyed.

After downing two brownies and half a dozen cookies provided by a bakery down the street, Saba boldly marched to the study door and knocked on it. She had to go home and resume eating tofu and bean sprouts before she got too big to fit through the door.

To her surprise, Malcolm invited her in. He sat in front of his computer, tapping on the keyboard, but she was too tired to be curious about what was on the screen.

"What have you been doing in here all day?" she asked, throwing herself onto the love seat. The leather, soft and fine as anything he owned, caressed her. She was drained and still shaken by what had happened, not to mention horny, but by the somber look on his face, Malcolm wasn't interested in sex.

"Making arrangements." He turned in the swivel chair.

"The apartment will be transferred to your name, as will the assets in all my bank accounts."

Saba sat up, her eyes widening. "What apartment?"

"This one. You will live here after I'm gone. Your apartment is too cramped. Mine has plenty of room for your circles and spell working."

"After you're gone." She repeated the words dully. She hadn't expected him to stay here, now that he could return to Dragonspace, but some part of her hoped that he'd want to.

"Yes." He said the word without inflection.

"I can't afford this apartment," she tried.

"I own the house. Now it is yours."

"Malcolm, I can't . . ."

His dark eyes narrowed. "Stop bleating that you can't. I saw you break Donna's spell to release yourself to help Caleb. You are a damn powerful witch. The house is yours along with all my money. I have no more use for it. Tell your short-sighted mother and father that you landed yourself a good job programming your software and it's paid off. They should have more respect for you. I have an acquaintance who has agreed to hire you into his computer firm. You'll have all the money you need."

She sat numbly. "Malcolm, don't."

"I built up a fortune during the eight hundred years of my enforced confinement. If I disappear without making arrangements, the banks and brokers and tax-collectors will get all the assets. I'd rather it be in your hands, so I put everything in a trust for you."

"You sound like you're never coming back."

"I'm not."

"No," she said. "Why should you?"

"You'll do better without me," Malcolm said, sounding reasonable. "Once I remove the mark and your dependence on me, you'll blossom. I know this."

"So you're leaving me for my own good? Terrific."

Malcolm pushed himself from the desk and walked to the window that overlooked the green of the square opposite the house. "I don't belong here, Saba. I never did. I belong in Dragonspace, with the wind under my wings and all the time in the world to *think*."

"Without human concerns and annoying witches to drag you down."

He didn't seem to hear her. "Dragonspace is my home. I need to be there."

"I know." Saba uncrossed her legs and moved to him. "I'm being selfish because I'll miss you."

He didn't turn as she approached. "Once I remove my mark, you won't miss me. You'll forget all about me."

Her heart burned. Dragon mark or no, she doubted she'd ever forget Malcolm, for many reasons. She slid her arms around his waist from behind, leaning her head on his strong back. "In that case, before you take away the mark, can we . . ."

She let the words dangle, but she had no chance to finish the sentence. Malcolm swung around, lifted her in his arms, and carried her back to the leather sofa. Kneeling beside her, he stripped off her shirt and jeans and pressed his mouth to the join of her thighs.

She squirmed and lifted her hips as dark feeling flowed through her. She would most definitely never forget *this*.

Lisa awoke in the dark hours later. Caleb slumbered next to her on the broken bed, the mattress more or less flat on the floor. He'd curled his left arm under the pillow, his right arm lying limp on the bedcovers. The gold armband glittered softly in the moonlight.

Lisa touched it with light fingers, but he didn't wake. She thanked God that Saba had been close enough to Caleb to pull off the armband, that she'd been able to break Donna's spell surrounding her to do so. Saba had kept her head while Lisa the powerful being had been crazed with grief. Caleb might have died if he hadn't been able to shift into a dragon, and Lisa would have lost him. If that had happened, she would have killed Donna with the orb and let the world go to hell.

The strength of her feelings alarmed her. As a normal person she could say that she'd give up the world for him, but as the silver dragon, she knew she could literally make that happen. She smiled faintly. Better confine herself to baking cookies to show her affection.

He'd been so brave for her, willingly putting himself into Donna's power to help with the plan when he hated and feared witches, Donna most of all. After what they'd done to him and what they'd done to his son, he'd allowed Donna to use him and to chain him, knowing that Lisa needed him to. He'd been through so much and yet, he'd given more. He was an amazing being.

Even now, he could sleep hard, knowing the danger was gone, while Lisa shifted restlessly. Outside the window, the lights of the city glowed softly against the sky, and beyond them, the stars beckoned her. She sat up and smoothed her hair, the silver streak warming her hand.

She loved Caleb and wanted to stay with him forever. She knew the silver dragon liked the golden, and yet they still did not quite connect. What would she do if the silver dragon did not want him, and how could Caleb stay with her in any case? Lisa's heart ached even as the silver dragon said, *Worry not. All will be as it should be.*

The stars glittered, bright even behind the thousands of lights of San Francisco. Lisa rose from the bed, careful not to disturb Caleb, and walked unclothed into the living room. All was silent here except a faint murmur of the wind chimes. The orb, quiet now, rested in its form as a dragon bowl with the charms inside on the shelf in the living room with all Grandma Li Na's Chinese things, where it belonged.

Lisa turned to the spare bedroom door and opened it. The way to Dragonspace lay misty and dark before her, cool wind ruffling her hair. She stretched out her arms, her whole being responding to the pull of the other world. She longed to feel the air of Dragonspace sliding over her silver body, longed to see the deep darkness of the sky untainted by human lights.

"Lisa-ling?" Caleb wandered out of the bedroom, hair tousled, moonlight shining on his bronzed, naked body. He saw her near the spare room door and stopped, his body still. He watched her a moment, then casual words came out of him, forced and light. "If you can't sleep, want to watch some television?"

"No." Lisa reached to the darkened doorway. "Come fly with me."

"In Dragonspace?"

Lisa smiled. The morning paper had carried a nice outline of a lighted silver dragon over the bay, the reporter wondering who had been shooting off fireworks.

"We'll stick to Dragonspace for now," she said. "The night is calling us, can you hear it?"

Caleb glanced at the open door, his look neutral. "If you say so."

She held out her hand to him. "Come on."

Caleb touched his armband, regarding her with an odd look in his eyes. At last he nodded and joined her at the door, sliding off the armband as they stepped through and to the rocky ledge.

He tossed the armlet to the floor behind him, then Lisa took his hand and they leapt from the ledge together, both of them elongating and becoming dragons. One flashed silver in the moonlight, the other gold.

Lisa stretched her wings, propelling herself upward into the night. She had no destination in mind, she simply wanted to soar over the dark land and feel the stars on her wings. She heard Caleb behind her, sensed hot air whooshing as he pumped his wings to keep up with her.

Lisa followed the path of stars stretched in a hazy smudge across the sky. Her wings flashed, the moon, a little larger than Earth's moon, warming them. She laughed for the joy of flying and knowing that Caleb was behind her. She loved being in love with him, both as a human and a dragon. She sang out a dragon song to him, urging him to keep up as she soared higher and higher.

The stars called to her, telling her to lose herself in

them. Without realizing she did it, Lisa changed her body to the swirling lights, moving faster and higher. Starlight engulfed her, the air growing colder by the second.

She knew she could become starlight, and the silver dragon in her told her exactly how to do it. The dragons that had turned to stardust and constellations millennia ago called out to her, promising her untold wonders if she joined them. Lisa stretched her senses, drifting farther toward them, her body a pale streak of lights in the heavens.

She wanted this freedom away from the pain and grief of life, to become pure magic and light. Her life as Lisa— her parents far away in Hawaii, her disastrous marriage, her sadness at losing Li Na, her hard work grubbing for a living—fell away. She could become the silver dragon alone and have nothing but peace.

"Lisa!" Caleb shouted behind her.

The silver and gold threads which had twined when they'd fought Donna hadn't dispersed. They pulled her sharply, solidifying her body into its silver dragon shape. Suddenly she was very cold.

It is not cold here, the stars promised. *Join us.*

Caleb seemed to know exactly what was going on. "Lisa, you need to stay in the human world and protect the orb."

No, the stars answered. *You have protected it long enough. Time to pass the task to another.*

Lisa wavered, wondering if she could let her grandmother Li Na down by leaving the task behind. Saba, though a strong witch, could not protect it like a silver dragon could. Ming Ue, another strong mage, likely wouldn't be able to either, and it wasn't fair to ask her after the help she'd already given.

Caleb, then. Caleb could spend his entire life watching television in Lisa's apartment, making certain that no one touched the orb. She had given up her silver dragon existence long enough.

"Lisa!" Caleb's call was desperate now. "*I* need you."

Lisa turned, her body glittering and almost insubstantial.

She felt her pull to Caleb, not enslavement, not the binding threads of the mark, but something deeper that bound her more tightly still.

Caleb hovered far, far below her, a golden speck in the rising sun that was just visible on the horizon. His words were faint as he projected them to her.

"I love you," he said, anguish in his voice.

Dragons don't love, the stars told her. *We are logical beings with no need of love.*

"The hell we are," she answered.

Lisa arrowed her body straight toward Caleb, her heart giving her the answer. She descended at a rapid rate, ice sheets forming on her wings and breaking off in chunks that sparkled in the rising sun's light. Caleb moved, a flash of gold, and she dove for him.

At the last minute, she veered around him, making him swerve. He growled and snapped his teeth at her, and she nipped him back, avoiding the downward push of his wings.

"You're mine." His dragon voice filled the air around them. "Stardust dragons can find their own women."

Lisa laughed. She flew away from him, but slowly, wanting to be caught. Caleb spiraled around her, rolling on currents of air, his gold scales glittering in the sun. She followed him, letting him draw her farther and farther away from the stars, heading back to the portal to the human world.

They flew almost leisurely to the gap that waited for them, enjoying flying together over Dragonspace, rolling over one another and playing impromptu games of tag. At last, Lisa streamed toward the gap that led to the Earth world and plunged through it, changing shape and landing on her backside on the living room carpet.

A few seconds later, Caleb burst through and landed on top of her, human once more, his gold armband in place.

"I want you," he said, holding her down with his strong arms. "I love you."

She touched his face, loving the warm, strong feel of it. "I want you, too, Caleb. And I love you."

"I want to stay here with you. You'll need my help."

"But can you stay? Saba said the magic would wear off once I'm safe. And now that Donna's gone and Malcolm can go home . . ."

"I don't want to go." He kissed her, his very male body hard under her touch, his eyes deeply blue. "The silver dragon has enough magic to let me stay, doesn't she? If she wants me, that is."

"Dragonspace is your home."

Caleb shook his head, his golden hair brushing her face. "It is lonely there. Here I have you, and television, and delivery pizza."

He was trying to make her laugh but she couldn't quite yet. "Dragons don't mate for life."

"They don't fall in love either or protect their children, but I've learned to do all that. I've found my life-mate, and it's you."

She traced his lips, her heart aching and full of hope at the same time. "I saw all the silver dragon's mates when we restored the balance. Not one of them was a dragon. Li Na must have known I was destined to fall in love with a dragon, since she disguised the orb as a bowl with a golden dragon on the bottom. She could have chosen any dragon, but she picked a golden."

"Goldens are the strongest dragons."

"She knew it would take a pesky golden to keep a silver dragon at home." Lisa snuggled into his side. "You need to teach me how to be a dragon, how not to get lost in the stars."

"I will if you teach me more about being human. Which will include having lots of sex."

She laughed. "I think I can make that bargain. The silver dragon was never alone through the centuries, you know. She always had someone she loved nearby."

Caleb growled. "Now it will be me." He nipped her

neck, as he liked to do as a dragon and moved her thighs apart to enter her.

"I love you, Caleb," she whispered as excitement took her. "Love you so much."

"I love you, too, Lisa," he murmured. "My magical, beautiful *mate*."

24

One more task had to be performed. At noon, a knock on the door woke them, and Lisa answered it to admit Malcolm. Saba, looking unhappy but resigned, entered behind him.

"Are you certain you want to go?" Lisa asked in a low voice as she and Malcolm stood in front of the doorway to Dragonspace. Malcolm had removed his clothing and now stood straight and tall in front of the door.

"Yes," he answered, laconic as ever.

Caleb watched, leaning on the door frame to Lisa's bedroom, the golden armband gleaming against his bronzed skin. He no longer needed the armband because the silver dragon had infused the doorway to Dragonspace with enough magic so he could come and go as he pleased, but he kept the armband because Lisa liked how it looked on him. The gold glistening against his bicep reminded her what a sexy warrior he was.

"Do you want time to say good-bye to Saba?" Lisa asked Malcolm. "I'll give you a minute alone."

"We have already said our good-byes," Malcolm said.

Lisa glanced at Saba. She waited by the shelves of Oriental curios, Malcolm's leather coat folded over her arms, her face white. Lisa touched her mind softly so as not to disturb her and found no trace of Malcolm's dragon mark. He'd removed it.

"May we get on with it?" Malcolm asked tersely.

Lisa sighed. She extended her power to the door and drew a line of silver fire that would allow Malcolm to pass through unharmed. "Good-bye, Malcolm. And thank you."

Malcolm nodded once, his gaze sliding to her and away. Lisa smiled, realizing he was embarrassed at the reminder that he'd changed into one of the good guys.

Malcolm raised his arms above his head and dove into the opening. As he did he became *dragon*, blacker than night, dark velvet on the darker sky. He looked back once, his silver eyes luminescent. Hot wind from his wings washed through the portal, stirring the wind chimes across the room, then the slit in the air vanished, leaving nothing but the ordinary spare bedroom. Malcolm was gone.

Lisa closed the door. Saba had drifted out to the balcony and stood at the railing, looking out at the city. Lisa shared a glance with Caleb, then she joined Saba on the balcony, inhaling the warm summer air.

"It's stupid to cry." Saba stared out over the rooftops, her cheeks wet. "I knew from the first he didn't want to stay."

"He'll be back," Lisa said.

Saba wiped away the quiet tears. "I don't think so. He's found his freedom. It's what he wanted."

Lisa slipped her arm around the other girl's shoulders. "Don't punish yourself too much. You're allowed to miss him and wish things were different."

"He won't come back."

"Yes, he will. I feel it."

Saba reached into the pocket of the leather coat Malcolm had given her and pulled out two crystalline spheres. "He gave me these."

Lisa touched one interestedly. "What are they?"

"Black dragon's tears. He said if I ever needed him, the

direst necessity like the world coming to an end, I could use them to call him. Long distance to Dragonspace or something." She tried to smile.

"He means it."

"I know." Saba dropped the dragon's tears back into the pocket. "But I don't think he'll consider it a dire emergency if I'm lonely at night."

Lisa said nothing, knowing Saba wouldn't listen to reassurances that Malcolm would one day return for her. Saba's heart was too tender right now, and she didn't want hope. But Lisa knew even without her silver dragon magic that he'd be back. She'd seen the way Malcolm looked at Saba when he thought no one observed him. He'd come back.

Lisa smiled to herself as she gathered Saba in a comforting hug. The silver dragon in her hoped she'd be around to see Malcolm and Saba finally get themselves sorted out.

"There's a rerun of *Buffy* on," Caleb called from the living room. "It's the one where they become their Halloween costumes. Want to watch?"

Lisa and Saba exchanged a glance, laughed, and drifted back into the house.

"Caleb," Lisa said a month later. They sat on the sofa late in the darkness, the television playing, Lisa's head on Caleb's shoulder. He trailed his fingers through her hair, once in a while turning his head to softly kiss her.

"Mmm?" he asked.

"We should get married."

He smiled into her hair. "Like humans do? That sounds nice."

"Nothing fancy," Lisa said, stretching her legs. On the television, the audience roared at Conan O'Brien's quip. "Just a few friends, some cake, some champagne. We can ask Mrs. Bradley to make cookies."

"Mmm," he said, chest rumbling under her ear. "I like those."

"That will make things easier when we make the announcement."

His lips grazed her forehead. "What announcement, love?"

"About the little dragon on the way." She laid her hand across her abdomen. "My doctor is amazed how strong she is. It will be a girl, of course. To carry on the silver dragon legacy."

Caleb went motionless. Lisa raised her head and found him staring hard at her, eyes fixed, his pupils pinpricks of black in the blue. "Little dragon?"

"Yours and mine." Lisa touched his face. "Remember all that dragon mating? Not to mention all the mating here in our bedroom. We already broke one bed."

"I thought . . ." He trailed off, voice strangled, then cleared his throat. "I thought lady dragons went off and laid a clutch of eggs in hiding."

"Nope." She took his broad, shaking hand and placed it on her belly. "The silver dragon chose to take human form and reproduce the human way. So you and I are going to have a little human child. Who will also be a dragon. It will be interesting explaining that to her."

His gave her a frozen stare. "You're telling me—I'll be a father?"

"Yes. Again. You did a wonderful job the first time. I'm sure you'll be fine this time, too."

Caleb's face was sheet white. "Oh, sweet gods."

Lisa tilted her head and kissed his cheek. "You'll be *fine*."

She watched his eyes widen in fear then soften as he thought of his son taken from him long ago. Hope entered his eyes, then fondness, and love. Last of all, the wicked Caleb gleam returned.

"Our child," he said, his voice strong. "Half-golden, half-silver dragon. She'll be insufferable."

"Just like her father," Lisa said, and kissed him.

Author Bio

Allyson James writes historical, contemporary, and paranormal romances, mysteries, historical fiction, and erotic romance under several different pseudonyms. She lives in the warm Southwest with her husband and cat and spends most of her time in the world of her stories. More about Allyson's books can be found on her website: www.allysonjames.com. Or contact Allyson via e-mail at allysonjames@cox.net.

Penguin Group (USA) Online

What will you be reading tomorrow?

Tom Clancy, Patricia Cornwell, W.E.B. Griffin,
Nora Roberts, William Gibson, Robin Cook,
Brian Jacques, Catherine Coulter, Stephen King,
Dean Koontz, Ken Follett, Clive Cussler,
Eric Jerome Dickey, John Sandford,
Terry McMillan, Sue Monk Kidd, Amy Tan,
John Berendt…

You'll find them all at
penguin.com

Read excerpts and newsletters,
find tour schedules and reading group guides,
and enter contests.

Subscribe to Penguin Group (USA) newsletters
and get an exclusive inside look
at exciting new titles and the authors you love
long before everyone else does.

PENGUIN GROUP (USA)
us.penguingroup.com